PRAISE FOR *THE HAUNTING OF BRYNN WILDER*

"The action builds to a satisfying and uplifting ending . . . Webb consistently entertains."

—*Publishers Weekly*

"Endearing and greatly readable . . . [a] tale that is both warm and poignant."

—*Kirkus Reviews*

"Webb's chilling tale of a woman running from a tragic loss will put a spell on you."

—E! Online

"Prepare to lose yourself in Wendy Webb's lusciously written *The Haunting of Brynn Wilder.*"

—POPSUGAR

"Enchanting."

—The Nerd Daily

"Wendy Webb weaves a searing gothic tale with elements of horror, mystery, and romance . . . It is incredibly absorbing and atmospheric."

—Bookreporter

"Wendy Webb is a rising voice in thrillers, and we can't wait to see what she does next."

—CrimeReads

"Suspenseful and engrossing, *The Haunting of Brynn Wilder* is a ghost story, a love story, and a chilling fireside tale in one. Readers will be drawn in from the first page, and they won't want to stop until they read the eerie conclusion, probably in the wee hours of the night."
—Simone St. James, *New York Times* bestselling author of
The Sun Down Motel

"Evocative and beautifully haunting, Wendy Webb's latest transports you to a location you'll soon want to call home, in a story you won't want to put down. It's no exaggeration to call this the standout gothic novel of the year."
—Darcy Coates, *USA Today* bestselling author of
The Haunting of Ashburn House

"A haunting tale of grief and loss that is beautifully layered with new beginnings and woven into a gothic ghost story both bone chilling and heartwarming."
—Melissa Payne, author of *The Secrets of Lost Stones*

PRAISE FOR *DAUGHTERS OF THE LAKE*

"Simultaneously melancholy and sweet at its core."
—*Kirkus Reviews*

"Well-delineated characters and a suspenseful plot make this a winner."
—*Publishers Weekly*

"*Daughters of the Lake* has everything you could want in a spellbinding read: unexpected family secrets, ghosts, tragic love stories, intertwined fates."
—Refinery29

"Perfect for anyone who loves a good ghost story that bleeds into the present day."

—Health

"*Daughters of the Lake* is gothic to its core, a story of ghostly revenge, of wronged parties setting history right."

—Star Tribune

"*Daughters of the Lake* provides an immersive reading experience to those who love ghostly mysteries, time travel, and lovely descriptions."

—New York Journal of Books

"*Daughters of the Lake* is an alchemical blend of romance, intrigue, ancestry, and the supernatural."

—Bookreporter

"Eerie, atmospheric, and mesmerizing."

—Novelgossip

"Haunting and heartbreaking . . . A masterful work of suspense . . ."

—Midwest Book Review

"In Wendy Webb's entrancing *Daughters of the Lake*, dreams open a door between the dead and the living, a lake spirit calls to a family of gifted women, and a century-old murder is solved under the cover of fog. This northern gothic gem is everything that is delicious, spooky, and impossible to put down."

—Emily Carpenter, author of *Burying the Honeysuckle Girls*, *The Weight of Lies*, and *Every Single Secret*

"The tentacles of the past reach out to threaten Kate Granger in this atmospheric tale set on the shores of Lake Superior. Filled with all the intrigue of old houses and their long-buried secrets, this gothic tale will make you shiver."

—Elizabeth Hall, bestselling author of *Miramont's Ghost*

"Wendy Webb's deftly woven tale hits all the right notes. A lost legacy of lake spirits, restless ghostly figures, and a past shrouded in fog and regret blend in delicious harmony in *Daughters of the Lake*. The queen of northern gothic does it again with this quintessential ghost story [that's] every bit as compelling and evocative as her fans have come to expect."

—Eliza Maxwell, bestselling author of *The Unremembered Girl*

THE
KEEPERS
OF
METSAN
VALO

OTHER BOOKS BY WENDY WEBB

The Haunting of Brynn Wilder

Daughters of the Lake

The End of Temperance Dare

The Vanishing

The Fate of Mercy Alban

The Tale of Halcyon Crane

THE
KEEPERS
OF
METSAN
VALO

A NOVEL

WENDY WEBB

LAKE UNION
PUBLISHING

Text copyright © 2021 by Wendy Webb
All rights reserved.

Published by Lake Union Publishing, Seattle

www.apub.com

Amazon, the Amazon logo, and Lake Union Publishing are trademarks of Amazon.com, Inc., or its affiliates.

ISBN-13: 9781542021623
ISBN-10: 1542021626

Cover design by Damon Freeman

Printed in the United States of America

For my Finnish ancestors, especially my gram,
Elma Herrala Maki

PROLOGUE

She huddled next to the trunk of an ancient tree and gazed up at the stars shining through the canopy of impossibly tall pines. They looked black against the night sky, brooding, plotting. She had wandered into the forest earlier in the evening, long before the blues and purples of twilight turned to inky darkness. The night had been safe, then.

She knew better than to leave the house when nightfall was near—her grandmother had always warned her about that—but the light had caught her eye. It was faint and flickering low, but as she stepped onto the path and followed it into the woods, then deeper still to the forest glen where she had encountered the bear and her two cubs earlier that spring, the light became brighter.

It looked like the flame of a tiny torch dancing through the trees, flitting this way and that. She was mesmerized by it, not realizing how deep in the forest she was until she turned around and saw she had strayed from the path. She couldn't see it anywhere. She didn't know which way she had come. And now the light was gone.

As the darkness fell around her like a shroud, she began to hear whispering voices floating through the pines. She couldn't make out what they were saying, but they seemed to be coming closer. Were they happy voices? Malevolent ones? Were they singing? She listened closely, holding her breath as though the very act of breathing would drown them out. As they came nearer, she tried to disappear into the tree trunk, not wishing to see whatever was whispering.

She closed her eyes. When she opened them again, they were all around her.

CHAPTER ONE

The key refused to turn. Annalise pulled on the door and jiggled its wrought-iron handle, a massive thing with intricate whorls and swirls, forged in another time. The door, too, was formidable: solid, well-aged oak with a curved top. It wasn't budging.

"Sometimes it sticks."

Annalise looked over her shoulder at Martin, the caretaker, who seemed as ancient as the door itself.

"I remember," she said, smiling at him. "Maybe that's why it was never locked."

"Let me try," he said, taking the key from her hand. He gave the door a mighty pull and turned the key at the same time. She heard a heavy snap as the key hit its mark. Martin pushed the door open and stepped aside. To Annalise, it was like he had opened the door to her childhood.

Metsan Valo. Her great-grandparents had named this fortress of a house "Forest Light" when they built it on Ile de Colette, an island in Lake Superior just off the coast of Wharton, a popular tourist getaway. They had come to the island to put down roots in a time when the forest that surrounded the house was deeper and darker and even more foreboding than it was now. And, to hear her grandmother tell it, full of spirits and demons and danger. Metsan Valo was new when the ancient trees had not yet fallen to the lumberman's axe, when mystery and wisdom still permeated the land and the water and the sky.

Annalise held her breath and stepped into the grand entryway, gazing upward to the ceiling two stories above. As she walked into the main room, she saw it was much the same as she remembered—dark-wood floors, weathered with age. Enormous wooden beams along the ceiling, hewn generations ago from the ancient trees. Turning to the kitchen, Annalise remembered the formidable stove always seemed to be warm. A wood-burning oven was built into the wall. The massive wrought-iron chandelier hung from a chain above the dining-room table, large enough for twelve. The fireplace, crafted from stones her ancestors had gathered on the property, stretched all the way up to the ceiling.

And the view, one entire wall of floor-to-ceiling windows overlooking the sprawling lawn—still meticulously maintained by Martin, Annalise saw—surrounded on two sides by thick forest and leading down to the dock and the great lake below. The enchanted wood, her grandmother used to call it. The lake was angry and gray and roiling today, hitting the rocky shoreline with crashing waves. It took her breath away, as it always did.

The place reminded Annalise, Anni, as her friends called her, of something out of Lord of the Rings or, more recently, *Game of Thrones*. Ancient, solid, heavy construction, made of entire logs, stones, and the other bounty of nature around it, built not just to withstand the wind and rain, but to command it.

The bones of the room were the same as Anni remembered, but the feeling wasn't. When Anni was a child, this house had seemed to be a fortress of protection between her and the outside world. It still was, she supposed, but the place felt diminished somehow now. Sagging with age. The overstuffed sofa and chairs all dipped slightly in the middle, their decorative pillows faded by the sunlight that had streamed in from the front windows for decades. And the air smelled musty, as though it had been trapped in the room forever. But that couldn't have been the case. Mummo had just passed, not more than a week prior.

Anni's eyes grew wide as she spied a flat-screen television on the coffee table near the fireplace. When had they broken down and conceded to modern conveniences? She turned and glanced into the kitchen. Sure enough, a dishwasher was built into the cabinets by the sink. Were those cabinets new, too?

It had been a long time since Anni last visited.

Martin shuffled around, opening windows, inviting the fresh air inside. A whoosh of chill swirled through the room, as though the breeze were making itself at home.

"It gets stuffy in here so quickly," he said to her, holding her gaze with his penetrating blue eyes, still as clear as the lake, though his face was lined—a testament to a lifetime working outside in the sun and wind. "The place will come to life again, now that you're here."

As if it had been waiting. A chill shot up Anni's spine, but she shook it off. Not today.

As she walked from room to room, her footsteps echoed along with the lifetimes of love and loss that lingered in the air here. She could almost hear her twin brother, Theo, laughing as the two of them ran back inside after a day on the water, trailing sand and sun with them.

Theo was light to her darkness, both in temperament and appearance. Where he was blond and blue eyed, with fair skin that freckled and burned in the sun, she was dark haired and dark eyed, with a darker complexion that seemed to soak up the rays. Theo was ever the optimist, brightening even the most serious of situations with a well-placed phrase. Outgoing and gregarious and warm, he lit up any room he walked into. Anni was more serious than her brother, quieter. She kept her own counsel, even as a small child. She was content to play alone in the woods, where the wind whispered secrets to her. He wanted only to be with her, swimming, gathering small stones along the lakeshore, or exploring the acres and acres of land their grandmother owned, creating adventures along the way.

Their mother called them yin and yang. Opposite, yes, but interconnected.

He would be here soon. As would the rest of the family.

"I'll take your suitcases." Martin's words broke her memories apart, and they fell to the floor like shards of glass. He grasped the handles of her two oversize cases and started up the stairs.

"I can manage those, Martin," Anni protested, reaching for the bags.

He smiled over his shoulder at her. "Nonsense. It's my pleasure. Always has been."

Anni followed him up the great staircase, each rung a log cut in half and varnished until it shone. She ran her hand along the black wrought-iron banister that had been twisted into a swirl by a blacksmith long ago, cool and smooth to the touch. Anni took a moment and gazed over the railing onto the great room below.

"Will the others be coming today?" she asked, imagining the quiet house filled with people, a lifetime of . . . everything . . . dredged up between them like sludge from the marshy bays. Her stomach tightened at the thought of it.

"Soon enough," Martin said, giving her a look as they made their way down the long hallway. "Not tonight. Maybe tomorrow or the next day. You'll have some peace for a bit until the horde descends." He opened the door to the master bedroom.

"Oh no," Anni said, peering inside at the enormous bed, its ornately carved headboard as heavy and formidable as she remembered. "I don't want Mummo's room."

"It's been cleaned," Martin told her, a slight affront in his voice. "When we got word you were coming, Meri and I made sure all of the rooms—"

Anni put her hand on his arm. "Of course you did. The house looks wonderful. Maybe Mom or Aunt Gloria will want this room. I just can't imagine sleeping in here."

He smiled. "You did, plenty, when you were a girl. The first clap of thunder, and you'd fly down that hallway."

Anni saw herself then, piling into bed with her grandmother. Mummo, the Finnish familiar word for *grandma*, which she and Theo had always called her, would be in her ever-present flannel nightgown, summer or winter, and would gather Anni into her arms and pull her close.

"No need to fear the thunder," she would say. "It's just the sky rumbling. The gods might be angry. But not with us. Now I suppose you want a story."

And Anni would snuggle down next to her as she told the old tales, of spirits and elves and sprites. Soon, she'd be asleep, lulled by the lavender scent of her grandmother's sheets. She could smell it now. But the scent dissipated into the air as Martin pulled the door shut.

"Your usual room, then?" he asked her.

"Perfect." She managed a smile.

They walked down the hall to the next door. When Anni stepped inside, more childhood memories came rushing back. The same red-and-black quilt still covered her bed, its headboard hewn from logs felled on the property, too. The round rug, woven by her grandmother out of old clothes, still lay in the middle of the room. The desk sat by the window, just as it always had. Anni wondered if the journal she had kept as a teenager was still in the bottom drawer.

A flat-screen television hung on one wall. It gave Anni a start. Like the one in the living room, it seemed strange and out of place. As though it had time-traveled there from the future.

"What's with the TVs?" Anni asked Martin.

He shrugged. "Last year the county finally got here with broadband internet," he said.

Anni's mouth hung open. "You're kidding me. All the way out here?"

"It's a new state initiative, running broadband into far-flung, remote areas. Something about closing the skills gap. Or education gap. Or some kind of gap." He chuckled. "They want kids who live out here to have the same opportunities as kids in the cities."

Anni squinted at him. She supposed it was great for people who lived on the island full-time, if a bit unsettling for her, as though harsh reality had intruded into her retreat from the rest of the world. And didn't explain the TVs.

"Did Mummo watch television?" she asked him.

"Your grandmother thought it was time to haul Valo into the twenty-first century," he said. "So she broke down and got the internet and the televisions. She loved her British detective shows. Especially the ones with priests in little parishes doing end runs around the constables."

This brought a smile to Anni's lips, the thought of Mummo curling up with a hot brandy and *Father Brown*. She smiled up at Martin but saw he was brushing away tears. She put a hand on his arm.

"I know," she said.

He cleared his throat and gazed into the room. Silence descended then, like a summer rain, and filled the room with everything unspoken. A lifetime at Metsan Valo, summed up in that moment of silence.

"I'm happy you're here," he said finally. "We both are. You, coming from the opposite side of the world, got here first. Someone else might ask why that is. They might wonder why the rest of them didn't hop into their cars and come immediately."

Anni shrugged.

Martin set down her suitcases and turned to go. "Need anything else right now? Something to drink, maybe?"

This man was a caretaker in every sense of the word. "I'm good, I guess."

"Meri's got a chicken roasting for dinner. Should be ready at about five. Beyond that, you know where everything is, honey."

Anni held Martin's gaze for a long moment. "It's so empty without her here," she said.

He nodded. "It always will be. But you're filling it up now."

Tears stung at Anni's eyes. "It's just . . ." She caught her breath. "I was coming to spend the next couple of months with her," she said, the words coming out in one long stream, a sob choking in her throat. "We had made all the arrangements."

Martin put a hand on her shoulder. "I know," he said. "We were preparing for your visit. Everyone is in shock. It was so sudden. Not unexpected, but sudden. We all thought we'd have more time."

Anger bubbled up inside Anni then, just as it had after she had originally taken the call from Martin. Her grandmother had died suddenly after an illness she had told no one about.

Martin gave her shoulder a squeeze and closed the door behind him. Anni listened to his footsteps echoing down the hall. She stood still for a moment, looking around the room, not knowing quite what to do next. Finally, she sank down onto the bed and stretched out, her head on the pillow. From that position, she could see the top limbs of the pines and the two enormous black walnut trees swaying in the breeze. Her trees, she had thought when she was a child. How often had she been mesmerized by that sight out her window while lying in bed over the years?

Now, it was almost like the trees were waving to her in greeting. They had been waiting for her. The forest itself had. As if it were saying, *Welcome home, Annalise.*

CHAPTER TWO

As Annalise was putting her clothes away, hanging her shirts and tucking her underthings into drawers, she heard a rumble of thunder. Somehow, it made her feel at home. Peaceful. Thunderstorms were common in this part of the world. Her room at Metsan Valo was situated on the corner, affording her windows on two sides, and she opened them all, letting the sweet, fresh scent of rain waft in on the breeze.

She sank into the chaise near the windows and put her feet up, pulling a light afghan around her. She leaned her head back, and soon her eyes began to get heavy, too heavy to fight. Anni wasn't sure if it was jet lag or the enormity of losing her grandmother so suddenly, just when she had been planning to visit, but whatever the cause, it overtook her, and she fell into a fitful sleep.

She dreamed of Mummo, and of Theo and the summers of their childhood, which were simple and uncluttered without the trappings of age, the drama of greed, and the passage of time.

When she opened her eyes again, all was dark. She rose from the chaise and walked out into the hallway, not bothering to flip on the light. She padded down the hallway to the stairs and saw a soft glow coming from the kitchen. Martin and his wife, Meri, were sitting at the table, deep in conversation. Anni stood at the top of the stairs and listened.

"I don't like it," Meri said.

"Nor do I, love," Martin said, putting a hand over hers.

"Do you know anything?"

Martin shook his head. "She didn't share the specifics with me."

Don't like what? Anni wondered. But she was uncomfortable eavesdropping any further, so she cleared her throat and started down the stairs. Martin and Meri both looked up at her and smiled.

"There she is!" Martin sang out.

"Wow, I guess I sacked out," Anni said, joining them at the table. "Sorry I missed dinner."

"Are you hungry, child?" Meri asked. "I've been keeping the chicken warm for you." She pushed herself out of her chair.

Child. Meri and Martin had always called her that. She was a bit long in the tooth for that name now, but she didn't mind. It made her feel like she was home.

"I can get it, Meri," Anni said.

Meri shook her head. "Nonsense. I'm delighted."

Anni pulled out a chair next to Martin and slid onto it while Meri fussed with the roast chicken and vegetables. She returned with a plate and set it in front of Anni, then grabbed a bottle of wine from the fridge and three glasses.

"This looks delicious," Anni said, hunger pangs rumbling in her stomach. She couldn't remember the last time she had eaten. On the plane? That was nearly fourteen hours ago. She took a bite and smiled at Meri. "I've missed your cooking."

Meri beamed. "We've missed you here, child."

It had been a long time. Years had passed since Anni had been to Metsan Valo. When Anni thought of it, the time away seemed like an eon and the blink of an eye at once. She had meant to get back to visit more often. A shroud of guilt wrapped around her and cinched in tightly. Anni had been feeling it ever since she'd heard the news of Mummo's passing.

Meri poured the wine.

"Here's to your return," Martin said, lifting his glass.

The three of them clinked.

As Anni devoured her roast chicken and vegetables, the three of them chatted about her trip, and current events, and anything else that wasn't the topic at hand. So many elephants were in the room, it was getting rather crowded.

Meri gathered Anni's empty plate and silverware, loading them into the dishwasher before adding a soap packet and turning on the machine. Anni smiled at this. She never thought she'd see Meri operating a dishwasher. A concession to the modern age. *Time marches on,* she thought. Even at Metsan Valo.

Martin glanced at his watch. "I guess we should be turning in," he said, pushing himself to his feet with a groan. "Sleep well, my girl." He ruffled the top of Anni's hair and smiled down at her.

"We'll be at the cottage if you need anything," Meri said, following him.

"Good night," Anni said. "Thank you for everything. It's good to be home." Her words caught in her throat.

"It's good that you're here," Meri said, nodding.

And then the door shut behind them. They were gone. And the silence, the aloneness, filled up the room.

What to do now? Anni toyed with flipping on the television in the living room but settled instead on doing the same in her bedroom. A close nest of four walls around her. Anni had never been alone at night at Metsan Valo, or anytime, really, and the emptiness was tangible. At the same time, the house seemed full of movement, breathing, rustlings down dark hallways. She shivered as she climbed back up the stairs and exhaled as she closed the door.

She found the remote control and turned on the out-of-place television, local news from the nearest big city dominating the airwaves. Anni changed into her pajamas and slipped into bed, propping her pillows behind her.

A moment later, she found herself awakening. It was that strange and otherworldly time between wake and sleeping, and she felt herself, her inner being, rising from wherever it had gone in her dreams, back into her body.

She felt a roughness beneath her, a scratchiness she didn't understand. What was it? She opened her eyes and saw what was pricking her. Pine needles. She scrambled to her feet and whirled around—she was outside. In the forest. *What in the world?*

Anni's heart was beating hard and fast in her chest as she got her bearings. The forest was dense and dark, but looking up, she saw a million stars twinkling in the universe. The full moon hung low in the sky.

She heard it, then. Voices. Tiny voices. Laughter all around her.

"She is here!" the voices said. "She has returned!"

"Follow us!"

"Come! Can't you hear the music?"

Anni did hear it. Ancient music, seeming to come from another place and time. But she knew better than to go toward it.

There were things in these woods, strange and frightening things. She'd known it since she was a child. Mummo had told her the old stories, time and time again, about the folk who lived in the forest and in the water. *Vaki*, she called them. There were vaki in the trees and rocks and water, unseen folk that could make you sick or make you well, harm you or help you, depending on their whim. They were guardians of everything in nature, from the animals in the forest to the trees to the plants to the rocks and the soil, the water and all the fishes and animals living in it. They were guardians of the wind and fire and earth and the sea. Everything in nature had vaki. Except mankind.

Tonight, they did not seem particularly benevolent.

Mummo had cautioned Anni and Theo to respect the vaki. To give a silent thanks for their protection when they walked into the forest. To ask for calm seas when they set out in their canoes. As children, she and Theo would see Mummo tossing flower petals into the lake, or setting out food and drink in the forest. To Mummo, vaki were real beings, not simply folktales. The Halla women had made a pact with the vaki long ago, Mummo had said, and brought that pact with them to this new land, to this house, to this property.

As a child, Anni believed these tales to be true and, more than that, unique to her family. Only the Hallas had vakis in their own magical world at Metsan Valo, she had thought. As she grew a bit older, Anni learned that many cultures had tales of little folk. She was stunned when she heard the cautionary and terrifying stories of Irish faeries, of people stumbling into their faerie rings in the forest and never being seen again, or joining a dance party in the woods late one night and being cursed to dance there forevermore. Those stories sounded so similar to Mummo's tales.

Was it truth, or was it legend? Anni didn't know the answer to that, but she felt that Metsan Valo was a place where truth and legend became entangled.

As an adult, Anni had all but forgotten about these tales, but now, here, they came rushing back in vivid detail. Anni ran, stumbling on roots and rocks, her bare feet burning with pain. Soon she burst out of the forest and into the yard, and there was Metsan Valo, standing sentinel. Her safe haven. All the lights were on, shining brightly in contrast to the inky sky. But as she stared at it, she saw it didn't look right. The house seemed larger, had an almost hulking, menacing presence. It was vibrating, as though the house itself were alive, breathing in and out.

Who had turned on the lights? Martin? It had been dark when Anni had gone to sleep.

At that point, Anni didn't care. She didn't care who had turned on the lights; she didn't care that the house seemed strange and enchanted. It was home, whatever strangeness had overtaken it, and she needed to get there, now. She sprinted toward the house and had almost reached the deck when she felt a sharp tugging on her pajamas. She was jerked backward and fell, hitting her head on the hard ground.

The voices surrounded her. And then she saw them, the vaki, tiny, flitting things, dancing around her in a circle to ancient music played in another time. Maybe she was in that time now. She closed her eyes to accept whatever fate had in store for her.

Anni opened her eyes and sat up with a start. Her sheets were twisted around her legs. She was drenched with sweat. She reached for the lamp on her nightstand and flipped it on. Her heart was beating hard and fast, and as she caught her breath, she noticed the television was droning softly.

It was a dream, then.

The clock read 4:44 a.m. Anni took a sip from the glass of water on her nightstand and slipped out of bed, padding to the bathroom to splash some water onto her face. She walked over to the windows and drew the curtains to the sides. There were the woods, just as they always had been. The yard. The lake shimmering beyond it. Nothing strange there. No vaki creeping around in the trees, bedeviling her. Playing tricks.

She took a deep breath and let it out. Those were just old stories Mummo used to tell. It was folklore, not true to life. She hadn't been back to Metsan Valo in a decade . . . of course those old tales were on her mind. Swirling around in her subconscious. It made perfect sense she'd dream about it.

Anni was feeling calmer, but she knew no more sleep would come tonight. It was already late morning in Paris, where she had been living for the past decade. Her body would take a while to adjust to the time change. She thought about Madame Troiveau, who ran the café down the street where Anni would stop in for a coffee every morning. She could almost taste the café au lait. Was Madame missing Anni today? What about Monsieur Bertrand, who Anni would see walking his dog every day? Was he wondering where she was this morning? She sighed.

Probably not. Her Paris neighborhood had come to life without her today. It had been her home for nearly ten years. But, as Anni looked around her darkened room, she knew this was home, too. Metsan Valo held a deeper, ancestral sense of home.

Anni wrapped her robe around her and slid her feet into her slippers. Madame's wasn't the only café au lait in the world. She made her way through the silent house, down the stairs and to the kitchen. Starlight shone in through the big windows in the living room, and Anni shivered just a little, remembering her dream.

She found the beans and filled the pot with water. Soon, the smell of brewing coffee wafted through the room. Anni poured some into her favorite mug, added a splash of cream, and headed into the living room. She had intended to settle down on the sofa, but then she thought, no. No, she would not. She grabbed a cozy throw off the couch and strode through the room to the french doors, flipped the bolt, and pushed the door open, a bit too dramatically. She was going outside. No dream was going to scare her away from what was hers. Her family's. No imaginary vaki were going to run her off.

She walked with purpose out onto the deck and sank down into one of the Adirondack chairs that sat in a neat row overlooking the lawn and the water, pulling the throw around her. Steam wafted up from her mug into the chilly air. Anni gazed into the woods. Nothing so frightening. Only ancient, massive trees, which had always felt like her guardians. She took a deep breath and heard a wolf howl in the distance. It was a mournful sound, and Anni wondered if it, somehow, was grieving along with her.

Anni sipped her coffee and watched the landscape come to life. As the first light hinted on the horizon, birds began their morning songs. She saw motion in the grass, little critters starting their daily routines. A long, lonely call of a loon pealed through the morning air, answered by another, farther away. She reveled in the sound, utterly a part of this place. She had never heard it anywhere else.

Anni watched as the friendly gray-and-white Canadian jays alit on the feeder, tweeting their thanks when they took a seed. When she was a child, she would sit as still as a stone on the deck, holding a few peanuts in her outstretched hand. A cautious jay would circle and then fly toward her, perching on her fingers while it took the peanut. She could still feel the scratchy talons and the weight of the bird as she tried to remain as still as she could so as not to scare it away.

The sky slowly lightened, the gray of morning twilight warming as the minutes passed. Anni noticed movement in the woods, scurrying. Was it the vaki? As the light of day dawned, the notion seemed to dissipate. The old legends from her memory had just messed with her head. That was all. She looked closer and saw the black and brown stripes of a chipmunk skittering through the grass. Anni smiled. *Vaki indeed.*

Stepping inside to refill her mug, she didn't hear the laughter in the woods.

CHAPTER THREE

"I've been here three and a half minutes, and A, I don't have a beverage, and B, I haven't hugged you yet. What kind of welcome is this?"

Theo.

Anni was reading on the deck when the sound of his booming voice pulled her out of the story's plot and back into the present moment. She dropped the book and shot out of her chair. There he was, in his faded jeans and striped sweater, looking like he had just stepped out of a Ralph Lauren ad.

She hadn't seen him in more than a year.

"What?" she cried, running toward her twin brother and throwing her arms around him. "You weren't supposed to get here until tomorrow!"

"I came early," he said, kissing her cheek and then pulling back. "Let me look at you! It's been way too long. You changed your hair!"

Anni lifted her hand and brushed the hair from her face, a guilty smile creeping onto her lips. "I colored it myself before I left. Too much?"

"It looks great! I like the red. You always used to get those crazy auburn highlights in the summer when we were kids. So, really, one could say you're just going back to your natural color."

Anni's delight engulfed her entire body. It had always been the two of them, growing up. Anni and Theo. They were the calm for one another in the bohemian miasma that had been their childhoods—their mother moving them from place to place every few years before they reached school age, each time a new interest, religion, or, more often than not, man caught her eye. Their father had never been in the picture. Indeed, Anni and Theo bore their mother's last name, Halla, rather than their father's, a man whom they had never met. Anni had stopped asking about him when she was still a child, and now, frankly, she never thought of him at all. She had relegated him to the "sperm donor" column and moved on with her life. He was as unreal and imaginary as the stories Mummo used to tell her.

And there had always been Metsan Valo to retreat to. Anni and Theo had spent almost every summer of their lives in the big fortress of a house, while their mother was off painting in France or taking a cooking class in Italy or living with a new man on his boat in the Caribbean.

Theo took her hand now and led her back through the french doors into the kitchen.

"How was your trip?" he asked her, opening the fridge and poking his head inside.

"Long," Anni said. "I'm just getting past the jet lag now. Did you drive up?"

"I made the mistake of flying," he said, taking the lid off a dish of leftovers, smelling it, and putting it back on the shelf. He closed the fridge door. "I always seem to block out the fact that O'Hare is the tenth circle of hell. When I finally got on the plane, I could swear I saw Hannibal Lecter in 7B."

Anni laughed out loud. Theo had such a way of lightening her mood. He had always played that role, even when they were children. Whenever Anni was upset, internalizing the slightest of things, afraid, fretting over nothing, it was Theo who would always bring her back to herself. As though he was a lifeline to reality when she was drifting away from it.

She held his eyes for a moment. That was what he was doing now, deliberately. Small talk, chatter, banter, laughs. But there was something bigger floating in the air between them, something unspoken and so painful that both of them wished with all their souls it wasn't there.

Anni saw it in his eyes; he was thinking the same thing. He enveloped her in a hug, and Anni felt Theo sigh into a sob. It let loose the feelings she had been holding in. They stood that way for a long time, literally crying on each other's shoulders.

"I was coming to spend the next few months," Anni blubbered out. "It was all set. She asked me to come, and I was coming."

"I know," he whispered.

They held each other until the tears dried up and only the love remained.

Finally, Theo cleared his throat. "Okay, I need a tissue, or this is going to get ugly," he croaked out. They pulled back and smiled at each other. "Oh, it's already ugly," he said, reaching for the paper towels on the counter.

"Speak for yourself," Anni said.

"It's really the end of an era, if I could be any more of a cliché," Theo said, reopening the fridge and pulling out a beer and a bottle of wine. "I was going to get a bottle of water, but to hell with that. It's five o'clock somewhere, right?" He poured a glass for Anni and popped the top off the beer for himself, taking a long drink.

"Did she tell you she was sick?" Anni asked.

Theo shook his head, a darkness falling over his face for a moment and then disappearing just as quickly.

"I would have told you immediately."

Of course he would have, she thought. It was a silly question. Anni and Theo hadn't talked much since they had learned their grandmother had passed. The shock of it had taken the wind out of both of them, and they had agreed to regroup after they both got to Metsan Valo, where they could see each other's faces in this place that meant so much to both of them.

"I was the closest to her, geographically," Theo said. "Well, not closer than Mom when she's at the house in Wharton, but how often is she there these days? God only knows. Let's just say I was the closest sane person to her. I could've arranged to be here during—" His words trailed off into a sob. He covered his eyes with his paper towel. "I would've been here."

"I know," Anni said.

Theo nodded. "Any of us would've come running. Even Big Edie and Little Edie."

Anni squinted at him for a minute until the joke sank in. "You mean Mom and Aunt Gloria?" she squeaked out, laughing. "That's so perfect."

"They would've Grey Gardened this place within five minutes of being here while Mummo was sick."

"Totally," Anni said. "I'd have found a family of raccoons in the bedroom when I got here yesterday."

It was a joke between them, but it had some truth in it, too. Anni and Theo had always felt a thread of otherworldliness ran through their mother and her sister, something deep in their souls and their psyches.

When they were very young, Anni and Theo began to feel as though they needed to be the ones to take care of their mother, rather than the other way around. It was as if she was so fragile, the world might break her at any moment. Anni remembered when that realization had first hit her. They were crossing the main street in Wharton, where they had settled during the twins' school years. They were only about five years old. Their mother was blissfully unaware of anything going on around them—traffic least of all—and Anni and Theo, at the exact same time, grabbed their mother's hands so she wouldn't walk out into the street and get hit by a car. The twins had exchanged a look then, and a knowing passed between them.

But there was something else, something darker than their mother's ethereal, scattered nature. Something the twins could never quite put their finger on. A vulnerability. . . Somewhere along the line, they had stopped trying to define it. In adulthood, when both were out of the house and forging their own lives, it seemed less threatening, less immediate. Let their mother muddle along just fine, drifting off into her own hippie fairy land. It didn't have much to do with them anymore. In recent years, Anni had likened it to how a parent might feel when a child left the nest and embarked on his or her own life. Yes, you always worried, but you needed to trust that they could handle things without you. That was how she felt about her mother now. Theo did, too.

Now, they walked over to the big sofa and settled down into its soft cushions.

"It's weird to be here without Mummo," Theo said, sighing.

"Everyone feels that way, I think." She shuddered and took a sip of wine. "Martin and Meri, at least. Especially them. It feels completely different. I was here by myself last night. I had a nightmare."

Theo grimaced. "Not surprised. It does feel different in here, you're right. Empty. Like the house's spirit is gone. Being here alone for the first night must've been creepy. I should've come yesterday to meet you. I don't know what I was thinking."

"Neither of us was thinking," Anni said. "I could've flown into Chicago, and we could've come together."

Theo shook his head, his bright-blue eyes shining with tears. He ran a hand through his blond, curly mop. "That's what happens when the heart of the family passes," he said. "Nobody thinks clearly for a while."

"You're exactly right about that, son." It was Martin, standing in the kitchen with Meri. Anni hadn't heard them come in.

Theo pushed himself up and crossed the room, hugging both of them in turn.

"Your grandmother knew people wouldn't be thinking too clearly now." Martin exchanged a charged glance with his wife. "So she did some thinking for you. That's what we've come to talk with you about."

"Why don't we sit down?" Meri said, gesturing to the big dining-room table.

The energy in the room seemed to sizzle. Anni and Theo exchanged a glance of their own as the four of them made their way to the table and took their places.

"Well, this is all very dramatic," Theo said, more of a question than a statement.

Martin cleared his throat. "We wanted to talk to the two of you, before the others arrived."

"About what?" Anni asked.

"About your grandmother's wishes, child."

They sat there in silence for a moment until Martin again cleared his throat. It was clear to Anni that the two of them were uncomfortable. That the words themselves were a struggle.

"When your grandmother fell ill, she came to us to talk about her final wishes and arrangements," Martin began.

"You should have told us she was sick," Theo said flatly, his eyes brimming with tears. "Why didn't you tell us?"

Martin held Theo's gaze, but Meri looked away. "She specifically asked us not to tell anyone," Martin said. "She didn't want people fussing, coming around, hovering. Not so much you two. The others."

Mom, Anni mouthed to Theo. He nodded.

Meri reached into the front pocket of her apron and pulled out an envelope. "She wrote down her wishes," she said. "We sat right here and talked about the particulars, and then she put it to paper, so you'd know it was coming from her, not us."

Theo squinted at them. "Why would we think that?"

23

Meri glanced at Martin. "Well, some things she specified are a little unusual."

They were silent for a moment, taking that in.

"What?" Theo said, finally. "Does she want some sort of pagan funeral where we all have to dance around naked in the woods? Because there's not enough mosquito repellent in all of Wharton for me to agree to that. No and no."

Anni couldn't help laughing. Even Martin and Meri shared a grin. Dear Theo. Breaking the tension once again.

His smile fading, Martin took the envelope from his wife. "When you put it like that, her requests don't sound that odd. Your grandmother wants you, Annalise, to write her obituary."

He pulled a couple of sheets of paper out of the envelope and handed one to her. "She got you started with dates, facts, all of the whos, whens, whys, whats, and wheres. She wanted you to fill in the color."

Anni looked at the page and smiled at Mummo's neat handwriting. "I can do that," she said.

"She wants an open house here next week," Meri continued. "It's up to you two to pick the day, depending on the weather. Many people will be coming and going, and we want to have a nice day for it. I'll cater it, so you won't have to worry about that."

"These don't sound like strange requests," Theo said.

Martin smiled. "Just wait. As far as her final resting place is concerned, she has been cremated already, per her wishes."

Anni and Theo nodded. "Yeah, we had all talked about that years ago. We knew that's what she wanted when the time came."

"It's what she wants done with her ashes that perplexed us a little," Meri said, wincing.

Anni and Theo were silent for a long moment.

Martin cleared his throat. "Her ashes, in their urn, have been placed in a small kayak," he said. "Almost like a child's toy. She had it made a few months ago. You two are to take that, along with a few of her most precious possessions, out into the lake and . . . set it on fire."

Anni and Theo stared at him, openmouthed.

"The mistress of Metsan Valo wants a Viking funeral," Theo said, grinning. "Unreal."

"In a manner of speaking, yes."

There was something about Theo's devilish grin, Meri's and Martin's grave expressions, and the very idea of setting the boat on fire with Mummo in it, like an ancient Viking funeral, that made Anni want to burst out laughing. It was one of those "laughter in church" moments. She tried to hold it in with a serious expression befitting the topic at hand, but it bubbled to the surface, and she couldn't stop it. The others joined in, and she laughed until she cried, at one point leaning her head on Theo's shoulder.

"That was the big unusual drama you wanted to share with us?" she squeaked out, finally. "I'm happy to do that for Mummo. What a moving tribute to her."

"Okay, but how are we going to do this?" Theo asked, looking out the window toward the lake and narrowing his eyes. "I suppose we could take the canoe. Or the boat. And drag the little kayak alongside until we got out a ways."

"How are we going to set it on fire in the middle of the lake?"

"Flamethrower?"

This made Anni laugh even harder.

"You know it's illegal," Theo said, brushing some unseen lint off his shoulder.

"Can you see the headlines? 'Halla grandchildren arrested in bizarre funerary rite.' You are totally taking the fall for it. I'll just tell you that right now."

Anni was wiping her eyes, and she realized Meri and Martin weren't laughing anymore. Their faces were grave. A seriousness settled in between them.

25

"There's something else, isn't there?"

"Your grandmother made a video will," Meri said, rolling her eyes just a little. "That's why she wanted all of you gathered here, now, before any funeral or wake or doings of any kind. Her lawyer is coming with it tomorrow evening, after the rest of the family gets here, for everyone to view together."

CHAPTER FOUR

Anni and Theo sat on the dock, dangling their feet over the side. The water below was crystal clear, and Anni gazed at their reflections, distorted and shimmering. They didn't speak for a long time. Like many twins, they didn't need words to know what the other was thinking.

"It's weird she didn't want to be buried in the forest, don't you think?" Theo said, finally. "It makes sense she'd want to be laid to rest there. Or, you know. Scattered." Anni had been thinking the same thing.

"All of her old stories, they're all about the forest," she said. "Some about the water, but not many."

"Although Lake Superior is an entity unto itself in all of her tales. Maybe she wanted his protection as she passed from one world to the next."

Anni eyed her twin and smirked. "Now you sound like Mummo."

"Well? That was her, you know."

Anni did know. Even her name, Taika, meant *magic*.

"And what about this video will?" Theo asked, splashing the water with his foot. "Who was she, Agatha Christie? All the heirs assembled, and the dearly departed gets the last laugh."

Anni was the one who laughed.

"I hadn't even thought about the will until they brought it up," Anni said.

"Me, neither," Theo said. "That's not the first thing that comes to mind when someone you love dies. Well. It's not the first thing that comes to our minds. But you can bet the others are thinking about it."

Anni snorted in the back of her throat. "Salivating is more like it. Who all is coming? Do we know?"

"The usual suspects," Theo said. "Mom and Gloria, for sure."

"Probably," she said. "There will be money involved. Vicky and her family, too. I wonder if she's bringing Yale."

"If he starts talking politics, I'm going to put him in the kayak and set it on fire."

"I'll create a diversion."

Theo gave her a sidelong glance. "You know, they're probably why Mummo didn't want anyone to know she was sick. Why she didn't tell even us. Maybe she didn't want them around at the end."

Anni shrugged. "We'll never really know, so I'm not going to get caught up in speculating. It is what it is, to use a phrase I absolutely hate. And as for the video will, maybe she just wanted everyone to know her wishes from her own mouth. That could be all it is."

"Yeah, but the question is: Why?"

Anni shot him a look. Theo humphed. "Maybe she gave all the money to charity and wanted to prevent somebody from filing a lawsuit or something . . . If Vicky gets disinherited, you know that Yale will be at his lawyer's office in a nanosecond."

"He probably already has, in prep."

Their cousin Vicky had married a man nobody in the family got along with. Anni couldn't remember one interesting or even civil conversation with him. It happened in every family, she supposed, but it stung especially cruelly since theirs was so small. But, to be fair, they hadn't spent much time together as adults, especially during the past decade. She and Theo didn't really know their cousin, let alone her husband.

Theo lay back on the dock with a thud and soaked up the sun, exhaling loudly. "This feels really good. I'm so glad to be away from everything. I needed a break. Although this isn't really much of a break, is it?"

Over the past months, Theo had been telling Anni all about the stressors of his fast-paced life as the owner of a marketing firm in Chicago, with clients making ever-increasing demands on his staff, and on him. It was indeed a world away from Metsan Valo.

"Things not easing up at all at work?" Anni asked him.

"No," Theo said, his eyes closed. "It's crazier than ever. I'm putting out fires every minute of the day. And Jenny isn't making it any easier," he said, referring to his wife of fifteen years, whom Anni adored.

"Why? What's wrong? Don't tell me—"

Theo shook his head. "Everything's fine. I think. Or not. These past few months, we've been arguing all the time."

"You never argue."

"I know! It's like everything about her was pissing me off. She'd go brush her teeth at night, and I would get annoyed. She's similarly annoyed with me. What is that?"

Anni squinted at her brother. "You tell me."

"I don't know," Theo said. "All marriages have ups and downs, right? That could be all this is. Maybe we're just in one of the downs."

Anni sensed there was more he wasn't saying.

"Or?"

"I don't want to think about the 'or' right now."

"I was wondering why she wasn't here."

Theo ran a hand through his hair and sighed. "I thought we could use a little time apart. She's going to drive up for the funeral in a few days. Why didn't Jean-Paul come? I know the ticket is expensive, but it's not like you can't—" Theo's words evaporated in the air when he saw her expression.

"What?" he asked.

Anni lay down next to him. "Jean-Paul and I broke up two months ago."

He was the man Anni had met in Paris a decade earlier and stayed to be with, upending her old life and laying the foundation for a new one in the process. He was a professor at the Sorbonne, and they had met when Anni was auditing one of his art history classes.

Theo shot up and stared down at her, openmouthed. "What? And you didn't tell me?"

Anni felt tears escape her closed eyes and trickle down into her ears. "I didn't admit it to myself for a while. I felt like it wasn't happening."

"What *did* happen?"

Anni grimaced. "We were arguing all the time, too. Just like you and Jenny. I was picking fights about nothing. I don't know. Maybe I sensed something because he finally confessed he was seeing someone else, packed up, and left."

"What?" Theo repeated.

"He gave me the apartment. Literally. Not just to live there. It's mine now."

"What?" His eyes grew wide.

"And moved in with her. She's one of his students."

"Whaaaaat?"

Anni looked up at her twin and couldn't help smiling at his horrified expression. He slumped back down next to her, shaking his head. Several minutes passed in silence, neither of them speaking aloud what they both were thinking—Anni had been a student of Jean-Paul's when they met, too. After flailing around from job to unsatisfying job in her twenties, she had decided to go back to school to get a master's in French language and art history with the idea of teaching one day. At the urging of her mother, she had enrolled at the Sorbonne. She met Jean-Paul and suddenly the few years she had intended to spend in Paris became a decade with the man. At least she had her degree to show for it.

Anni felt Theo's hand grasp hers. He didn't need to say a word. She knew it all. His incredulity, his grief, the fact his heart was breaking for her, his anger at Jean-Paul for being so blind as to leave his sister. Anni felt it all, with that one touch of Theo's hand. At that moment, Anni felt like everything in the world that mattered was right there.

"Hello, my darlings!" Their mother's voice pierced the silence, breaking the peace between them.

Anni and Theo pushed themselves up and turned around to see their mother, Arden, standing a few feet away. True to form, she was wearing a long flax-colored linen dress with a colorful, flowing scarf wound around her neck, her tangle of thick blonde hair blowing in the breeze behind her. Anni had always thought their mother looked like she had just stepped out of a magical tale—she seemed not quite of this world—and given that she was named after the forest in a Shakespeare play, that characterization wasn't far off the mark. Theo meanwhile had always thought she was more Ophelia than Arden.

"Mom!" Anni and Theo scrambled to their feet. Arden walked toward them, arms outstretched, and enveloped them both in a hug. She smelled like the same musky perfume she used to wear when Anni and Theo were children.

She pushed back and looked at each of them in turn. "My children," she said, a sad smile on her lips. "Taika, gone from this world. It's hard to fathom."

Arden never called her mother Mom or Mummo. Always her first name. Anni always felt it was a sort of distancing between mother and her eldest daughter that she never quite understood. But Arden, ever the hippie, defied understanding.

"You loved your grandmother fiercely, and you two were the loves of her life," Arden went on. "I can say that to you now, before everyone else gets here. I don't want to cause hurt feelings. But you kids were her whole world. Vicky"—Arden waved her hand—"she's too concerned with handbags and social media and *influencing*. She never had any idea who Taika was, not really. What this place is. You two got her, and Metsan Valo. Even more than my sister and I did."

Anni took this in. Her mother was right. She and Theo had shared an especially close relationship with Mummo. They did get each other, instinctively. And though Anni hadn't been to Metsan Valo in a decade, the house lived in her bones. And vice versa.

"It's good to see you, Mom," Theo managed. "How's everything in—where in the world are you now?"

Arden smiled. "I'm home in Wharton for a while," she said, taking a few steps toward the end of the dock and gazing down at the water. "You both know that. I sent an email last month when I arrived."

Anni and Theo exchanged a glance. "I never got an email from you," Theo said.

"Oh?" Arden turned her big blue eyes on him. "I could've sworn I sent it. I'm sorry, dears."

Typical, Anni thought.

"Mom, you were here before Mummo died," Theo said. "Why didn't you tell us she was sick?"

"I didn't know," Arden said. "I had been here only a couple of weeks before she passed, and I was busy getting the house in shape. I'd been here to see her, of course. I noticed she had slowed down a bit, but she put on a good show. I had no idea."

Anni couldn't even look at Theo, knowing they were both roiling inside over how oblivious Arden could be.

"Anyhoo, I'm taking a class in horticulture at the university," Arden went on. "I've never been good with plants or landscaping, and I felt I should brush up on my skills. It's artistic in a way I didn't realize before. So I'm having fun with it!"

Thank goodness for that, Anni thought. God forbid their mother not be living in a constant state of delight.

"Are you and Gloria staying at the house in town?" Anni asked, hoping for an affirmative answer. But Arden shook her head.

"Heavens, no," she said. "Gloria and I agreed that we'd stay here at Metsan Valo with everyone. A real family reunion for the first time in forever."

Theo was staring straight ahead, and Anni could tell what he was thinking. *God save us all.*

CHAPTER FIVE

Standing between her children, Arden threaded one arm through Anni's and one through Theo's and led them from the dock. "Meri and Martin have prepared some hors d'oeuvres and wine for us on the deck. Dinner is in an hour or so. Let's enjoy each other, darlings, until the others arrive. We have so few moments together, just the three of us, these days."

They walked slowly toward the house, and Anni's stomach seized up. Wine. She needed wine. She shot Theo a look, and he stifled a laugh.

After they were seated at the shady table on the deck, nibbling on the cheese, crackers, and salami Meri and Martin had assembled for them and sipping on cold white wine, Anni fidgeted in the silence that had descended over them. What to say to their mother, whom she hadn't seen in who knew how long? Arden had come to Paris a while ago to visit but spent most of her time haunting the museums and the cafés, and little with her daughter. When had that been? Two years ago? Three?

"Are they coming today?" Anni asked, finally, breaking the silence.

Arden shook her head. "I've spoken to Gloria, and her wing of the family won't be here until tomorrow."

Small miracles, Anni thought.

"Do you know who all is coming? Is Vicky bringing Yale?"

"Oh, you can count on Yale being here," Arden said, a chuckle in her voice. "There's money at stake! Of course he's coming." *Funny,* Anni thought. It was exactly what Theo had said.

"What about their daughter?" Theo asked. "What's her name? Urchin?"

Anni choked on her sip of wine and let out a laugh. Even Arden was amused.

"You know very well it's Lichen, Theo," Arden said, mock admonishment in her voice. "Be nice, for goodness' sake. Yes, she was quite a handful early on, but according to Gloria, she's becoming a lovely young lady. Apparently, she's very shy. Quiet."

"How old is she now?" Anni asked. "Five? Six?"

"More like twelve or thirteen," Arden reported. "Time passes so fast, children."

At least she's right about that, Anni thought. She felt a twinge of something, guilt perhaps, creeping into her around the edges. Had it really been that long since she had seen her cousin?

They chatted for a while about the news of the day, how Arden was liking being back in Wharton, and other safe topics until Martin and Meri appeared with their dinner, a platter of grilled steaks and baked potatoes, and a salad, no doubt picked from the extensive garden on the sunny side of the house.

"It looks lovely!" Arden smiled as they dished up their plates.

Martin and Meri retreated, as they oftentimes did, despite pleas for them to sit down and enjoy dinner with the family, and the three of them were left on their own with the delicious meal the couple had prepared.

As Anni watched them go through the doors back into the house, she thought about this couple who seemed as old as time. She didn't know how long Martin and Meri had been at Metsan Valo, but it seemed like forever. All her lifetime, certainly.

"Were they here when you were growing up, Mom?" Anni asked between bites of her rib eye. "Martin and Meri, I mean."

"Oh my, yes," Arden said. "They've always taken care of this property. The woods. The lake. And us."

"Even when Pappa was alive?" Theo asked, referring to their grandfather, Arden's father, who had died before the twins were born.

Arden nodded. "They've always helped out here," she said. "I can't remember a time they weren't at Metsan Valo. They are part of the fabric."

"It's like they haven't aged a day in the whole decade I was away," Anni mused, taking a sip of her wine.

They ate in silence for a bit, and then Arden shook her head. "No more of this old family talk," she declared. "Let's catch up, darlings! What's the scoop with the two of you? What's happening in your worlds?"

✦

Later, after the three of them had talked about the latest events in their lives, Arden announced she was retreating upstairs to bed. Anni and Theo walked up with her, as was their family's long-ago custom. Anni had all but forgotten the ritual of a kiss on the cheek and a hug before bedtime. It was a nice way to end the day, settling down filled with the love of family. But, this time, she winced as she noticed Arden had taken Mummo's room instead of the one she had always slept in over the years, down the hall.

Anni couldn't help wrinkling her nose as she caught a glimpse of the chaos within the room as she and Theo said good night to their mother. Arden had been there all of five minutes before the contents of her luggage were strewn everywhere in Mummo's tidy nest. It was as though Arden's suitcase had exploded. Caftans here, wide linen pants there, long strands of beads littering the nightstand.

"Good night, dears!" she cooed, kissing each of them on the cheek. "I am so happy to be with my children again. Even under these circumstances. We can make it about love, my pets. Taika would've wanted that."

That was their mother—eccentric, frustrating, and though Anni could all too easily forget it, loving and warm, too. Such a dichotomy. It had been that way all their lives.

As she and Theo descended the staircase, Anni gave her brother a sidelong glance. "Do you know what just ran through my mind?"

Theo smiled at her. "What, pray tell? There's so much gold to mine from the conversation with Mom just now. Are you talking about the Greek restaurant owner or the hotelier in Venice?"

"Neither," Anni said, lowering her voice. "Mom is the elder of our family now."

This stopped Theo midstair, a horrified look on his face. "You're right. That's a wild thought."

He took a breath in. "Do you think she's going to inherit this house? That's what's going to happen, obviously."

Their *Grey Gardens* joke from earlier didn't seem quite so funny now.

Back down in the great room, they saw through the wall of windows that Martin had started a fire in the heavy wrought-iron firepit out in the yard. Anni loved how its cutouts of animals and birds gave off shadows in the firelight.

Anni and Theo made their way out the french doors, across the deck, and onto the lawn, and sank into chairs around the fire.

"Perfect, Martin, thank you," Anni said, feeling the warmth of the fire on her face. These late-summer evenings could turn cold very quickly here on the island after beautiful, warm days. It was as though summer and fall were fighting for dominance.

"If you don't need anything else, kids, I'm going to hit the hay," Martin said.

Anni and Theo bade him good night and turned their eyes to the fire, watching as the flames danced and swayed, casting eerie, long shadows onto the grass. Neither spoke for a long time. Instead, they gazed at the fire or up at the millions of stars that blanketed the night sky. Anni had grown up under this sky. It looked like home to her. But it still took her breath away. The vastness of it. The sheer number of stars. The constellations. The Milky Way. No wonder people made up stories about heroes immortalized in those stars. Or maybe the stories weren't made up at all, but handed down.

She, Theo, and Mummo would sit outside, right where they were sitting now, and look up while Mummo spun those tales of the past. Her absence ached in Anni's bones. She knew Theo felt it, too.

She sighed and pulled the throw blanket that was folded in her lap tighter around her. Looking out into the woods, she noticed the tiny on-and-off glow of fireflies. She nodded her head toward the forest. "The fireflies are out tonight."

Theo glanced into the woods and smiled. "I love those. They seem so magical, don't they? Little flickering lights bobbing around in the dark woods."

Anni smiled, but soon that smile faded. Something about the scene seemed off. Her skin began to crawl. More fireflies appeared in the woods. And still more. It was like they were reproducing in an instant. The woods were lit up with hundreds of them. Behind every tree, by every bush. All at once, it was as light as day.

Theo narrowed his eyes. "That's weird."

Anni leaned forward to get a better look. The fireflies were creating a neon light show in the woods. "Have you ever seen anything like that?"

"No," Theo said.

A heaviness descended between them then. "Maybe we should go inside," Theo said, pushing himself up from his chair. He wasn't looking at Anni. He had his gaze trained on the fireflies.

All at once, the bugs shot out of the forest and descended on Anni and Theo, flying this way and that with lightning speed, whirring around the twins' heads and bodies like a biblical swarm. The noise was unimaginable, as though a squadron of fighter pilots had taken aim around them. The twins began swatting the flies away from their heads.

"What the hell . . ." Anni whispered.

Anni wanted to scream, but the flies would've swarmed into their mouths, choking them. Theo grabbed Anni's hand and pulled her up from the chair. The two pounded through the yard and up to the deck, squishing so many fireflies beneath their feet that the deck's wooden slats began to feel slippery. Anni reached for the handle and flung the french door open, slamming it shut when she and Theo were inside.

They looked at each other, stunned expressions on their faces. Theo bent at the waist and panted, finally letting out a long roar.

"What in the ten plagues of Egypt was that?" he said, collapsing onto the couch.

Anni shook her head and made her way into the kitchen on unsteady legs. She washed her hands—all that swatting—and opened the freezer. She grabbed a large bottle of the Finlandia vodka that Mummo always kept on ice and poured two generous shots for herself and her brother, and joined him on the couch.

It was dark inside the house; the two hadn't bothered to turn on the lights when they had stormed inside. *No need for illumination,* Anni thought as she handed Theo his glass. It was only then she noticed his face, a mask of confusion. He was staring out the window.

"What?" she asked.

"The fireflies," he said, his voice dropping to a whisper. "They're gone."

Anni whipped her head around to look outside and saw her brother was right. She couldn't see a single firefly, let alone the battalion that had just swarmed them. She pushed herself off the couch and made her way to the french doors. She gasped when she saw the deck was just as clear as it had been earlier in the day. They had stepped on a legion of bugs on their way back to the house. Hadn't they? It should be covered with slime. But it wasn't.

What had just happened?

CHAPTER SIX

Finally curled up in her bed, Anni tossed and turned. She couldn't get those fireflies out of her mind. What had really happened out there?

She and Theo had grown up *almost* believing Mummo's tales about spirits that protected or bedeviled the woods and the water around Metsan Valo. As Anni punched her pillow and turned onto her side, it occurred to her that she had never felt afraid here, even if the woods *were* filled with beings—which she didn't really believe, not with her rational mind, at least. She knew they were only folktales, spun on dark, cold winter nights in the old country, tales that Mummo had passed down to Anni and Theo as her mother and grandmother had passed them down to her, long ago. Lots of families did that, right? Nothing so unusual there.

But somehow, she felt like something strange and otherworldly was happening now. For real. There in her bed, in the deep and profound quiet of a Metsan Valo summer's night, all sorts of unexplainable possibilities floated through her consciousness as she drifted between wake and sleep.

First it was her dream of awakening in the woods—if it really was a dream. And now the fireflies. She could explain away the dream with the slightest bit of rational thought. Being back here again after so long,

Mummo's death rocking Anni's foundations. It made perfect sense she'd dream of the old tales, that they'd come to life in her mind.

But those fireflies were definitely real. Tangible. Buzzing. She had swatted them away. They had wriggled into her ears and buzzed around her eyes. She had stepped on hundreds of them on the deck, so many it was slippery as she and Theo ran toward the safety of the house. The flies were there. And then they weren't. Theo was there, too. He was a witness to it. This wasn't in Anni's imagination or her dreams. They had experienced it together.

Theo's room was next to hers, their beds sharing a wall. Anni wondered if he was still awake. She knocked softly. Two quick raps came back in return. Just like when they were children. *I'm awake, too. You're not alone.* It made her exhale with relief, just knowing he was there.

She smiled, thinking of those childhood years when, after days filled with swimming in the cold lake, boating, rummaging through the forest, and making forts in the trees, they had fallen into bed and knocked on the wall to each other when they couldn't sleep. They had made up a sort of language of knocks. One soft knock meant, *Are you awake?* Two soft raps in return meant, *Yes, all is well.* One hard one meant, *Angry, don't bother me.* Three: *I'm coming to talk to you.*

Anni rapped three times. She slipped out of her bed and padded into the hallway and to Theo's door. She opened it slowly. What she saw sent a chill throughout her body. Theo wasn't in bed. He hadn't been in bed. It was still made.

So who had knocked?

Anni walked down the hallway toward the grand staircase, her heart beating harder with each step. Where was Theo? As she reached the stairs, she looked down into the great room and, in the darkness, saw a figure at the fireplace, his back to her. He was poking at some embers, stoking the fire back to life. But they hadn't lit a fire before going to bed. Had they? They had been outside, in front of the firepit, with the fireflies.

"Theo?" she called out in a harsh whisper. Then, louder, as she descended the stairs: "Theo?"

Halfway down, Anni stopped. It wasn't her brother. She was frozen to the spot, gripping the railing as she watched the figure in front of the fireplace slowly turn toward her.

It was a man Anni didn't recognize. His clothes looked old and threadbare, like something from another time. Her heart jumped into her throat, but her voice didn't find the scream she was expecting. Something in the man's eyes silenced it. A gentleness, a fondness. Those eyes twinkled at her. He smiled, his grizzled face showing a life hard lived. And then his image flickered and faded from view, as the poker he was holding fell to the ground with a clank. The embers faded, too. The fire was dark and cold.

Anni stood there for a long time, staring at the enormous fireplace, its stones, which ran all the way to the ceiling. Those rocks had been gathered on this property generations ago.

She descended the stairs, one at a time, holding her breath as she moved closer. The poker lay on the floor where the man had dropped it. Anni bent down and picked it up, expecting it to be warm from tending the fire. But it was cold as the grave. She placed it back into the iron set where it belonged. It clanged softly as it came into contact with the other tools.

Anni shook her head. What had just happened? Had the man even been there at all?

Something caught Anni's eye, taking her gaze away from the fireplace. Movement, outside, beyond the wall of windows. She crept over to the french doors and peered out. Had the man returned? Or was it an animal? A bear, maybe? That was more likely. Bears were quite common in the woods around Metsan Valo and even ventured onto the property from time to time. Anni remembered Mummo having to chase bears away from the bird feeders more than once. She smiled as she thought of her grandmother running outside clanging pots and pans together, telling the bears to "shoo!" They would always comply with Mummo's orders, although to Anni they looked slightly affronted.

Anni squinted into the inky darkness but didn't see anything. No more movement. No bear, then, foraging in the bird feeder. She was turning to head back upstairs to her bedroom when the lights illuminating the dock flickered on. They were motion activated. Something had to be out there.

Anni peered outside and saw it was a person, walking out onto the dock. Theo. Even at this distance, she knew her brother's gait.

Anni flung the doors open. "Theo!" she called out. "Hey! What are you doing out there?"

But he just kept walking, one slow step after another.

A coldness wrapped around Anni then. It was the way he was walking. Like he was in a trance. Or asleep. She bolted outside and across the deck. "Theo! Wake up!" He didn't respond. She hurried down the stairs, jumping two at a time, and thundered through the yard toward the dock, calling Theo's name with every step.

But he didn't turn around. It was as though he didn't hear her. He was at the very end of the dock by the time she reached it, screeching his name. "Theeeeo!"

And then he simply walked off the dock, took one more step as though he were walking down the sidewalk, and hit the water. He submerged instantly. Anni let out a strangled scream. She knew it was a deep drop-off. And ice cold. She couldn't count how many times she and Theo had jumped from the dock into the cold water on blisteringly hot days. Or on winter days after spending time in the sauna their great-grandfather had built on the water's edge. This was not like that. Not in the least.

Anni pounded down the dock and, without any hesitation, jumped in after her twin.

The water was inky black and stung her with its icy cold. She opened her eyes beneath the surface but couldn't see—she knew she wouldn't be able to make out anything in the dark lake but tried any-way—so she flailed around with her limbs, hoping to hit Theo's arm or leg or torso—something she could grab on to.

She came up for air and saw him, splashing to the surface as if propelled up from below, coughing and spitting out water. She was on him in an instant, wrapping her arm around his neck and kicking with her legs to get him to shallow water, where they could both find their feet. He tried to fight her off, flailing and kicking in a panic.

"Calm down! I'm saving you! Go limp! Help me! You know what to do!" She locked eyes with him, and in a moment, she saw his panic cede to recognition.

Mummo had made them practice saving each other before she'd consent to letting them swim off the dock. One thing to never do was what Anni had just done—jump in after someone who may be drowning. The danger of being pulled under by their panic is great. But Anni didn't care. She gave a silent thanks that Theo understood, calmed down, and together they could make their way toward shore.

It was then Anni noticed Martin standing at the end of the dock and Meri hurrying toward him with two big towels.

When they could touch bottom, Anni and Theo waded onto the shore before collapsing onto the rocky beach. They sat there, panting, gasping, and catching their breath as Martin and Meri wrapped them in towels.

"What in the hell happened?" Theo said, coughing.

"I was going to ask you the same question," Anni said. "What were you doing out here?"

Theo shook his head. "I have no idea."

The twins exchanged a long look. Anni noticed Martin and Meri did the same.

"Come on, now," Meri said. "Let's get you inside."

Anni let Meri help her up as Martin hoisted Theo to his feet, and the four of them slogged through the yard, across the deck, and into the house.

"You two peel off those sodden pajamas, have a good rinse, and dry off," Meri said. "Theo, you go into the mudroom. Anni, you take the bathroom. You'll find more towels. I'm going to nip upstairs and get you some fresh pajamas to change into."

"I'll start a fire," Martin added.

Anni and Theo did as they were told, and soon, rinsed, toweled dry, and in fresh PJs, Anni's hair turbaned up in a towel, she and Theo sank onto the couch in front of the fire, side by side.

Martin appeared with big shot glasses of ice-cold vodka and handed one to each of them. "Do you mind telling me what happened out there? We heard the ruckus and came running."

Theo shook his head. "All I know is, I was sitting down here on the couch. I couldn't get the fireflies out of my mind and didn't feel like going to bed."

Meri wrinkled her brow. "Fireflies?"

Anni waved her hand. "We'll tell you about that later. What happened then, Theo? Why did you go out to the lake?"

"I have no idea," he said, staring off into the dark night. "I must've fallen asleep on the couch. The next thing I remember is waking up in the water."

Anni shivered and leaned into him. "You easily could've drowned out there."

He ran a hand through his thick mop of wet hair. "It's crazy."

Anni sat up straighter and looked him in the face. "It's like my dream the first night I was here," she said.

"What dream?"

"I told you I had a nightmare. In the middle of the night, I woke up in the forest and had no idea where I was or how I had gotten there. I found my way back, and the house itself seemed . . . I don't know.

Menacing isn't the right word. It was like it was breathing in and out or something."

Meri sat down, hard, in one of the dining-room chairs. Martin put his hand on her shoulder.

"Then what?" Theo wanted to know.

"I hurried back to my room and crawled into bed. The next morning, I didn't know if it was a dream or what."

"You were called," Meri said, her voice wavering.

Anni and Theo turned to look at her, their mouths agape. Her face was like stone, and Martin was ashen.

"Called?" Anni managed to squeak out.

"It has begun."

CHAPTER SEVEN

Anni reached for her brother. What had begun? Whatever it was, it wasn't good. A feeling of dread descended around her. All she wanted was to run from this room, this house, and catch the next flight back to her apartment in Paris.

Martin threw a harsh glance at Meri and shook his head. "Now is not the time to speak of this," he said under his breath.

"Speak of what?" Theo asked.

"My husband is right," Meri said. "Perhaps we should—"

"What are you all doing up at this hour?" Arden's lilting voice echoed from the second-floor railing. She flounced down the stairs in her long white nightgown, which was embroidered with daisies and black-eyed Susans. "Are we having a party?"

Why did Arden have to appear now, for the love of God? Anni hissed inside her own head. She wanted more than anything to hear what Meri and Martin had been about to tell them. What had begun?

"Meri, what—" Anni tried. But Meri locked eyes with her and shook her head quickly, almost imperceptibly.

"We'll talk about this later," Meri said to Anni, scrambling to her feet. She turned to Arden. "We were just going back to our cottage, ma'am. There was a little—" Her words evaporated.

"Incident," Martin offered, raising his eyebrows. "But all is well now."

"Oh?" Arden said. "An incident? But you have it handled?"

"Yes, ma'am."

"That's good. You two are so wonderful, taking care of all of us." She turned to the fridge. "Anyone else feel like ice cream?"

Obviously, Arden hadn't heard Anni's screaming as she ran outside or seen anything of the "incident." Anger and irritation bubbled up inside Anni—those old, familiar feelings that always seemed to grip her when she spent too much time with Arden. *Theo could've drowned, Mother. But by all means, investigate the ice-cream situation before asking about it.* But Anni held her tongue. Instead, she turned to Meri and Martin.

"Thank you so much for your help," Anni said to them, her voice thin. "Can we continue our conversation in the morning?"

Martin nodded. "We'll set aside a time to talk after the reading of your grandmother's will. You kids should head to bed now and get some rest. You've got a big day tomorrow." They scurried out the front door and shut it behind them.

Theo pushed himself up off the couch with an exaggerated groan. He extended his hand to Anni and pulled her up, too.

"I don't know about anyone else, but I'm beat," he said, a little too loudly. "Come on, sister. Let's be off with us."

"No ice cream, then?" Arden said, her face crestfallen. She was holding a carton of chocolate caramel swirl.

"Not tonight, Mom," Theo said, leading Anni to the stairs. "You enjoy it, though. We'll see you in the morning."

"Shall I walk you up?" Arden said.

"That's okay, Mom," Anni said.

Anni and Theo made their way up in silence, and then rushed into Anni's room like they used to do as children. Theo plopped down on the chaise by the window, and Anni sank into her bed. Their usual places.

"One: I've never sleepwalked in my life," Theo began. "Neither have you. Two: What in the name of *The Haunting of Hill House* did Meri mean by saying we were *called*?"

"It sounds really creepy when you think about it."

Theo gazed up at the ceiling. "Why did Arden have to flounce downstairs at that exact moment? Meri never tells us anything—the woman is as silent as a stone—and now when she was just about to—"

"Martin swooped in and stopped her," Anni said, lying on her back with a thud. "Did you notice that?"

"Yes. I. Did," Theo said, overenunciating every word.

"I have never been as annoyed with our mother as I was just now."

"The Queen of Bad Timing strikes again. But we've had plenty more to be annoyed about over the course of a lifetime."

"True," Anni said, pausing for a moment before she continued. "If we were *called*, as Meri said, who called us? You went to the water. I went into the forest."

"If you're insinuating that she meant the spirits, you're going Metsan Mad," Theo said.

"That might be the case," Anni said, "but there's no denying the fact that we were both sleepwalking out into the night."

"What's to prevent it from happening again?" Theo wanted to know. "Do we need to put bells around our necks so someone will hear us if we stray off like wayward cats?"

This brought a smile to Anni's lips.

"Do you think she'll tell us what she was about to say?" Anni asked. "Or was the moment broken, and now we won't get it out of her?"

Theo ran a hand through his hair, a favorite gesture when he was trying to think. "No idea. They said they'd talk with us after the reading of the will. But who knows? They can both be so secretive, Martin and Meri. Creeping around, giving each other meaningful looks when certain subjects come up but never divulging anything. Nothing of substance anyway. I had forgotten how much drama it all used to be."

"Like they're guarding the secrets of the dead, isn't that what we said when we were kids? There was always an undercurrent of strangeness with those two."

Theo nodded, and gave Anni a grin. "We'd want to bike into town, and they'd get all gothic and strange about it as though they were privy to something deep and dark and dangerous, like the local werewolf—"

"Secret identity known only to them—" Anni added with a laugh.

"—had undergone the 'big change' the night before."

They shared a laugh, remembering.

"I had sort of forgotten how *Grimms' Fairy Tales* Metsan Valo seemed to us back then, largely because of them," Theo said, peering out the window. "And the old stories. This is all that is. Don't you think?"

"I do," Anni said, although her voice wavered a bit. "Both of us having weird experiences on our first night back here—even if mine was only a dream—could be chalked up to the fact that we're twins, and the same kind of stuff happens to us."

Theo nodded. "And you're right, yours might have just been a dream. We really don't know. There's no doubt I walked off the dock like some kind of zombie, though."

"Mummo would say the vaki are running amok. Enchanting us. Teasing us."

Theo huffed. "Well, somebody better tell them to stop. Because I'm not amused."

The twins looked at each other, neither knowing quite what to say. A feeling washed over Anni just then. Was that what Meri had been talking about earlier? Something mystical and folkloric? She shook her head at the thought of it.

"I'm a little afraid to go to sleep," Theo admitted, wincing. "It was really dangerous, what happened out there."

"I know," Anni said. "Don't do it again."

Anni didn't want to tell her brother about the ghost—or whatever it was—by the fireplace earlier.

"Okay, I'm going to bed," Theo said, pushing himself up and off the chaise. "Do you think you'll be able to sleep?"

Anni yawned in response. "I hope so. What about you?"

"Probably not," Theo said. "I'm really shook up. I think I'm going to call Jenny to talk about what's going on back home. It'll be a distraction."

Anni's eyes brightened. "Oh! Yes. Do that. Give her my love."

Theo crossed the room and opened the door. "I'm just a knock away."

Anni was snuggled beneath her covers when she heard a soft rap from next door. She rapped twice in response. It was only then she remembered what had happened earlier. A chill whispered its way under her blankets, and she pulled the quilt tighter around her, wondering if she'd get any sleep at all.

⚜

Anni awoke the next morning to the sun streaming into her room. She rolled over and looked at the clock. Nine thirty. Late, by Metsan Valo standards, where everyone typically rose for an early breakfast. But she gave herself credit for not sleeping the day completely away, after the strangeness of the night before combined with her jet lag. She pulled her robe around her and stepped into the hallway. Voices wafted through the air, and upon realizing the origin of the loudest among them, she groaned. Aunt Gloria had arrived.

Instead of heading downstairs, disheveled and in her pajamas, Anni quickly slipped back into her room. If she was going to be greeting relatives she hadn't seen in a decade, she might as well look presentable.

After a quick shower, Anni dressed in jeans and a white-cotton shirt she had bought a few weeks earlier in Paris, and took the time to dry her hair. She put on a dab of makeup and surveyed the situation in the mirror. Despite her efforts, her tired eyes reflected the two sleepless nights she had spent here. She sighed. It was as good as it was going to get.

Standing at the top of the stairs looking down, she saw Arden, Gloria, and Theo sitting at the big table, mugs of coffee in front of them. Meri was clearing their plates. She looked up and smiled as she saw Anni descending the stairs.

"Darling Annalise," Gloria said with a toothy grin. "How lovely to see my niece again. Even under these circumstances."

Anni gave Theo a questioning look. *Darling Annalise?* He shrugged. Gloria held her arms out wide, and Anni let herself be enveloped in a hug. Gloria air-kissed both of her cheeks.

"It's good to see you, too, Auntie," she said, eyeing Theo over their aunt's shoulder. He stifled a laugh, taking a sip of coffee and looking away.

Anni slid into one of the chairs as Meri set a plate of sausage, eggs, hash browns, and grilled tomatoes, along with a mug of coffee, in front of her. Only then did Anni realize she was ravenous. It felt like she hadn't eaten in days.

"You must tell us all about Paris, dear," Gloria said, taking her place at the table again and eyeing her coffee mug with a sigh. Meri took that cue and was there in an instant with a warm-up. "How is your delicious Jean-Luc?"

Anni winced. She had known it might come up, but she didn't have any desire to deal with their breakup so quickly, and publicly, before she had even had her first cup of coffee.

"Jean-*Paul* is good," she answered and took a sip of her steaming brew. It wasn't quite a lie, just an omission. He likely was good, for all she knew. Theo raised his eyebrows at her over the rim of his mug.

"Are Vicky and Yale here yet?" she asked, desperate for a change of subject.

Gloria shook her head. Only then did Anni notice her aunt's perfectly cropped bob and that she was wearing a colorful Lilly Pulitzer sundress with pearls, despite the fact she was in the Northwoods on the cusp of autumn. *A preppy Anna Wintour on Lake Superior,* Anni thought. So very different from Gloria's usual slightly unhinged–hippie vibe. She shot Theo a look. He raised his eyebrows. She knew he had noticed it, too.

"Vicky, Yale, and Lichen should arrive by noon or so." Gloria lifted her head and smiled broadly over Anni's shoulder. "Oh, good! Here's Charles! My darling, come and meet my niece and nephew, Annalise and Theo."

Anni turned and saw a tall, elegant man in his seventies trotting down the stairs. His thick hair was completely white, and his tanned face glowed with health and vitality. His blue eyes shone. He was dressed in crisp khaki shorts and an ecru polo shirt. Boat shoes on his feet. An expensive-looking watch on his wrist. He radiated wealth, or the appearance of it.

Anni and Theo both pushed their chairs back and got to their feet, Theo coming around the table to greet the man.

"Delighted," Charles said, shaking Anni's hand first, then Theo's.

"Welcome to Metsan Valo," Theo said.

"Thank you," Charles said. He smiled broadly. "But I've been here before."

"Oh?" Theo responded, as Gloria sidled up to them and threaded an arm through Charles's.

"I brought him to meet Mother a few months ago." Gloria beamed. "Shortly before we were married."

CHAPTER EIGHT

The room fell so silent that Anni could hear the ticking of Mummo's old clock that hung on the kitchen wall. She caught a glimpse of Arden's face—a mask of sheer disgust. She wasn't even trying to hide it. Tension hung in the air like fog.

Theo broke the silence. "In that case, I should've said welcome to the family!" he said, a bit too loudly. "Congratulations!" He kissed Gloria's cheek.

"Wow," Anni said, slowly. "We had no idea you were even seeing anyone. Here you were, asking about my life when you had this monumental news to share."

"Oh, it was a whirlwind," Gloria said, waving her hand. "A total, utterly romantic whirlwind. Would you like some coffee, darling?"

"Coffee?" Arden scowled. "This calls for champagne, don't you think?" Turning to Meri, she asked, "Will you get a bottle or two from the wine cellar?"

Soon Meri returned, Martin in tow, with trays of glasses. When everyone had a glass of bubbly, Arden stood up.

"To my sister and her new husband," she said, raising her glass. Anni took a sip and could feel the bubbles slide down her throat.

"Tell the kids how you two met!" Arden said, a dark sheen in her eyes.

Gloria held a hand to her cheek in a mock blush, as Charles chuckled. "Online!" Gloria admitted. "A dating site, if you can believe that. Just like the young people are doing these days."

Theo raised his eyebrows. "Tinder?" he squeaked out, stifling a laugh.

"Oh goodness, no, whatever that is," Gloria said. "It's a site for people our age. Over fifty."

Fifty? Anni thought, noticing Arden rolling her eyes. Gloria hadn't seen fifty in a couple of decades.

Oblivious, Gloria continued. "It was love at first sight!" she cooed, gazing at Charles. He nodded and took a sip of champagne.

"Yes, indeed," Charles said, his voice low. "How could I not fall for this lovely lady?"

"Oh stop," Gloria said, waving her hand again, which Anni now noticed was perfectly manicured.

"And tell the kids how long you knew each other before getting married!" Arden prompted, a little too brightly. "It was definitely a whirlwind!"

Gloria squinted her eyes at Arden. "It was a bit sudden, yes," she said. "What was it, darling? Three months? Four?"

Theo and Anni stared, neither finding any words.

Charles reached over and took Gloria's hand, bringing it up to his lips and kissing it. "When it's right, it's right."

"As he said to me, at our age, why wait? He whisked me away, and we eloped."

Gloria was beaming, but Anni thought she detected an undercurrent of . . . something. Hesitation? Fear?

Finally, she found her voice. "What a romantic story," Anni said, and raised her glass. "Here's to many years of happiness."

"Hear, hear," Theo said, taking a sip.

Anni noticed Arden crossing the room and filling her glass again from the bottle Martin had set on the sideboard.

The room fell silent, then, a heavy cloud of uncertainty and wariness swirling in and out between them.

"So," Theo started, changing the subject, "does anyone know when the lawyer is coming today?"

"Five o'clock," Arden said, glancing down at the watch pendant that dangled on a chain around her neck. "Gloria, you said everyone will be here by then, right?"

"Oh, goodness, yes," Gloria said. "They should be arriving early this afternoon, if not before."

"So we've got some time," Arden said. "Kids, how about we leave these two lovebirds alone and take the ferry into Wharton? I haven't seen my babies in so long, it'll be good to spend some time together."

Anni and Theo exchanged a glance. "Sure," Anni said, glad to have this whole strange episode with Gloria and Charles come to an end. She pushed herself to her feet, and Theo popped up, too.

"Let's do it!" he chirped.

Soon, the three of them were in Arden's convertible, driving on the winding forest roads leading away from Metsan Valo. In a few miles, the forest opened up and gave way to grassy fields and rocky beaches as they followed the lake's shoreline toward town.

Metsan Valo had been built on Ile de Colette, the only island in Lake Superior that had year-round residents. It was a small community of a few hundred people, which swelled tenfold during the summer season. Hundreds of families had summer homes here, going back generations. Tourists could find high-end resorts, rustic campgrounds, and everything in between. At the marina, you could find huge yachts and tiny fishing boats moored side by side. Despite the money that clearly populated the place, the whole island had a laid-back hippie vibe. It had always made sense to Anni that her mother, growing up as one of the locals on Colette, would have inherited the island's eccentric, bohemian nature.

Saint Michel, Ile de Colette's only town, had a couple of high-end restaurants, a good burger joint, a spot known for pizza, and shops geared mainly toward summer people and tourists. But the most popular gathering place for tourists and locals alike was Jimmy's, a bar that had partially burned down years earlier. The owner, Jimmy, had simply put an enormous tarp where the roof had been and opened back up for business. Musicians who regularly sold out massive arenas would take the stage there for an impromptu acoustic set, celebrities seeking an out-of-the-way vacation could be found drinking beer at the bar, and barefoot twentysomethings who had pitched their tents in one of the island's campgrounds would line up for one of the showers in the back bathrooms. The slogan "no shirt, no shoes, no service" was definitely not enforced there. A far cry from Anni's favorite Paris bistros.

"We've got to hit Jimmy's one night while we're both here," Theo said as they drove past it, mirroring Anni's thoughts once again.

Arden had been silent on the drive. They pulled onto the ferry and climbed out of the car, then took the metal steps to the upper deck of the ferry. Arden sighed as the three of them looked out over the vast, glittering lake and the chain of Redemption Islands in the distance.

"I've traveled all over the world and have never seen anything as breathtaking as this," Arden said. "Well"—she paused and squinted—"the Greek islands rival it. But this is home."

"Is it, Mom?" Theo asked. "You're always traveling. It's almost like you don't consider anyplace to be home."

Arden smiled, but it didn't reach her eyes. "Wharton and Metsan Valo will always be home to me." Her look brightened. "But there's a whole big wide world to explore! So many experiences to have! People to meet! I've been lucky to have been able to do it." It was as though, after the unpleasantness with Gloria earlier, the free-spirited, bohemian Arden had awakened and was bubbling to the surface.

As the ferry neared Wharton, she turned to her children and smiled. "How about getting a little bite of lunch at the Flamingo? Who wants nachos?"

Anni had breezed through Wharton on her way to the ferry a few days prior, but now, as the hilly town came into view, her heart swelled with anticipation of spending some time there. Arden had told her long ago that Wharton was magic, and Anni knew this was true.

If Colette was a hippie enclave, Wharton was a town plucked out of a moment in time and preserved. There were no fast-food or chain restaurants, no strip malls, no big-box stores. No buildings over three stories tall, or as some liked to say, none taller than the church steeple. Instead, there were locally owned restaurants with chefs that New York or Paris would envy. Little shops that sold locally made items like candles and stoneware and jewelry and artwork, crafted by the many artisans who called Wharton home.

Oddly temperate in summer and winter, Wharton defied Lake Superior's harsh weather, much to the amazement of meteorologists, who had no good explanation as to why Wharton wasn't twenty degrees below zero on any given winter day when its nearest neighboring town was in the deep freeze.

It was a place where people fell in love—with the town, with life, and with each other.

As Arden drove off the ferry, Anni felt a flicker of that love in her heart, wishing she had someone to share it with. Jean-Paul floated through her mind, but here, in this place, all she could feel for him was sadness and regret. Ten years, lost.

When driving past the homes in town, they saw no modern architecture. Nothing ever changed in Wharton, or not much, at least. Grand homes of the past might have been turned into inns, but none were ever torn down to build an office park. This wasn't by any zoning order of the city, but simply by resident preference. Nobody who chose to own one of the old homes in Wharton would ever tear it down and build something more modern in its place. Anni had always known that, but after having been away for a decade, the strangeness of it was just now hitting her. Most of the homes in town were small Victorian cottages with front porches, peaked roofs, and carefully manicured gardens, built a century ago and lovingly maintained. Some grander homes still remained as well and had been converted into inns. Harrison's House stood sentinel on the top of the hill, looking down over the water with its wraparound front porch, widow's walk, and long, scandalous history. Built a century ago by the wealthiest man in Wharton, it had harbored family secrets, murder, cover-ups, and a legion of ghosts before the great-grandson of the original owner turned it into the toniest inn in the region. And the ghosts? Some said they remained.

In town, they drove past LuAnn's, another century-old inn and restaurant, which had been a boardinghouse back in the day. Locals called it the most haunted place in town, but even so, everyone congregated there for LuAnn's famous happy hours and Friday-night fish boils.

They pulled up in front of the Flamingo, an eclectic restaurant that featured the bird as a motif, and some of the best food in town. Their nachos were legendary.

"Shall we?" Arden asked, her smile broad and warm.

As they slid into a booth by the window, a woman behind the bar caught a glimpse of Arden and walked over.

"Hi, girl." She smiled, putting a hand on Arden's shoulder. "Good to see you back in town. You don't have to tell me who these two are." She turned to Anni and Theo. "The twins."

"We are indeed," Theo said, extending his hand to her and flashing his best smile. "I'm Theo, the twin who got all of the brains and beauty, and this swimming-in-the-low-end-of-the-gene-pool twin is Anni."

"Hello," Anni said, laughing. "I tried to absorb him in the womb, and he has never gotten over it."

They all shared a laugh. "Kids, this is Jan Billings," Arden said. "She owns the place."

"It's so nice to meet you both. It's a great day when Arden's back in town, and for you two to be here, even better." But then her smile faded into a look of concern and sympathy. "I was so sorry to hear about Taika. Everyone here feels the same. She was a great lady. A force of nature. Colette and Wharton won't be the same without her."

Arden nodded. "Thank you. It was quite a shock, but not unexpected. She had been ill."

Jan nodded. "So we've now heard. She didn't tell anyone, though, did she? Rode it out on her own. So like her. Independent and stubborn until the end."

"True." Arden nodded. "She didn't even tell the family. It's maddening, if you want to know the truth. We could've been here. Helped her. Just been with her."

"Are you all having a service, or a wake, or anything like that?"

Arden shook her head. "That's all still up in the air. We haven't planned anything right now, but we'll put the word out. I'm sure people will want to come and pay their respects."

"Absolutely," Jan said.

Arden folded her napkin in her lap, her eyes filled with tears. "The three of us came for a quick bite and a drink before we head back to Colette later," she said. "We have some family business to take care of this afternoon, but we fancied a getaway before diving into all of that stuff."

Jan pulled out her notebook. "So what can I get you?"

Nachos ordered, glasses of wine in front of them, Theo broached the subject on all their minds.

"Gloria," was all he said. "Discuss."

"Don't get me started," Arden said, taking a sip of her cabernet.

"Oh, we're getting you started, lady," Theo said. "It's a big reason we came. Did you know about this?"

Arden nodded. "Taika called me after Gloria brought Charles"— she drew his name out until it had several syllables—"to meet her."

"So Mummo was . . . what? Surprised?"

"Suspicious is more like it."

Theo squinted at his mother. "Why, exactly, was she suspicious?"

"Well, come on." Arden smiled and shook her head. "You have to admit the transformation is pretty profound."

Theo's eyes grew wide. "Profound? It's like she's a different person. Even her accent has changed. Have you noticed that?"

"Suddenly she's Katharine Hepburn with that made-up mid-Atlantic accent," Anni said. "And what's with the 'darlings' all the time? Have you ever heard her use that word before even once?"

"And her outfit!" Theo added. "Who is she, Jackie O? The last time I saw her, she was literally wearing an old tablecloth she had sewn into some kind of weird caftan with several strands of pearls around her neck."

"News flash, Charles," Anni said, taking a sip of wine, "Gloria is from a tiny island in Lake Superior. Not the Hamptons."

Brother and sister were having a laugh, but their mother's expression was grave.

"You've hit on the problem with Gloria," Arden said.

This stopped Anni and Theo's laughter. "What problem?" they said at the same time.

"She becomes other people."

"What do you mean? How?" Theo asked. Both he and Anni stared at their mother.

Arden sighed. "You've never noticed it before because, for many years, the other person she became was me," she said. "That's all you knew of her."

Theo gasped. "We thought you two were just peas in a pod."

Arden shook her head. "I thought so, too, at first. But then I realized what she was doing. It started small, borrowing a sweater, getting the same haircut as me. Little by little, her whole personality was gone."

Anni and Theo shared a look. "That's creepy," Anni said.

"Indeed," Arden said. "It's like she wanted to become me. All of that kind of fell to the wayside when she married Phil. Oh, she still dressed like me, but I thought she just adopted that style after mimicking me for so long. Phil saw through all of that. Saw who she really was."

Anni and Theo looked at each other. They sat in silence for a moment.

"And now?" Anni asked.

"She's at it again," Arden said. "She morphed into Charles the instant she met him. She wanted to be what he was. So she just became that, just like she became me all those years ago."

CHAPTER NINE

Arden, Anni, and Theo nibbled on the enormous plate of cheesy nachos piled high with smoked chicken, black beans, *pico de gallo*, and all. With so much to talk about, they just couldn't let the subject of Gloria go.

"Uncle Phil died, what, twenty years ago?" Theo said, pulling a cheesy chip off the plate. "Vicky was in college, I remember that. Has Gloria dated anyone since then? We've certainly never met anyone."

Arden waved her hand. "Oh, a man here and there. Someone to go out to dinner with, or to take in a play or a concert with. Nothing serious. Nothing like this. Phil was the love of Gloria's life. It takes a while to move on from a loss like that. He was the only one who really saw her. The true Gloria. We all know her, but she puts on such an affectation for everyone else. Phil saw through that, though. When he died, nobody else did."

"Why does she do it?" Anni wanted to know. "I can't imagine changing my whole persona for someone else."

Arden ran a hand through her hair, and Anni saw shades of Theo in the gesture. She was stalling.

"We all have such strong personalities," Arden began. "Starting with my grandparents, then Mummo and Pappa. That trait has been handed down to the three of us. I could never tell you two anything." She smiled at them.

"But Gloria was different. She blended into the woodwork at Metsan Valo. She never wanted to stand out too much."

After a long silence, Theo said, "Are you worried about her? Do we have a situation here?"

Arden shook her head. "I really don't think so. I have been suspicious, just like Taika was. I have a lot of worries, even today during their grand revelation. I thought, what are his motives? What are *her* motives?"

"Money is always the only motive," Theo said. "Convenient, him whisking her off to elope just after visiting her ailing mother at Metsan Valo."

"But, unless Gloria is a complete idiot, he would have no way of knowing Mummo's net worth," Anni said. "A beautiful home on Lake Superior is one thing. What Gloria—and all of us—stand to inherit today is another."

"Well, we'll see what happens this afternoon," Theo said, narrowing his eyes.

"Just talking it out with you two has made me feel better about it all somehow," Arden said. "I've been aching to talk to you about it ever since I met him."

"There is this newfangled technology called the telephone," Theo said. "Maybe you've heard of it."

"No, smart guy," Arden said, grinning. "I wanted this to be in person. When you could see it, too, and really have an opinion. I was going to bring it up when you came for your visit, Anni. But your Mummo gave us that opportunity instead." Anni saw her mother's eyes well with tears again.

Arden took a breath. "Could there be an upside? A reason not to worry?"

Anni narrowed her eyes. "What sort of upside?"

"Yes, this thing with Charles was a whirlwind, as she keeps saying," Arden said. "But as Charles said, at their age, who cares? Whatever age she admits to, Gloria is seventy-six years old. If she has found companionship at this stage of the game, that's great. It's pretty obvious he isn't after her for her money, right?"

"How do you know that?" Theo asked. "We don't know that."

"The man exudes old money," Arden said. "I can feel it oozing out of his pores." Theo and Anni exchanged a look.

"Don't you two say something in your silent twin language." Arden squinted at them.

"If he's rich—and do we even know if that's true?" Theo asked. "Then maybe it's Gloria who's going after *him*, not the other way around."

"What does Vicky think about this?" Anni asked. "Has anyone talked to her?"

Arden sniffed. "Vicky's so caught up in her own world that she wouldn't notice if her mother married Harrison Ford."

"True," Anni said, chuckling. "There are so many layers to our family drama that it's like we're living in an onion."

After lunch, the three of them wandered around Wharton, stopping into favorite shops, talking to shopkeepers, and just enjoying the town's vibe.

"Let's stop at the house," Anni suggested. "Do we have time?"

She was referring to the house where she and Theo had spent much of their rather bohemian childhoods, a white house with a big front porch on Wharton's Front Street, its back porch facing the lake. It was where Arden alit when she came back to Wharton.

Like many homes in town, this house had its own long and scandalous history, having been the site of Wharton's "crime of the century" more than one hundred years prior. A pregnant woman had been killed. Her husband, an executive with the town's biggest employer, was on trial for her murder when the woman's father killed him on the courthouse steps.

Arden had bought the house shortly after the twins were born, not wanting to doom them to the island lifestyle she had viewed as constricting when she herself was growing up. The family of three used that house as a home base when Anni and Theo were in school and traveled worldwide whenever they could. Anni and Theo had grown up with the Louvre, the pyramids, and the Colosseum as regular field trips.

Arden fingered her watch pendant. "It's two o'clock. Remind me, what time is the 'event' back at Metsan? It's at five, right?"

"Right," Theo said. "We've got time."

"Great!" Anni said. "It's been years since I've seen the old place."

They headed down the street toward the water and their former home. When they turned onto Front Street, childhood memories came flooding back to Anni, thoughts of running through the yard with Theo, playing hide-and-seek at night with a gaggle of neighborhood kids, being constantly admonished to stay out of the water unless Arden or one of the other mothers was nearby.

"Do you remember the lady?" Theo asked her as they neared the house.

Anni nodded. "She would tuck us in at night sometimes." As kids, Anni and Theo had asked Arden about the lady, who seemed to be dressed in clothes of the past. But their mother had always brushed it off with a wink and a smile. As Anni grew up, she came to believe the lady was just a product of the twins' imaginations, but with all the odd happenings, she began to wonder if it had been real, after all.

As they got nearer to the house, Arden gasped and broke into a run toward the front door, which was standing wide open.

Anni and Theo caught up with her before she crossed the threshold. Theo took her arm.

"Don't go inside, Mom. Whoever broke in might still be there."

Anni fished her phone out of her purse and called 9-1-1. In just a moment, a squad car pulled up, and an officer got out.

"What's happened, Arden?"

"Oh, Bill, thanks for coming so quickly," she said. "This might be nothing, but as you can see"—she pointed to the door—"we just got here and found it like this. The door's wide open. My children wouldn't let me go inside."

Bill smiled at Anni and Theo. "Good. You all wait here. I'll check it out."

He disappeared inside the house, and a few moments later, a second squad car came roaring down the street and stopped in front of the house. A tall man with a decidedly Idris Elba vibe about him got out of the car and smiled broadly at Arden.

She raised her eyebrows. "When you come calling, it's got to be serious," she said, smiling at him.

He trotted up the front porch steps and gave her a kiss on the cheek. "Hey, lady, this is your safety somebody may be messing with. You bet I'd be here."

Arden gestured to Anni and Theo. "Kids, meet Nick Stone. He's the chief of police in Wharton. Nick? My children, Annalise and Theo."

"Good to meet you." Nick smiled. "You've got a nice mother. She really adds to the color of Wharton."

"Tie-dye, no doubt," Theo said, and Anni knew he was stifling an eye roll.

"And my condolences about Taika," Nick said, touching Arden's arm. "She was a force of nature. A truly great lady. It was my pleasure to know her."

Arden whisked away a tear.

"Thank you," she said. "We're all still figuring things out, but we'll have some sort of reception at Metsan Valo soon."

"Kate and I will be there," he said. "As will everyone else in this town."

Arden gave a sad smile as her eyes filled with tears. She nodded, unable to speak her response.

Nick cleared his throat. "Let me pop inside and see what's going on."

As Anni, Theo, and Arden waited outside, Anni noticed a few people trickling down the road. LuAnn, a grizzled older man wearing a chef's apron, and Beth St. John, whom Anni knew was the owner of Just Read It, the local bookstore. Their faces were not simply curious, but concerned.

"We saw the lights and heard the sirens," LuAnn said as they neared. "Is everything okay here, honey?"

Arden hugged her. "I'm not sure what's going on," she said. "The kids and I had lunch at the Flamingo, and we were stopping by the house before we headed back to Metsan Valo. We found the front door wide open."

"Any chance you could've left it open?" said the man, raising his eyebrows and wincing. Anni had been thinking exactly the same thing. Her mother was nothing if not absentminded.

"Oh, Gary, stop," LuAnn said, slapping him lightly on the arm. "Of course she didn't leave it open." She glanced at Arden. "Right?" It was clear to Anni these people knew Arden's eccentricities.

Arden shook her head. "I suppose it's possible, but—" Her words were stopped midsentence by the two officers emerging from the house.

Nick scanned the assembled crowd. "What, has LuAnn's happy hour taken to the streets today?"

"No, smart guy," LuAnn said, her eyes narrowed in mock indignation. "We saw the lights and wanted to make sure the Keystone Kops were doing their jobs."

"Thank you for your vigilance," he said, nodding his head. "But now I'm going to have to ask you to vamoose. We need to talk to Arden for a bit, and we don't need an audience for that."

LuAnn, Gary, and Beth each hugged Arden in turn, said goodbye to Anni and Theo, and were on their way. After a few steps down the road, LuAnn turned and pointed two fingers at her eyes, and at those of Nick Stone and back again, nodding.

"Okay!" he said. "Arden, let's talk about a time line. When were you last here in the house?"

"Yesterday."

"What time?"

"Midday, I'd say," Arden said, squinting off into the distance. "I took the noon or twelve-thirty ferry over to the island. I'm not quite sure which. I wasn't really watching the time."

Nick turned to Anni and Theo. "Were either of you here in the house before or after Arden left?"

Anni and Theo both shook their heads. "We were at Metsan Valo," Anni said.

Nick nodded but squinted at both of them. "Did you stop here in Wharton to see your mother as you were coming through town or go over on the ferry with her?"

Anni fidgeted, and Theo cleared his throat. "We didn't know she was here," Theo said finally. "Of course we would have stopped to get her."

"I sent an email!" Arden protested.

Anni shook her head quickly, locking eyes with the chief. He nodded, seeming to get the gist of what she was trying to convey.

"Okay, so none of you has been in the house since Arden left yesterday." It was more of a statement than a question.

"That's right," Anni confirmed.

"Then let's go on inside. Bill did a thorough sweep of the house, so we know nobody is still here. I want to get your impression of the state of things. I'll ask you not to touch anything."

"Okay," Arden said, looking from Anni to Theo and back again.

The three of them followed Nick through the door. No lights were turned on, but the sun streamed through the six-paned windows, illuminating the dust that was floating in the air.

The scene was typical Arden disarray, scarves flung here, jackets tossed there. A strand of pearls was hanging from the banister. Nothing unusual.

It was Arden's office that caught Anni's eye.

It was in utter chaos. The desk was on its side. Papers strewn everywhere. Books pulled from their shelves and thrown on the floor; some were opened, as if pages had been ripped out. Arden's crystal vase, a prized heirloom she had been given by Mummo's mother, was shattered in the center of the room, its shards glinting in the rays of sun.

Arden started to step into the melee, but Nick stopped her.

"No," he said, simply. "Don't go in, Arden. We're going to dust for prints. I just wanted to make sure this wasn't how you left it."

Arden shook her head. "I'm a bit messy. But not anything like this."

"I figured as much but had to ask."

Nick put a hand on Arden's back and led her outside. Anni could see her mother was shaken. Arden sat down, hard, in one of the Adirondack chairs on the porch.

"Why would anyone do this?" she said, to no one in particular.

"That was going to be my next question," Nick said. "Wait until we get the scene all buttoned up and fingerprinted, but then I want you to go through and see if anything is missing. Did you have any valuables in your office? The rest of the house is undisturbed. That room was your thief's focus, for sure."

Arden shook her head. "I don't have any valuables, per se. Family heirlooms that have been passed down, artwork I've either created or picked up in my travels. Photographs. Those are the things that are valuable to me. I don't even have a television or any other electronics that someone could sell. There's some jewelry upstairs in my bedroom, but not the Hope Diamond or anything like it."

Nick took a breath in and exhaled. "You're not going to want to hear this, but that does not surprise me, and not in a good way," he said.

"I'm sure you didn't notice this, Arden, but there was no forced entry. I'm already thinking this wasn't a stranger break-in."

Anni turned her eyes to the front door. He was right. None of the panes of glass were broken. The lock looked intact. There was no sign anyone had kicked in the door.

"Those family heirlooms. What would they be?"

Arden fixed her gaze on him.

"You're not suggesting anyone in my family—"

Theo and Anni exchanged a look.

"For the record, Officer, Anni and I have been at Metsan Valo," Theo said. "Anni was on the island two days before Mom caught the ferry, and I arrived one day before."

"Of course, darlings," Arden said. "Nobody is accusing you of anything."

"Plus, if we wanted something, we'd just ask Mom for it," Anni said. "Why go through the drama of a break-in?"

"Too much effort," Theo said.

"Yes, Nick, you can cross my children off your list," Arden said, smiling. "They know everything I have is theirs."

"Duly noted. Now, Arden, about those family heirlooms."

"Well, the vase for one," Arden said, scowling. "Silverware that belonged to my grandparents. Some lamps from the turn of the century."

"When Bill's done inside, you can go back in and check it out to see if anything is missing," Nick said.

"We can't," Theo piped up. "Not right now, anyway."

Nick cocked his head and squinted at him. "Why not?"

Arden answered the question for him. "We have to be back at Metsan Valo at five o'clock for the reading of Taika's will."

CHAPTER TEN

They left Arden's house in Wharton locked up tight. Her office was still a shambles, but she would deal with that another day. Anni and Theo had promised to help her clean everything up.

The twins stood on the ferry deck, leaning on the railing, looking out over the water. "What were they looking for, do you think?" Theo asked.

"No idea," Anni said, eyeing their mother, who was sitting on a bench on the upper deck, lost in thought. "It's just crazy."

"And not a break-in!" Theo said. "The person had a key. Or Arden just left the door open. Which isn't outside the realm of possibility. But still. 'Let me use my key to get in and then leave the place completely undone so it's totally obvious that I took something,'" he said. "That's not exactly a career criminal's thinking."

"Unless that was the point," Anni said, raising her eyebrows and lowering her voice.

"What do you mean?" Theo whispered.

"Whoever did this wanted Mom to know," Anni said. "This feels kind of hostile, doesn't it? An assault in a way? It's like, 'I can get into your house whether you like it or not, and I'm going to trash it.'"

Theo grimaced, his eyes following a cormorant that was flying along with the ferry. "The way you say that, it's like you're thinking someone has a grudge against Mom. Or wanted to make her afraid. An assault on her safety."

Anni felt it was true, deep in her bones, but didn't quite know how to respond. "Who could ever feel that way about Mom?" she said finally.

Theo shook his head. "We're the only ones who have any grievances against her." He chuckled, but his smile betrayed sadness.

"I know," Anni said. "I am totally on board with circling the wagons. Somebody did this purposefully. Somebody close enough to her to have a key to her house."

Theo stole a glance at their mother. "Or maybe not," he said, his voice low. "Like I said, she very well could have left the door unlocked."

"No," Anni said, shaking her head. "Well, not that she's not capable of leaving her door unlocked, because we both know she is. But it couldn't have been some random break-in. Like, someone walking by and wondering if he or she should try the door. It's so unlikely."

"Right," Theo agreed. "Plus, why ransack the office if you weren't looking for something particular?"

"The question is, what?"

～❦～

As the three of them pulled into the driveway at Metsan Valo, Anni noticed a fancy SUV in the driveway along with a luxury sedan. One belonged to Vicky and Yale, no doubt. The other, Anni presumed to be Mummo's lawyer's. Theo, who was in the back seat of Arden's car, audibly groaned. Anni turned around to him and laughed.

"Oh, was that out loud?" He smirked. But then, a seriousness came over him. "Mom, I don't think we should tell anybody about the break-in."

Arden turned around to look at him in the back seat. "Why do you say that, Theo?"

Theo shook his head. "It's not what this afternoon is about," he said, slowly, as though he was thinking through every word before he said it. "We're gathering to hear Mummo's will. That's enough for everyone to deal with right now. Our news about the house in Wharton can wait."

Arden was silent for a moment, considering this. "Of course it can wait," she said. "You're right. This is about Taika and her wishes. We can update everyone later if we choose to."

Anni beamed at her brother. She knew keeping the break-in secret in respect to Mummo was only part of it. She could sense what Theo wasn't saying. Nick Stone hadn't specifically asked them to keep the news of the break-in quiet, but Theo didn't want to bring it up because someone in Metsan Valo right then could very well have done it. Who else but Gloria's family would have a key? Theo didn't want to tip their hand if that were true.

The walk from the car to the house seemed to take an eternity, like one of those bad dreams in which you're trying to get somewhere, but despite walking and walking and walking, you don't get any closer.

Once they were finally inside, Anni noticed everyone was congregated in the living room. Gloria and Charles were chatting by the windows with Vicky and Yale. Lichen was sitting in a corner engrossed in her phone. Martin and Meri hovered in the kitchen. The man Anni assumed to be Mummo's lawyer was younger than she had expected, with jet-black hair and a crisp suit. More Manhattan than Metsan. She wondered what had happened to their longtime lawyer, Jacob Saari.

Vicky rushed up to Anni and enveloped her in a hug. "It's been way too long," she cooed. Anni couldn't remember the last time the two of them had seen each other. The hug lasted a bit too long, Anni thought, as though Vicky were hanging on for dear life.

Theo and Yale exchanged an obligatory wave.

"Hey, man," Yale said, smiling broadly and crossing the room to give Theo a hard pat on the back. Theo winced a little.

"Are we late?" Arden said to no one in particular, fingering her watch pendant. "We said five o'clock, right?"

The lawyer sprang off his chair. "No, you're not late! You're right on time, Ms. Halla. I had some other business to attend to here on the island, so I've been here all afternoon. I just arrived at Metsan Valo, a few moments before you did."

Arden's face lit up. "Patrick, dear," she said, taking a few steps forward to air-kiss him on both cheeks. "How are you?" Then she turned to Gloria. "You know Patrick, don't you?"

Gloria smiled tightly. "We hadn't had the pleasure before today."

"You must remember my grandfather, Jacob Saari," he said to her. "He was your family's lawyer for many years. Generations."

"Of course we do, darling." Arden looked around the room. "Old Jack. My sister and I remember him well, don't we, Gloria?"

"Oh, yes," Gloria piped up. "He and Dad used to play cribbage, to the death, if I recall."

Patrick grinned. "That sounds like him. You may know he retired a few years ago, and I took over his practice."

"Jack and Sonja moved down south, isn't that right?" Arden said, prompting him. "Florida?"

Patrick nodded. "They have a place in a senior-living community down there. They thought it was time to escape the winters."

Gloria narrowed her eyes at him. "You're the grandson. Jim's son. But why don't we all know you? This is a pretty small community."

Patrick smiled, and Anni got the feeling he'd had to answer that question more than once. "I didn't grow up in Wharton. I came for visits, but I lived in Seattle. My parents moved out there before I was born. My dad worked for Boeing."

Gloria looked off into the distance, nodding her head slightly. "Oh, that's right. I had forgotten about that. I moved away about the same time."

Anni smiled at the small-town suspicion. It was so alive and well here. The people in Wharton and on Colette would give strangers the shirts off their backs, but if you claimed to be one of them, you needed to prove it.

"Patrick and I have recently met," Arden said to everyone, as if to put this line of questioning to rest. "He's a dear, just like his grandfather."

The room fell silent for a moment, everyone's eyes trained on the grandson. He cleared his throat.

"We're set up in the back study. Now that everyone's here, let's proceed. I'll just make sure everything is up and running back there, so give me a second." He disappeared down the hallway.

So this is it, Anni thought. She couldn't wait to see Mummo again on her video will. But at the same time, she felt her stomach tightening.

"Seems like a good time for a drink," Yale said, making his way to the sideboard where Martin and Meri had set up decanters of Scotch and vodka, white wine chilling in an ice bucket, red wine breathing.

Charles followed his lead. "Capital idea, Yale," he said, dropping an ice cube into a glass and pouring himself a Scotch.

Anni helped herself to a glass of wine, as did Theo. Both noticed Arden was fiddling with her watch pendant. "Mom? Wine?" Anni asked.

Arden looked at her, as though she had no idea what Anni was talking about, but then the realization unclouded her expression.

"Sure, honey," Arden said, accepting the glass Anni was holding out to her. She drank it down in a gulp.

Tension was swirling. Gloria sidled up to Charles and took his arm. "We should probably go in," she said softly, her eyes brimming with tears.

Drinks in hand, all of them filed through the great room and down the hallway to a suite of rooms Anni didn't often frequent, three guest bedrooms and Pappa's study, a long, dark-paneled room lined with bookshelves. The books themselves looked ancient, tomes from another time, likely brought there by Anni's ancestors who had carved Metsan Valo out of the deep, dark forest.

Anni saw that some of the furniture had been moved out of the way and chairs were set up in rows. A large TV monitor was perched on her grandfather's enormous antique desk, with a laptop connected to it.

The family settled into the chairs, some chattering nervously, others sitting with their hands in their laps, lost in thought. The air felt thick with anticipation.

Theo took Anni's hand and squeezed it. He leaned over to whisper in her ear. "I don't care what's in the will," he said, his voice low. "Just seeing Mummo again, even if it's on TV, is going to make me bawl like a baby. Smother me if I begin to make a scene."

Anni grinned and squeezed back. She, too, was steeling for the moment Mummo came onscreen. Conflicting emotions were swirling through her mind. Sitting there, waiting for the video will to begin, Anni wished with all her heart that Mummo had confided in her. Maybe that was why she had invited—more than invited, summoned—Anni to spend the months of fall with her.

Anger bubbled up inside, and Anni tried to beat it back. The thought of it was almost too much. Being so close to getting on a plane to have that long visit, and Mummo died before it could happen. It was as though Mummo had denied her the chance to say goodbye. To care for her. To spend time and let her know how much she loved her. To help her feel peace at the end.

Anni put her face into Theo's arm and tried to stifle her tears.

He put that arm around her and patted her shoulder. "I'm the one who's supposed to be making the scene," he said into her ear. "You're just trying to steal my thunder."

The lawyer cleared his throat. "Okay. Thank you all for coming to honor Taika's last wishes. I've been the great lady's lawyer for the past several years. She has named me as the executor of her will."

"You're the executor?" Yale asked, a bit too loudly.

"Yes," Patrick said. "You all probably know what that means, but if you don't, I'm to carry out her wishes, disburse any funds to heirs, and generally make sure things go as she planned and stipulated in her will."

"Got it," Yale said, crossing his arms in front of his chest and leaning back.

"Taika contacted me when she got her diagnosis because she had the desire to get her affairs in order," the lawyer continued. "As you all know, when this lady wanted something, she got it."

Everyone chuckled.

"She directed me to cross all of the t's and dot all of the i's on her will, and one of the other things she wanted me to help her do was create this video message. You all should know that the video in itself is nonbinding, in a pure legal sense. It is not Taika's last will and testament. That's on paper, signed, witnessed, tight as a drum. This video is a message from Taika to you, her loved ones."

Anni squeezed Theo's hand. He squeezed back.

"Although video wills are nonbinding, they are becoming more and more common," Patrick went on. "It's a way for people to demonstrate, in no uncertain terms, that they're of sound mind and body when the will was written. In the past, families have contested wills in ugly disputes when someone didn't get what they expected. She wanted you to know that she was completely lucid, if anyone in this room needed confirmation of that. And because she chose not to share her illness with any of you, she had specific things she wanted to say, in addition to the bequests, and she did not get the chance to do that in person with most of you."

He cleared his throat. "If everyone is ready—"

Martin turned down the lights, and the lawyer started his laptop, which whirred to life. Mummo's smiling image came into view.

Anni's stomach was tied up in knots, tears stinging at the backs of her eyes.

"Hello, Taika," Arden whispered.

Mummo was sitting on one of the couches in the great room, the wall of windows behind her. She was wearing her signature turtleneck with a black shawl draped over her shoulders. How many times had Anni seen her in that same outfit on chilly nights as they sat outside in front of the firepit, watching the flames and the stars? The tears began to flow.

And then Taika Halla began to speak.

CHAPTER ELEVEN

"Hello, dear ones," Mummo began, a slight smile on her lips. "If you're watching this, you're assembled in the back study at Metsan Valo, and I have passed into the next world. I know you are grieving for me. Take your time with that, your own time. Nobody else can tell you how to grieve. It is a solitary burden. But I believe all of you know I was not afraid of this journey. I have known, all of my life, that there were spirits in the air, in the forest, and in the water. All around us, guarding us, bedeviling us, teasing us, threatening us. Our ancestors, along with the spirits of nature, all of them together here at Metsan Valo. I have taken my place among them now.

"However, that knowledge won't help you when something happens in your life, and you instinctively pick up the phone to call me. Or when you spend time here at Metsan Valo, and I am not with you, sitting in front of the fire, sharing stories of the past, doing puzzles on the big table. Laughing and crying together. You will grieve for my presence during those times. I know. I have felt the same for my darling husband, and my parents, and those who came before. But please do not grieve for my spirit. It has been set free."

Arden dabbed at her eyes with a tissue as Gloria rested her head on Charles's shoulder.

"I also know some of you are a bit angry with me, or hurt that I did not tell you about my diagnosis or allow you to come here to say your goodbyes or, heaven forbid, take care of me. A few of you certainly would have upended your own lives, put everything on hold, to be with me as I withered away. I just couldn't have that, dears, but I know who you are."

It was as though Mummo looked around the room, then, at each one of them in turn. Her eyes seemed to rest on Anni and Theo, and she smiled a conspiratorial smile. How could that be? It couldn't. It had to be Anni's imagination.

"Now," Taika went on. "Before I get to the reading of my will, please allow me to tell you one last story. You know how I love passing down the old tales. Indulge this old woman by listening as carefully as you can."

Anni and Theo glanced at each other and smiled, tears glistening in their eyes. Gloria and Charles shared a look as well. Gloria shook her head and shrugged.

Lichen fished her phone out of her pocket and leaned back in her chair. Vicky nudged her daughter in response. "Give me that," Vicky said in a harsh whisper, opening her palm. Lichen grudgingly handed it over, and her mother tucked it away.

"The old ones had the power of darkness and the power of light," Mummo began, her eyes flashing. "In the ancient times, we were the wizards, the sorceresses, the ones who heard the whispers of nature.

"We had the power of dead spirits in our hands, the mastery of the air, the water, the forest and everything in it. Long, long ago, our people had forged alliances with these spirits, folk, and vaki. Those alliances were strong and unbreakable."

Anni and Theo leaned into each other, settling down for a story the way they had done so many times before.

"During the old times, our people lived in the north, in the harsh land of windswept plains, high mountains, and dense forests that bordered the sea. When the Vikings raided and pillaged and conquered, they were not afraid of anything or any people. Except for us."

Mummo sat up a little straighter, leaning toward the camera.

"The Vikings feared us because they knew they had no chance of survival, let alone victory, if they stepped onto our soil or sailed on our waters. We defeated them in the forests, setting the very trees and stones and animals upon them. We defeated them on the seas, commanding the enormous and fearsome creatures that dwelled in the deep, dark corners of the ocean bottom to attack their boats as the water engulfed them. We defeated them in the skies, summoning the heavens to rain down on them, the clouds to rise up, and the winged beasts to take flight against them.

"If this sounds familiar, it should. J. R. R. Tolkien used the collection of Finnish mythology, the *Kalevala*, as the inspiration for his epic tales. Gandalf is said to have been patterned after a Finnish hero in the *Kalevala*. The blood of sorceresses and wizards runs through your veins. This is who you are."

Theo eyed Anni. "So I'm Gandalf, apparently," he whispered. "I don't know who that makes you."

"If you say a troll, I'll kick you."

Mummo took a sip of tea and continued. "Now I will tell you one last story, an epic tale from those long-ago days.

"During these times of darkness and light, a girl called Kaija lived in a remote village in the north. Her father tended the reindeer, and her mother kept the home fires burning, as was typical of most households in the village. The women knew the secrets of the forest and its plants and herbs. The girl learned about nature from her mother and about the sea from her father, as did all the children in the villages that dotted the windswept northern seacoast lands.

"As she grew older, Kaija loved to walk to the sea, dressed in warm furs on frigid winter mornings, accompanied by the nature spirits who followed her wherever she went. She had the power, more so than most.

Young though she was, not yet a grown woman, the people of the village came to respect her for her easy and effortless way with the forces of nature.

"One morning, the air itself felt jittery and strange. Birds were flying in circles, and the forest elves refused to venture out of their lairs. But the rock spirits were jumping with excitement, and the water folk splashed against the shore. Then Kaija saw what all the fuss was about. A young man had washed up from the sea. She ran to him and turned him on his back, his clothes sodden. He was alive, but barely. Kaija waved her hand in the air, sending a bird to alert her father, who soon arrived with a horse and cart. Together, they loaded the man into the cart and took him back to their home.

"He slept for a long time, tended to by the women of the village as Kaija looked on. They mixed potions and made poultices. She called upon the spirits of the air to breathe life back into the man and the spirits of fire to warm him.

"When he finally opened his startlingly blue eyes, the people found he did not speak their language. He could not tell them who he was, where he had come from, or how he had ended up in the water. But they gave him refuge nonetheless. They were a people who assumed the goodness in those around them, until they had reason to believe otherwise.

"He stayed in the village, making no attempt to return to his home. Because it was Kaija who found him, she was given the task of teaching him the language of their people and the ways of their village. On their first day together, she put a hand on her chest and said, 'Kaija.' He made the same gesture and said, 'Calder.' And their communication was off to a good start.

"They spent days, weeks, and months together, an hour or more every day practicing the language. After, he worked with the men tending the reindeer and hunting and fishing. He became a skilled blacksmith, forging swords and tools for the people. Years passed. Soon, the people forgot the strange circumstances surrounding Calder's arrival to their village. He had become one of them.

"All was well until one day, Viking warships, called the *dreki* because of the fearsome dragon heads on their prows, sailed into the bay. The Vikings disembarked and stormed into town, swords drawn, shouting in a language nobody could quite understand. But Calder did. He stepped forward and began speaking in the foreign tongue. After a heated exchange, the Vikings took hold of him and began to drag him away.

"The people of Kaija's village were peaceable, choosing not to unleash their power unless threatened. They were threatened now. The Vikings moved in with their swords, and several villagers fell to the ground. Cries and screaming filled the air.

"Kaija ran into the fray and opened her arms wide.

"'Unhand Calder. Leave this place. Sail away,' she shouted. 'Or you will never reach your destination.'

"One of the Vikings laughed and grabbed her as well, brandishing his sword at the villagers. But Kaija just kept on speaking.

"'We, as one people, call upon our friends, the mighty spirits of the air and water, to stop you. We call upon the vaki of the forest and the mountains and the hills to stop you. We summon the power of dead spirits that we hold in our hands to destroy you.'" Mummo's voice was deep and powerful.

"The Vikings continued to chuckle, until it began.

"The sky turned dark, and the air itself buzzed and crackled with life. Lightning sizzled through the gray clouds. A waterspout formed in the bay and moved toward one of the dreki ships and then stopped, waiting for Kaija's command. The Vikings stopped, too, and looked around at what was happening before them, amazement and horror on their faces. The one who was holding Kaija loosened his grip for a moment as he watched the spectacle unfold. She hurried away from them and opened her arms wide, throwing her head back and gazing toward the sky."

Mummo was painting a picture with her words, and Anni could see it clearly in front of her, as she always had.

"And then, they heard the flapping of great, muscular wings, and all of nature fell silent in reverence. This was the age of dragons, the most fearsome creature on earth. The entire village watched as the beast materialized over the hilltop and flew toward the sea, circling above the Vikings, who ducked and screamed, unhanding Calder as they ran. They scrambled through the water back onto their ships, and sailed off, the waterspout following to ensure they wouldn't return.

"Calder ran to Kaija and took her in his arms for the first time. 'How?' he said. She shrugged and smiled. 'It is who we are.'"

Mummo took a sip of tea and looked back into the camera, as though she could see right into their souls.

"This isn't just a folktale," she continued, raising her eyebrows. "It is the story of our family, as far back as we can reach. Calder and Kaija married. They are our ancestors, as alive in our hearts today as they were back in the ancient times. Some of you sitting here today do not see the point of this story. To others, it has reached your heart. Kaija and Calder live in you."

Tears stung in the backs of Anni's eyes. She did feel it in her heart.

"And now, Patrick," Mummo went on, "you might want to pause this so everyone can stretch, refill their drinks, and settle back in for what they've all been waiting to hear."

CHAPTER TWELVE

"Okay, well, that was weird," Lichen said to her mother, a little too loudly. "I thought this was supposed to be a will or something."

Vicky just shook her head. She stood up and stretched.

"I'll go refill your glass, babe," Yale said to Vicky, taking the wineglass out of her hand. "Does Lichen have to stay? She's really bored. She can watch TV in the living room or something."

Lichen's eyes brightened, but Anni could practically feel Vicky's blood pressure starting to surge. Anni leaned forward and touched her cousin on the shoulder.

"That's probably fine," Anni said. "Don't worry about it, Vic. If there's anything specific for her in Mummo's will, you can tell her about it later."

"Agreed, darling," Gloria piped up. "This is for grown-ups from here on out."

Patrick, who had been standing in the back of the room with Meri and Martin, cleared his throat. "I'm going to be sending all of you links to this, so you'll have it. She can watch it at another time. If she chooses to."

"Oh," Yale said. "So we didn't really have to be here after all? We could've just done this on Zoom or something?"

Finally, Vicky found her voice. "For heaven's sake, Yale, have a little respect for my grandmother. And my family. For once in your life."

"Okay, okay," he said, smiling sheepishly at the room. "I'll go get you some vino, and we'll get back to it." He took his leave, with Lichen following close behind. Charles filed out, too.

Anni noticed Arden, sitting alone, wringing her hands in her lap. She didn't seem to have heard the latest Yale boorishness. Or if she did, it didn't register with her. Same story, different day.

"You okay, Mom?" Anni said. "Can I get you anything?"

Arden turned to her daughter, a somewhat surprised expression on her face, as though Anni's words had pulled her back from elsewhere. "Get me anything?"

Theo and Anni exchanged a worried glance. "Mom, why don't I go and get you a glass of wine?" he said. "Or water, if you'd rather?"

"That would be fine, honey," Arden said, holding out her glass toward Theo. He took it from her, and he and Anni slipped out of the room, leaving their mother with a lost expression on her face.

"Do not even say the word *Yale*, or I'm going to lose it," Theo said, his voice low.

"Tell me about it," Anni said. "And what's wrong with Mom? It's like she's in a daze or something."

Theo shrugged. "Any more than usual?"

Anni humphed.

"It's been a big day for her," Theo said. "First the house in Wharton, and now this. I know she's—well, Mom—all the time, but I'm thinking we should just give her a pass on this one."

Anni nodded. He was probably right. Still. Anni's stomach tightened, but she didn't know why.

They reached the sideboard in the living room, and Anni noticed Lichen was already sprawled on the couch, television remote in hand. Yale and Charles were talking in hushed tones by the window, each sipping a Scotch.

Anni and Theo refilled their glasses and poured one for Arden. "Okay," Anni said, loud enough for Yale and Charles to hear. "I guess we should get back in there."

No response from either of them. She cleared her throat and tried again. "I said, it's time to get back in there."

At this, both men turned toward Anni and Theo. "Give us a minute, guys," Yale said.

Anni and Theo stared silently at him for a moment.

"What?" Anni said.

"A minute," Yale said, annoyance oozing from his voice. "We're in the middle of something here."

"Oh! By all means!" Theo shot back. "Let us just wait for you. No problem! Whatever you're talking about is way more important than my grandmother's last will and testament. Obviously."

Charles looked down into his glass as Yale stared at Theo, openmouthed.

"Give you a minute, my ass," Theo continued. "It's time for the reading of your wife's grandmother's will. Get back in there right now and support her."

Charles put a hand on Yale's arm and nodded.

"Listen, I didn't mean anything by that," Yale said, looking from Theo to Anni and back again.

Anni put up a hand to silence him as she and Theo started down the hall, drinks in hand.

"Unreal," she whispered to Theo.

"They're certainly cozy," he whispered back, catching her eye.

In the study, Gloria had moved down a few chairs to sit next to Arden, and the two sisters' heads were together. They were talking in low tones. Theo handed Arden her glass.

"Here you go, Mom," he said, his voice filled with gentleness.

"Thank you, honey," she said. Anni thought she looked a little more herself. Her eyes were brighter, her smile more engaged.

Yale and Charles filed in after them, taking their seats. When all of them had settled in, Martin turned down the lights once more.

"Ready to continue?" Patrick asked.

A moment later, there was Mummo again, smiling her familiar smile.

"Okay," she said. "Now it's time to get down to the nitty-gritty. I wanted to make the will a part of this goodbye video so nobody would think I'm off my rocker. Not that you'll find anything too dramatic in what I'm about to say."

She cleared her throat.

"I, Taika Halla, being of sound mind and body . . ." She stopped and chuckled a bit. "Well, that's a stretch, even on a good day."

Both Anni and Theo smiled at this, remembering Mummo's good-natured complaining about getting old.

"Let's begin here," Mummo continued. "I have named my lawyer, Patrick Saari, as the executor of this will. Any concerns or questions you have should go to him. He will handle the disbursement of any funds you have inherited."

People were fidgeting in their seats. Mummo continued.

"You should all know that I have created a college scholarship fund for Ile de Colette high school seniors in the Halla name. Growing up on this island can be isolating—my two daughters know this only too well—and most of the year-round residents do not have the means we do to send their kids to college. This will help the island youth see the big, wide world and get an education. I've also made a sizable donation to the animal rescue in Wharton. That all said, let's get down to it."

Electricity sizzled through the room, but Anni wasn't quite sure why. It seemed to her as though everyone was on the edge of their seats, hotly anticipating finding out what kind of inheritance was coming to them. Would they leave this room rich? She looked around, her lips a tight line. She didn't even try to hide her disgust.

"It's like they're on a game show," Theo whispered to her, once again echoing her thoughts.

Mummo took a deep breath and spoke.

"To Martin and Meri, keepers of Metsan Valo. This house would not still be standing without you, and it would certainly not be the refuge we all enjoy today. You are so much more to us than caretakers. You are the hearts and souls of this place, and beloved family members. Your company, wise counsel, and good humor have buoyed me over the years. You have always made me feel loved and cared for.

"I have transferred the house where you live on this property into your name. It is now yours. If you choose to do so, and knowing you, I know you will, you may live there until you join me in the next world at the end of your days. You will continue to be paid as usual from the estate for your work, and Patrick has an envelope for you containing a sum that will allow you to live out your retirement without a hint of worry when that time comes. If you choose to leave Metsan Valo— which I know you will not do—your cottage will be transferred back to my estate. All of this is specified in my paper will and is legally binding."

Anni turned and smiled at Martin and Meri. They were embracing and wiping away tears.

"Now, to my dear daughters, Arden and Gloria. You have been an endless source of fascination, love, and, at times, exasperation for me over the years."

Everyone chuckled at this, as did Taika. It was like they were sharing a laugh again.

"Your baby days were the most fun and fulfilling time of my entire life. Watching you learn about the world and everything in it. Discovering a new skill every day. Do you remember me reading to you at night?"

Arden reached over and put an arm around Gloria's shoulders. An audible sob came from one of them.

"My love for the two of you is boundless. Gloria, when Philip died, you lost your soulmate, your whole heart, but you soldiered on, put one foot in front of the other as best you could and made a good life for yourself. You helped Vicky navigate that tumultuous time when all you wanted to do was cry.

"Arden, you raised Theo and Anni on your own as a single mother. Brava, my darlings. Job well done."

Gloria's shoulders were shaking. She held a tissue to her nose.

"Traditionally, Metsan Valo has been passed down from mother to eldest daughter," Taika continued. "But, my dear Arden, you never stay in one place long enough to make it a home. You are a child of the world. I will not burden you simply to uphold a tradition. And you have always been vulnerable to the vaki, my dear. Your sweet nature. Your gentle soul. They have always bedeviled you, haven't they? My eldest daughter and I talked about this long ago, just so you all don't think I'm springing it upon her now. Arden, you will not be burdened with Metsan Valo. It was your choice as much as it was mine."

Anni watched her mother nod her head in . . . was it agreement, or resignation? What was this about the vaki? She exchanged a glance with Theo. He shrugged, a puzzled look on his face.

Taika continued.

"My two daughters, you inherited a sizable amount of the estate when your father passed away all of those years ago. You are both wanting for nothing. Gloria, with your recent marriage, I see that you are well taken care of."

It was like she sucked the air right out of the room.

"I know you don't want to inherit this house and the responsibilities that come with it any more than your sister does. You left Metsan Valo, Colette, and Wharton long ago. You have no desire to come back to stay. Be that as it may, you and Arden are my heirs. Patrick has envelopes for you as well, that will allow you to live as you do for the rest of your days. No worries, my darlings. All of my love to you. But along with this, I do have one stipulation."

Gloria and Charles exchanged a glance. She looked at Arden, who shrugged her shoulders.

"The funds I am passing down to you now must and will go to your sister if one of you should die. In other words, if Arden passes away, her inheritance from me goes to Gloria. And vice versa. This is written in stone and not revokable."

"Can she do that?" Yale asked, out loud.

"Yes," Theo shouted.

Mummo continued.

"To my granddaughter Vicky, her husband, Yale, and my great-granddaughter, Lichen," Mummo went on. "You have been visitors here, but never knew what Metsan Valo was all about. Vicky, I know it is not really your cup of tea. You haven't been here in years. Like your mother, you have chosen to carve out your life away from this place and have done an outstanding job creating your own world. You need nothing from me, nor from Metsan Valo. Nonetheless, Patrick has an envelope for you, a token that you can disburse to your daughter as you so choose. I would encourage you, dear, to use part of it to bring her here more than you have been. Lichen is named for this forest and should know its power."

"What in the hell?" Vicky said, out loud. Gloria shushed her.

"Finally, we come to Anni and Theo," Mummo said, seeming to smile directly at them again.

Theo took Anni's hand and winced. "After that smackdown, I hope we get nothing," he whispered into her ear.

"I saved you two for last because this announcement is going to be the most dramatic," Mummo said, a concerned smile on her face. "Anni and Theo, my beloveds, to you, I leave the entirety of my estate, including Metsan Valo, other than the funds already given to Martin and Meri, your mother, aunt, and cousin. You two, more than anyone, love this place as I do. You love the land and the forest and the water. You love the old stories that bring it to life.

"Theo, you have created a wonderful life for yourself and Jenny in Chicago. A business of your own employing dozens of people, a home of your own. You do not need this house and the grounds, nor do you want it. Owning a home with your sister might complicate things that may be on the horizon with your marriage."

Theo furrowed his brows at Anni. Both of them wondered how she could have possibly known that.

"That is why I am entrusting Metsan Valo to Anni alone. That includes the house and everything in it; the grounds, excluding Martin and Meri's cottage; the boats; and a trust that will keep Metsan Valo running in perpetuity. All the rest of my estate, Theo and Anni will split equally. That means savings, retirement accounts, life insurance, stocks and bonds, and whatever the hell else I have. Patrick will unsnarl all of that for you. Now, if someone is especially fond of something in the house for sentimental reasons—I know Arden loves some of the artwork in the great room—I'm sure you can work it out so they can have it. But, Anni, the decision is yours alone."

Anni gasped aloud. She looked at Theo, who was giving her the side-eye.

"Unreal," Vicky mumbled. "Not that I'm surprised."

Mummo went on. "Darling Annalise, you are the mistress of Metsan Valo now, the keeper of our history. You know what that means. I have told you the old stories. Take heed of them. Remember their wisdom. Remember Kaija and Calder. And above all, remember who you are. You will learn more of what you need to know in the coming days. I know I have picked the right successor."

Theo took Anni's shaking hand into his own. "It's okay," he whispered. "It's right."

"Now, I think it's time for me to bid you farewell. I have loved you all, with the ferocity of this inland sea. A love as vast as the sky. As deep as the forest and as gentle as the animals within it. You have been my whole world. And now it's time for me to travel to the next. Don't be surprised to see me again. I will be watching over each and every one of you, keeping you safe. Above all, please remember that all of you have *sisu*. It will get you through anything life throws at you, dears."

The word she used had no translation in English. It was the zeitgeist and character of the Finnish people. It meant nothing could get the best of you. You had the determination, strength, and power to take anything life dished out, and triumph over it. It was bravery and courage in the face of adversity. Strength in the face of fear. The will to take you anywhere you wanted to go.

It buoyed Anni from the inside.

And then, the video went dark. The room was deathly quiet.

Martin flipped on the lights as Patrick Saari moved through the room with white envelopes, handing them out, as discreetly as he could, to everyone.

Vicky opened hers immediately and sneered at the check it contained. "Why does this not surprise me?" she said, her voice in tatters.

"Vicky," Anni started.

"Honey," Gloria tried.

"Oh, don't even," Vicky said, tears welling up in her eyes. "Anni and Theo have always been the golden children in this family, and I've always been an afterthought. That's how I've felt our whole lives, and this just confirms it." She hurried out of the room. Yale gave them all a seething look and followed her, his footsteps clomping down the hallway.

Anni's whole body went taut and tense, every cell preparing for what was to come.

CHAPTER THIRTEEN

"Well, that's a lot to unpack, right there," Theo said finally. "Mummo did not spare the drama. Suffice it to say, it did not go remotely how I thought it was going to."

"I really thought she was going to do something like make Metsan Valo into a heritage museum," Anni mused.

Theo grunted.

"Vicky seems happy about it all," Anni said, grimacing.

Theo winced. "Yeah, that was brutal. I don't know what she was expecting, but I thought it was a total smackdown in a 'You don't get it, you're not getting much' sort of way."

A few moments passed, neither knowing quite what to say.

"What should we do?" Theo said. "Anything? She seems really hurt."

"Nothing," Gloria interjected, pushing herself to her feet as Charles hovered nearby. "Let her be."

"But—" Theo tried.

Gloria shook her head. "She'll be fine. The truth is, Mother was right. And it's not her fault. Or yours. Or Vicky's. It's mine."

"Yours?" Anni asked.

Gloria nodded. "I didn't bring her here as often as I should have. As often as your mother brought you. I wanted to take her away from all of this, give her a bigger life in the city. Goodness, you grew up in Wharton, for the most part! You could be here all the time when you weren't globe-trotting, and you spent every summer here. Of course you'd be closer to Mother than Vicky was. I'll put that all on me." Gloria wiped away a tear.

"Darling, don't," Charles said, draping a protective arm around her shoulders. She gave him a small smile.

"It'll all be fine," Gloria said. "In time. Give her a little time. Maybe invite her here for weekends. Make her feel more a part of this place than she has in the past."

The idea of Vicky and Yale spending weekends at Metsan Valo made Anni's stomach turn, but Gloria was right. They were all family. Everyone should enjoy this place that their great-grandfather had built.

"Ever the peacemaker, darling," Charles said to Gloria, leading her away. "Let's go and find your daughter."

Patrick Saari crossed the room and sat next to Anni. "We should talk within the next few days," he said. "I can give you the info on things like upkeep, bills, utilities, and other things that need doing to keep this place running."

"Okay," she said, still not believing it. She was the owner of this fortress of a house now. How could that possibly be?

He held her gaze. "I know," he said. "It's a lot."

She nodded, still looking into his blue eyes. She didn't quite trust her words to reach over the tears that she was trying to keep inside. But something about being there, held in his gaze, made her wish the two of them could stay like that for a while. A long while.

"Get in touch tomorrow," Patrick said, breaking the spell. "Or the next day. Or whenever you're ready."

He pushed himself to his feet and handed his cards to both Anni and Theo. Theo took it into his hands and turned it over, as if he had no idea what it was.

"I should head out to catch the ferry," Patrick said. "I knew this was going to be a little rough, and you all don't need me hanging around right now."

Theo stood and stretched. "I'll walk you out," he said. Anni watched as they disappeared out the door.

That left Anni and Arden, still sitting in their chairs. Arden was looking straight ahead, her hands wringing in her lap. Anni slipped out of her chair and sat down next to her mother.

"Are you okay, Mom?" Anni asked.

Arden nodded, still staring straight ahead.

"Do you want this burden?" Arden said, finally, her voice reed thin.

"Burden?" Anni asked. "What do you mean?"

"This house," Arden said, snapping her head around to look at Anni. Her face was a mix of anger and concern. "It's not just a house, you know. It's all consuming. I'm upset your grandmother saddled you with it."

Anni shook her head and furrowed her brow. "I don't understand what you mean."

"I mean, this isn't just a nice vacation home to come to a few times each year. You have a life in Paris. What will Jean-Paul have to say about this? Will he want this albatross around both of your necks?"

Anni took a deep breath and let it out again. It had to be said, though she really was not looking forward to opening this can of worms.

"Jean-Paul and I aren't together anymore," she said finally.

"Wha-a-a-t?" Arden asked, elongating the word as though it had many syllables. She took Anni's hands in hers. "Since when?"

Anni felt her face begin to heat up. "A couple of months ago."

"Oh, honey. What happened?"

Anni squeezed her mother's hands before pulling hers away. "He was cheating on me," she said, shrugging. "I don't want to—"

"How did you find out?" Arden wanted to know.

"A couple of months back, we started arguing more than usual, and it just came out that he had been seeing someone." Anni pushed herself up from her chair. "But I don't really want to talk about it."

Arden clasped her daughter's hand. "Where are you living now?"

"Jean-Paul gave me the apartment," she said.

"And you want to stay there after living with him in those four walls for a decade?"

Anni shrugged. "I haven't had time to really think about it, Mom. I love the neighborhood, but I've toyed with the idea of selling the apartment and buying something new. Now I guess I have the means to do it. I'm not sure. I'm sort of at loose ends, if you want to know the truth. Lately I've been wondering if I want to stay in Paris at all."

Arden squinted at her for a moment, looking deeply into her daughter's eyes. Anni's skin began to crawl under the scrutiny. "What?" she asked.

"That's convenient, isn't it?" Arden said, raising her eyebrows.

Anni shook her head. She was regularly puzzled by Arden's off-the-wall comments and opinions, but this one came straight out of left field, and she had no idea how to catch it.

"What does that mean, Mom? Convenient?" she asked.

"Wel-l-l," Arden said, fingering the watch pendant around her neck. "It's a pretty big coincidence, wouldn't you say? Your nice life in Paris getting upended just before Taika dies and leaves you Metsan Valo?"

This caused Anni to sit down, hard. "You don't believe in coincidences."

A sly smile crossed Arden's face. "Exactly, my dear. The universe— or something—paved the way for the next chapter in your life. It cleared all obstacles out of the way for you to be the mistress of this place. Tied it up nicely for you in a big bow."

"Oh, Mom, you can't possibly think—"

Arden shook her head and pushed herself up to her feet, extending her hand to Anni, who took it and let herself be pulled up, too. Arden patted her daughter's back.

"Dear heart, there is no such thing as a little coincidence, let alone one this huge. Things happen the way they do for a reason."

Not this again. "I hate it when you say things happen for a reason," Anni said, furrowing her brow. "What's the reason behind a child getting cancer? What's the reason for Hitler to have existed? And never mind our free will to make things happen in our lives."

"I'm talking about coincidences, Annalise, not tragedies and horror stories. If you and Jean-Paul were still together, it would be a big obstacle for you right now. A problem. You would have no idea what you should do. But as it is, you're at loose ends. There's nothing keeping you in Paris . . . other than the fact that it's Paris, and who wouldn't want to be there?" Arden chuckled. "It would seem that the universe has opened the doorway to the next chapter of your life."

As much as she wanted to, Anni couldn't argue with that. The problem was, she wasn't sure if she wanted to walk through that door.

CHAPTER FOURTEEN

Anni and Arden walked arm in arm back into the great room, where they found Theo staring out the wall of windows, sipping on a glass of wine. Anger seemed to be floating through the air.

Vicky, Yale, and Lichen weren't anywhere to be seen, nor were Gloria and Charles.

Meri and Martin were busy in the kitchen. Plates and silverware, along with a loaf of homemade bread and butter, sat on the table. Martin was tossing a salad, and Meri was stirring a pot on the stove. It smelled to Anni like the dish Mummo used to call "meatballs swimming in their own gravy," which was basically Mummo's version of Swedish meatballs. Anni hadn't had a taste of that in years.

She walked to the stove and peered over Meri's shoulder. "This smells delicious," she said. Meri turned to her and smiled.

"Apparently, it's just going to be us," Theo said, joining Anni in the kitchen. "Everyone else is having dinner in town."

"Did something happen?" Anni said. "I mean, other than how the reading of the will went."

Theo shook his head, pulling out a chair from the table and sinking down into it with a thud. "Charles and Gloria thought it would do everyone good to have a little distance tonight," he said.

Arden plopped into her chair. "That's probably a good idea," she agreed.

"Did Vicky say anything else?" Anni wanted to know.

"No," Theo said. "They all pretty much just left in a hurry. I didn't even see Yale and Vicky. They were already gone by the time I was walking out with the lawyer."

Theo broke off a piece of bread and buttered it as Martin and Meri set the bowls of meatballs and salad on the table.

"Will you two join us tonight?" Arden asked.

Martin smiled but shook his head. "I think we'll retreat to the cottage," he said. "You should talk among yourselves, now that you know what's to come."

"It was an eventful afternoon," Meri added. "We'll be back to clean up later."

"Don't you dare," Theo said, wagging a finger at them. "I think we can handle putting the dishes in the dishwasher. Go enjoy your evening."

"Yes, please do," Arden said. "And thank you for this wonderful dinner."

"If you need anything, we'll be in the cottage," Martin said, and they took their leave.

Arden looked down at her plate and sighed. "I haven't had Taika's Swedish meatballs in years, and it is so fitting that this is our meal now, tonight. Funny. You can travel the world over and eat every cuisine known to man, but it's the food on your own table that speaks to your heart."

Anni covered her face with her napkin and began to sob.

Arden reached over and rubbed her back. "Oh, honey. I'm sorry. I didn't mean—"

"No," Anni said, her voice wavering. "It's not that. What you said was beautiful. And true. It's just—" She wiped her eyes with the napkin and sniffed. "Everything feels so messed up. She gave all of this to me, and the rest of the family is—"

"Don't, Anni," Theo said. "You didn't do this. It was Mummo. And whether Vicky and Yale like it or not, this is what she wanted. They're just going to have to deal with it and move on. Maybe they were expecting a big payout. It's pretty clear that was what Yale thought was going to happen."

"I don't think it was the money for Vicky," Arden said. "This has been simmering for a long time. If anyone is to blame for Vicky not feeling connected to this place, or to Taika, it's her."

Anni dipped her bread in the gravy on her plate. "I guess you're right," she said.

They ate in silence for the rest of the meal. Arden seemed off in another world, staring at nothing and everything, likely thinking about times past.

Theo and Anni both seemed to sense this was not the time for idle conversation, so they were quiet as well. When they had all finished their meals, Anni cleared the table and loaded the dishwasher while Theo scrubbed the pans and tidied up the kitchen.

Arden pushed back her chair and got to her feet. "Darlings, I'm going to retire to my room. It's been a long day. I'd like to call Nick Stone and ask if he has any thoughts on the break-in. He'll want me to come back to Wharton and go through my office to see what's missing, but that can wait for another time."

"We'll walk you up," Anni said, wiping her hands on a towel.

"Not tonight, loves," Arden said. "I'd like to be alone with my thoughts."

Anni and Theo kissed their mother, and she ascended the stairs, stopping midway to turn around and look at them, her long, flowing dress seeming to blow in an unseen breeze.

"I love you, my darlings. We don't say it enough. Or show it enough. But you two live in my heart."

"We love you, too, Mom," Theo said, his voice catching in his throat.

With that, Arden turned and made her way up to the second floor, disappearing down the hallway. Anni thought she heard her humming a tune as she went.

Theo turned to Anni. "Well, that was unusual."

Anni smiled. "Vintage Mom. She's ready for her close-up for sure. But it was still nice to hear."

"It's like the world has turned upside down when our mother is the sanest one in the room." Theo flopped down onto the couch. He glanced at the ancient clock that stood on the far wall. "It's almost eight o'clock already," he mused, running a hand through his hair.

Anni walked to the windows and gazed outside. It was summer's end, and the days had begun to shorten. Darkness fell early now. Twilight had already descended around them. The sky over the lake was turning shades of red and purple, and the first of the stars were beginning to twinkle in the sky. So like any other night at Metsan Valo. But now everything had changed.

She turned to her brother. "Feel like taking a sauna?"

"Why not?" he said. "I'll go turn it on and meet you down there in an hour."

As Theo trotted down to the stone sauna, which had been standing where the edge of the woods met the lakeshore longer than Metsan Valo itself, Anni headed up to her room. She was grateful for the nearly empty house. She had no desire to run into any of her other family members. She needed a few minutes alone to digest what had happened during the day or, more pleasantly, not think of it at all. She shut the door behind her and slumped onto the chaise. She was the owner of this magnificent home now. She had no idea how much money was in Mummo's estate, but she knew finances were never going to be an issue in her life again.

She sat there for a long time, staring out the window, watching the sky turn from pinks and purples to deep blue to inky black. A million stars shone down, and the moon was like a beacon, high in the sky.

Anni glanced at the clock and saw it was almost nine. The sauna would be hot by now. The heat and steam would soothe her, as they always did. An ancient Finnish tradition, the sauna offered staggering health benefits. Some reports said you could burn five hundred calories during twenty minutes in a sauna, that it increased blood flow to muscles, and sped recovery after a workout, that it could reduce cardiac problems, improve skin health, and a whole host of other benefits. One of the traditional rituals after taking a sauna was jumping in a cold lake, rolling in the snow, or taking a cold shower while you were still hot and sweating. Many Americans who took a sauna at the gym skipped this step, but to Anni (and all Finns) that was missing the whole point. The feeling of clean that came from immersing oneself in cold water after sweating out all the toxins in one's system was unparalleled and invigorating to the max. It always took Anni's breath away.

Anni dug her swimsuit out of the dresser and changed into it, then wrapped a robe around her and slipped her feet into a pair of flip-flops. She grabbed one of the enormous white towels in the bathroom and headed downstairs.

The great room was dark, so Anni flipped on a couple of lamps as she went. She glanced around for Theo but didn't see him, so she pushed open the french doors onto the deck. Before taking the stairs, she scanned the yard and the forest beyond. No fireflies.

She held tight to her towel and hurried down the yard toward the sauna, which she saw was lit up. Theo was pouring some water onto the rocks inside when she opened the door. The rocks sizzled, and steam wafted into the air.

The twins sank onto the benches. Anni leaned back and sighed aloud. "This feels really good after the day we've had."

"Day, month, year."

"No doubt," Anni said, the heat baking into her bones. "Crazy, what went down today with the will."

Theo shrugged. "It is what it is. Even though I hate it when people use that expression. It just seems to sum up the situation this time. Obviously, Vicky is hurt. Obviously, Yale is his usual, delightful self."

"Do you think Mom is upset she didn't inherit this place?" Anni wondered, grimacing.

"Not at all," Theo said, pushing his hair back from his face. "What I said about Big Edie and Little Edie still stands. Even though Little Edie seems to have turned into Jackie O for the time being. Mom would convert this place into an artist's commune in five seconds, and every dead relative on our family tree would rise up from the grave in protest."

Anni grinned, but then a seriousness fell over her face. "Are you upset?"

Theo narrowed his eyes at her. "Oh, for God's sake, Anni. Why would you even ask that?"

"Well?" she said, shrugging. "I mean, it's a lot."

"One: you know me better than that. Two: Mummo was right. I have a life in Chicago, a business to run, and a home of my own that I have no intention of leaving. I'm not the person to inherit this house, this place, this tradition. And she knew it. I'm the one who comes here to vacation. To stay all summer if I want. Not the keeper of the flame, so to speak."

"You make yourself sound like Yale."

"Say that again, and I'll summon the fireflies," Theo said, a mock scowl on his face. He reached over and dipped the ladle into its wooden bucket and drizzled more water over the hot rocks. Steam filled the air between them.

Anni breathed in the steam and exhaled. Her whole body was beading with sweat. She could almost feel all the toxic energy of the day pouring out of her. Which, after all, was the point. At least her brother wasn't angry with her. The rest she could deal with.

"There were a couple of weird things about what Mummo said today, though," Theo started. He looked at Anni, a hesitancy in his eyes.

"What things? Us being Gandalf? I'm not down with that wardrobe, if it's true."

Theo grinned. "It would look great on me, sadly. Especially the hat. Seriously, though, do you think she really believed all of that, or was the whole story some sort of metaphor?"

"Like, she was referencing our ancestors coming to this country and conquering this harsh land to build Metsan Valo, you mean?"

He shrugged. "I'm not sure. It was a cool story, though."

The heat was making Anni's skin tingle. She was sweating from head to toe.

"I was actually talking about something else," he said, leaning back against the wall. "Did you catch what she said about it not being wise to own a house with you because of what might be coming down the pike with Jenny?"

Anni had caught that but hadn't wanted to bring it up. But now that Theo had, she figured the subject was safe territory. "The night you got here, you talked a bit about how you guys were arguing more than normal. Is there more to it than that?"

Theo ran a hand through his wet hair.

"Have you called her since you've been here?"

He sighed. "No. I mean, I tried once but didn't reach her. And yes, I think there might be more to it than I've said. I don't really know. I'm going to try to ride it out. Not do anything drastic. They say not to make any big changes in your life right after a loved one passes away, so I'm going to take that advice."

Anni leaned forward, toward her brother. "Are you saying that you've been thinking about making changes? Splitting up?" She hated to even say the word that came out in a whisper. "Divorce?"

Theo put his head in his hands. "It's just not working, Anni."

"Since when?"

"Since a while."

"Why didn't you tell me?"

Theo groaned. "I suppose I didn't want to say it out loud. Give it a voice. I've been hoping things would change. We've been sort of coasting along for some time now, leading quasi-separate lives, but within the last couple of months it has become totally unworkable. I've told you that everything she does annoys me. It's strange. I don't know why. It's just like I've hit the wall."

"What are you going to do?"

He shook his head. "I don't know. Nothing right now, I guess. We've been married forever. Every marriage goes through rough patches, right?"

"Of course," Anni said. "It's not wine and roses for a lifetime. But you're right. You don't have to make any rash decisions right now. I like the idea of riding it out for a while. You should call her tonight. Tell her what's going on. I know she's concerned about you."

"How do you know that?"

"Because she loves you, you dope."

"I'm not sure about that anymore." Theo lay back on the bench and stretched out. "It's just the weirdest thing. I feel so detached from her." He sighed and leaned back against the wood-paneled walls. "So I ride it out?"

"I vote for riding it out. But what did Mummo say to you about it?"

Theo sat up and looked at Anni, his face dripping with sweat. "What do you mean, Mummo?"

"You obviously told her about what's happening in your marriage."

"That's the thing," Theo said. "I didn't. But in the video, she said she didn't want to give Metsan Valo to both of us because of complications that might arise with Jenny. Or some version of that, anyway."

"And you hadn't talked to her about any of this?"

"No! Not one word. I might be reading way too much into this, but the way I heard it, it's like she foresaw a divorce on the horizon for me and Jenny. If Metsan Valo was partially in my name, like if you and I owned it together, that would be something for Jenny to go after in a divorce."

Anni looked at her brother, openmouthed. "That can't be right."

"That's what I heard," Theo said. "But we should watch it again to be sure."

A gnarling began to twist in Anni's stomach. "I didn't tell her about Jean-Paul, either. But it's like she knew I was available. Or something."

"This is getting too weird."

"It's weirder," Anni said. "Mom thinks *the universe* opened the door for me to come back here."

Theo groaned. "Oh no, for the love of God." He wiped his brow. "Not the universe at work in our personal lives again. You'd think it would be busy handling world peace and global warming."

Anni laughed at this. "Race relations in this country could use some help, if it's not too much trouble. Cancer, too."

They sat in silence for a moment, breathing in the heat, feeling it in their bones.

"Do you think it's about time we jump in the lake?" Theo asked, mopping his brow. "I mean literally, not figuratively. We've been in here, what, twenty minutes?"

Anni pushed herself to her feet. "Let's do it."

Theo got to his feet, grabbed his towel, and pushed on the door. And then pushed again. And again. He turned to Anni. "I can't get the door open."

Anni tried, pushing the door with all her might. "I wonder when this was used last. The door is obviously stuck."

Theo joined her, and the two of them pushed, putting their whole bodies into it. It didn't budge an inch. Theo sat back down on the bench. "Now what?"

Anni looked around. The sauna was made of stone and wood. The door was the only way in or out, but it didn't have a lock on it, so it had to be stuck shut because of . . . what? Humidity? Heat? That was ridiculous. This sauna had been standing in this same spot for more than one hundred years. It had seen its fair share of heat and humidity. But if Mummo hadn't used it in a while . . . who knew how the wood of the door would react? Would it expand?

"So, before you start panicking like we're in an episode of *Law & Order*, we're not going to die in here," Theo said, breaking Anni's train of thought, the amusement buoying his voice. "The would-be villains are misinformed. This sauna doesn't have a wood fire anymore. Mummo broke down and dragged herself into the modern age a few years ago. It's electric and has a timer. The controls are in here."

He switched the dial to off. "Boom. Problem solved. It'll take about half an hour for it to cool down in here."

He settled back down on the bench. Anni took her place next to him. "Why did you go right to that?" she asked.

"To what?"

"To the scenario that someone was trapping us in here?"

Theo looked at her. "Why else would the door be blocked?"

CHAPTER FIFTEEN

The sauna was still warm but had cooled down considerably by the time Martin opened the door from the outside. Anni and Theo were both lying on their backs on the benches.

"Oh!" Anni said, sitting up. "Thank goodness you came. We couldn't get out. The door was stuck."

"I saw the light was on for longer than it should be," Martin said. "I'll take a look at this door tomorrow to see what's wrong with it."

Theo sighed. "I don't even feel like jumping in the lake now. I'm cooled down. It sort of defeats the purpose."

"Agreed," Anni said. "Thank you again, Martin."

As the twins gathered their things and made their way back to the house, Anni looked back over her shoulder and saw that Martin stayed at the sauna watching them until they reached the french doors and were safely inside.

Later, after Anni had taken a quick shower and pulled on her pajamas, she found herself looking out her bedroom windows from her perch on the chaise. The night was bright with stars, and the moon was shining down, a shaft of light illuminating the forest. She listened to the singing of frogs through her window, a sound that always calmed her. The lake was lapping softly on the rocky shoreline. It spoke to her in an ancient language that seeped into her bones. She closed her eyes, leaned her head back, and listened, and she could almost feel her blood pressure dropping, her heartbeat slowing.

But then a sound awakened her. Anni's eyes fluttered open. Were the frogs still singing? She listened closer but couldn't make out what the sound was. It wasn't exactly a song, or even a tune. But it was coming from outside, that was for certain. She took a deep breath and leaned forward.

It sounded mournful. Like an awful keening or a dirge. As Anni listened, the sound surrounded her. It seemed to seep inside her. She had to know what was making that ungodly music.

Anni gazed out her window into the forest below, still illuminated by the moon and the starlight. She squinted, at first not believing what she was seeing, and then gasping aloud at what she was sure she saw.

Figures, cloaked in flowing white garments, floated among the trees. Anni had no idea what they were. Spirits of the dead? She could see their distorted faces, mouths that were more like gaping maws. Black holes where eyes should be. They were the ones singing these mournful cries, keening as though their very souls were breaking. She noticed garlands or wreaths around their heads, long, sheer, flowing scarves around their necks.

Anni watched as they circled among the trees. It was almost a dance. A ghostly parade. They swayed and bobbed in and out of the ancient trees, this way and that. All the while singing their mournful songs. But then they turned as one, and focused on her, on the window where she was standing. They began to float slowly toward her, one after another.

Anni was glued to the spot, watching. All at once, they sped toward her as one. She broke free and ran across the room and out the door.

"Theo!" she screeched, bursting into his room.

He opened his eyes, squinting. "What? What's going on?"

She rushed past him to the windows. "Look!" she hissed, in a whisper. "Look out there."

He scrambled out of bed and looked over her shoulder, out into the night. "What?"

Anni just stood there, staring. Nothing. Just the starlit night. No creepy floating specters, no bodies clothed in white gowns.

"What did you see out there, Anni?" Theo asked, his face filled with concern. "Fireflies again?"

She shook her head and sat down, hard, on the bed across from Theo's.

"You wouldn't believe me if I told you," she said.

Theo curled into his bed and pulled the covers around him. "What is it with this day? It can end already."

Anni lay back. "I know. I want to say 'what else can happen,' but I feel like that would be tempting fate. More like daring it."

She was silent for a moment. The thought of going back into her room, alone, was making her skin itch.

"Can I sleep in here?" she asked.

Theo yawned and snuggled down into his pillows. "Sure. But I'm imposing some house rules. There is to be no snoring. And no peering dramatically out the window. And no wandering off to investigate strange phenomena."

"Agreed," Anni said, pulling back the bedclothes and slipping down inside. "Did you call Jenny?"

"And no talking."

~❧~

The next morning dawned, and the sun streamed in through the windows. It took a moment for Anni to realize where she was. She sat up and looked around. *Oh, that's right.* She had spent the night in Theo's room. He was still asleep, snoring softly. *Just like when we were children,* Anni thought. She didn't want to wake him, so she slipped out as quietly as she could and went back to her own room.

She turned on the shower and let it get warm before stepping into the spray and standing under the stream for a long time. She remembered that, growing up, showers here at Metsan Valo meant "step in and step out." It was a matter of conserving hot water for others. But apparently a few years ago, Mummo had upgraded to an unlimited hot-water system, along with putting solar panels on the roof to cut down on energy costs, so that wasn't an issue anymore.

And that was when it hit Anni. She had been preparing this house for the future. For her. Mummo had spent the last few years making it easy for Anni to step in and become the owner. She'd have no ancient, quirky boilers to deal with. Nothing major needed to be replaced. Even the sauna had been upgraded to an electric configuration that didn't require an all-day fire to get hot, like it did in the old days. Anni would be surprised if Mummo hadn't replaced the roof within the last few years while she was at it. The televisions!

Meri and Martin would know about all the improvements Mummo had made. Anni finally stepped out of the shower and dried off, intending to pop downstairs and ask them about it.

She was just finishing dressing for the day in her jeans and long-sleeved T-shirt when she heard her phone buzzing in her purse. She picked it up and looked at the number. She didn't recognize it, but from the area code, it seemed to be from Wharton. Maybe Patrick?

"Hello?" she said, furrowing her brow.

"Hey, is this Annalise?"

"Yes," Anni said. "Who's this?"

"It's Nick Stone," he said.

The police chief, she remembered. "Oh! Hi! What can I do for you?"

Anni could hear him shuffling some papers around. "I've been trying to get ahold of Arden," Stone said. "Her phone keeps going right to voice mail."

Anni smiled. "She tends to turn her phone off when she's here. Something about the cell-phone energy messing with nature."

"Not surprised by that," Stone said, a lightness in his voice. "That's why I called you. You're still on the island with her, right?"

"Yes," Anni said, peering out the window. "Everyone's still here, as far as I know. I just woke up and haven't been downstairs yet. Yesterday was a long day."

"I can imagine." Stone sighed.

"Are you calling because you have some news?" Anni wanted to know.

"No," Stone said. "I was just wondering if she—or someone—was going to ferry over to Wharton today to take a look in her office. We're done in the house in terms of getting any fingerprints. I'd sure like to know if something is missing, and if so, what that something is."

"Are you usually this attentive to nonviolent crimes, Chief?" Anni could feel herself smiling.

He chuckled. "Nope. This is someone messing with Arden. I want to know who it is. Your mom's a great lady."

"Kooky, but great," Anni said, a laugh in her voice.

"You probably don't know this, but I have a connection to the house, too," he said. "It's another reason I don't take too kindly to people breaking in and trashing the place."

That was news to Anni. Her mother had owned that house for decades, and, from what Anni had heard, Nick had moved to Wharton within the past few years.

"Really? How so?"

"My wife's great-grandparents built it," he said.

Anni took a breath in. "You're kidding! That's wild. Who were they?"

Nick chuckled. "That's a long, strange, and highly scandalous story you should talk about over dinner sometime with my wife, Kate. In a nutshell, Kate's great-grandmother was murdered when she lived in the house on Front Street. The body was never found until a century later. It washed up on the beach in front of Kate's house, if you can believe that. It was my first case when I came to Wharton, investigating her murder. It took a while to figure out—well, Kate figured it out—that the murder had taken place a century earlier."

"A century? But the body—"

"I know," he said. "I told you it was strange. It took a lot of convincing, and proof in the form of newspaper articles and photos Kate found that ultimately made me believe it. Or rather, suspend my disbelief. I have since learned that there is nothing usual about my wife, or the women in her family. Or Wharton, for that matter."

Anni understood that better than the chief knew. "It sounds like my family." A chill went through Anni then, as a memory she had shared with Theo earlier swam back into her mind.

"I think I've met her."

"Who? Kate?"

"No," Anni said. "Her great-grandmother. You may not know that Theo and I grew up in that house. A beautiful lady in a white gown used to tuck us into bed at night when we were little. She was so lovely and kind. It wasn't until we were much older that we realized the lady wasn't really fully there, if you get what I mean."

Nick let out a whistle. "Kate is going to love to hear that. We've got to get the two of you together sometime."

"It's a date."

"For now, let's find whoever is messing with that house, and your mother."

"That sounds good to me. I'll track down Mom and make sure she calls you."

Anni had always known this place was filled with strange coincidences that weren't coincidences at all. This kind of synchronicity, like that the police chief investigating a crime at your mother's house would have a deep connection to that very house, didn't happen often elsewhere. But in the Wharton/Colette community, it happened all the time. Anni was beginning to think nothing was random in this part of the world. Then something else occurred to her. "Nick? I'm wondering if I could ask you a favor."

"Sure. What is it?"

"My mom, Theo, and I, and Taika for that matter, are a little suspicious about my aunt Gloria's new husband. They apparently had a whirlwind romance and married quite quickly. With the amount of money she's worth . . ."

"I see. So you're wanting me to run a background check on the guy."

"Could you?"

"Of course," Nick said. "It's good to know your suspicions. He could be involved in the break-in, for all we know. What's his full name?"

Anni winced. "I don't know. But I can find out and call you with it."

⁂

Anni kept her phone in her hand and stepped out of her room. Her stomach tightened. Would Vicky and Yale be downstairs? Were they still at Metsan Valo, or had they left in a huff? She had no desire to see the extended family after yesterday's events. Anni hesitated at Theo's door for a moment, wishing he was up and around to offer some moral support. She put her ear to the door and listened. No signs of life.

Hearing voices downstairs, she realized she couldn't hide from her family forever. Nor should she. She had done nothing wrong and hadn't even known about Mummo's plans. She took a deep breath, pasted a smile onto her face, and headed for the stairs.

They were all seated at the table finishing breakfast—Yale and Vicky, Gloria and Charles. Lichen was slumped in the big armchair, engrossed in her phone.

"Morning, all!" Anni said, a bit too cheerily.

"Good morning, dear," Gloria said, taking a sip of coffee.

"Aunt Gloria, with all of the excitement yesterday, I didn't have a chance to ask if you have a new last name," Anni said, casually taking out her phone. "I should update your contact info if so."

Gloria beamed at Charles, and then looked back at Anni.

"It's Wellington, honey. Gloria Wellington."

"I like the sound of that, my dear," Charles said.

Vicky pushed her chair back from the table and stood up, crossing the room toward Anni.

"I'm so sorry about how I reacted yesterday," she said, taking Anni's hands. The two cousins smiled at each other. *Maybe this isn't going to be so bad after all,* Anni thought.

"Like hell," Yale growled under his breath, throwing his napkin on his plate. "You have nothing to apologize for."

At that moment, Theo came trotting down the stairs but stopped midway, sizing up the room.

"Well, good morning to you, too, Yale," Theo said. "What did I miss? Bloodshed?"

Anni grinned at her brother, then turned back to Vicky.

"I don't know what to say," Anni began. "Except that I had no idea what Mummo was going to do. It was a total surprise to me."

Meri poured some coffee into a cup, added a splash of milk, and handed it to Anni.

"Thank you," Anni said, taking the cup. She pulled out a chair at the table and sank into it. The air was thickening, and Anni could feel the tension hanging in the room. A change of subject was definitely in order.

"Has anyone seen Mom today?" Anni asked, as Theo joined her at the table with a cup of his own.

"She left for one of her famous early-morning walks here in the Metsan forest when I was coming downstairs," Gloria said, her voice bright and lilting. "Why?"

They hadn't told the rest of the family about the break-in, she realized. She turned to Theo, and he nodded in answer to the question she didn't pose.

He cleared his throat. "There's something you all should know," he said, a catch of hesitation in his voice.

"Now what? More drama about the will?" Yale said.

"No. As a matter of fact, Yale," Theo said, a sharpness in his voice, "the three of us stopped by the house in Wharton yesterday and found that it had been broken into. Mom's study was ransacked."

"Ransacked?" Gloria said, putting a hand to her chest. "Arden didn't say anything about this to me."

Anni shrugged. "There really wasn't time. When we got back, the lawyer was already here."

"True, true," Gloria said. She and Charles pushed their chairs back and got to their feet. He put a protective arm around her shoulder. It was a familiar gesture by now.

"Did they loot the place?" he asked. "Take valuables, that sort of thing?"

"The police came and had a look around," Anni went on. "We didn't have a chance to figure out what was taken because we had to get back here for the reading of the will. But nothing like TVs or any other electronics were missing."

"Kids." Gloria sniffed under her breath. "I hear they've been having a problem in Wharton with random break-ins and minor sorts of vandalism."

Anni furrowed her brow and shot Theo a look.

"The police didn't say anything about that yesterday," Theo said. "But maybe that's all it is. I hope so."

"I'm sure the police will get it all sorted out," Charles said, deep and authoritative. "As long as nobody was hurt, that's the important thing." He cleared his throat. "Darling, we were going to take a drive this morning, remember? You were going to show me some of your favorite spots on the island."

"I'll get my purse," Gloria said. "Maybe we'll do some shopping in town later!"

When those two had gone, and Yale, Vicky, and Lichen had slipped off somewhere, Anni slid over to the table and carefully picked up the teacup Charles had been using. She retrieved a plastic bag out of the cabinet and wrapped the mug in it before sinking into the deep sofa with a groan.

Theo squinted at her. "What are you doing with that mug?"

"He called this morning," Anni said, looking over her shoulder at Theo, who was pouring the last of the coffee into his mug.

"Who?"

"Nick Stone."

Theo joined her on the couch. "Why, does he have news?" He settled back and crossed his legs.

"No. But while I had him on the phone, I asked him to look into Charles's background."

Theo's eyes lit up. "I was wondering what that business was about just now, you asking for Gloria's new last name."

Anni grinned. "Yep. Nick asked for Charles's full name, and it occurred to me that we didn't know it. So . . ."

"The mug. Fingerprints. You crafty minx."

"If I had a nickel for every time someone called me that . . ."

"You'd have a nickel," Theo said, chuckling, then furrowing his brow at Anni. "If Stone wasn't calling with news about the break-in, why was he calling?"

Anni winced, knowing her brother was not going to like what she was about to say. "He was wondering if we were coming to Wharton to go through her study."

Theo laid his head on the back of the couch and groaned. "I really don't feel like going all the way over there today and sifting through Mom's books and papers. Do you? After yesterday—good Lord, what *didn't* happen yesterday? I'm sort of exhausted from it all. You coming into my room shrieking in the middle of the night didn't help." He gave her a side-eye and grinned.

"It's a lot of upheaval for one day," Anni said, wondering if she should tell him what had caused her to wake him up in the middle of the night. The cause of the shrieking.

Anni couldn't get it out of her mind. The scene replayed over and over, as though it was on some sort of mental loop. It was like a procession. Or a march. Spirits in flowing white gowns. A ritual of some kind? But she wasn't sure she had even really seen it. It might have been a dream, for all she knew.

She sighed and gazed out the window, sipping her coffee. What was happening at Metsan Valo? It was like she was getting gaslighted by her own home.

The business with Theo blundering off the dock in the middle of the night. And her, the night before, waking up in the woods—or had she? Again, it was like something, or someone, was playing with her mind. Were all these happenings real? Or just dreams? Or something else entirely?

One thing she couldn't deny: the fireflies. Both she and Theo were there. They experienced it together. And they had just disappeared into thin air as quickly as they had swarmed.

And then there was the sauna.

Theo was staring out the window, as lost in thought as she was. She suspected he was mulling over the same strange things in his mind.

"Do you think someone deliberately trapped us in the sauna?" Anni asked him, her voice low. "Not being able to open the door from the inside. That doesn't just happen. There's no way to lock it. That's been a safeguard of saunas for hundreds of years. Thousands, even."

He held her gaze for a long time without answering. She knew what he wasn't saying. If it were true, it had to have been someone in their own family. Just like what Nick Stone said about the break-in.

"I want to say no," he said finally. "But that's just me, wanting to say no. What do you think?"

"I think if someone intentionally locked us in there, it would've had to have been a dumbass, who, one: didn't know anything about saunas because it's really hard to die in a sauna—just lie on the floor, heat rises, duh—and two: someone who hadn't been here in a few years and didn't know Mummo converted the sauna to electric and we could just turn it off."

Anni sighed. "It's sort of ridiculous when you think about it. What would be the motive?"

"What's always the motive? Money."

Anni smirked at him. "You always say that. But there's nobody up or down the food chain in this family who would inherit anything if I died except you. You know that. We did our wills together."

"Jenny gets it all if I go to the great beyond," Theo said, running a hand through his hair. "Maybe I should rethink that. But what happens to your money if you and I were to exit together, so to speak?"

"Mom is my beneficiary in that case," Anni said. "And I seriously doubt the queen of the summer of love is killing either of her children."

"Bad karma."

"Aura destroying."

They both sighed at the same time.

"It makes no sense," Theo said, finally. "It had to have been a fluke. Some kind of accident. The door expanding because of the heat. I don't know."

Both of them stared out the window, watching the pines sway in the breeze and the lake glistening in the distance.

All these unusual, eerie happenings. It seemed to Anni that a sort of strange enchantment had fallen around them, the house, and the forest beyond. As though they were shrouded in a fairy tale. Decidedly Grimm's.

"It just sort of feels like this place is out to get me," Anni said finally. "Doesn't it? I've never felt this way here before."

"That's because you've never been here without her."

Anni whipped her head around to see Meri and Martin standing in the kitchen. How long had they been there?

"I didn't mean to startle you two," Meri said, a small smile on her lips. "I'm very sorry about that."

Anni's heart was pounding, but she managed a smile as she put a hand to her chest. "No! You didn't startle me. I just didn't know you were there."

They looked at each other in silence for a moment.

"I don't quite understand, Meri," Anni said, pushing herself to her feet. "Is it just that things are weird here without Mummo? Because they certainly are. You started to say something yesterday about us being called? That things had begun? What did you mean by that?"

"I don't think—" Martin began. But Meri shook her head. A look that spoke volumes passed between them. But Anni couldn't read what those volumes said.

"All I meant was, your grandmother has been mistress of this house since her mother left this world. Taika passed down this place, and all that comes with it, to you. Now it's your turn."

That didn't really seem to answer Anni's question. It just raised more.

"We need to sit down and have a talk, very soon," Meri said. "Later today. Or tonight. You need to let what you've learned sink in. You need to think about how it may change your life. This is a big step for you.

You must make some decisions right away. There is much for you to learn about running this house. Keeping the grounds. Of course, we will be here to help, every step of the way."

"Okay," Anni said, shaking her head. "I guess I'll look forward to that?" She shot Theo a look. He shrugged.

Meri is right, though, Anni thought. She did have some big decisions to make, now that this place was hers. Her living arrangements were on the top of that list. Was it incumbent upon her to move to Metsan Valo now?

Meri broke Anni's train of thought. "What would you like for dinner tonight?" she asked, smoothing her apron.

Anni furrowed her brow. "Dinner?"

"Yes," Meri said, smiling slightly. "That's up to you now."

So that was one thing. Deciding the menu for the day. Not so hard and mysterious. But the realization that Mummo was gone and Anni was now charged with doing things that she had done settled onto Anni's shoulders like a heavy shroud. The fact that she was the one being asked about dinner made her sadness, her grief, the monumental loss, somehow more tangible and real. All at once, she had no desire to do it.

Theo sensed her trepidation. "I suppose lobster thermidor is out of the question."

His comment broke through her mood, as he always managed to do. Anni chuckled, and then had an idea. "What about barbecued spareribs?" she suggested. "Mummo always used to love those."

Meri nodded. "Done. I'll make her favorite slaw and baked potatoes to go with it."

Anni wasn't sure what she was supposed to say now. "Great!" she ventured. "Thank you."

"Is there anything you need?" Martin asked, his eyes expectant.

Anni looked at Theo, who shrugged again in response. "I think we're fine," Anni said.

Meri gave her a quick nod. "Very good, then," she said. "We will be off. Martin is going to keep an eye out for the lawn crew to get here. They're mowing and weeding today. I'll be in the cottage if you need me."

Martin opened the front door, and Meri followed him out, leaving Anni and Theo staring at each other.

"Apparently, you're lord of the manor now," Theo said. "You should probably start wearing an ascot."

"That's *lady* to you, smart guy." Anni smirked. "And ladies don't wear ascots."

But his joke couldn't lighten her mood this time. Her skin was still crawling. "Seriously, that was weird. Wasn't it?"

Theo poured himself a glass of water. "It might feel weird," he began, taking a sip. "But the fact is, you own this house now. They've had a lifetime of taking direction from Mummo. So now they're looking to you. Like it or not, sister, you are in charge of Metsan Valo."

Anni nodded. "I suppose that's true. Of course it is. But what about their creepy 'It has begun'? What has begun?"

"Morticia and Gomez are always dramatic," Theo said. "But you're right. That was creepy, even for them, and she deflected it just now when you asked about it. Maybe she just meant your reign as queen of the castle?"

"Fireflies. Sauna. Creepy visions in the woods. The break-in."

Theo squinted at her. "What creepy visions in the woods?"

"You don't even want to know," Anni said. "My point is, we need to talk to the gruesome twosome and find out what they meant. Because something *has* definitely begun. And I don't like it."

CHAPTER SIXTEEN

Anni was at loose ends. Martin and Meri were nowhere to be found. Gloria and Charles still hadn't returned. Vicky, Yale, and Lichen were similarly absent. Theo wanted a day to himself and had retreated to his favorite beach on the other side of the island to soak up the last rays of the late-summer sun, read, and decompress. Anni suspected he had a lot on his mind, mainly Jenny. It sounded like they were headed for rocky shores. She wanted to be there for her brother but not be intrusive, either, so she let him go off on his own without insisting she go along, which she would have loved to do.

After rattling around the house on her own for a while, she pulled Patrick Saari's card out of the folder of documents he had given her the previous day and dialed his number. It seemed as good a time as any to take care of business with him.

"This is Patrick." His voice sounded lower than she remembered it.

"Hi!" Anni said, a little too loudly. "It's Anni Halla."

"Hey, Anni," Patrick said. "How are you holding up after yesterday? It was a lot to deal with."

She nodded into the phone. "Yes, it was. A lot," she said. "Everyone in the family has retreated to neutral corners today, so I thought it would be a good time to follow up with you. You said you had some things to go over with me? About running Metsan Valo?"

"I do," he said. "Do you want to make an appointment to get together and talk?"

Anni looked around at the empty house. "Is today good?"

A few minutes later, Anni was in her rental car, driving toward the ferry dock. She figured she could do double duty in Wharton, meeting with the lawyer first and venturing to the house on Front Street to go through Arden's office in the afternoon. Anni could clean it up and see if she could discern what, if anything, was missing. Arden still hadn't resurfaced by the time Anni left Metsan Valo, so she had called Nick Stone and they arranged to meet at the house after Anni's appointment with the lawyer. She could get a start on the room, anyway.

Arden's phone was still going right to voice mail—she probably hadn't charged it in a while. So, before Anni left the house, she stole into Mummo's room, now Arden's, and left her mother a note explaining where she was and what she was doing.

Cleaning up Front Street. If you want me to look for anything in particular, call me!

How Arden would see the note in the shambles of clothes strewn everywhere, jewelry hanging here and there, the unmade bed, and books spilling off the bookshelf, Anni had no idea. But she had made a good effort, anyway.

Standing on the deck of the ferry, it was Anni's turn to exhale. It was as though, as she watched the island fade into the distance, she was leaving the previous day behind, too. More than that, her whole previous life—Paris, Jean-Paul—was fading. As Wharton lay in front of her and the ferry chugged toward it, a new life was waiting for Anni.

Now that she was alone, she had a moment to digest her new circumstances. She owned Metsan Valo. What did that mean? How would it change her life? Would she leave Paris and move back here? Did she want to? Did she have a choice?

She couldn't sell the house, of course. Wouldn't even think of it. The house had been built by her ancestors and belonged in her family for generations to come. She was just the steward of it, for the time being.

Anni hadn't thought of any answers as the ferry pulled into the dock in Wharton. Just the fact that she was thinking about the questions had to be good enough for now.

Patrick Saari's office was in an old brick two-story building with a flat roof just off the main street. As Anni pulled up, she saw that it had a rooftop deck overlooking the lake. Patrick was sitting up there at a patio table with an umbrella, and he waved when he saw her get out of the car.

"I'll be right down," he called out. A moment later he was at the front door with an enormous white dog at his heels.

"Hi!" he said, holding the door open for her. "Thank you for coming. I've got everything set up in my office."

The dog nuzzled up to Anni, and she gave it a scratch on the snout. "Who's this?" she asked.

"This is Pascal," Patrick said, a grin lighting up his eyes.

"*Comment ça va*, Pascal," Anni cooed, scratching behind the dog's ears. He wiggled and wagged his tail in response. "Is he a white shepherd?"

Patrick nodded. "He came to me from a rescue organization down south. I was visiting friends, and I saw him, and . . . well, one thing led to another. I couldn't leave without him."

Anni smiled. She had a bias toward animal lovers. She and Jean-Paul had a French bulldog, Mitzi, who had left with Jean—it was a nonnegotiable. She had been Jean's dog before Anni had come into the picture and was now nearing the end of her days. Sometimes Anni wondered who she missed more.

As Pascal trailed behind them, Anni followed Patrick through the building, which she now saw was also his home. The living room was at the front of the house, with textured plaster walls, dark wooden beams spanning the ceiling, and big windows overlooking the lake. It was furnished with a mix of antique pieces—a lamp here, a sideboard there—and comfortable modern décor, like a soft leather couch and a flat-screen television. A leather armchair, a reading lamp next to it, sat near the window, with a stack of hardcover books and a coffee mug on a side table.

The brick fireplace with a wrought-iron grate looked well used, its utensils and a stack of wood standing ready by its side. A big, comfy dog bed sat next to the fireplace, a well-loved stuffed sheep guarding the lair until Pascal returned.

Passing by the dining room, Anni saw a long table, its top worn with age. She imagined it had been handed down from generation to generation in Patrick's family.

"This is a great house," Anni said. "Really beautiful."

He turned and smiled at her. "Thank you. Lots of character. It's my grandparents' house. They lived here for sixty-five years. I've blended some of their old things with my new stuff, and it sort of works."

Anni looked around the room and grinned. "We have something in common. Inheriting our grandparents' homes."

"Yes, indeed." Patrick nodded. "Although this house isn't as grand as Metsan Valo. Or complicated. There's a lot of upkeep where you are."

Martin and Meri took care of that, Anni thought to herself as they walked through the kitchen. An impressive AGA stove stood on one wall, a collection of copper pots and saucepans hanging above it. A wide scrubbed wooden table sat in front of the window, a couple of dog-eared cookbooks open, as though Patrick had been going through recipes before Anni arrived.

She smiled as she followed him through the warren of rooms.

They settled into his office, which was lined with bookshelves. An enormous mahogany desk stood in the center of the room.

Patrick had a stack of paperwork on his desk, documents for Anni to sign. Transfer of the house, Mummo's accounts, investment information. Life insurance. He explained all of it to her, but she knew she wasn't taking it all in.

"Okay," he said, clearing his throat. "Martin and Meri can give you a rundown of the day-to-day stuff, but I've got everything here that you need to know about running the house. The cadence of the bills, which we need to transfer into your name, the list of all of the maintenance people and what they do—lots of fat to trim there, if you ask me—the pay schedule for the household help. All of the receipts for the last time things like the fireplace, HVAC systems, and appliances were serviced. Taika left no stone unturned for you. She even updated—"

"I noticed that!" Anni broke in. "The sauna is electric now."

"And the hot-water heater. And the roof. All of the major mechanicals are new. She wanted the place to be in great shape for you. Nothing major for you to handle, except for day-to-day maintenance and bills."

Anni stared down at the desk filled with paperwork and sighed. Tears filled her eyes. "So like her. Taking care of me until the end. Still. It all seems complicated."

"Yes and no. Taika set up a fund, a separate account, for all of the household bills and taxes. You won't have to worry about it. It's autopay. And every ten years, it will replenish automatically from the trust she left for you. So it really is set it and forget it."

"She had been planning this for a while," Anni said, locking eyes with Patrick. "How long had she been ill?"

"Two years," he said, his expression grave.

Anni took this in. It was like a shot in her heart. All that time and never a word.

"What was it?"

He looked at her and bowed his head. "Cancer. Pancreatic. She was adamant that no one was to know."

"Theo and I would've come in a minute," Anni said, her eyes filling with tears.

"I know. And she did, too."

Anni sat back and ran a hand through her hair. "Stubborn Finn."

He smiled. "Aren't we all? Independent and strong to the last. Be that as it may, and I know these were her wishes, but I'm sorry. I need to say that to you. I felt terrible about her keeping everyone in the dark. Still do."

"Oh no," Anni said. "Not at all. Please don't feel that way. You were honoring her wishes. And I can't begin to thank you for that."

"I tried to talk her out of it. Several times."

Anni chuckled. "I can imagine how well that went."

"She did tell me you two had made arrangements for you to come for a long visit," Patrick said. "I assumed she was going to confide in you then."

Anni nodded, not able to say any words in response.

Patrick smiled at her then. A warm smile, wrapped in remembrance and sadness. He truly cared. Anni smiled back at him, and in doing so, noticed his eyes—perhaps the deepest blue eyes she had ever seen. Almost indigo. All at once, she didn't know what to say.

"Have you had lunch?" he asked, breaking the silence.

Was he asking her to lunch? "Well . . . no, I haven't eaten lunch," Anni stammered.

"I have some roast chicken left over from yesterday, and I was going to make a salad. Nothing fancy, but would you care to join me? We could eat on the rooftop and continue talking, if you'd like."

Anni glanced at the clock on the wall—it was about noon. She wasn't supposed to meet the chief at the house until one thirty. Why not?

"It sounds perfect."

Patrick buttoned up all Anni's paperwork, and the two of them traipsed into the kitchen. He opened the fridge and pulled out a couple of roasted chicken breasts and a tub of salad greens. On the counter, he found some grape tomatoes, fresh basil, and a red onion.

"How about you slice all of this up, and I'll make the dressing?" he said.

With Pascal curled up under the window, Anni started slicing the tomatoes and onion as Patrick minced some garlic and herbs and slid them into a mason jar with olive oil, balsamic vinegar, a teaspoon of fancy mustard, and a squeeze of honey. He screwed the top onto the jar and shook it.

She had never seen anyone make salad dressing that way. "What a great method," Anni said, smiling at him.

He gave the jar one last shake and set it on the counter. "I've learned a thing or two from the cooking shows that I may or may not be watching constantly when I'm not working."

Patrick assembled the salad ingredients in a bowl, drizzled the dressing over it, and tossed, sprinkling blue cheese crumbles on top when he had finished. He handed the bowl to Anni. "You take this." He reached into the refrigerator and grabbed a bottle of white wine, along with a loaf of crusty bread that had been sitting on the counter. "I'll take this."

He nodded toward the back door. "The stairs are there. I've got plates and things up on the roof."

Anni and Patrick, followed by Pascal, made their way up the staircase toward another door, which, Anni found, led out onto the rooftop.

She was stunned to see a full-on kitchen, with a grill, small fridge, sink, and countertop under an overhang next to the house. A brick oven that Anni imagined was for pizza, bread, and anything else that could be cooked with a hot flame, was built into the wall. There was a hutch where Anni could see plates and glassware, and she noticed it could all be enclosed by a set of what looked to be old barn doors that slid on a heavy wrought-iron bar.

Toward the center of the rooftop, she saw a rectangular table that held candles in glass jars, with six chairs around it. Vibrant flowers sat in pots here and there. Tucked into one corner, there was a chiminea and two Adirondack chairs with ottomans. On the other side of the rooftop was a raised garden containing what Anni thought were lettuces and herbs. She set the salad bowl on the table and walked over to get a better look. She spied squash, pumpkins, and zucchini.

"You are quite the gardener."

He shrugged. "It keeps me off the streets," he said, grinning. But Anni could tell he was pleased by the compliment.

And then, there was the view. The building overlooked the lake, and from this height, Anni could see the sunlight dancing on the water, glistening and glinting far into the distance.

Anni couldn't mask her delight. "This is magnificent. I'd never leave this rooftop."

Patrick looked around and smiled. "I must say, it's not too bad," he said. "My grandparents didn't use this rooftop space, which I always thought was a shame. My first mission when I moved here and took over his practice was to make it usable. It really adds a lot of living space, don't you think?"

"Oh, definitely," Anni said. "It doubles the downstairs footprint, for sure. How did you get started?"

"The table and chairs. I wanted to sit up here and view the lake. Then it sort of snowballed," Patrick said. He had the delightful look of a guilty little boy. "I got a couple of basil plants and noticed how much direct sun this rooftop gets, so I decided to try lettuce, too. I still can't believe you can just grow it at home."

Anni laughed, remembering a trip she had taken to Florida when she was in college. She could not get over the lemon tree in front of the hotel. It was like she had walked into the garden of Eden.

Patrick went on. "Then I got tired of running up and down the stairs making dinner, so I built the kitchen a couple of years ago. The pizza oven is new this year. I haven't used it yet."

He retrieved a corkscrew from the hutch, opened the wine, and poured two glasses, handing one to her. He slid plates out of the cabinet and grabbed silverware.

"Can I help with anything?" Anni said.

"Not a thing," Patrick said. "Got it handled."

They settled into chairs, and he served the salad.

"I'm assuming all of these greens are from the garden here?" Anni asked, taking a bite.

Patrick nodded. "'Tis the season. Rooftop salad."

Anni smiled at him. Being here with Patrick like this, enjoying a casual lunch, felt at once like the most normal thing in the world . . . and extremely odd. She wasn't even sure if she should call him by his first name. What was the purpose of the lunch? Would she be billed for it? Was she a client?

Maybe it would be best to ask.

"Am I your client now?"

This stopped him midbite. "Do you need a lawyer?"

Anni shook her head. "I'm just not sure of the protocol. I mean, you were my grandmother's lawyer and are the executor of her estate. Now it has all come to me. I don't know if that means you're my lawyer, too, or . . . what the situation is, exactly."

"Of course, I'm at your disposal for anything you need," Patrick began. "But if you have someone who handles—"

"No," Anni broke in. "I don't have anything to handle, or anyone to handle it. I mean, now I do, I guess, but I really don't know what 'having a lawyer' might entail."

Patrick smiled and refilled their wineglasses. "I'm not certain if you're asking if I've been on a retainer or anything like that with Taika, but the answer is no."

Anni could feel her face redden. The last thing she wanted was for Patrick to think she thought they were "on the clock" during their lunch, even if she had been wondering exactly that.

"Great," she chirped. "So maybe we can say you'll be on call if I need anything related to Metsan Valo?"

"Perfect. And if you rob a bank, I can defend you, too."

The two of them shared a look then. A grin, but something more, too.

"Good to know if I should ever decide to begin my life of crime. But I think I have all the money I need now, so there's really no point."

Patrick took a bite of his salad. "What will you do? Other than robbing the odd bank here and there, I mean."

Anni sighed. She looked out onto the wide expanse of the great lake and sipped her wine before answering. So many things ran through her mind, each image overlapping the other like a slideshow. She and Theo at Metsan Valo as children. Arden greeting them on the dock when she arrived. Curling up with Mummo in front of the firepit when she was a child, grilling hot dogs over the flames. Martin and Meri, standing quietly in the background, handling everything. Her apartment in Paris. So many memories, spanning a decade.

"I have no idea," she finally admitted.

CHAPTER SEVENTEEN

After they had lingered at the table much too long, the dishwasher was whirring, the countertop had been wiped down, and everything else had been put away. Anni hung the dishrag over the faucet to dry and turned around to find Patrick standing there, leaning against the counter smiling at her. All at once, she didn't know quite what to do with her hands.

"Lunch was lovely," she said, pushing the hair back from her face.

"So was the company. Thanks for all of the help cleaning up."

They stood there for a moment, like awkward teenagers, smiling shyly at each other.

Patrick cleared his throat. "What's on your agenda for the rest of the day?" he said finally.

That snapped Anni back into reality. She had all but forgotten her other errand in Wharton.

"I guess I hadn't mentioned this to you, but my mother's house on Front Street got broken into. We discovered it yesterday."

Patrick's eyes grew wide. "Is everything okay? Nobody was hurt?"

His concern warmed Anni. "No, we're all fine," she said. "The house was empty when it happened. Arden was with us at Metsan Valo."

Patrick ran a hand through his hair and shook his head. "I don't think there's been a break-in like that in Wharton for close to a millennium. I haven't heard anything about it, and you know the Wharton gossip mill."

Anni did know. "I thought the news would be all over town by now. LuAnn and Gary saw the squad cars and wandered over."

"It might well be, now that I think about it," he said. "I haven't been anywhere since I got home from Metsan Valo last night." He touched her shoulder. "What happened, if you don't mind my asking?"

Anni told him about how she, Theo, and Arden stopped by the house on their way back to the island the day before and found the door standing wide open. Anni could still feel the emptiness, the violation in the pit of her stomach that came with the thought of someone rummaging through her childhood home. But with everything that had occurred since then, it seemed strange that it had happened only the day before. Only hours. It seemed like a lifetime ago.

"Was anything taken?"

"That's what I'm about to find out," she said, glancing at the clock above the stove. It was nearly one thirty. "I'm heading over there right now, actually. Nick Stone asked me to look around and see if I can figure out what's missing."

"Wouldn't it be quicker to have Arden do it? I mean, she'd be the one to know if anything was gone."

Anni smiled at this. "You don't know my mom very well. She's rather . . . I'm just going to call it *scattered*. I'm really not sure if she has any idea what's been accumulating in her office. I want to clean the place up, mainly for Mom. She shouldn't have to come back to all of that."

"Would you like some company? After all, you helped me clean up after lunch. It's the least I can do."

It sounded like a very good idea to Anni. She didn't relish going into the house alone, or at all, but it had to be done.

"Do you have time?" she asked.

He nodded. "Of course," he said. "Nothing but. Such is the life of a small-town lawyer."

Anni plucked her phone from her purse and called the chief, letting him know she had arrived in Wharton and was ready to go through the house.

"Do you want me to meet you there?" Nick asked.

"Sure," she said, "but Patrick Saari is coming with me."

Nick chuckled. "You need a lawyer to go through your mother's house?" he teased her.

"You never know," she said, grinning at Patrick. But then her smile faded. "Nick, does everyone in town know about the break-in by now?"

"I'd go ahead and assume yes," he said. "LuAnn, Gary, and Beth were there. That's as good as alerting the media in this town. If you sneeze in Wharton, someone shows up with chicken soup five seconds later."

"One of the loveliest things about Wharton," Anni said. "People take care of each other. But in this case—"

"I think the rumor mill is a positive in this case, too," he said. "If anyone in this town saw anything, I can guarantee we'll find out about it."

That made sense to Anni. A town full of eyes and ears. Speaking of which, something else occurred to her.

"I got a last name for Charles," Anni said. "Wellington."

Nick chuckled. "The guy sounds like an English lord."

"Let's hope he is," Anni said. "For Gloria's sake."

"I'll get somebody on it," Nick said. "And since you won't be alone, I'll finish up some things here and swing over to Front Street in a bit."

"Sounds good," Anni said, ringing off and dropping her phone back into her purse. After Patrick locked up, they set off down the block, Pascal trotting a few steps ahead, as if he knew where they were going. The house on Front Street was just a short walk away, and as they rounded the corner, they saw Gary, the grizzled cook from LuAnn's inn, sitting on the front porch in one of the Adirondack chairs, taking a swig of beer. When he caught sight of them, he scrambled to his feet and waved.

"Hi, kids!"

Pascal took off in a run and greeted him by doing a few quick circles on the porch as Anni and Patrick made their way down the block.

"Hey," Anni said, slowly, furrowing her brow. "Fancy meeting you here."

Gary cleared his throat. "We're all taking a turn," he said.

"Taking a—"

Gary gave her a quick nod, his lips a straight line. "You bet we are. We're making our presence known. Making it look like someone is here all the time. In case whoever it was thinks about coming back."

Anni wanted to hug the old man. Her face must've said it all, because he enveloped her in his arms. "Arden isn't here in town all the time, as you well know, but she's one of our own," he said, his voice gravelly in her ear. "So are you and your brother. You don't mess with Wharton's own."

In that embrace, she could feel the town's protection around her, as though it were a tangible thing.

"I don't know how to thank you," she said.

Gary pulled back and looked at her, amusement lighting up the lines on his face. "Thanks are not necessary."

Patrick put a hand on the porch rail. "Gary, I'm assuming everyone knows about this by now. Did anyone see anything?"

"No, damn it all," Gary said. "Not a thing. But we're all on alert now."

"Thank you again for standing guard," Anni said. "I know my mom will appreciate it, too."

"Now that you're here, I'll head back to LuAnn's," he said. "Gotta start the dinner prep. I've got a pork shoulder in the slow cooker for burritos."

Although he didn't quite look the part, Gary was one of the best chefs in Wharton. As he lumbered back up the road to the inn, he turned around midway and waved.

"Don't you worry, Anni," he called. "It'll all be okay."

She hoped it would. She fished the house key out of her purse and turned the lock. As she pushed the door open, Anni felt that same emptiness wafting through the rooms as she had felt the previous day. There was no life in this house. No living energy. None of Arden's spirit or joie de vivre. It was cold and gray, as though a cloud had descended over it all. Anni didn't even want to step inside.

"Shall we?" Patrick said, apparently not feeling what Anni had sensed. She took a step through the doorway, Patrick behind her. But Pascal stood at the threshold, growling.

Anni and Patrick shared a glance, her eyes questioning, his worried. He put a hand up and shook his head at her, as if to say, *stay where you are.*

He snapped his fingers at Pascal, jutting his chin up and making a clicking sound with his tongue. The dog knew exactly what that signal meant and roared into the room barking, a loud, angry, threatening bark. Anni watched as he raced from room to room, snarling and barking. He stormed up the stairs, and Anni could hear him barking there, too. A hard and fierce bark. A bark meant to intimidate.

"Should we follow him?" Anni whispered, taking a few tentative steps into the room.

Patrick shook his head. "He wouldn't be barking like that if all was clear." He put a hand on Anni's back and led her out of the house and onto the porch, and then down the steps to the sidewalk. He slipped his phone out of his pocket and dialed.

"Hey, Nick, it's Patrick Saari. We're at Arden's house. I sent Pascal in before us, and he is going nuts."

It would be only a moment before Nick arrived, but to Anni, it was one of those out-of-time experiences that seemed to last a lifetime.

Pascal's relentless barking pierced the air, echoing down the block. Doors opened, and neighbors ventured out to see what all the commotion was about. Curious faces looked through windows.

"What do you think he's barking at?" Anni said, her voice harsh and tattered.

"I don't know," Patrick said, his eyes trained on the house. "But we're not going in there without Nick."

Moments later, the squad car arrived, and Nick, along with another officer, Bill, the same one from the day before, jumped out. Anni noticed they were armed, a rarity in Wharton.

They could hear Pascal snarling as though he had something—or someone—cornered.

"You two stay out here," Nick said as they blew past Patrick and Anni into the house, guns drawn.

"Pascal!" Patrick called, and in a moment, the dog ran down the stairs to his side. Pascal was panting furiously, and the fur on his back was standing up straight. He was still trained on the staircase, growling low in his throat.

A few moments passed, and finally Anni saw Nick descending the stairs. "I need you to have a look at this," he said to her.

Her hand flew to her neck. "What is it?" she asked, her voice thin.

"I'm not sure," Nick said. "It might be nothing."

"Pascal didn't think it was nothing," Patrick said under his breath. He gave Anni's shoulder a squeeze, and they entered the house, Pascal at their heels. His steady, low growls accompanied them up the stairs.

Bill was standing in the hallway outside Arden's bedroom door. Anni rushed past him but was stopped short by what she saw.

It was a set of clothes, laid out on Arden's bed. A long linen dress and a string of pearls positioned as though Arden herself, wearing the outfit, were lying there, in repose. Except there was no body. Pascal stood poised next to Anni, growling low in his throat.

A thread of chill wrapped itself around Anni.

"What is this?" she said, turning to Nick, her voice a whisper, knowing he wouldn't have an answer for her.

"I don't know," he said. "It wasn't here yesterday."

"But the house was locked," Anni said. "Wasn't it? The whole house was locked up tight."

Nick nodded. "Yes, it was."

"And Gary was outside. For how long, we don't know."

The four of them stood there for a moment in silence, all seeming to be coming to grips with what they were seeing.

"You know I'm going to have to ask you to leave the premises," Nick said. "We need to do another sweep for fingerprints."

Anni took a deep breath in. "I'm going to say no," she said.

Nick furrowed his brow at her.

"You didn't get anything the last time you dusted for prints," Anni said. "You're not going to get anything now. It's the same person. Obviously."

Nick led Anni down the stairs, with Pascal and Patrick following behind.

"You won't like what I'm thinking," Nick said to Anni as they walked outside onto the front porch.

She just looked at him in response, not able to utter a word.

"Anni, it's pretty clear that whoever did this had to have a key to the house," Nick said.

CHAPTER EIGHTEEN

For much of the day, Anni had been trying to get ahold of her mother, annoyed when she couldn't reach her. Now, the last thing she wanted to do was talk to Arden and tell her about this latest development.

Nick continued. "The house was locked, and there's no sign of forced entry. I hate to say it, Anni, but this feels very personal."

Anni winced at what he was implying. It was someone in the family, then. "Only a few of us have a key," she said. "Me, Theo . . ." She squinted into the distance. "I'm not sure who else. The caretakers at Metsan Valo, Martin and Meri, probably have one."

"What about Gloria?" Patrick said, leaning on the porch rail.

Anni didn't know quite how to answer that. Based on what Arden had told her and Theo the day before, about Gloria slowly assuming Arden's personality, it seemed unlikely she would've given her sister a key to her house.

"It's possible," she said, chewing her lip. She wasn't sure whether to bring up that conversation or not. Telling strangers their private family business seemed like a betrayal, especially since it would bring Gloria's . . . eccentricities . . . into the light of day. Nobody had to know about that.

But, to Anni, what she had learned the day before, coupled with Gloria's strange morph into Jackie O inspired by her brand-new husband, in addition to her basically being written out of Mummo's will . . . It all was congealing into a miasma of doubt and suspicion in Anni's mind.

She had no idea what, or how, she was going to tell Arden about this. She needed to talk to Theo.

"Will you guys excuse me for a minute?" she said, retrieving her phone from her purse and taking a few steps down the sidewalk away from the house. She dialed her brother, but his phone went right to voice mail, too. *What's with this family today?* Anni thought.

"Call me," she said, her voice low. "I'm at Front Street, and I need to talk to you. It's important."

She looked up at the two men standing on her mother's porch and shrugged. "I tried to call Theo to get any insight he might have," she said. "But no luck."

Her stomach tightened as she dialed Arden's number, but somehow she knew her mother wouldn't answer. Arden always unplugged at Metsan Valo.

She dropped her phone back into her purse and joined the others on the porch. "Now what? Should I still go through Mom's office?"

Nick nodded. "Yeah. If you can figure out what's missing, we'll be closer to uncovering who's behind this."

"Okay," Anni said.

"Let's do this," Patrick piped up. "I'm happy to help with whatever I can. We can clean up for your mom, if nothing else."

Anni smiled at him, a warmth rising in her chest. *This* was a nice guy. What a concept. She had grown so accustomed to Jean-Paul's narcissism—always needing to be listened to with bated breath, always needing to dominate the room with his stories, always needing to be right—that she had forgotten a man could be simply nice, good hearted, and kind without wanting the attention and adoration that Jean so completely needed and craved.

When she thought about it, of course their union had been destined to fail. When she became his partner instead of his adoring student, when she began to challenge him on points he'd make or put forth thoughts she'd have about the day's news, politics, or the world . . . It was almost as if, when she became fully herself, his attraction to her had worn off. His love for her had withered. Looking back, she could see it drain away, little by little, until it was gone, replaced by annoyance and even a touch of disdain. No wonder he had sought the adoration of a student's eyes and heart again. Ever the Pygmalion. The molding of a young woman's mind and heart was what made him happy, gave him the sustenance he needed. What Anni needed was so much more than that.

It made her feel, for the first time, a bit sad for him. To never know the peace of being with a true partner in life. When this thought hit her, it was as though her grief for their decade together melted away. He was her past and always would be. But there was a future on the horizon, too.

"I need to head back to the station, but I'm going to tell Bill to stick around," Nick said, rousting Anni from her remembrances. "He'll check the house to make sure nobody is here, and then settle out here on the porch. I don't want you being surprised if whoever did this comes back."

Anni shrugged. "It has to be a family member, though, right? I mean, we're not talking about a stranger breaking in anymore or kids vandalizing the house?"

"Families can get pretty ugly at times," Nick said. "Especially when there's money involved. Have you thought about installing a smart cam?"

"I don't think Arden has internet here, but we can check it out," Anni said. "It would be nice to get a shot of whoever is doing this."

She and the chief locked eyes for what seemed to her like forever.

"I don't like to say this to you, either, but I need to," he said. "To me, they're trying to scare or intimidate Arden. And you and your brother. The trashing of the office was one thing. But this macabre scene they staged on the bed—that's something else again. That was done to frighten you."

Anni put a hand on the chief's shoulder. "Don't go just yet," she said, turning to find her purse. She retrieved the bag containing the mug Charles had been using that morning. She held it out to Nick.

"I'm not sure if this is going to be useful to you or not," she said. "But you might be able to get Charles's prints off this mug. He was using it this morning."

Nick took the bag and gave Anni a grin.

"You're going all CSI on me."

Anni shrugged. "I'm not saying it was Charles, but someone is messing with my family. You don't get away with that."

~❧~

As Anni and Patrick sifted through the papers and books strewn everywhere in her mother's office, Pascal sat sentinel by the door, his back to the room, his gaze trained on the rest of the house. Every so often, Anni heard a low growl.

"That's a really good dog you have there," she said to Patrick as she hunted around for the pages in a ream of her mother's poetry, a manuscript Arden had been working on for as long as Anni could remember.

She found a sheet, handwritten, rather hastily, it seemed, by her mother.

Twins?
How could it be, two little hearts beating inside of me?

Born of mystery and of love, emerging from the ethers

My children, evermore

My children of the night, the wind, the forest, and the water

My children

Anni held the sheet with shaking hands. A surge of anger was taking hold. It bubbled up inside her and spilled out before she could contain it.

"How dare they?" she spat, not really to Patrick, but to the world at large. Tears were pricking at her eyes. "These are my mother's things. My mother's words. How could someone come in here and do this?"

Pascal circled Anni and curled up by her side, resting his great head on her leg. He sighed.

"It's a violation," Patrick said. "Not to point out the obvious. But we haven't found anything missing. You would've said so, right? It seems like they came in here only to trash the place."

"That's exactly what it seems like," Anni said, her voice harsh. "I mean—what, were they looking for a first edition of Dickens in here? My mom's got nothing like that."

"Considering the events of yesterday, they could've been looking for her will," Patrick said.

This stopped Anni. "I think she's leaving everything to Theo and me. In fact, I'm sure of it. So would taking the will somehow negate that?"

Patrick shook his head. "I've got a copy of it. She filed it with me when she got back to Wharton a couple of weeks ago. That's how we met."

"Whoever broke in here might not know about that, though," Anni said, not liking where this conversation, and this whole incident, was leading. Right down a path to her own bloodline.

Anni shook those thoughts out of her head and began gathering the rest of the sheets of Arden's poetry into a neat pile. "I need to find something to keep all of this paper in. Like a folio or a box or something."

She started opening drawers in search of a box for Arden's papers, while Patrick placed books back onto the built-in shelves that lined the room. Anni felt a smile bubble up inside her, despite her frustration and anger, as she remembered how excited Arden had been to install those floor-to-ceiling bookshelves in what had been the guest bedroom.

And then it hit her, a revelation that showered over her like rain. Why hadn't she thought about it earlier?

"Patrick, stop," she said. "Don't put any more books on the shelves."

A memory had come flooding back of Arden, more than twenty years earlier, standing by an empty shelf in the bedroom she had just renovated into her office. She was wearing a long linen dress (nothing so odd about that) and looking as though she was keeping a delicious secret.

"You won't believe what I've done," Arden had said to Anni, all Cheshire cat. She slid her hand onto one of the shelves and pushed something, her eyebrows raised. "*Et* voilà!" she cried, as the entire shelf opened up, revealing a staircase.

And then Anni remembered. There had been a door to the basement in this room before her mother converted it into the office. She had simply made that door into a bookshelf.

Anni had followed her mother down the stairs, which were lit by electric sconces that looked like candles on the walls of an ancient castle. She remembered being afraid of going into the basement as a child because it was so cold and dank, but Arden had renovated it into a reader's lair. The walls were lined with bookshelves. An old, wooden desk sat in the middle of the room, a comfy leather armchair and an oversize ottoman tucked in a corner next to an antique lamp. What looked to be an ancient Oriental rug covered the floor. Candles were everywhere.

Anni had stared at her mother, openmouthed. Arden had laughed.

"This used to be an old root cellar," Anni had said, grinning. "I hated coming down here when I was little. You made it into a gorgeous den."

"It really wasn't so hard," Arden had said. "What do you think?"

Anni had looked around, delighted. "I love it. Mom, you never fail to amaze me. I can't wait to tell Theo!"

The memory dissipated as Anni stood in her mother's disheveled office and ran her hand over the shelves. Where was the switch? Anni couldn't remember. But in a moment, she had found it.

"Get a load of this," she said to Patrick, grinning. She pressed the button, and the shelf swung open.

Anni's grin faded as Pascal began to growl.

CHAPTER NINETEEN

The fur on Pascal's back stood straight up. The dog's gaze was fixed on the staircase, every nerve poised to strike.

"Go," Patrick said, low and under his breath. The dog took off down the stairs, barking and snarling.

"Should we get Bill in here?" Patrick asked.

"No," Anni said, following the dog. "Not a soul alive knows about this basement room outside of my family. If somebody is down there, it's one of my own, and I want to be the one to confront them."

She stomped down the stairs, that same sense of rage bubbling up in her chest. How dare they? Whoever it was. How dare they terrorize her sweet, kooky, New Agey mother?

When she reached the basement room, she gasped, and all her bravado faded into the air. Even in the darkness, she could see something wasn't right. Anni flipped on the light. Books on these shelves were strewn about, just as they had been in the office. The chair was overturned, its cushions cut open with a ghastly slash. Even the rug had been pulled back. The back door was ajar, an eerie, slim shaft of light from the back stairway streaming into the room.

Pascal was standing in the doorway, tail down, growling a low growl.

Patrick put a hand on Anni's shoulder. "We're going back up now," he said, with an eye toward the secret door. He clicked his tongue and snapped his fingers for Pascal, who reluctantly tore himself away from the doorway and hurried to Patrick's side.

Anni wanted to object, wanted to go through that door to follow whoever it was and demand to know why they had come into her mother's house and threatened her family. But something about the way the dog was growling, so protective and on point, made her reconsider that notion. Pascal did not want her to go through that door.

She did the next best thing. She hurried up the steps to her mother's office and burst out the front door, surprising Bill, who was sitting on the porch.

"What's happened?" he said, jumping to his feet.

Anni didn't bother to answer. She raced around the side of the house to the back door, where the steps from the secret room led. Anni looked around wildly. Nothing. Nobody.

Bill, Patrick, and Pascal had been following close behind. Anni stood there, looking at the open door.

"Don't touch it," Bill said. "That was *not* open before you two went inside. I did a full sweep of the house, inside and out."

As he put his phone to his ear and called the chief, Patrick turned to Anni.

"That means whoever did this was in the house with us."

Anni wasn't sure what to do then. She looked around, from Patrick to the door to Bill, a few paces away. Pascal circled between them.

"I need to get back home," she said, pushing her hair back from her face. "To Metsan Valo." She hurried inside to retrieve her purse and rejoined Patrick and Bill out on the porch.

"Please call me, or have the chief call, with any news," she said to the officer.

As they walked to Patrick's house, Anni's thoughts swirled. She wanted to hurry back to the island to talk to Theo and Arden. And yet, she was coming to grips with the reality that someone in her family had been here, trashing this house for a second time. It made her want to stay on the mainland to find whoever it was. They couldn't have caught the ferry this quickly.

Why would they do this? What were they looking for?

"It isn't about valuables," Anni said, voicing her answer to the question in her mind. "I know that's what everyone is thinking about after the reading of the will, but I'm sure it's not about that."

"Why?" Patrick said. "It makes sense. Even I could feel people were rather . . . *put out* isn't exactly the right term. But nobody was happy after the reading of the will. Especially you."

"That's true," Anni said, wincing as she remembered the tangible cloud of anger that settled over the house.

"It's not so unreasonable, somebody wanting to get what they think is theirs."

No, Anni thought. That wasn't right. It couldn't be. "My mom doesn't have anything of value," she said, looking back over her shoulder at the house. "She's not into accumulating things, especially expensive things. She'd love a painting by a street artist she happened upon one afternoon in Paris or New Orleans, but would never buy anything expensive like a Van Gogh."

Patrick nodded, smiling. "Yeah, that sounds like Arden."

"Even her jewelry. There's nothing precious, nothing expensive."

"And then there's the laying out of her clothes," Patrick said. "That's just weird."

Gloria popped into Anni's mind then, her transformations. She didn't like this. Not one bit.

"I'm even more convinced of it now. It's the scare factor they're after."

On the street in front of Patrick's house, Anni fished her keys out of her purse and leaned against her car. "I'm sorry to run off like this," she said. "But I really need to get back."

"Do you want me to go with you?" Patrick asked. "Like you said, whoever did this is one of your own. Confronting them alone might be risky."

All at once, Anni realized she would very much like Patrick to come along with her. But this was family business. Very ugly family business.

"I won't be alone," she said. "Theo is there. So is my mother. Meri and Martin, too."

Anni noticed she omitted Gloria's family from that list. She hadn't done it on purpose, but when she thought about it, her aunt and cousin weren't her safe haven and never had been. The fact was, someone among them had done this. And it certainly wasn't Theo or Arden. That left Gloria and her brood.

"Okay, then," Patrick said, reaching up and pushing a stray tendril of hair out of Anni's eyes. The gesture was so intimate, it made her blush. But she didn't pull away.

"What are you planning to do?" he continued. "Confront them?"

"I will," she said. "This is ridiculous. Why anyone would do this to my mother's house—to my mother—it's insane. I'm really angry about it." She let out a small laugh. "Theo always says I don't suffer fools gladly, and I'm going to force whoever it was to confess."

"So a full Agatha Christie situation then," he said.

Anni could imagine it, her acting as Poirot in a roomful of suspects, laying a careful, intricate trap for the guilty party to fall into. But somehow, she knew it wouldn't go as smoothly for her as it always did for the master sleuth.

"I guess so," she said, wincing a little. "I don't know what this person wants, but they're not getting it. This is going to stop today."

Patrick smiled at her. "I don't envy them. Are you going to press charges?"

Anni hadn't thought about it. The notion of taking any sort of legal action against family was abhorrent to her. But so was trashing a family member's house. Terrorizing her mother. "Maybe," she said. "We'll see how it goes."

She arrived at the ferry dock just in time to drive on before they closed up and shoved off. She climbed out of her car and made her way up to the deck, where she glanced around, hoping she wouldn't see Yale or Vicky. She stood at the rail and watched the hills of Wharton fade from view. She had always loved that sight, and on this day, it did what it always did—made her blood pressure drop a few points, calming her heart, her anxiety, and her anger. The temperature dropped as it always did when the ferry chugged away from the dock and into open water, and Anni wished she had brought a sweater to wrap around her to stave off the chill.

An eagle soared across the bow. Anni watched as it dove down toward the water, stretched out its talons, struck, and, with a great flap of its wings, flew away with a fish. She would need some of that eagle's power when she arrived back at Metsan Valo.

"Thank you, my friend of the skies," she said aloud.

When the ferry docked on the island, Anni drove carefully off and turned onto Colette's main street. An eerie emptiness swirled around the shops and restaurants. It was the late summer, early fall exodus that happened every year, when tourists and summer residents went back to their everyday lives, their children back in school, summer vacations over. This was the time of year when the island settled into itself again, the slow turning of the trees and the yellowing and browning of the countryside setting the backdrop of life for the year-round residents. It was the prelude to winter, with its harshness and isolation. It was as though the residents and the island itself were taking one last gasp.

As Anni drove past the coffee shop, she spotted Theo sitting at a table outside reading a book, a mug of coffee in front of him. She pulled up alongside the row of tables where he was sitting and stopped.

"Hey," she said as she slid out of the car. "Fancy meeting you here."

Theo looked up from his book and gasped, his eyes wide.

"Did I startle you?" Anni said as she pulled out the chair across from him and sank down into it.

"Yes, you did," he said. "Where have you been?"

"Where have I been? Where have you been? I tried to call you a thousand times today."

He narrowed his eyes at her. "You tried once. I have the message on my phone."

"Once, a thousand, whatever," she said, waving her hand. "The point is, I wanted to talk to you."

"Sorry," he said. "I was under radio silence. I had a lot of thinking to do."

Anni knew exactly what he was thinking about. She reached out and gave his forearm a squeeze.

"I was thinking about Jean-Paul today, too," she said. "Coming to terms with it all."

Theo simply nodded, frowning. He didn't have to say anything. Anni knew her brother was struggling to make a decision about his marriage.

He took a sip of his coffee. "So why did you try to call me a thousand times? Or, more accurately, once?"

"Mom's house was broken into again."

Theo set his book onto the table with a thud. "You're kidding me."

"No," Anni said, leaning in. "You're not going to believe what happened."

She told him about the second break-in, and how Arden's clothes were arranged on the bed just so. And how Pascal was so on point and growling the whole time. And the books strewn about in the basement.

"The basement reading room," Theo repeated, smiling. "Mom did such a good job renovating that. I haven't thought about it in years."

"Neither had I," Anni said. "Remember the back stairway leading to the back door?"

"Yes," Theo said. "I made use of it a time or two when I came home on spring breaks."

"That door was open."

Theo's mouth dropped open. "Nobody knows about that room being anything but a skanky root cellar but us. I'm guessing it wasn't you."

"And I'm guessing it wasn't you."

They held each other's gazes for a long moment, both running through the list of possible suspects in their minds. Anni's stomach tied up in knots. Was she going to have to confront Gloria and her family? It was looking more and more like it.

"The clothes on the bed is a really sick gesture," Theo said. "It gives me the chills."

Anni took a deep breath and let it out again in a long sigh. "I want to get back to Metsan," she said. "I'm calling a family meeting."

CHAPTER TWENTY

As Anni drove down the long driveway toward Metsan Valo, Theo's car following behind, the knots in her stomach tightened. The idea of confronting her family about the break-in was eating at her core, but she knew it had to be done.

As she rounded the corner and the house came into view, it took a moment for her to comprehend what she was seeing. Mummo's cabin cruiser was sitting in the driveway, hooked to Yale's SUV. Yale was beside it, making sure the connections to his trailer hitch were sound.

Anni and Theo parked and got out of their cars at the same time, giving each other a look.

"What's going on, Yale?" Theo asked, baring his teeth in a smile and walking slowly toward the boat. "Taking her in for repairs?" He propped one foot on the trailer hitch.

Yale shrugged at him. "Yeah, something like that."

"What exactly do you think you're doing?" Anni said to Yale. "Why is the *Kalevala* hooked up to your car?"

"Vicky wants it," Yale said.

Theo let out a strained laugh. "Is that so?"

"It's so," Yale said. "She is packing up, and we're leaving. With this. Taika said we could have whatever we wanted. And we want this."

Anni stood there for a moment, not quite believing what she was seeing or hearing.

"No, actually, she did not," Anni said, her voice even, her steely gaze trained on Yale. "She said that if anyone wanted any special item, we could probably work it out."

Yale smiled. "This boat is special to us."

"Oh, really?" Anni said, narrowing her eyes. "When's the last time you were out on it?"

"Last summer," Yale said, jutting out his chin. "My family has spent many happy times on it. It means the world to us."

"You and Vicky weren't here last summer," Anni said, taking a step forward.

"How would you know that?"

Anni shook her head as Theo groaned. "There's a newfangled thing called a telephone. I talked to Mummo every week."

Yale's face was reddening.

"The fact of the matter is, Yale, everything here is mine, whether you like it or not," Anni said, her voice even. "What in the world are you thinking? What's wrong with you?"

"Yeah, whatever," Yale said, mumbling something under his breath that Anni knew was an insult.

That was when Anni noticed Vicky standing in the front doorway. How much had she heard? "Come on, honey," Vicky said, pulling his arm. "She's right. You can't be mad at her. This is what Mummo wanted. And we're not taking the boat."

Yale wrenched his arm away from hers.

"We're going for pizza at Jimmy's," Yale said to Vicky. "I'll get Lichen and meet you back out here in five minutes."

He stormed into the house, slamming the door behind him so hard, Anni was afraid it might shatter.

Vicky stood there for a moment, her face a sea of shame and anger and confusion. Anni reached out and opened her arms to her cousin.

Vicky melted into them. She let out a strained sob. "He is such a good man. And you never get to see that. I don't know what has gotten into him."

"Do you want the boat, Vic?" Anni said, pulling back and looking her cousin in the eye.

Vicky shook her head. "What would we do with it? Yale is just being stupid."

Anni sighed. "I hate to add to the tension, but you can't go to Jimmy's right now," she said. "Something has happened in Wharton, and we need to have a family meeting."

Vicky furrowed her brow. "A family meeting? What is it?"

"It's serious," Anni said. "We have to do it now."

Just then, Yale opened the front door and strode outside, Lichen behind him. He began tugging at the trailer hitch to unhook the boat from his vehicle.

"Yale, we're not going just yet," Vicky said, her voice tentative. "We can't."

Her husband didn't even look up at her. "Yes, we can. Get in the car."

Vicky recoiled, as if stung by his words. Anni glanced over at Theo, who was walking toward Yale.

"I'm sorry to break up this delightful moment, but we're having a family meeting right now. Everyone needs to be in attendance," Theo said. "That means you, Yale."

Yale shook his head.

"Come on in the house, honey." It was Vicky, her faced flushed with anger. "You are still part of this family."

Yale sighed a great sigh, but followed Vicky into the house.

Theo put an arm around Anni's shoulders. Only then did she realize she was shaking. "Could he be any more of a jerk?" Theo said.

"At least it's good to know some things never change," Anni said, taking a deep breath in. "Are you ready to go inside and do this?"

"Let's do it," he said, and together they walked into the house.

Night fell early as the air grew crisper this time of year, and the first hint of dusk was filtering into the sky as Theo and Anni made their way into the living room, where they found Vicky perched on the couch and Yale standing by the window, looking out into the twilight. Lichen was engrossed in her phone on the couch, as usual.

Gloria and Charles glided down the stairs, both dressed in northern chic casual wear—a designer version of Northwoods attire—new jeans and flannel shirts with fancy logos on them.

"What's this about a family meeting?" Gloria asked as Martin and Meri came in through the side door.

Theo cleared his throat. "It's just that something more has happened at the house in town, and we wanted to talk it over with everyone, now that we're all together."

He looked around the room. "Wait. Where's Mom?"

CHAPTER TWENTY-ONE

A sense of dread settled like a brick in Anni's stomach.

Gloria and Charles exchanged a glance. "We've been out for much of the day," she said. "I haven't seen her."

"Vic, have you?" Anni asked.

Vicky shook her head. "Not since last night."

"So she hasn't been around the house at all today?" Anni shot a glance toward Theo, a simmering panic rising quickly in her throat. "Nobody has seen her?"

Theo turned to Martin and Meri. "Surely, you two—"

But Martin's grave expression stopped his words in midair.

"We assumed she had gone to the mainland with you," Meri said. Her voice was as thin as a reed. "The last we saw her was when she went for her morning walk."

Something was not right. Arden loved her time in the forest, but she'd flit back to the house throughout the day for lunch or to get a bag to store the wild herbs she had gathered or to retrieve her journal so she could write poetry or take some of her crystals out to meet the trees or any number of Ardenesque reasons. She had never stayed away for an entire day.

An understanding passed in an instant between Anni and Theo.

Theo hurried up the stairs, taking two at a time. Anni could hear him opening the door to the master bedroom. "Mom?" His voice was high and thin, as though he was calling to her from his childhood. Anni heard him opening and closing all the doors in the hallway, still calling her name. A moment later, he appeared at the railing, his face ashen. "She isn't here."

Anni took off down the back hallway, looking in every room, hoping against hope she'd find Arden in the study at the end of the hall. It was empty. More than that. Cold. A heaviness descended out of that coldness and buried her, as swift and terrible as an avalanche.

She turned and walked back out into the living room, every agonizing step seeming to take an hour as she carried that cold heaviness with her. She looked at the concerned faces of her family and shook her head.

Everyone's gaze fell on Martin and Meri then. Meri grasped her husband's hand and squeezed it, her face as white as the snow that was blanketing Anni.

"It's the vaki," Meri whispered.

"What do you mean, the vaki?" Anni said, louder than she had intended. All this fairy-tale business was getting old. They had a real-life crisis here. Not some enchanted mischief.

Meri took a deep breath. "Look for her in the forest," she said.

Something tangible to work with, at least.

"Meri's right. Mom could be hurt out there," Anni said. "Not able to get back to the house."

A silence filled up the room for a terrible moment. And just like that, they sprang into action. Meri grabbed flashlights and jackets from the mudroom and handed them out to everyone. Martin hurried outside and lit a fire in the firepit.

Soon, the family was gathered on the deck, suited up, flashlights in hand, gazing out into the twilight, not knowing exactly what to do. Darkness was falling, and here, when it fell, it took everything else with it.

"Okay," Theo said, taking charge. "Gloria, your troop has the waterfront. You go down there and look around. Walk all of the shoreline in both directions. Yale and Vicky, you go one way. Gloria, you and Charles go the other."

"Make sure to look in the sauna," Anni added. "The door stuck last night, and Martin had to get us out of there."

This was greeted with a quizzical look from Gloria, but Anni didn't want to take the time to explain it to her at that moment.

"Anni and I will head out into the woods," Theo continued, and then squinted off into the distance for a moment. "Martin, you come with us. There are three trails through the forest, so it makes sense to have three of us searching there. Meri and Lichen, you stay here so that someone is at the house if she comes back."

Lichen looked up and nodded, putting her phone away.

Martin turned to his wife. "If she does come back, build the fire bigger and brighter to let us know."

As Gloria, Charles, Vicky, and Yale headed down to the lakeshore, Anni, Theo, and Martin forged off toward the woods. All ten acres of them. Anni knew they couldn't possibly cover them all on foot. The trails would have to do. She prayed her mother hadn't strayed too far off the paths. She knew how easy it was to get disoriented in these woods, even if one had grown up playing in them.

The entrances to three well-used trails lay at the edge of where the lawn melted into the forest. Each was a three-mile loop that wound through different parts of the forest, up hills and cliffs, down to the bubbling creek, across flat, grassy expanses. This was not a walk in the park, as Mummo liked to say. People came from all over the country, sometimes the world, to trek on trails like these in the state parks of Colette and the mainland. Anni's family had their own.

They had been cut out of the forest generations ago by their great-grandfather, and maintained ever since, mostly by Martin himself. In the early days, markers showed the way. But now, those markers had fallen away, because of time, weather, and vaki mischief, as Mummo would say. But even without those guideposts, the trails had been so well used, by both humans and animals, they were more apparent. It was easier to find your way and not take wrong turns into unfamiliar territory.

"Martin, you take the Upper trail. I'll take the Pine trail. Anni, you take the Creekbed trail," Theo said, setting off at a trot toward the trailhead. He stopped for a moment and looked back at Anni. He put his hand to his heart, and the look he gave her, an expression of hope wrapped in fear as though he were a frightened little boy, broke her heart into a million tiny pieces. She nodded, managing a smile, although every cell in her body was screaming, before turning toward her corner of the woods.

Anni had spent a lifetime playing in this forest and knew much of it as well as she knew her own name, or the plot of her favorite children's books, or the layout of her room at Metsan Valo. She had followed all the trails through these woods since she was a child. But it was still more than possible, in fact, easy, to get turned around and disoriented if you strayed from the trails, as she had found out in heart-thumping detail a few nights prior.

She felt none of that disorientation now. She knew the Creekbed trail best of all. It snaked through the forest to where the creek bubbled through the pines on its way to the lake. It was a magical place, as magical as Anni had ever seen. The trail was filled with little outcroppings and cozy nooks, large boulders that sat on the edge of the creek—perfect for reading—and massive trees that seemed as old as the world itself. They had big, low-lying branches that stretched out over the creek, and Anni used to lie on one of the great tree limbs and watch the creek flow by below.

Here in the forest, Anni would always have encounters with animals. A turtle sunning on a partially submerged log. A deer that quietly crept to the creek for a drink. Squirrels that chased each other through the leaves. Sometimes, she saw wolves and bears, who never meant any harm.

Anni had spent countless hours exploring every inch of this trail, reading by the bubbling creek, making little houses for the vaki the way people in the city put tiny doors and other ornaments at the bases of massive trees, creating a make-believe community for fairies. It was undoubtedly why Theo had suggested she search it. She had always felt like Snow White in this corner of the forest, with all the animals friendly and ready to help. Even the air here seemed charged with magic. But this wasn't Disney's version of the old tale, not today. More decidedly Grimm's.

This had been her favorite place in the world when she was a child, a place she had all but forgotten as she grew older. And now she was looking for her mother here, terrified of what she might find.

As she hurried along the path, twilight began to fade into night. She heard the singing of the frogs and the chirping of crickets, adding their music to the darkness. It brought to mind thoughts of the otherworldly scene she had witnessed taking place in this very forest the night before. Spirits, keening, wailing, floating in a procession.

As the thought wrapped itself around her, Anni stopped short, her breath labored, her heart beating hard and fast in her chest. A funeral procession?

She had no choice but to press on. Anni reached the creek and made her way along the water's edge, breathing in the fresh forest air mixed with water and reeds and grasses and pine.

The heaviness, the dread she had felt a moment earlier was gone. A strangely peaceful feeling washed over her. Almost an enchantment.

Her cells were buzzing with life, not just her own life, but the life contained in everything around her. In the grasses, as they swayed quietly in the breeze. The rocks, standing sentinel to eons of night following day. The trees, protecting it all, they alone having an unencumbered view of the night sky and the stories told in the constellations. Their leaves, holding on to their color for a few more days until succumbing to the change that we all must go through. The water, as it adjusted to the cooling of the night instead of the warmth of the day. The animals, creeping from their lairs and sniffing the cool, sweet air. Anni felt it all inside her as she walked. She was a part of it. Inside it. And it was inside her.

Everything would be okay now, she began to believe. She would find her mother. All would be well.

The little voices in the forest joined in with the frogs' chorus. Whispers on the wind. Laughter.

A feeling began to grow in the pit of Anni's stomach. A gnarling, a questioning. *What have you done with her? Where have you hidden her? Give her back to me.*

"Help me find her," Anni said out loud, to the forest itself.

"Here," she heard, the voice scratchy and ancient, as though it was coming from another time. "Follow me. Follow."

It was the same sound she had heard in her dream a few nights before. But this time, she felt powerful, not pursued. She began to run.

Anni ran down the path by the creek, tripping on rocks and tree roots that seemed to jut their way into her path at just the moment before she passed. Branches closed in, their scratchy fingers seeming to reach out for her.

"Stop it," she growled, with a force she didn't quite feel inside. "Stop it and help me."

Anni burst through a tree-lined section of the path into an opening. Which way to go now? She looked around wildly, unsure of her next steps.

Just then, a wolf stepped out of the shadows and locked eyes with Anni. She held her breath and could feel her heart beating in her chest, her pulse racing. It was the largest wolf she had ever seen, at least 130 pounds, if not more. Anni knew she was supposed to look away—you're never supposed to look a wolf in the eye—but she could not. It was like she was transfixed there, staring into the wolf's deep, yellow eyes.

It turned and began to trot, quickly glancing over its shoulder toward Anni. Was it leading her someplace? Anni felt certain that it was. She followed it out of the clearing and back into the dark woods that led to the creek. She stopped when she saw the wolf standing at the base of the bridge her grandfather had built decades ago to allow people to cross when the water was high. It was high now.

A shaft of moonlight illuminated the water.

And then, she saw her.

Arden. Floating on her back in the creek, her long cream-colored dress billowing out around her. She had a garland of flowers around her head like a crown, and a long strand of pearls was wound around her neck and dripping down into the water, where they shimmered in the moonlight.

Arden's hands were clasped across her chest, as though she was praying. Her eyes were closed, her face the picture of peace and contentment. Except her lips were blue.

Anni began to scream.

CHAPTER TWENTY-TWO

Anni rushed into the water. The icy cold stung her legs like a thousand tiny pinpricks. She grabbed Arden under her arms and began to pull her toward the shore. Anni couldn't tell whether she had a pulse. She struggled to drag Arden out of the creek and onto the bank—she felt like deadweight, immensely heavy. Anni gave a massive tug and tumbled into the water herself before scrambling back to her feet.

"Mom," she said, shaking Arden's shoulders. "Mom!"

Arden's head flopped toward the side, her mouth opening to let a school of tiny silver fish stream out and into the water.

Anni recoiled, but then doubled down. "No!" she growled. "Get out of there. Get out."

She turned her mother's head to make sure every last minnow was gone. How they got into her mouth in the first place was unclear, since Arden was floating on her back, but Anni didn't want to think too much about it.

"Theo!" Anni screamed out. "Martin! Help me! I found her!"

Anni was struggling, trying to pull her mother out of the water, when she heard pounding footsteps coming toward her. It wasn't Theo, but Yale who burst through the woods. Of course, he had been checking the shoreline. He had to have been nearer to Anni than either Theo or Martin.

"Oh, dear God," Yale said, his voice low, his expression grave. "Here, let me."

He pushed past Anni and sloshed into the creek, scooping up Arden into his arms and carrying her out of the water. He rushed up onto the bridge and laid her down flat. He began CPR.

After a few moments, he stopped and looked at Anni. "She's breathing. On her own."

Anni shook her head at him. "So why . . . ?"

Yale gathered Arden into his arms again and stood. "Let's get her to the house," he said.

They hurried up the forest path, twisting and turning, as Anni yelled for Theo.

"We've got her! We're going to the house!"

It was a long trek through the woods from the creek to the house. Longer now. Going back the way Anni had come, the trees seemingly reached out for them, as they had earlier for Anni, grasping their clothes with limbs that were more like claws. But Yale pounded through, almost bulldozing his way past the branches. He didn't have the first idea of the enchantment of this forest, and wouldn't care, even if he did. He had one goal, and that was to get Arden back to the house. Quickly. Safely. While she was still alive.

Behind him, Anni watched her mother's head loll back and forth as Yale loped along. It gave her a sick feeling to see Arden so helpless, so incapacitated. But still, her mother's expression of serenity and peace never left her face.

Finally, Anni could see the lights of the house through the trees. They were almost there. Yale tripped on a tree root and went down on one knee, but held on to Arden for dear life, perhaps literally. He regained his footing and pressed on. Anni cursed the root as she passed.

They emerged from the forest and into the yard, and a great rush of wind swirled around them. Yale broke into a run toward the house, with Anni close behind.

"Anni!"

She looked over her shoulder and saw Theo and Martin bursting out of the forest at their trailheads. They came running toward the house as well, and all of them followed Yale up the deck steps and through the french doors.

Yale laid Arden on the couch, her long linen dress dripping water droplets, like beads, onto the floor. One tiny silver fish flopped on her chest. Yale kneeled next to her and placed two fingers on her neck. Everyone held their breath.

He turned to the family and nodded his head. "She has a pulse. She's breathing." Yale reached up to one of Arden's closed eyelids and, putting a finger under her lashes, carefully pushed it open. Her blue eye startled Anni. But there was no recognition. No awakening. Yale lifted one of her arms, and it dropped down, like a rag doll.

"Call the paramedics," Yale said to Vicky, who ran for her cell phone.

Meri and Martin stood in a corner of the room. Meri shook her head. "This is not a case for doctors," she said, her voice barely audible above the fray.

Theo flew to Anni and clung to her, both of them staring at Arden, wide eyed.

"Why isn't she responding to anything?" he asked, his fingers like talons, digging into Anni's arm. "Why is she like that?"

"It looks like a coma to me," Yale said. He slid a hand behind Arden's head and felt around. "Or something like it. But it doesn't feel like there was any trauma. No bumps that I can feel right now."

Gloria knelt down beside her sister and stroked her hair. "What did you get into?" she said, her voice singsongy and childlike. "What happened to you out there, Ardie? Who put this spell on you?"

Anni watched as Gloria pulled the strand of pearls from around Arden's neck and wound them around her own.

As Yale pushed himself to his feet, Anni noticed a growing blood-stain on his pants. His knee. He had fallen on it a moment before.

"Yale," she said to him, pointing at his knee.

He looked down and grimaced. "Oh, yeah. I knew it wasn't going to be pretty when I went down."

It was only a few minutes, but it seemed like a lifetime until the paramedics arrived. All at once, the room was engulfed by the sound of propeller blades, as loud as a freight train. Or a tornado. Blindingly bright light streamed in through the wall of windows facing the yard as a helicopter landed on the lawn.

Meri rushed over to the door and pulled it open as a team of paramedics hurried in with a stretcher.

"She's there," Anni said to the paramedics, pointing to Arden. "On the couch. I found her in the creek a few minutes ago."

They transferred Arden to the stretcher and started checking her vitals, buzzing around her with gauges and equipment and monitors.

"Possible coma," Yale said. "But no signs of trauma."

One of the EMTs nodded his head. They pulled a blanket over Arden and started back out the door.

"Okay," one of them said. "We're airlifting her to the hospital in Salmon Bay."

Salmon Bay, or Sammy, as the locals called it, was a much bigger town than Wharton about thirty miles down the shoreline. That was where everyone went to do their grocery shopping, go to the movies, get their cars serviced, or buy new clothes that didn't come from a boutique, among other things. Big-box stores, fast food, chain hotels, but also a quaint, historic downtown. It also had the best hospital in the region. It was a short flight across the water but would take at least two hours, maybe more, to get there by car and boat from Metsan Valo.

"We'll go with you," Anni said to the paramedics.

"No," one of the EMTs said, putting up his hand. "I'm sorry, but nobody goes in the chopper. She is stable right now, breathing on her own. We'll get her to the hospital safely. You'll have to meet us there."

A moment later, they were gone, out the door, into the helicopter, and away into the sky. The darkness fell around the house like a shroud as the sound of the blades grew fainter and fainter. As Anni watched, it seemed to her the blades might have been the wings of a great dragon, flying away to another land. Like it had in the story of Kaija and Calder. Though this time it took an enchanted princess with it. This realization sent a chill up her spine.

She shook those thoughts out of her head. "Okay, we need to get going," Anni said, looking around for her purse. But Gloria put a hand on Anni's arm.

"You're soaking wet," she said, brushing a sopping tendril of hair from Anni's face. "You've had a long day and must be exhausted."

"But my mother—"

"And my sister," Gloria said, locking eyes with Anni. "Charles and I will go. We'll stay as long as we can with Arden tonight and then get a room in that delightful inn across from the hospital, so we're close by. Won't we, Charles?"

"Let's pack our bags, dear," he said, heading up the stairs to their room, with Gloria close behind.

Anni looked at Theo, her eyes pleading with him. "We should go," she said.

"I hate to say this, but Gloria is right," Theo said. "You're totally exhausted. You need a hot bath and a good night's sleep. We'll go first thing in the morning."

The last thing Anni wanted was to be away from her mother, but she had to admit she was bone tired. This day had taken it out of her. Getting to the hospital was a long slog from Colette. She didn't know if she could even stay awake for the drive to the ferry, let alone wait for it, take it across to Wharton, and then drive another half an hour to the hospital through the dark forest that lined the lakeshore cliffs.

Anni never liked making that drive at night. It was a two-lane highway that clung on one side to a high cliff. The road twisted and turned—Anni had driven it countless times, but it always seemed different and new, especially at night. Curves where there had been a straight-away. Twists in odd places. Debris like tree limbs always happened to be in the roadway, causing you to swerve at unexpected moments. Many unsuspecting motorists had plunged unaware off the cliffs in the dark as the ancient trees themselves seemed to shift positions to bedevil drivers.

But there was something else about that stretch of forest between Wharton and Salmon Bay. Something evil that lurked there. All the Wharton townspeople knew it. An old tuberculosis sanatorium had been built on those rocky cliffs generations ago. When Anni and Theo were growing up, it had been converted into a retreat for artists and writers. But it had burned to the ground mysteriously a few years back. Most everyone who was there that night got out alive, but it was said that a sense of madness had followed them back into their lives and homes.

Nobody in either Wharton or Salmon Bay would venture onto the site, even though the views from the trails on that property were said to be breathtaking. It had always seemed to Anni that the forest on Metsan Valo's side of the lake was enchanted and filled with spirits. But the forest on the mainland was home to demons and evil and lost souls. She knew she should get to the hospital for her mother, but she had no wish to venture into those woods at night, especially on this night.

Charles and Gloria hurried down the stairs with their bags. Finally, Anni relented. *Let Gloria carry the ball for once in her life*, a voice seemed to say in Anni's head. *And you take care of yourself, for once in yours.*

"Call us when you get there," Anni said. "And be careful. Especially by the old sanatorium. You know how dangerous those roads are at night."

Gloria put a hand to Anni's cheek. "Aren't you sweet," she said. Her eyes had a strange sheen, as though a lunacy or delirium lurked behind them. She followed Charles out the door and pulled it shut behind her, without looking back.

Anni exhaled as she heard Charles's car roar to life, and the crunch of the tires on their gravel driveway as they pulled out onto the road.

Theo was at the sideboard pouring a couple of drinks, and he handed one to Anni as both of them slumped down onto the couch.

Yale and Vicky joined them, leaning into each other with a sigh. Lichen hovered behind them. Yale had his pant leg rolled up and was dabbing at his knee with a cloth.

"It's not too bad," Yale said. "What do they say in movies? It's just a flesh wound?"

Anni smiled at him, a wave of guilt washing over her about their harsh words earlier in the evening. "Thank you for what you did tonight, Yale," Anni said. "I don't know how I could've gotten Mom out of the creek without you."

He ran a hand through his hair. "Arden's alive. That's the main thing. I'm glad I was there to help."

Theo leaned forward, putting an elbow on his knee. "How do you have all of this medical knowledge? You were like a full-fledged doctor just now."

"Not quite. I'm just a volunteer firefighter," Yale said. "We're all trained as EMTs."

Anni and Theo stared at him, openmouthed. "You're a firefighter? Seriously?" Theo asked.

Yale shrugged. "Seriously. Our burb west of the cities is bordering on rural, so we're all volunteer. I've been doing it for twenty years. As a side hustle."

"Side hustles usually pay," Theo said, raising his eyebrows.

"This one pays," Yale said. "Just not in the way you'd think."

Anni noticed Lichen smiling with pride. Yale pushed himself up off the couch and extended his hand to Vicky. She took it, and he pulled her up, too. He wrapped his other arm around his daughter. "Let's get to bed," he said to his family. "It's been a long day."

As they walked toward the stairs, Anni turned toward them. "Yale? Thank you."

He put up his hand and shook his head.

Vicky smiled at Anni over her shoulder. Anni watched them walk up the stairs together as a family, each step seeming to hurt all of them, not just Yale.

Anni and Theo sat in silence for a while, watching the flames outside in the firepit dance and sway.

"The world has gone crazy," Theo said. "Mom went all Ophelia on us. Yale is the hero of the day. Gloria steps up and takes charge. What kind of alternate reality have we fallen into?"

Anni shook her head and sighed. "What do you think happened to Mom? Was this an accident? First her office was torn apart, and now this."

"Somebody was obviously trying to send her a message by trashing her office, not once but twice. If what happened to her today was an accident, it's an awfully big coincidence, wouldn't you say?"

"I don't believe in coincidences," Anni said, but the words seemed to wither and die as a terrible realization hit her. It wound around her chest and squeezed tighter and tighter until she could barely breathe. She looked at her brother, not knowing how to say the words.

"What?" he said, leaning forward. "What is it?"

Anni felt her body go cold. She began shivering, deep in her core.

"Theo," she said, her voice a thin rasp. She reached over and took his hands. It couldn't be. It just couldn't.

"Anni, you're scaring me."

"The clothes that were laid out on her bed today," she managed to squeak out. "It was basically the same outfit she was wearing when I found her. I mean, she always wears that same style. But . . ."

The twins looked into each other's eyes for a long moment, the possible implications of that reality settling into them, seeping into their skin.

"What are we dealing with here?" Theo asked.

"I don't know. But I think it's time to call Nick," Anni said, pushing herself off the couch. "He needs to know what happened to Mom."

Theo followed her to the dining table, where she had left her purse before the search for Arden. Anni grabbed her phone and dialed.

"Nick Stone."

"It's Anni Halla," she said.

"Hi, Anni—" he began. But she cut him off.

"Something's happened."

Nick took an audible breath in. "What is it?"

Anni told the chief the whole story, about how they discovered Arden was missing, the search, and how she had found her mother floating in the creek, unresponsive. The EMTs. The helicopter.

"Okay." Nick drew the word out. "So that's what the chopper dispatch to the island was for. Arden."

"Yeah."

"She's on her way to the hospital in Sammy?"

"Yes," Anni said. "But there's something else. This is going to sound really odd, but she was wearing an outfit just like the one that was laid out on her bed today. Pearls, linen. Everything."

Nick was silent for a moment. "What do you think that means?"

"I don't know," Anni said. "But all of it together doesn't feel good. It feels like there's an intention. A thread connecting it all."

"Are you on your way to the hospital now?" Nick asked her.

"No," she said, a twinge of guilt fluttering through her chest. "My aunt and her husband are headed there." Anni glanced at the clock.

"They're probably on the ferry right now, or waiting for it. Theo and I will be at the hospital first thing in the morning."

More silence from the chief. Anni could hear him tapping his finger, or maybe a pen, on his desk. "Listen, you may think this is overkill, but I'm sending someone to the hospital to guard her room."

"But my aunt—"

Nick cut her off. "Anni, remember what we said today at Arden's house? Remember who you asked me to investigate?"

And then, Anni did remember. The break-in had to have been done by someone with a key. She and Theo hadn't had a chance to confront the family before they went looking for Arden. Right now, after everyone came together to look for her, it seemed silly to suspect one of them for the break-in and the macabre display on Arden's bed.

But all at once, Anni realized that Gloria and Vicky had been in the house when she and Yale got there with Arden. Had they even been looking at all?

He was sending the guard to protect Arden from Gloria.

"Should Theo and I come right now?" Anni asked, the words catching in her throat.

"No," Nick said, a little quicker than Anni would've expected. "Come tomorrow as you had planned. I'm going to head over to the hospital myself right now, so that I can be there before your aunt arrives. I'll reassure her that we're on the job."

And then he hung up. Anni just held her phone for a moment, not knowing what to do with it.

"What did he say?" Theo wanted to know.

"He's going to put a guard outside Mom's door," Anni said.

Theo furrowed his brow. "Why would he do that?"

Anni locked eyes with him, knowing he would understand without her even saying it. Theo's eyes widened when the realization hit him.

"And he's sure we shouldn't go there now?"

"He's going himself," Anni said. "He wants us to stick to the plan we made. He didn't say it, but I think he wants to send a message to Gloria. Like, he's there, on the job, and aware of what her intentions might be."

Theo's face melted into confusion. It was one thing to have their mother's house ransacked. It was another to think a family member did it. A family member who was staying at Metsan Valo with everyone else. But things had just ratcheted up in severity. A break-in was one thing. Real harm was another.

Arden was, likely, at the moment, lying in a hospital bed in some sort of coma. What had happened to her? Who had put her there?

As Anni walked up the stairs toward her bedroom, all these thoughts were swirling through her mind. But then something else hit her. She turned and looked over the balcony into the great room as she realized she hadn't seen Martin and Meri leave. It was as though they had evaporated during all the confusion. A chill ran through her as she hurried to her room, shutting the door behind her.

CHAPTER TWENTY-THREE

Anni soaked in her claw-foot tub for a long time, letting the water wash the day away. She tried to read a novel she had plucked from the bookshelf before retreating up to her bedroom, but it was just no use. There were no other worlds to retreat into that night. She couldn't get the image of Arden floating in the river—serene, ethereal, eerie—out of her mind. Anni toweled off and changed into clean pajamas. But before crawling into bed, she had a longing to see something, anything of her mother's.

Anni stole down the hallway and opened the door to Mummo's room, now Arden's. She was greeted by the typical Arden disarray— clothes strewn everywhere, jewelry hanging from dresser drawer pulls, a scarf draped across the curtain rod. Normally, the mess would annoy Anni, but now she smiled at the familiarity of it. Her scattered mom. Anni lay down on the bed and pulled the covers around her, smelling the faint scent of patchouli that always seemed to waft around her mother.

Arden, what happened to you? First, the break-in, and now this. But why? It made no sense. Anni couldn't fathom what anyone would have against her hippie mother, who drifted around the world seeking only pleasure and happiness and love. Anni and Theo had their own issues with her, mainly because she wasn't as concerned with them as she was with herself, but that affected nobody but them.

Growing up, Anni and Theo had wished they had a more typical mother, someone who helped with homework (other than theater, which she insisted they participate in, much to Anni's chagrin), imposed rules and boundaries, and reined them in. But more often than not, it was Arden who untethered Anni and Theo, setting them adrift, floating in whatever sort of world they chose with not a whole lot of supervision. It seemed to them, at times, that Arden cared more about Arden than she did about her children.

It seemed to be a theme running through Anni's life, she realized just then. Trying to coax love out of people who loved themselves more.

Mummo, by contrast, couldn't have loved them more if she'd tried. She was their grounding force, pulling them back to earth, tying them to the land and the lake and the forest at Metsan Valo when their mother would go spiraling off into her own delights and enjoyments.

But they never doubted Arden loved them in her own way. Both Anni and Theo had acted out in the sullen ways only teenagers can. But those teenage resentments had faded for both of them, and now they looked upon their mother with good-humored annoyance and, yes, love. Was it a typical relationship? No. But nothing was typical in the Halla family. Would Arden always be more concerned with Arden? Yes. Her children had accepted that and decided to just let it go and let it be.

As Anni lay in Arden's bed, childhood memories swam through her mind. She thought of the time when she and Theo and Vicky were little, all at Metsan together. Gloria had organized a scavenger hunt through the woods . . .

Gloria. All at once, it occurred to Anni that Gloria hadn't yet called her from the hospital. She glanced at the clock. Nearly four hours had passed since she and Charles had left. More than enough time to get there.

Anni fished her phone out of her purse and checked for any missed calls. None. She called Gloria's number. Right to voice mail. Anni groaned as she pushed herself off Mummo's bed. She padded down the hallway to Theo's room and knocked.

"It's me," she said, pushing the door open a crack.

Theo was reclining on his bed with a book, pillows propped under his head, the ubiquitous black-and-red checked comforter pulled snugly around him. He smiled when he saw her.

"What's up?"

"Gloria," Anni said, settling down onto the foot of his bed. "Has she called you?"

He furrowed his brow. "No," he said. "I thought she was going to call you." He glanced at the clock on his bedside table. "It's late. They should be there by now."

Anni dialed Gloria's number again, but after a few rings, it went to voice mail. Not that she expected anything different.

"She's not picking up," Anni said, staring down at her silent phone.

"Call the hospital," Theo said.

Anni nodded. "Good idea." She looked up the hospital's number online and dialed. After identifying herself as Arden's next of kin and jumping through a few more hoops, Anni was connected with the nurses' station on her mother's floor.

Arden was stable but not responsive. The doctor had done an initial exam and assessment, and concluded there was no sign of trauma. The cause of her coma-like condition was unknown. She was on IV fluids for dehydration and scheduled to get a round of tests in the morning. She was resting comfortably.

Yes, there was a police officer outside her door. No, she had not had any other visitors.

"Gloria and Charles haven't been there," Anni said to Theo.

"Maybe they stopped at the hotel first," he offered. "Maybe visiting hours are over?"

Anni began to get a tingling on her skin. Nothing felt good about this.

She dialed Nick Stone.

"Hey," he said. "I'm here at the hospital outside your mother's room. She seems to be doing okay, considering."

"And my aunt hasn't been there?"

"No," Nick said. "But I wouldn't worry about that just yet. It's getting late, and visiting hours are winding down."

As Anni had suspected. Still. Something was nagging at her.

"The road between Wharton and Salmon Bay is so treacherous, especially at night. You don't think . . ."

"Do you mean an accident?"

"I hate to suggest it, but that could explain why they haven't been to the hospital yet."

"We've had no reports of any accidents," he said. "But I'll send someone to drive that stretch of road, just in case."

Anni exhaled. "Okay. Thank you. Theo and I will be there in the morning."

"We'll be in touch," Nick said. "I'll call you if there's any news."

Anni let out a great yawn. Exhaustion had seeped into her very cells.

"I'm going to hit the hay," Anni said, getting to her feet with a groan. She opened the door to the hallway. "We can take this up tomorrow. Maybe both of us can get a decent night's sleep for once."

"Put a bell around your neck so I'll hear you if you wander off," Theo said. "Knock if you need anything."

Back in her room, Anni was getting ready to settle down for the night when the desk underneath the window at the far end of the room caught her eye. Moonlight was streaming in, illuminating an enormous book.

It hadn't been there earlier. Not that she had noticed, anyway. She stepped closer to the desk to get a better look.

The book seemed ancient, and it was one of the largest volumes Anni had ever seen. Hundreds and hundreds of pages. Anni picked it up—it must've weighed at least ten pounds. Maybe twenty. The covers were held together and locked by silver hinges tooled with swirls and whorls and eddies.

The book reminded her of the Gutenberg Bible—the first book printed using metal type in the 1450s—she had seen years earlier at the Library of Congress. It was ancient. Holy to anyone who loved books, Christian or not. Was that what this was? A long-lost copy of the Gutenberg? Anni had heard a few copies still remained in private hands. Could it be? If so, it was worth a fortune.

Anni flipped on the desk lamp and took a breath in when she got a good look at the cover. Decidedly not the Gutenberg. It was well-worn leather, hand tooled with designs depicting scenes of some kind. Definitely not Judeo-Christian scenes from the Bible. When Anni looked closer, she saw they were images from the stories Mummo used to tell—vaki in the woods, hiding behind mushrooms and trees. Small folk dancing in a ring around a blazing fire. People working the land, cutting down trees, fishing in crude boats. The sun shining on the water, something poking its head just above the surface. Birds soaring with vaki on their backs.

Anni unlatched the hinges and carefully opened the book to the first page. It was an illustrated story in another language. Finnish? Anni was reasonably sure that was what it was. She spoke only a few words of Finn that Mummo had taught her, *mummo* for one, meaning *grandmother*.

Her exhaustion melted away as she sank down into the desk chair and began paging through the ancient volume. The illustrations, though hundreds of years old, were vibrant and colorful. Illuminated. They drew Anni in, with their depictions of vaki and small folk and elves, even trees that seemed alive and animals whose faces held wisdom and courage.

Some of the stories were pages-long narratives. Others were more like poems. She wasn't sure how long she sat there, enraptured by the book. Her room had become pitch black, but for the desk lamp. At one point, she heard a wolf howl in the distance, answered by another, then another.

"You are the keeper of it now."

Anni whipped her head around to see Meri standing in the shadows next to the door. Anni hadn't heard her come in. How long had she been there?

"Meri, you scared the life out of me," Anni said, her heart beating in her throat.

But then, the hairs on the back of Anni's neck stood up, and her skin began to tingle as the realization set in. It wasn't Meri. It was a much older woman, an ancient woman, wearing a black dress.

Anni shot up from her chair and flipped on the ceiling light. She looked all around the room. But nothing was there. Nobody was there. She opened her door and peered out into the hallway. All was quiet. She crept down the hall to the railing overlooking the main floor. A small fire burned in the fireplace.

It was then she noticed Martin and Meri seated together at the dining-room table. Meri snapped her head up to look at Anni, and a small smile came to her face.

"Hello, my dear," she said. "The time has come for us to have a talk."

CHAPTER TWENTY-FOUR

A cold whisper of fear settled onto Anni's skin, gripping tighter as she walked down the stairs, taking each step slowly and carefully. She felt like a rabbit making its way out of a hedge, not knowing a wolf was quietly waiting nearby.

Meri and Martin were illuminated by a single shaft of light that shone down upon them, and both were gazing at her now with strange, blank looks on their faces.

Anni wanted to run, to cry out, but . . . that was ridiculous. Wasn't it? These were the people who had cared for her all her life. She shook off the feeling.

"What's going on?" she managed to say, her voice wavering. She stood at the bottom of the stairs, holding on to the wrought-iron handrail, as though it could protect her. But from what?

"Join us," Meri said, motioning to a chair across from the two of them. "I'll brew a pot of tea."

Anni did as she was told, sliding onto the chair at the table where her family had congregated for generations. In this great room, where she had spent countless happy hours over the course of her life. Yet everything about it felt new.

As Meri fussed in the kitchen, Martin simply sat in his place, smiling at Anni. A blank smile, devoid of any of his usual warmth and wit.

It was as though his body was there, at the ready, set to go, whenever Martin's spirit returned to it.

Anni fumbled with her hands in her lap.

Meri poured steaming cups of tea for the three of them and settled back down into her chair.

"You saw the book?" Meri asked, peering at Anni over the rim of her cup.

Anni nodded but couldn't respond in words.

"It belongs to you now. You are its keeper. This is what your grandmother wanted to pass on to you. It was the purpose of your planned visit."

Anni gazed around the darkened room. It was like a strange, dreamlike version of itself. The same as it ever was, but slightly off. Askew somehow. The house itself seemed to be buzzing with life. Breathing in and out. Watching her. All at once this home that had been her refuge all her life felt like the most haunted, sinister place on earth. She wanted Theo with her. But she stayed where she was, glued to the spot.

Finally, she found her voice, buoyed by anger. "What is going on here, Meri? First, I wake up in the forest in the middle of the night—or dreamed I did—then fireflies attacked Theo and me, he walks off the dock and into the water, we get trapped in the sauna, ghosts and laughter and whispers are everywhere, you two are acting like characters in a Stephen King novel right now, and my mother is lying in a hospital bed in some weird kind of unexplained coma after her house got broken into."

Martin and Meri just sat there, across from her, smiling their blank smiles.

"Say something!"

Finally, Meri spoke. "Your grandmother's absence has left a void."

Anni huffed. "No kidding." She set her teacup down on the table with a thud. "Obviously. It's a great loss for all of us. What does that have to do with—"

Meri held up her hand. "She passed along that legacy to you," she continued. "You are the mistress of Metsan Valo now."

"Again, we all know that. We all heard Mummo's last will."

"Child, what I'm trying to tell you is that you don't simply own this house, you are the keeper of all that is here. The vaki have been restless since the death of your grandmother."

Anni closed her eyes and shook her head. "If you're trying to tell me that the spirits in my grandmother's folktales are real, in the woods right now and *restless*, I'm going back to bed. I love the old tales as much as anybody, but I need to get some sleep before Theo and I head to the mainland tomorrow."

Anni pushed her chair from the table.

"It's all in the book," Meri said.

"What is?"

"The story of our people, Annalise. Your people. Your grandmother told you the story of Kaija and Calder for a reason. She was telling it specifically for you to hear. It was Kaija who first had the idea to write down our stories, our tales. She documented our spells and remedies and incantations. She wrote how to summon the wind and the rain and the sun. How the vaki were in everything.

"It's all there, in the book. Handed down through generations of women. It is a great gift your grandmother has given you. It is in your hands now. Read it. Let it become a part of you."

Anni didn't know quite how to respond to this. That the book on her desk was a history of her family was fascinating. But all the business about the supernatural . . . she knew Mummo believed it. But nothing in Anni's rational mind could even begin to comprehend it.

"I can't read it," Anni said, finally. "I can look at the pictures. But it's in Finnish, and, if what you're saying is true about how long ago it was written, an ancient form of the language at that. I can't possibly understand it. I'm not sure anyone but a scholar of the ancient history of the region could translate it."

Meri held Anni's gaze. The electricity between them began to take on an ominous force, as though a shaft of blackness was holding them together.

"You can read it," Meri said. "You alone, now. Study the pages. The language will begin to make sense to you as it seeps off the pages and into your body. You need to take control of the world around you, Annalise. You and the women of Metsan Valo. It is your charge."

Meri and Martin exchanged a glance.

Anni shook her head and pushed herself to her feet. All at once, she wanted very much to be away from Meri and Martin. Exhaustion was overtaking her, and she was done with all this. At least for the moment.

But when she turned to hurry back up the stairs, she saw that the room was filled with people.

Their faces were hazy; even their forms lacked crisp edges. Many were dressed in black, others in furs and hats. One young, dark-haired woman had an enormous hawk perched on her arm. A man standing just behind her held a wooden bow and a quiver filled with arrows. Another brandished a silver sword that glinted with a light that was not shining on it, but from within. A woman held a basket filled with herbs and plants. Another knelt next to a small fire, breathing in the aromatic smoke. All at once, Anni saw that they were here, in the great room at Metsan Valo, but at the same time, on a windswept hill, its grasses blowing in the breeze. Anni saw the forest beyond and the ocean in the distance. She could smell the fresh salt air.

These were her ancestors. Their stories were in the book on her desk upstairs. It had kept them alive, in a way, filled with their tales of adventures, powers, magic, and wonder.

At the far edge of the group, Anni saw Mummo and Pappa, standing with an older man and woman. Anni didn't recognize the woman, but the man? She looked closer and watched as he picked up the fireplace poker and stoked the fire. He turned to her and smiled, nodding his head. This was the man she had seen a few days before. It was as though this was his job, the fire here at Metsan Valo. It was up to him to keep the home fires burning.

Anni turned to speak to Martin and Meri, but they seemed to be in another place and time, far away from her. The dining table seemed light-years away, as hazy and unfocused as her group of ancestors had been. Meri was pouring more hot water into their cups. Anni could see the steam rising up, almost as though it was alive and animated. The two of them were talking to one another, but Anni couldn't hear what they were saying.

All at once, they seemed to change and morph, as if they were aging backward. Soon, the young Martin and Meri were there at the table, which seemed new and freshly hewn. An older couple came through the door. She was carrying a basket of carrots and potatoes, and he was holding a great fish on a line.

Martin and Meri scrambled to their feet.

"Beautiful catch, sir!" Martin said, taking the line.

"We'll have a fine dinner tonight," Meri said.

But Anni knew, somehow, they were not speaking English. The words were longer, the cadence more musical. Yet she could understand what they were saying. As if she had always known the language, as though it lived inside her.

The scene, along with Meri and Martin themselves, faded into darkness. She turned back to her ancestors, but they were gone as well. The great room at Metsan Valo was as it had always been. Now it was cold and dark, save for a small fire humming along in the fireplace, stoked by a man who had built it in another time.

CHAPTER TWENTY-FIVE

Anni awoke, twisted in her sheets. She was in her room, safely tucked into her bed, although she did not remember coming back up the stairs after the strangeness of the night before. Had it even really happened? Why was everything about this time at Metsan Valo wrapped in doubt? Anni had been constantly wondering what was real and what was fantasy, dreamed up in her imagination. It was as though her mind and reality were not on the same plane.

One thing was real. The book was still sitting on her desk. That was a tangible thing, at least.

She was tempted to sit and spend all day reading it, until she remembered. Arden. Theo. They were going to the hospital. She checked the time. Nine thirty. Anni shot out of bed and grabbed her robe before hurrying out into the hallway. Theo was downstairs, clearing his plate from the table. Meri and Martin were nowhere to be seen.

"Why didn't you wake me?" she said, hurrying down the stairs.

"Coffee?" He retrieved a cup from the cabinet and poured, handing her the pitcher filled with cream. "When I got up, you were sleeping so hard I didn't want to wake you. We've both been exhausted, you even more than me. So I let you sleep."

"But we've got to get over to the hospital," she said, and took a gulp of coffee. "We should be there by now." The image of Arden, lying serene and motionless in a hospital bed, played in her mind.

"I've been on the phone with her nurses," Theo said. "They're running some tests this morning. So we've got some time. We'll catch the ten-twenty ferry and be there around noon."

Anni rummaged around in the fridge and found a container of yogurt. "Did you talk to Gloria?" she asked, grabbing a spoon from the silverware drawer.

"I haven't been able to reach her," Theo said, wincing. "And the nurses said she hasn't been there yet this morning."

Anni's mind went in different directions at once. Gloria was supposed to call when she got to Salmon Bay last night. She hadn't. Did they get there?

But at the same time, it was only nine thirty. It could be that Gloria and Charles just hadn't made it to the hospital yet. Maybe they were exhausted when they got to Sammy, went right to the hotel, and slept in that morning, just like she had.

Vicky and Yale came through the front door as Anni was finishing her yogurt.

"Vic, have you heard from your mom and Charles?" Anni asked.

"Not since they left last night, no," Vicky said, exchanging a glance with Yale. "Why?"

"They were going to call me when they got there," Anni said, "and they haven't been to the hospital today. Theo and I are just on our way there now, but it's sort of weird they haven't checked in. Isn't it?"

Vicky didn't respond immediately, but the look on her face was annoyance mixed with worry. Anni wasn't very close to her cousin, but she knew enough about Gloria to know that Vicky had to have similar frustrations with her mother as she and Theo did with theirs. Vicky's father had no doubt been her grounding force, as Mummo had been for them.

"It's not totally out of character for Mom to space out about things like this," Vicky said, wrinkling her nose. "She's always been sort of . . ." Her words trailed off, as though finishing the thought was just too exhausting.

"Oh, we know, believe me," Theo said. "Arden has always been 'sort of,' too."

Vicky fished her cell phone out of her purse and dialed. She rolled her eyes and hung up when her mother didn't answer. "She just doesn't get the concept that carrying a cell phone is so that people can reach her if necessary, especially when she travels. She's always turning it off or leaving it in the hotel room or something."

It sounded all too familiar to Anni. "The Halla sisters are nothing if not consistent," she said, pushing her chair back from the table. "We'll check in with you when we get there."

Anni headed back up the stairs, turning to Theo over her shoulder. "I'm going to hurry up and get dressed," she said. "And then let's head out."

"Ready when you are," Theo said.

Back in her room, Anni ran a brush through her hair and splashed some water on her face. Moisturizer and a little under-eye concealer would have to do. She pulled on a long-sleeved shirt and jeans, and grabbed her jacket. She was about to race back downstairs when she remembered—they might stay overnight. So she took a minute to throw pajamas, a change of clothes, and her makeup case into a bag. Before she walked out the door, she glanced back at the enormous book on her desk. The pull to sit and read it was almost overwhelming, as though it was calling out to her, drawing her in. But she didn't give in to it. First things first.

Out in the hallway, she closed the door behind her, turned around, and jumped back with a gasp. Meri was standing there, next to the railing.

"I'm sorry," Meri said. "I didn't mean to startle you."

Anni managed a smile, her heart beating hard in her chest. "That's okay. I'm glad I ran into you. Theo and I are on the way to the hospital, and there's an outside chance we'll be staying overnight. Just so you won't worry if we're not around later. I'll call you from the hospital to update you on Mom's condition."

"Very good," Meri said with a quick nod, reaching into the pocket of her dress. She drew out a black skeleton key. "Let's lock your room in your absence." Her voice was as low as a whisper, her expression grave.

"The book?" Anni whispered.

Meri nodded, inserting the key into the lock on Anni's bedroom door and turning it. *Chock.* She held the key out to Anni.

"We've got a duplicate in our cottage," Meri said. "You take this one."

Anni reached into her purse for her key ring and threaded the skeleton key onto it.

"Why, though?" Anni asked as they walked down the hallway together.

"You saw its power last night," Meri said. "Best to keep it in your hands only."

They parted ways at the staircase, with Meri continuing down the hallway and Anni descending the stairs. When she looked back over her shoulder, Meri was gone.

A few moments later, after saying their goodbyes to Vicky and Yale, and offering assurances they'd call with any news, Anni and Theo were driving down the road to the ferry dock. The day was crisp and clear, and the leaves were just beginning to turn. Anni couldn't remember the last time she had seen the sky that blue.

"A book appeared in my room last night," she blurted out.

He furrowed his brow. "What do you mean it appeared? Like, out of nowhere?"

Anni grinned. "That wouldn't surprise me at this point. But no. Someone put it on my desk. Someone, meaning Martin or Meri. And my money's on Meri."

"Then I'm assuming it's not *Fifty Shades of Grey*," Theo said.

Anni let out a laugh. "No, it's not that. At first I thought it was the Gutenberg Bible. For real. It's that old and that huge."

They reached the dock and drove onto the waiting ferry. When they climbed up the metal staircase to the observation deck, they saw they were the only ones aboard.

"So what's with the book?" Theo asked as they settled onto a bench.

"It's where Mummo got all of the old tales," Anni said, looking out over the water. The sun was making it shimmer, like diamonds were dancing on its surface. "Meri told me it was written generations ago. By the woman in Mummo's last tale, the one she told us about in the video."

"What was her name? Kaija?"

Anni nodded, pulling her jacket closed. The wind had picked up, and it carried a bite with it. "Apparently, she got the idea to write all of the folktales down in one place. Others added to it over the years. There are spells, too, like for controlling the elements and communicating with the vaki. The whole nine yards. Everything Mummo used to tell us."

Theo gave her a side glance. "No way."

"Way."

"Unreal!" Theo said. "I've never seen that book before."

"I know! I'd never seen it before, either. But Meri told me it's the story of our people. She said it's mine now because I'm the 'mistress of Metsan Valo.' I wish people would stop saying that."

Theo leaned forward and put an arm on the bench in front of them, to look her in the face. "You're telling me all of this happened after you went to bed last night? You found this book and had a conversation about it with Meri. For real?"

Anni wanted to tell him about the ancestors in the great room, shadows of them, or whatever they were. A vision into another time. That she had possibly seen Kaija and Calder from Mummo's story. And Mummo! And Pappa! And their great-grandparents. And that their great-grandfather still tended the hearth at Metsan Valo to this day, keeping the home fires burning throughout eternity. But she simply could not find the words. The book itself was strange enough. She didn't have to go down the rabbit hole completely.

"Exactly," she said. "I found it and looked through it, and then started thinking about who might've put it in my room. Of course, the usual suspects, Martin and Meri. I went downstairs to look for them, and sure enough, they were sitting at the table. It was like they were waiting for me."

"That's really wild," Theo said, staring out into the distance. The dense pine forests and rocky shorelines of the Redemption Islands chain, all unoccupied and undeveloped, now designated as a national park, came into view. "I want to take a look at it when we get back."

"The pages are illustrated," she said. "It's like an illuminated bible from the Middle Ages."

"Only it's a playbook on how to control, you know, everything in the natural world," Theo said, grinning. "It's like the pagan's answer to the Gutenberg."

Anni looked at him, openmouthed. "That's exactly what it's like," she said, her voice dropping to a whisper. "And, you know, Theo, Meri was lurking outside of my room this morning when I was getting dressed. She was standing there when I came out."

He wrinkled his nose. "Well, that's a little creepy."

"It's a lot creepy," Anni said, feeling the chill of it now.

"They are the king and queen of melodrama. What was she doing out there? Waiting for you, I mean."

"She was there to lock my bedroom door behind me. She gave me the key."

His eyes grew wide. "Why? Because of the book?"

"I guess she doesn't want anyone else to get their hands on it," Anni said, thinking out loud. She hadn't worked this out in her mind before this conversation, but it was all falling into place now. "But that seems wrong to me. I mean, if it's the story of our ancestors, then it belongs to you, too. And Vicky. And Mom and Gloria. Right?"

"That's right," Theo said. "But maybe it's about the book's value. You said it was really old, right? Ancient? Is it typeset?"

"Yes!" Anni said. "I wonder how they did that, out in the middle of what's now northern Finland."

"It's got to be worth a fortune. It could be the first book ever typeset in the Finnish language. I assume that's what it's written in. Or the first one typeset in eastern Europe."

"You don't think . . ." Anni started, a thought formulating in her mind.

"What?"

"Do you think the book is what the break-in was all about?"

Theo's hand flew to his mouth. "Because it's so valuable, you mean? But we don't know that it is."

"We don't know that it isn't," she said, raising her eyebrows.

They let that thought simmer between them for a moment.

"Why would they tear everything apart, though?" Theo asked. "You said the book was enormous, right?"

Anni nodded.

"One look in Mom's library would tell them if it was there or not."

Anni remembered the utter disarray in Arden's library. All her papers, strewn everywhere. Her poetry, ripped from its journals. Her beloved books, thrown on the floor like garbage.

And then the realization hit Anni like a wave. It was anger. An assault on Arden's favorite, most precious belongings. Her words.

She looked at Theo, wide eyed. "This is one of two things," she said. "Either they came in looking for the book and were angry when it wasn't there, so they trashed the place. Or—"

"Or what?"

"Or they were just angry."

CHAPTER TWENTY-SIX

The ferry chugged into the Wharton bay and glided toward the dock. Anni saw the town's streets were bustling with people making their way in and out of the shops. Some were sitting at outdoor cafés, others merely enjoying the town's quaint atmosphere and the particular Wharton magic that swirled through the air.

She looked down the shoreline and could see the house on Front Street, which had stood on the waterfront for a century. She could almost see her own childhood face peering out of the window of the corner room upstairs. Anni had loved to watch the ferries come and go when she was growing up. She and Theo had had so many happy times in that house.

"I know who the nice lady on Front Street was," she said to Theo, as offhandedly as she could.

He squinted at her. "How? How do you know who she was?"

Anni couldn't help the laughter that was bubbling up inside her. "I love knowing things you don't know."

"How?"

He was actually a little angry, Anni thought. It just made her more delighted.

"Nick Stone's wife, Kate? Her great-grandparents built the house more than a century ago."

Theo squinted at her. "Wait a minute. I thought her great-grand-parents built Harrison's House."

He was referring to one of the most magnificent inns in Wharton—they could see it as the ferry docked—that had started its life as the private home of the town's most prominent citizens. Kate's grandmother Hadley was still alive and very much a fixture in Wharton when Theo and Anni were growing up. Anni remembered her as a kindly old gal with a wicked sense of humor who gave out the best candy at Halloween.

"Nick said it's complicated," she said. "Apparently Kate's great-grandmother, the one who built the house on Front Street, was murdered when she lived there."

Theo raised his eyebrows. "You think that's who our 'lady' was? Is?"

"Who else?"

Theo shook his head and smiled a faraway smile. "Unreal. She used to tuck us in at night. I wonder if Nick's wife has any pictures of her. I'd love to see them."

"That's what I thought, too. Nick said we should get together with his wife sometime to talk about it."

As the ferry docked, Anni and Theo made their way back down to the car. When the ferry lowered its gate, they drove off and into town. As they drove by the house on the way to the hospital, they saw Gary and LuAnn were sitting on the front porch, he in his chef's whites, and she in full-on leopard print from head to toe. Theo pulled to a stop, and the two sentries came down to greet them. LuAnn's expression was grave.

"How's your mother?" LuAnn asked, leaning into the car through the passenger window, which Anni had opened. "Has there been any change?" Obviously, the word had gotten out in Wharton. It didn't surprise Anni a bit.

"We're headed to the hospital now," she said. "We'll let people know once we know."

LuAnn put a hand on Anni's arm. "We're all praying for her."

"We sure are, doll!" Gary piped up. "Beth is smudging in the bookstore. You can smell the sage all the way across the street."

Anni's eyes welled up with tears. People could be so kind. She couldn't even look at Theo, knowing the tears would come if she did.

"Thank you," she said, her voice breaking. "And thank you again for watching the house."

"The least we can do," LuAnn said. "It's a nice break, coming down here to sit on the porch."

They said their goodbyes, and Theo drove off toward Salmon Bay. Anni pulled her phone from her purse.

"Calling the hospital before we drive into the dead zone," she said to her brother, holding the phone to her ear.

That was another peculiar thing about the stretch of road between Wharton and Salmon Bay. As you drove out of town, there were only a couple of miles of cell signal until it completely cut off near the site of the old sanatorium. Nobody could ever explain why. It was as though the site itself was so dark, whatever pervaded it so sinister, that the cell signal couldn't penetrate it.

"This is Annalise Halla," she said into the phone. "I'm calling to check on my mother."

Anni listened for a minute and shook her head at Theo. *No change*, she mouthed to him.

She thanked the nurse and let her know she and Theo would be arriving within the hour.

She turned to Theo. "Okay, so no change. No visitors today—so Gloria hasn't shown up—and the police are still outside the room."

Theo took a long breath in and let it out in a sigh. "Where is Gloria?"

Anni settled back into her seat. A familiar sense of dread began to wrap itself around her, but Anni didn't know if it was because they were driving on this stretch of road she hated, with all its twists and turns, its energy dark and gray even on the brightest of days, or if something had happened to Gloria and she was somehow sensing it.

She clasped her hands together as they took turn after turn, the rocky cliff on the side of the road seeming to grow steeper and nearer with each twist.

"Is there no such thing as a guardrail in Wharton County?" Theo asked, his face focused and stern. "Is that so much to ask? A simple—"

As they rounded a corner, the sight they encountered stopped Theo's words in the air, and their car on the road at the same time.

Four squad cars, lights flashing, were parked at odd angles, askew, on the roadway. A fire truck and ambulance sat on the shoulder. Anni saw uniformed officers, EMTs, and even men with ropes and what looked like rappelling gear. What in the world?

Theo inched the car closer and rolled down his window.

"What happened?" he asked one of the officers.

"Accident," he said. "Move along, please."

But Anni didn't want to move along. She didn't want to go anywhere. Something about this didn't feel right.

"Theo . . ." Anni began. "I don't—"

Just then, Nick Stone emerged from behind the ambulance. He caught sight of the car and waved them over. Theo and Anni exchanged a glance and hopped out of the car as soon as Theo put it into park.

"What's going on?" Anni asked the chief.

"I was just about to call you," Nick said. He walked over to Anni and put a hand on her arm. "A car went over the cliff last night." He cocked his head in the direction of the cliff side, and it was then Anni saw the angry, black skid marks on the roadway, like a knife wound, cutting through the grass and disappearing over the edge.

She looked into Nick's face and couldn't understand why it was filled with such compassion. All at once, she knew.

Nick saw the recognition in her eyes. "The car was registered to a Gloria Bishop. That's your aunt, right?"

201

Anni and Theo caught each other's eyes for a split second before both of them rushed to the side of the cliff. They peered over, and there it was. A car, crumpled in a heap at the bottom. Anni wouldn't have been able to identify it as Gloria's, but she was sure the chief had his facts straight. EMTs were scrambling down the embankment with a stretcher.

Theo turned from the scene and ran a hand through his hair, taking a few steps down the road. Anni's mind was racing in all directions at once as she walked back over to the chief.

"Are they . . . dead?" Anni asked. "And why are you just finding out about this now? You said they went off the road last night. How do you know that?"

Nick put up his hands. "I know you have lots of questions," he said. "First, we're getting the driver out of the car right now. He's alive. We're not sure about the extent of his injuries, but he's alive."

"What about Gloria?" Anni asked.

Nick took a breath in. "Was she supposed to be in the car?"

Anni blinked at him several times, and then turned to her brother. "Theo?" He turned to her, and she motioned for him to come.

As he was nearing them, Anni gave him the news. "Charles is alive. Gloria isn't here."

He furrowed his brow. "What do you mean, not here? Did she get thrown from the car? Have you checked everywhere?"

Nick nodded. "She is not at the scene. Are you telling me she was a passenger in the car?"

"Yes," Anni said. "They left the island last night to come to the hospital. Just after the helicopter left with my mom. Charles is her new husband."

"You mentioned that last night. But are you absolutely sure Gloria was in the car? What I'm asking is, are you sure she left the island at all?"

"We both saw them leave together. They packed bags because they thought they'd be staying overnight."

"I'm going to have my people do a thorough search of the area," Nick said. "They'll scour the shoreline and the forest between here and Wharton. I'll call Gary and LuAnn to be on the lookout for her, too. There's some blood on the dash—maybe it's hers, and she's injured. I'm putting out a missing person's alert on her. Do you have a recent photo?"

"I do," Anni said, remembering she had taken a shot of Arden and Gloria the day before. "I'll send it to you when we're back in cell range."

Anni looked around at the chaotic scene. The scene of an accident. Maybe a crime scene. She wasn't sure what to do next. She wanted to help but didn't know how.

Just then, the paramedics came up over the cliff, carrying the stretcher. Charles. Anni and Theo rushed over to it and saw he was conscious, barely. Blood covered his face. He was gazing off into the distance, maybe into his own memories, smiling a ghastly smile.

"Charles," Anni said, leaning over the stretcher as the EMTs ran to the ambulance. "It's Anni. Gloria's niece. I'm here, and so is Theo. Is there someone we can call for you?"

Charles's eyes were rolling back in his head. "This is an outrage," he murmured.

"Where's Gloria?" Anni asked. "Was she in the car with you?"

He looked up at Anni and smiled, his teeth covered in blood.

"Where is Gloria, Charles?"

"Charles?" he said to her. "Oh, that's right. Gloria?"

And then his eyes fluttered closed. The EMTs slid the stretcher into the ambulance, and the doors slammed behind them. They went roaring off toward the hospital in Salmon Bay.

Theo and Anni walked back to the chief.

"We're on our way to the hospital," Anni said to him. "We'll call Vicky—Gloria's daughter—once we get into cell range again. She's his next of kin, that we know of. We don't know if he has any other family."

Nick shook his head. "Give me her number, if you would. I'll be the one to notify her."

"I'm sure she'll be on the next ferry," Theo added.

"I'm not sure she should do that," he said. "You said Gloria was in the car with her husband when they left Metsan Valo. She was nowhere to be found at this crash site. It makes you wonder if she ever got to the mainland, or if she was somehow left in Wharton. Someone needs to be at the house if she comes back."

The crash was the horrifying answer to the question of why Gloria hadn't reached the hospital. But it raised more questions than it answered.

Where was she?

CHAPTER TWENTY-SEVEN

Theo and Anni sped toward the hospital in Salmon Bay. The dense forest where the crash had occurred soon gave way to rolling farmland and orchards, which were bustling with people picking their own bushels of sweet apples right off the tree. Soon, the road veered back toward the lakeshore, where a marshy area separated the inland farms from the big lake. Anni always loved to see the wildlife in the marsh, migrating ducks of all kinds, snowy egrets, geese, even deer, and an occasional bear or two. On this day, she saw a pair of swans floating serenely in the calm waters. *Arden and Gloria*, she thought, *in better days.*

And then it hit Anni. First Arden disappeared. Now Gloria. A chilling thought began to slither into her mind. Something was happening to the daughters of Metsan Valo, something that Anni couldn't put her finger on. But she couldn't think about that right now. She pushed it into the back of her mind to attend to the situation at hand, the real-life situation they were dealing with. Not the otherworldliness that seemed to be draping itself around them, around her, at every turn.

Anni's phone buzzed. "It's Vicky," she said to Theo before answering.

"What's going on?" Vicky asked. Her voice, thin and higher than usual, seemed to be floating on an undercurrent of simmering panic. "The police said Mom wasn't in the car?"

"That's right," Anni said, as soothingly as she could. "We were at the scene, Vic. Gloria wasn't there. There was no indication that she was ever there. The EMTs are taking Charles to the hospital right now by ambulance, as I'm sure Nick told you. He was conscious, but not really coherent."

Vicky let out a sob, and Anni heard Yale in the background, comforting her. "I couldn't care less about Charles," Vicky said, taking an audible breath in. "That was unkind. Of course I care. But he's no more than a stranger to me, to us. I've only met him a few times. I'm more concerned about Mom."

"I understand," Anni said.

"We're supposed to stay here," Vicky said. "In case she comes back. Do you think that's the right thing to do? I feel like we should go out looking for her."

"The Wharton police have put out a missing-persons alert on her," Anni said. "Which I'm sure the chief told you, right? Maybe you and Yale should look around the island. Meri can wait at the house, in case your mom comes back. Martin can search the forest, but—"

"I know," Vicky cut her off. "He can search there all he likes, but Mom wouldn't go into the woods. And there's no earthly reason she wouldn't be with Charles. We all saw them leave together. It was *her* sister they were going to check on."

The cousins were silent for a moment. Theo glanced at Anni as he drove, shook his head, and shrugged. Nobody knew the best thing to do.

"Okay," Anni said, with more authority and decisiveness than she felt. "You and Yale do a sweep of the island, around the ferry dock. You're absolutely right—there is no reason to believe she didn't get on that ferry with Charles. But you should probably take a look around just to cover all bases."

"Okay." Vicky sighed a long sigh. "I think that makes sense. It will give me something to do, anyway. Other than just wait here, helpless."

They rang off, and Anni noticed that she and Theo were now entering the town of Salmon Bay. It was much more sprawling than Wharton; its population was tenfold larger, if not more. But downtown Sammy, Old Town, as it was known, was still as quaint and lovely as it had been when it was built more than a century earlier out of limestone quarried nearby.

Little mom-and-pop boutiques and local restaurants rivaled those big chains on the other side of town. People still frequented their local hardware store, pharmacy, and other local businesses. A one-screen movie theater built in the 1930s was more popular than the cineplex in the mall.

As they drove through town, Anni saw new buildings that hadn't been there the last time she was in Sammy, businesses with neon signs lining the roadway, expansion everywhere she looked. In a way, she was happy to see the town growing and thriving, but it also gave her an unsettled feeling in the pit of her stomach. As though time was marching on without her. The places of her childhood were changing, moving on, becoming something other than she had known when she was young. But in her mind, they had remained the same, frozen as they were the moment she last saw them. She supposed she didn't have the right to stave off the passage of time, and she'd forfeited her hold on the places she had called home as a child when she moved across the sea and built a life for herself for the past decade. Still. It didn't lessen the feeling of wishing things had stayed the same, grasping at vestiges of her childhood as they slipped away, and being left with empty hands, unable to stop the inevitability of evolution. She wasn't here to live through the changes.

Anni knew the hospital was about a mile off the main street but couldn't remember exactly where it was or where to turn. It had been so long since she had been there. She saw Theo was similarly at sea, squinting at road signs, trying to remember which way to go. She was pulling up her GPS app when they both saw the blue hospital sign on the roadway at the same time. "There," Anni said, pointing.

They pulled into the hospital parking lot a few minutes later.

"Okay," Theo said, reaching over and squeezing Anni's hand. "We've got this." They both got out of the car.

The hospital lobby was oddly deserted. A shiver ran through Anni as their footsteps echoed in the emptiness. She noticed Theo shuddered as well.

"I hate hospitals," he whispered, wincing.

Anni knew what he meant. Sickness, trauma, and death hung in the air in these places, if not the very spirits of the patients themselves, with loved ones' grief and worry snaking their way through it all like a tight black cord. And now, Anni's and Theo's worries and fears were wafting into that miasma of pain, feeding it anew. It followed them through the halls like a living thing, renewed and regenerated by everyone who sought help there.

On Arden's floor, they saw a uniformed officer sitting in a chair outside one of the rooms.

"I guess we found her," Theo said, raising his eyebrows.

They introduced themselves to the officer as Anni looked up and down the hallway for a nurse who could give them the latest updates on Arden's condition.

"The chief told me you were on your way," the officer said.

Anni smiled at him. "You can go ahead and take a break if you'd like," she said. "We're here now, so—"

But the officer shook his head. "Thanks for the thought, but no. I'm here until I get relieved in a couple of hours."

Anni pushed open the door.

The room was silent, but for an occasional beep from one of the machines that were hooked up to Arden. Blood pressure. Oxygen monitor. Heart monitor. Dappled sunlight streamed in from the window, bathing her in a warm glow. Arden lay on the bed, her hands clasped over her chest, just like they had been when Anni had found her. Only now, she was wearing a papery-thin hospital gown and looked as pale as the grave. No garland of flowers, no linen dress, no pearls dangling in the water.

"Mom?" Anni said in a whisper, laying a hand on Arden's shoulder. "Mom, can you hear me?"

The only response was a beep from her blood-pressure monitor. The low side of normal.

Theo hooked his arm through Anni's and laid his head on her shoulder. They both sighed, gazing at the woman who had been so many things to them, everything, over so many years. A couple of chairs were folded against the wall on the side of the room, and Theo pulled them up to their mother's bedside. The twins settled down to do . . . what? Wait. Sit with her.

"What are we supposed to do now?" Theo asked Anni, echoing her thoughts.

She shook her head. "Talk to her, maybe? Read to her? I don't know what people do in this kind of situation."

Neither had brought a book or a newspaper or anything to read, so Anni fished her phone out of her purse and downloaded an e-book. A sweet New Agey, self-help romance that had dominated the bestseller lists a few years prior. She thought her mother might like it. As she was beginning to read, the door pushed open, and a doctor came into the room. He was middle aged and balding, with dark hair and kind eyes.

"You're her children, I understand?" he said. "I'm John Baldwin."

Anni and Theo scrambled to their feet. Theo held out his hand, and Dr. Baldwin clasped it.

"How is she?" Theo asked.

Dr. Baldwin shook his head. "She's stable. Her vital signs are normal. She's doing as well as can be expected."

"As well as can be expected? That really doesn't sound good. Do you have any idea what caused this?" Anni asked.

Dr. Baldwin leaned against the bed. "That's what I was hoping to ask you."

Theo furrowed his brow. "Us? What do you mean? You're the medical professionals, here."

But Anni knew what he meant. He was going to ask them about Arden's mental state. Whether madness permeated their family tree. Whether Arden had done this to herself.

"She didn't try to commit suicide, if that's what you're insinuating," Anni said, a bit louder than she had intended.

The doctor cocked his head and looked from one to the other of the twins. "Are you sure about that?"

"Why would you even think that?" Theo asked, his neck reddening. Anni could almost feel the bile rising in his throat. "Did you find anything? Poison in her system? Drugs? Because we can tell you our mother never even took an aspirin, let alone anything strong enough to kill her."

Theo turned around and walked to the window, running a hand through his hair. Anni understood Theo's frustration at the doctor's questions, but the real frustration was that they didn't have any answers to give. Nothing helpful that would illuminate the mystery of why their mother was lying in a coma.

"My brother's right," Anni said, making an effort to keep her voice even. "Our mother wouldn't have tried to take her own life. Isn't there any other explanation? I mean, you know her house was broken into a few days ago, right? I'm sure you've noticed the officer in the hallway."

"We've been briefed by the police, yes," Dr. Baldwin said, crossing his arms over his chest. "We've run a battery of tests, including toxicology, but we can't find anything wrong with her. I was just hoping to gain some insight from you."

"So you're telling us you don't have any idea what caused this?" Theo asked.

Dr. Baldwin shook his head. "It's not a head injury. It's not drug induced. Her vitals are completely normal. Her blood work is completely normal."

"If everything is normal, why isn't she awake?" Anni asked.

Dr. Baldwin held her gaze for a long moment. "We don't know," he said finally. "This falls into the 'we've never seen this before' category, if I'm going to be totally honest with you. If we knew what caused it, we could treat it. But our tests are telling us nothing."

"So you were hoping we could provide insight into whether she had ingested something that you couldn't trace," Theo said.

"Exactly," the doctor said.

The three of them sat in silence for a moment, listening to Arden's monitors beep.

"What are you doing for her?" Anni asked, motioning to the bag of IV fluids attached to her mother's arm.

"Nutrition and hydration," he said.

The words made Anni's skin crawl. She looked down at her sleeping mother, and tears stung at the backs of her eyes. That was what doctors did for patients who were dying. Beyond care.

The doctor went on his way then, with the promise he'd return in the afternoon, leaving Anni and Theo sitting in the quiet of their mother's bedside, listening to the beep of her monitors.

CHAPTER TWENTY-EIGHT

After rapping softly at the door, Patrick Saari poked his head inside.

"Okay if I come in?" he said, a tentative smile on his face. "I don't want to intrude."

"Patrick!" Anni said, jumping up from her chair. "Don't be silly. You're not intruding."

He came fully through the door then, carrying a large bouquet of flowers in a vase.

"Oh, how lovely," Anni said, taking the vase and setting it on a shelf next to the window. "Thank you." She turned to look at him, a warmth radiating in her chest. She hadn't even thought about calling him to let him know what was going on, but she was absurdly glad to see him all the same. Anni supposed word about Arden being in the hospital must be all over Wharton by now.

Patrick's eyes fell on Arden, a look of deep concern on his face. "Hello," he said, his voice soft. "It's Patrick. I'm here with Anni and Theo, and we're all wondering when you're going to wake up and join this party."

Her monitors beeped. Patrick turned to Anni and Theo. "What do the doctors say?"

Theo pushed himself up from his chair. "You're not going to believe it, man," he said. "Anni, will you fill him in? I'll go down to the ER and see what's going on with Charles. There's got to be some news by now."

Anni gave him a weak smile as he left.

She motioned for Patrick to take a seat next to her, and told him the whole story of how Arden had gone missing and turned up in the creek, how Charles and Gloria had left Metsan Valo after the helicopter had gone, how no one had heard from them before she and Theo left for the mainland, and how they had come upon the scene of the accident as they were driving to the hospital an hour or so earlier.

Patrick nodded, a look of recognition on his face. "Okay, so that's what all the sirens were about this morning. I was wondering what had happened. I hate that stretch of road. It's so dangerous, especially at night, and especially at this time of year with the deer roaming all over the place."

"They could very well have swerved to avoid hitting a deer," Anni said. "The skid marks would indicate they swerved to avoid something."

"You said *they*," Patrick said, reaching over to put a hand over hers, a look of concern on his face. "Just Charles is here in the ER? Is your aunt okay, Anni?"

She took a deep breath. "That's the weird part of it," she said. "Gloria wasn't at the scene of the accident."

Patrick leaned back in his chair and sighed. "Wow," he said. "It's unreal. All of it. It must have been horrible for you. Especially being the one to find your mother."

"It was," Anni said, the scene replaying in her mind. Arden, floating serenely in the water under the light of the moon, her pearls shimmering like a thousand stars. Anni had the feeling that scene would haunt her for the rest of her days.

All at once, the scene in Arden's bedroom in Wharton, her clothes laid out on her bed in eerie similarity to what she was wearing when

Anni found her floating in the creek, played out in her mind, superimposing itself on the image of Arden lying in the creek.

"She was wearing the same outfit," Anni murmured, her voice as low as a whisper.

Patrick furrowed his brow. "What outfit?"

"The one we found laid out on her bed yesterday," she said. "It was nearly identical. A long linen dress. Cream. Pearls."

A thought was swirling around in Anni's mind, a thought she didn't want to give voice to. But she couldn't silence it. It had to be said.

"Patrick, it's almost like that scene, the macabre display on her bed, was a warning."

Patrick took a sharp breath in. "Or a preview of what was to come."

Anni stood up from her chair and stepped over to the window. She needed a second to think. To gather her thoughts. Her mind was running in several directions at once.

"Both sisters went missing on the same day," she said finally.

Patrick was silent for a moment, letting it sink in.

"What does it mean, though?" he asked her. "Do you think someone is behind it? If not, that's an incredible coincidence."

Anni could hear her mother's voice as clearly as if she were speaking aloud, there, in the room. *I don't believe in coincidences.*

"My mother didn't believe there was anything random in the universe," Anni said, slowly. She gazed out the window, trying to formulate her thoughts. "What if it's more real than that?"

A look of dread crept onto Patrick's face then. He winced, and said, "You mean, what if the two Halla sisters going missing on the same day, the day after their mother's will was read, wasn't random at all. It wasn't some New Age occurrence, but something more earthly. And sinister."

"Exactly," Anni said, crossing her arms in front of her chest.

Anni's phone buzzed in her purse. She fished it out and furrowed her brow when she saw who was calling.

"Theo?" she said, into the phone. "Are you calling from the ER?"

"Get down here," Theo said in a harsh whisper and hung up.

Anni stared at her phone for a moment and then turned her eyes to Patrick. "Theo wants me to come down to the ER," she said, pushing herself up from her chair.

"I'll stay here with Arden, if you'd like," he said. "Talk to her. Keep her company."

Anni reached down and squeezed his shoulder. He put his hand on top of hers, and they locked eyes. Anni felt she had so much to say to this man, and yet, she could think of only two words. "Thank you."

◌❧◌

The ER was a scene of controlled chaos, doctors and nurses rushing here and there, the light from machines bathing the area in red and blue hues.

Anni was directed to a room where Charles lay on a bed, his head bandaged, his arm in a sling. He was hooked up to a bag of IV fluids and various monitors, and Anni could see he had a barrage of sensors stuck to his chest. His heart activity was displayed on one of the screens. Theo was standing at his bedside.

"Hello, dear," Charles said as Anni entered the room. His voice was as thin as tissue paper. His eyes fluttered closed, as though the exertion of those two words had taken a great toll on him.

"He's got several cracked ribs, a broken arm and shoulder, and a concussion," Theo reported. "They have him on a morphine drip for the pain. They're monitoring him for internal bleeding, but otherwise, he's in fairly good shape. Considering."

Anni replayed the scene of the accident in her mind, the car at the bottom of a steep embankment.

"Thank goodness," Anni said, managing a smile. She leaned down and put a hand on Charles's good arm.

"Gloria was in the car," Theo said, his eyes holding hers for a long moment.

She pulled a chair next to Charles's bed. "What happened, Charles? Can you remember anything?"

Charles opened his eyes with great effort and nodded, slowly. "We were driving along," he said. "It was dark. The road is terribly dangerous." He sighed. Anni noticed his words were slightly slurred. *The morphine,* she thought.

"Did you lose control of the car, or hit a deer?"

Charles shook his head, slightly. "A woman."

Theo raised his eyebrows at Anni.

"You hit a person? There was someone walking on the road at that time of night?"

"It was dark," Charles said. "All of a sudden, my headlights shone on a woman standing in the middle of the road."

Anni was silent for a moment. Was this the result of his medication? Or had there really been a woman on the road?

"Charles, what happened then? Did you hit her?"

"No," he said. "I swerved out of the way. I'd never hit Gloria."

Anni shot a look at Theo, and he raised his eyebrows at her as if to say, *See what I mean?*

"Gloria? She wasn't walking on the road, Charles. She was in the car with you, right?"

Charles nodded, tears trickling down his face. "She was. But she was also on the road. Standing there in the middle of the road. Wearing a blue dress."

The alarm on his heart monitor began to sound, and a nurse rushed in. "He needs to rest now," she said.

Anni leaned over his bed. "Is there anyone we can call for you, Charles? Any family? Children?"

"Gloria is my family," he said, his eyes filled with fear and dread. "Did I kill her?"

CHAPTER TWENTY-NINE

Anni and Theo walked out of the ER, a haze of confusion and questions hanging over them.

"It has to be the morphine. Or the trauma of the crash itself. Don't you think?"

Anni said the words, but something about Charles's face, his earnestness, the fear in his eyes, made a chill go up her spine. Thoughts were swimming around in Anni's head, strange and otherworldly ideas, that she didn't want to entertain. What if he really *had* seen Gloria standing on the road? An apparition of her? What if that had caused him to go over the cliff?

What was happening?

But she didn't raise any of these questions with Theo. She could see that her brother was fraying at the edges. He looked disheveled, his usual pristine and tidy appearance seeming a bit off, not quite right. Gone was the air of a Ralph Lauren ad, the cool confidence of someone at home in his own skin, in charge, a funny quip at the ready for any situation, replaced by an undercurrent of . . . of what? Anni couldn't quite put her finger on it. It was a blend of fear and disbelief, tinged with a dose of being fed up with it all.

When they turned down the hallway toward Arden's room, they saw LuAnn and Gary standing outside the door, talking with the police officer.

Anni couldn't help but smile. These were such good people. LuAnn hugged Anni and Theo.

"I don't know how much this lady has to endure," LuAnn said, shaking her head. "Or you two."

"Kids, we're so sorry," Gary said. "We heard about the crash on the cliff. Word is Gloria is unaccounted for?"

Anni got them up to speed on the latest, that, yes, Gloria's whereabouts were unknown, Charles was in the ER, and Arden was still in the same coma-like state she had been in when Anni had found her the night before. She let them know there was no real prognosis on Arden. No way of knowing when she'd open her eyes again. Or if she would.

"The ER doc said Charles could be released as early as tomorrow," Theo added. "They want to monitor him overnight, but his injuries aren't that severe, miraculously enough."

This was news to Anni. "Are we supposed to take him back to Metsan Valo?" she asked.

Theo shrugged. "I guess so. Where else would he go? He said he doesn't have other family, which is odd. I mean, there have to be people somewhere, right?"

Theo was right. It did seem odd. They didn't know much about the man, other than he had preppy taste in clothes, he seemed wealthy, and Gloria was besotted with him. Hence the background check. She wondered what, if anything, the chief had uncovered. Despite having myriad questions about him, the fact was, one thing was for certain: Charles was married to Gloria. That made him family, for better or for worse.

"We'll have to call Vicky and let her know," Anni said. "I guess it will be up to her to help take care of him until he gets back on his feet again?"

He eyed Anni and wagged a finger at her. "And, yes, it's up to Vicky to take care of him. It's not up to you to do everything, you know. If it makes sense for him to stay and recuperate at Metsan Valo, fine. But that means Vicky and Yale need to stay, too. He's their responsibility. Not yours."

Theo strode off down the hallway, the phone to his ear.

Anni took a deep breath and let it out in a long sigh. LuAnn took Anni's hands into hers. "Things are feeling out of control, aren't they, honey? It's a lot right now. First Taika's death, and now all of this."

Anni nodded, tears stinging the backs of her eyes.

"Gary and I were talking on the way over here," LuAnn went on. "We're going to organize a group to go in and clean up Arden's house, with your permission."

The vision of the abject mess in Arden's study, and in the basement room, swam through Anni's mind. She and Patrick hadn't made much of a dent in it the day before. She didn't relish going back and completing that task.

"Oh, LuAnn," Anni said, her voice cracking. "You're so kind to suggest it, but you don't have to do that."

"Kind, my behind," she said with a laugh. "You have enough on your plate right now. This is Wharton, honey. It's what we do. We help each other."

Gary cackled out a throaty laugh. "You bet we do," he said. "It's what life is all about, doll."

The sense of security, of a family of strangers, of the kindness of neighbors in Wharton was wrapping around Anni and holding her tight.

"And, listen now," LuAnn went on. "There's no telling when Arden is going to come out of this thing. Might be tomorrow, might be three weeks from now. That's what I understand."

Anni nodded. "That's right."

"We'll organize a crew to come and sit with her. Take turns. So you don't have to be sitting vigil at her bedside twenty-four-seven. They say people in comas can hear what's going on around them. We'll talk to her. Read to her. Tell her the latest scandals and town gossip."

"Beth can bring some books," Gary piped up. "And movies! That way, she'll have stimulation all of the time."

Anni looked from one to the other of them, tears falling down her face. She felt lightened, from the inside. "You two," she said. "You're too much."

Gary laughed at this. "Too much of what, that's the question!"

Theo came walking down the hallway just then, slipping his phone back into his pocket.

"How's Vicky holding up?" Anni asked. "I assume there's no news on Gloria?"

Theo ran a hand through his hair. "No news. And she's a mess, if you want to know the truth." He sighed and leaned against the wall. "We should probably get back in there and sit with Mom," he said, letting out a great yawn and closing his eyes.

Gary squinted at him. "When's the last time you ate?"

"Or slept?" LuAnn added.

Anni echoed their concern. Theo looked exhausted.

He shrugged. "I didn't sleep much last night," he said. Anni knew the feeling.

LuAnn and Gary exchanged a glance. "You two aren't planning to go back to the island tonight, are you?"

Anni shrugged. "I packed a bag just in case we'd need to stay."

"Me too," Theo said. "I figured we'd get rooms across the street at the Salmon Bay Inn."

LuAnn's eyes popped, and Gary shook his head.

"Not possible, kids," LuAnn said. "They're full up this week. Some kind of environmental conference put on by the college."

So that was why the town was buzzing with people as tourist season was winding down, Anni realized.

"Come back to Wharton with us," LuAnn went on. "The suite at the inn is available, and you can stay in it at no charge."

"I've got pot roast in the oven," Gary added, raising his eyebrows. "It's been cooking on low all day."

Anni and Theo conferred, silently.

"Are you sure?" Anni asked LuAnn.

LuAnn shook her head. "We don't have guests in the suite right now, and you are more than welcome."

It seemed like a very good idea. Being taken care of by LuAnn and Gary at the inn would be a relief, even if they had to drive twenty miles down the shoreline to get there.

Anni turned to Theo. "I'll stay here with Mom for a few more hours," she said. "But you go ahead with them now. You're beat."

"Are you sure?" Theo asked her. She could see he was really hoping for an affirmative answer.

"Absolutely," Anni said, and she could feel a tangible sense of relief from her brother. It was all getting to be a bit too much for him. That was clear to her.

"LuAnn, maybe you and Gary could take Theo with you?" Anni continued. "That way, I'll have a car here when I'm ready to leave the hospital."

"Absolutely," Gary said. "We should be getting back now. Gotta check that pot roast."

Theo pushed open Arden's hospital room door and slipped inside, presumably to say goodbye for the night. Just then, Patrick emerged from the room. The four of them stood out in the hallway, giving son and mother their privacy.

"She was resting comfortably," Patrick said. "I read the newspaper to her. The doctor was in and said there's no change. He's going to find you later to give you an update."

"We'll give you some gossip magazines next time," LuAnn said with a laugh. "I think she'd probably like that better than the daily news."

Theo emerged from their mother's room, tears in his eyes. He threw Anni the car keys.

"Are you sure about this, Anni?" he asked. "I can stay."

Anni shook her head. "Go. Have a good dinner. Take a hot bath. I'll be there in a couple of hours, and we can get a good night's sleep before coming back here tomorrow."

Theo enveloped his sister in a hug. "I may be drunk when you get there."

"I'd expect nothing less," she said, giving his arm an extra squeeze.

As Theo, LuAnn, and Gary headed down the hall toward the elevator, Gary turned back to Anni and Patrick.

"You kids get something to eat, too," he said, wagging a finger at them. "Do not, I repeat, do not, go to the hospital cafeteria. The brewpub on Main Street has great food."

Anni watched the elevator door close as Theo gave her a small wave. The hallway seemed especially empty then. It struck Anni how fractured her family had become in the blink of an eye. Taika, gone. Arden, lying in a hospital bed, unresponsive. Gloria, missing after a strange and terrible accident. Yale, resentful, Vicky, unglued. All in the space of less than a fortnight.

Like it was a deliberate attack on their family.

CHAPTER THIRTY

Patrick and Anni sat with Arden for the next hour or so in her still, quiet room. She was so calm, lying just as she had been when Anni had found her. The serenity on her face seemed almost otherworldly to Anni. The look of utter peace . . . It wasn't a blank look as it would be if her body was simply an empty shell. She had a countenance of contentment. As though she were an enchanted princess in a fairy tale, knowing she'd be awakened someday and waiting patiently for the time to come.

Patrick read aloud from a book he had picked up in the hospital library. Anni leaned back in her chair and listened, nodding off more than once.

She fell into a fitful, shallow sleep. Her dreams were hazy and jumbled. Faces materialized and swam into view in the darkness behind her eyes. Voices were all around her, whispering in her ear.

"Tell my husband the will is in the third drawer of my desk. The third drawer. He won't think to look there."

A cold hand clutched at her arm. "Get me out of here," the voice hissed. "I need to go home."

"I'm all alone. I'm cold."

And then there were a thousand more, one on top of the other, a cacophony of last wishes, anguished cries, fearful pleas, resigned words. The keening of the dead echoed in her ears.

Anni awoke with a start.

"Anni," Patrick said to her, his voice low.

Anni pushed her hair back from her face with her hand and blinked a couple of times. "Wow, I really zonked out there, didn't I?"

Patrick smiled. "You did," he said. "It doesn't bode well for my oratorical skills."

Anni shuddered and rubbed her arms. She looked around, fearful of seeing the specters swirling through the room.

Patrick eyed her, a look of concern on his face. He closed his book and set it on Arden's tray table. "How about getting something to eat?" he suggested. "A walk down to the brewpub in the fresh air will do you good."

Anni wasn't sure she should leave Arden. She was about to say so when a nursing aide pushed open the door.

"Knock, knock!" she said, her eyes bright. "I'm here to freshen your mom up and work her muscles a bit. Is now a good time for that?"

Anni stood up and stretched. "A perfect time, actually," she said. "We were just heading out to get a bite of dinner. Is that okay?"

The aide smiled. "Absolutely. I was going to ask you to step out, anyway. I'll freshen her up, put on a new gown, and we'll change her sheets, too. So you've got some time."

Okay, then. Leaning over Arden, Anni said, "Mom, I'll be back later to tuck you in."

Out in the fresh air, Anni realized Patrick was right—the walk down to the brewpub did feel good. A nip of fall swirled through the air, previewing the season to come. Anni breathed it in and felt it infusing her body with the scent of the lake, turning leaves, and the hint of apples that always seemed to waft through the air here.

At the entrance, Patrick pushed open the door, and the two of them walked into a pub that might have been transported there from England or Scotland. There was an enormous curved bar with a gleaming wooden bar back that was intricately carved. Its swirls and whorls shone in the soft light of the Tiffany-esque lamps that hung above it. Wooden tables dotted the floor, and leather booths stood against the wall. It definitely had an old-world vibe, Anni thought, as the two of them sat on a couple of leather stools at the end of the bar. Much better than the hospital cafeteria, that was for certain.

A chardonnay for her, a Scottish ale for him, and they clinked their glasses in a toast before taking a sip. "To peace and boredom for your family, Anni," Patrick said. "You all deserve that, about now. You've had your share of . . . incidents for the time being, I'd say."

He wasn't kidding. She took a sip of the wine. It tasted restorative after this long day. Long few days.

"So what's next?" he asked her. "Do you even know at this point?"

Anni had to admit she didn't. "I guess it all depends on how long my mother is going to be in the hospital," she said, working the situation out in her mind as she spoke. "I'm feeling sort of in limbo. It doesn't make sense to go all the way back and forth to the island every day if Mom is here."

"You're at LuAnn's tonight, right?"

"We are," she said. "But if it's going to be a week or two, or longer, I guess we can stay in the house on Front Street. And for that matter, I don't even know how long my brother can stay, period. He has a wife and a business to run back in Chicago. I don't imagine he can be here indefinitely."

Her situation was different. She didn't have anything to hurry back to. Or anyone. She had been working as Jean-Paul's assistant at the university, but since the breakup, she had been at loose ends.

For Anni, everything depended on how long they expected this coma, or whatever it was, to last. A terrible thought was scratching at the edges of her mind. She didn't want to give it a voice, let it in. But it was there, scratching, making itself heard. What if Arden never woke up? What would happen then, to her, to Theo, to their family?

They were already fractured. Could they survive losing Mummo and Arden within such a short time of each other? And where was Gloria?

As that idea was draping a black shroud over her psyche, she wondered: Long-term coma patients didn't take up hospital beds, did they? From what Anni knew, hospital beds were for people they were actively treating, who were actively recovering, or not. But people in lengthy comas were usually transferred to a care facility or hospice, weren't they? Anni didn't know enough about the condition to even have a sense of what would come next. Would they suggest Arden go to a nursing home of some kind? When would that happen? Would she and Theo let it happen?

"I want to take her back to Metsan Valo," Anni said, answering aloud the question she was mulling in her own head, and surprising herself with her clarity. "We could hire nurses to care for her there. If they're not doing anything for her at the hospital but keeping her comfortable, I don't see why we can't bring her home."

"I've got to admit I don't know much about this kind of situation," Patrick said. "And it sounds like the doctors don't know much, either. Specific to Arden, that is."

Over dinner, their conversation drifted to other things. Anni was grateful for the distraction. Patrick was good at that, Anni was learning. He could infuse normalcy into the strangest of situations. Something told her that quality would come in handy if the two of them would be spending more time together. Metsan Valo was steeped in strange. She eyed him as she took a sip of wine. Would they be spending more time together? Anni decided to put that notion on the back burner, for the moment. She had more important things to focus on than what might be a budding romance with Patrick Saari. Still. It was a nice distraction. A beginning of something. A possibility.

They chattered on about politics, LuAnn and Gary's sweet late-in-life love story, and the changes Anni had noticed in Salmon Bay that had happened in the decade she had been away.

"I felt exactly the same way," Patrick said. "It's like I expected this area to be just like it was when I visited with my parents when I was younger. When I moved here a few years ago, Wharton was the same as it always had been, but in Salmon Bay, I saw that time had marched on without me. It didn't even ask! So much new development. The car dealerships were a special abomination."

After Anni had enjoyed her salad and Patrick gobbled up his fish and chips, they walked in the twilight back to the hospital. As they were about to enter the doors, she turned to him.

"You don't have to stay with me," Anni said. "It's getting late, and you've been here all day. You probably want to get home to feed Pascal."

Patrick smiled at this. "I know he's watching the clock right now, tapping his paw, impatiently wondering where in the name of Lassie I am," he said, chuckling. "But I'm happy to stay. I don't want you to be here alone."

Anni put a hand on his arm. "It's okay. It really is. I'm not going to stay very long myself. I want to get back to Wharton before the deer turn the highway into a gauntlet."

"Okay," Patrick said, enveloping her in a hug. Their faces lingered near each other's, cheek to cheek.

"Thank you for coming today," Anni said, softly, into his ear. "It meant the world to me."

"I'm finding it hard to stay away from you, Anni," he said. He pulled back to look into her eyes. "Is that okay with you?"

"It's more than okay," she said, kissing him on the cheek. So much for putting romance on the back burner.

They shared a silent moment then. An understanding. This was the beginning of something. Anni knew it, felt it deeply in her bones. They both knew it. She could see, in her mind's eye, or imagination, scenes played out: walks along the lake, quiet dinners on his rooftop. Watching the sunset at Metsan Valo. She wondered if Patrick was imagining the same.

But for now, she watched him walk to his car in the parking lot. He turned and put up a hand in a wave. "Let me know when you get to Wharton," he said. "I just want to know you've gotten there safely."

"I will," she called out to him. "I'll be careful." They didn't need another Halla car to go over the cliff.

⚜

Anni rounded the corner to Arden's wing and saw the officer was still there, reading something on his phone. He looked up when he heard Anni's footsteps as she walked down the hallway.

"Hi," she said to him. "How's everything here?"

"All quiet," he said.

All at once, something occurred to her. "I'm sorry!" she said. "I should've offered to get you some dinner while I was out."

He shook his head. "Kind of you, but not necessary. I'm getting relieved in about an hour, and my wife has a pot of spaghetti on the stove."

It sounded nice, being taken care of like that. Knowing someone was waiting at home. It had only been a few months since she and Jean-Paul had split, but even when they were together, she had never felt taken care of, not really. She had always been the one taking care of him that way.

"Thank you for being here all day," she said to the officer. "My family appreciates it."

She opened Arden's door and stepped inside, and there was Arden, lying just as she had been. The nursing aide had gone, and Anni noticed Arden's hair was freshly brushed, and she was wearing a clean gown. Anni sank down into the chair by her mother's bedside.

"Hi, Mom," she said, the sound of her voice disturbing the quiet. "I had dinner tonight with Patrick Saari. Just thought I'd let you know a little romance might be brewing. I think Taika would be pleased, don't you?"

No reaction, not that Anni expected one.

She reached out and tucked a lock of Arden's famously unruly hair behind her ear. "I don't know what's going on with this family, Mom," Anni said, a tear escaping from her eye and running down her cheek. She whisked it away. "You fell into this weird, unexplainable coma, and Gloria vanished into thin air. On the same day. What's happening to the Halla women? What kind of strange force is raining down on us?"

Those words caught in Anni's throat as she said them. More and more, she was realizing it did feel like that. An enchantment. And not the good kind. This felt evil and intentional. Anni was trying to fight against that notion, but it was winning.

"Mom, I know you're in there somewhere," she said. "Come back now. Things are getting out of control, and I could really use your help."

Still nothing. Anni sat back in her chair and sighed. She gazed out the window and noticed darkness was falling. She was not relishing that twisty-turny drive back to Wharton in the dark, knowing there wasn't so much as a streetlight for miles between Salmon Bay and Wharton. A shiver went up her spine. *That's it*, she thought. *Time to go.* She pushed herself up from the chair, leaned over, and gave her mother a kiss on the forehead.

"I love you, Mom," she said. All at once, an idea floated into her mind. It was as clear as if her mother had said it aloud. "Okay, Mom. I'll stop by the house and get you some pajamas to wear instead of this ghastly hospital gown. The cream-colored satin ones. In the second drawer in your dresser."

With that, she left the room and walked toward the elevator, her footsteps echoing in the empty hallway.

CHAPTER THIRTY-ONE

Anni climbed into the car and started it up, taking a deep breath. She could do this. It was just a road.

She drove slowly through town. Once outside of the city limits, darkness fell around her. No stars twinkled in the sky; no moon shone down. The overcast cloud cover took care of any light Mother Nature might have provided her. She'd have even welcomed fireflies at that point.

Anni flipped on her high beams and loosened her too-tight grip on the steering wheel. It was silly, she thought. The only part of the highway that was treacherous was the stretch just outside of Wharton. She had miles to go before hitting that, and once she did, she'd slow down and inch her way along. Nothing to be afraid of. She'd get there.

She passed the marsh. And there were the farm fields. There were the orchards. The landscape was more familiar now. Not threatening at all. She exhaled. Maybe this wouldn't be so bad.

Anni was keeping her eyes peeled for deer and other animals that might be creeping around the roadway. Hitting a deer could be catastrophic anywhere, but near the cliffs, deadly. She was so focused on scanning the landscape that she didn't realize she was nearing the dreaded part of her drive until she was upon it, taking the first curve.

She slowed to a crawl and sat a bit straighter in her seat, white-knuckling the wheel. A twist, then a turn, then another twist. She was doing it. Slowly, methodically, yes, but moving forward. Getting closer to Wharton.

Around the next turn, eyes shone in the glare of her headlights, small eyes, low to the ground. A raccoon, maybe. Or a fox. It made no attempt to run into her path. It simply watched the car as it went by, letting Anni pass without incident. Anni felt a chill go through her.

She didn't notice the area where Charles and Gloria had gone off the road. It was too dark to see the skid marks, she supposed, and she was grateful for that. She had no wish to see those awful, black slashes in the dirt.

Time slowed to a crawl. It seemed like an eternity to Anni, but it was only minutes of her inching along, twisting and turning, until the road finally straightened out and moved inland from the cliff. She exhaled a long breath she hadn't even realized she had been holding, and loosened her grip on the wheel. She had done it. She was safe.

Just then, a deer jumped directly into her path. Its face, illuminated by her headlights, was a mask of panic and fear, its eyes wild. Anni knew better than to swerve to miss a deer. The conventional wisdom in these northern towns was "hit the deer, swerve for the moose." That was because you're likely to survive an impact with a deer, but swerving to miss it could send your car out of control. *Over a cliff,* she thought with a shudder. Hitting a moose was more dangerous than swerving out of its path. It would total your car and you along with it. She had heard that adage so many times that her reaction was instinctual. She slammed on her brakes and closed her eyes, bracing for an impact that didn't come. She opened her eyes to see only an empty roadway. No sign of the deer, which had disappeared into the night. Anni scanned the sides of the road for others. When you saw one deer, there were likely to be more following behind. But she didn't see anything. Just the dark night.

Anni could feel her heart beating in her throat. *That was a close one.* She took a few deep breaths to regain her composure, gently pressed on the accelerator, and the car began moving again. Would this drive never end? It was less than thirty miles from Wharton to Salmon Bay, and yet Anni felt like she had been driving since the beginning of time. She made a mental note to leave the hospital well before dusk every day, if indeed Arden had an extended stay there, so she wouldn't have to travel this road again at night.

Finally, she pulled into the outskirts of Wharton, past the lovely Victorian-style bungalows that lined the streets there. The streetlights were replicas of old gas lamps of the past, and they flickered a warm, yellowish glow. Lights were on in many of the homes, illuminating family time inside their snug four walls, and Anni could see manicured gardens, buckets of deep yellow, red, and orange mums signaling the end of summer and beginning of fall. Some houses even had corn stalks and pumpkins. *The seasons are changing*, she thought, *in many more ways than one.* Anni rolled down her window to smell the fresh Wharton air, which people who had respiratory problems came from all over the country to drink in. It whooshed into Anni's lungs and lowered her racing pulse and pounding blood pressure in an instant. Home.

As she drove through the streets toward LuAnn's inn, she got the idea to swing by the house on Front Street. Arden wanted those pajamas, Anni was sure of it. She didn't know how, but she was sure. She'd stop by now, she reasoned, rather than having to remember it in the morning.

But, when she turned onto Front Street, she took a quick breath in and furrowed her brow, scowling at the house at the end of the block. She could plainly see a light burning in Arden's bedroom on the second floor. The rest of the house was dark, but for that light. Had she and Patrick left it on when they were there the day before? Or, was the person who broke in to send Arden's library into disarray and mess with her head in the process back for round three?

Anni pulled to a stop in front of the house. She was about to call Nick Stone when she heard the music.

She stepped out of the car to listen closer. It seemed to be coming from Arden's bedroom window, which, Anni now saw, was open. Anni recognized the familiar voice of a singer Arden loved when Anni and Theo were small. Carole King. Anni recognized the song. It was from Arden's favorite album, *Tapestry*. She had played it incessantly, dancing around the living room with her two toddlers. Anni and Theo had all the songs on that album memorized before they entered kindergarten. It was the soundtrack to their lives.

And now it was wafting through the air as if it were on Arden's record player, in their living room, long ago. Anni could hear scratches in the vinyl. The sound was decidedly not up to today's standards. But the music and the singing grabbed at Anni's heart and squeezed.

But then, there was something else. Anni cocked her head and listened. A voice, singing along with the songs on the record. Arden's voice.

Anni stole up to the darkened front porch and tried the door. It was open. She entered the house and held her breath, taking careful, silent steps into the living room. She hadn't imagined it, then. The music was still playing. Arden was still singing along. It was coming from upstairs. Could it possibly be that, somehow, Arden was there?

All thoughts of calling the police flew out of her mind. Anni crept up the stairs. Arden's bedroom door was closed, but Anni could see the light shining out from under it. The music was louder here. The singing, out of tune, just as Arden's had always been. It made Anni smile to remember her mother belting out her favorite songs, terribly off key and not caring one bit about it. It was about the experience of it, for Arden. Singing for the joy of being swept up in the moment, no matter if you were on key or not. Arden had been the epitome of "dance like nobody is watching" back then, in so many more ways than one.

Anni stopped at the bedroom door for a moment to listen, as though the whole thing were happening in her childhood somehow and might fade away, dissipate into nothingness, if she opened the door. And she desperately wanted to go on hearing her mother's voice. She wished she would step into her childhood when she opened that door.

Just then, Anni heard the scratchy sounds of the needle coming to the end of the vinyl. And the sound of someone turning it over. There was a person in the room. It wasn't in Anni's imagination. It wasn't a strange and mystical trip back in time. This was real.

She opened the door and gasped at what she saw.

It was a woman, with her back to Anni. She was turning the record over on the record player and humming a tune. She was wearing the same clothes Arden had had on when Anni had found her in the creek. A linen dress, dripping wet. Water was pooling on the hardwood floor where she stood. A long strand of pearls around her neck. A garland of flowers crowning her head.

"Mom?" Anni squeaked out, and the woman whirled around.

"You're here, darling!" she said. "Come and dance with me!"

Her face was made up in full 1960s flower-power fashion, blue eyeshadow and all. The lipstick was haphazard. And she had a terrible, angry gash on her forehead. Anni now saw blood on her dress. One arm was hanging limp, at an odd angle.

"Gloria," Anni said as softly as she could, walking up to her aunt, step by careful step, as though she were approaching a wild animal.

Gloria spun around again, teetering for her balance, when the music on the other side of the album began to play.

"I've always loved this song," she said, her voice now turning high, like that of a little child. "Mama loves it, too."

"Gloria," Anni said, holding her arms out in front of her. "It's me. Your niece, Annalise."

"Anna, Anna, Anna-leeeeese," Gloria sang out, just as Theo had when they were children. "Anna-fofanna." She turned back to the record player and began dancing to the music.

What was this?

Anni stepped back a few paces and drew her phone from her purse. She dialed Nick Stone. "I'm at Front Street," she whispered. "I found Gloria. She needs an ambulance."

CHAPTER THIRTY-TWO

Anni watched as Gloria morphed from Arden to Theo, to she herself, slipping into their different personalities and vocalizations as if she were trying on sweaters at the mall.

"Darling," she said, "we should really get some dinner, don't you think? It's about that time, isn't it? We can't sing the night away, for goodness' sake! What would you kids like?"

She was looking at Anni with an expression, for all the world, that was exactly like Arden's, down to the raised eyebrows, cocked head, and bemused countenance, as though dinner was the most complicated and vexing decision in the world. Anni remembered having to take charge of it at a very early age.

"Macaroni and cheese?" Anni offered, casting a quick glance out the window, hoping to see the chief's car pull up at any moment.

"You always want mac and cheese," Gloria said, in a lower tone, her face taking on Theo's mock annoyance, with a twinkle in his eye betraying his humor. She had him down.

"Please come sit over here," Anni said, gingerly grasping for Gloria's good arm, guiding her to the bed. "You're so tired from dancing."

Gloria sank down onto Arden's bed, wet clothes and all.

"Oh, you're right," Gloria said, in a tone that sounded more like Anni. "All of this on my shoulders. It's too much. Why do I have to handle everything?"

Gloria's arm hung at her side. Anni noticed her shoulder was out of joint.

"Are you in pain?" Anni asked her.

"Pain? Oh, heavens no, darling," she said. "Why would I be in pain?"

"Do you remember what happened? The crash?"

Gloria looked at her with utter confusion in her eyes. And then she stood up from the bed and began dancing, in slow circles, singing along with the music.

Nick was in the doorway a moment later. Anni hadn't heard the car pull up, hadn't heard him enter the house. The two of them exchanged a glance.

He cleared his throat. "Gloria?"

She whirled around and smiled when she saw him. "You're a hand-some man," she said. "Come and dance with me." She held out one of her arms, as the other flopped at her side. As she smiled broadly, Anni saw blood on her teeth. The gash in her forehead gaped open like a giant maw.

"Why don't you come with me instead?" Nick said, holding out a hand to her. She took it, and smiled coquettishly, a blush coloring her ashen cheeks.

"Where are we going?" she asked, her voice like that of a child.

"For a ride," Nick said.

"A ride? Together?"

Anni saw the lights of an ambulance turn onto Front Street.

"Yes," Nick said. "You and me. Come on. The car's pulling up now."

"I think I'd like that," she said, allowing Nick to lead her out of the room. He caught Anni's eye, and so many unspoken words and questions passed between them.

Anni followed as Nick led Gloria down the stairs. By that time, the EMTs had a stretcher on the front lawn.

"Why don't you relax here?" Nick said. "You'll be comfortable for the drive."

Gloria smiled at him and did as she was told, sinking onto the stretcher. Blood was oozing from the wound on her forehead. The EMT leaned forward to clean and bandage it, but Gloria pulled away abruptly.

"I beg your pardon, sir," she said. "Exactly what do you think you're doing?"

The EMT looked to Nick. "You've got a cut on your forehead, Gloria," Nick said, gently, but with an undercurrent of authority. "This nice gentleman is going to clean it up for you. You'll feel better when there's a bandage on it."

She nodded. "Very well," she said. "He's taking care of me."

"You let him do his job, now, Gloria," Nick said to her as the EMTs loaded the stretcher into the ambulance. In a moment, it took off, lights and sirens blazing. Anni watched as it turned at the end of the block and made its way up the hill toward the highway.

"I called Vicky on the way over here," Nick said to her. "She and her husband are on their way to the hospital right now."

Anni nodded. An emptiness seemed to fill her up inside. A numbness, pushing everything else away. She tried to think of something to say to Nick in response, but words were just out of reach.

"That must not have been fun," Nick said, putting a hand on her arm. "I'm sure you're feeling pretty stunned right now. But you found her. You may well have saved her life."

"It was terrifying," she said.

He took a deep breath. "There's something else you should know," he said.

Anni was silent, not wanting one more shoe to drop. But then, there it was.

"Charles Wellington is an alias," Nick said, gently, as if to soften the blow. "The prints match up to a long-time con man, Larry Smith. Anni, the man has made a career out of targeting rich widows and bilking them out of their money."

Anni went cold, deep on the inside. She knew Gloria would inherit Arden's money from Mummo if Arden died. And Charles would inherit the whole thing if Gloria died. But he would not, could not, have driven over the cliff to accomplish it. This had to be something else. Maybe he *had* married Gloria for her money, but he surely wouldn't have risked his own life . . . would he?

"Listen," he said, squeezing her arm. "I'm headed to the hospital. We can circle back on this Charles business. Right now, he is safely in the hospital. Not going anywhere."

Anni managed a smile and watched as the chief slid into his car and drove out of sight.

She put her phone to her ear and called Theo.

"We found Gloria," she said, her voice wavering. "She's in an ambulance right now."

"What?" Theo said, his voice raising an octave. "Where?"

"The house on Front Street," Anni said.

"How?" He couldn't seem to formulate complete sentences.

"I don't know," she said. "I'm coming to pick you up right now."

A few moments later, Anni was pulling into the parking lot in front of LuAnn's restaurant and inn, which had begun its life as a boarding-house more than a century earlier. It was a house that seemed to exist out of time.

Anni walked in, and saw it was exactly how it had been when she had last seen it, more than a decade ago. The restaurant on the first floor looked like a time-traveling 1950s diner. The linoleum bar, faced with red pleather barstools, held beer taps where the soda fountains used to be. A mishmash of tables, some tile, some wooden, some linoleum, populated the dining room. Old newspaper clippings of famous

Wharton happenings lined the walls, next to photos of celebrities from a bygone era. It was completely LuAnn, from soup to nuts. But that was where the diner comparison ended. Her husband, Gary, was the chef, cooking up some of the best meals that were decidedly not diner fare, and their daily happy hour, attended by town residents, inn owners, shopkeepers, and visitors alike, was legendary.

In a town of haunted places, LuAnn's was reportedly among the most haunted, with spirits regularly floating through the dining room and mischievous ghosts bedeviling guests by hiding their shoes or hairbrushes. Nobody meant any harm, as LuAnn liked to say. They were just passers-through.

Anni found Theo, LuAnn, and Gary sitting at the bar. The rest of the place was empty.

"Let's go!" Anni said, annoyed that he hadn't been waiting outside for her.

"Where?" Theo asked her, taking a sip of his drink.

She squinted at him. "What do you mean, where? Back to the hospital! Gloria's on her way there right now."

"Vicky and Yale are catching the next ferry," Theo said, a gentle tone in his voice. "I talked to her just now."

"And?"

"And, you've been on call at the hospital all day, not only sitting at Mom's bedside, but tending to Charles, too," he said. "It's Vicky's mother who is in the ER right now. It's her turn."

Anni couldn't believe what she was hearing, from Theo of all people. "Gloria is seriously messed up, Theo," she said. "It was scary. We have no idea how she got from the crash site to the house. It's not too far, so she probably walked. But she was completely whacked out. Not making any sense. It was like Gloria's spirit, her self, wasn't even there. She was morphing into Mom. You. Me. She was up in Mom's bedroom listening to Carole King records."

Theo winced, both of them, no doubt, remembering what Arden had told them the day of the reading of Mummo's will. How Gloria would assume other people's personalities. Their affections. Even their taste in clothes.

Gary and LuAnn exchanged worried glances. Gary pushed his chair back and retreated behind the bar.

"That's so sad, honey, and must have been awful to go through," LuAnn said. "But it's also true you made that drive between here and Sammy twice today, once in the dark. Your mother is resting comfortably, I'm told. Your cousin is on her way to see to her own mother. The Halla sisters are being taken care of in fine style. The way I see it, you're off the clock. What was it you said to your brother earlier today? Take a long bath, relax, get a good night's sleep, and get back at it in the morning."

Gary reemerged with a tray holding beer for Theo and a glass of wine for Anni, along with a decadent-looking dessert. "I'm assuming you had dinner at the brewpub, but the brownies are warm, and I've got the vanilla ice cream on top. Whaddya say?"

Anni slid down onto a barstool. She had to admit it. She was beat. And beaten. She didn't have any fight left in her and knew, deep down, they were right. She could take a few hours off. And she had no urge to make that dangerous drive yet again, in the dark.

"It takes a village, Anni," Theo said. "We've got one right now. You and I will rest up tonight and go to the hospital in the morning, bright eyed and bushy tailed."

She looked at her brother, her eyes brimming with tears. She took a spoonful of the brownie–ice cream concoction Gary had put in front of her. Heavenly. Only then did she notice her hand was shaking. "I'll call Vicky to give her the details on what I know," she said, reaching down for her purse.

Theo glanced at the clock on the wall. "She's probably on the ferry right now, but there's cell reception."

LuAnn and Gary retreated discreetly to the kitchen in order for Anni to make that call.

"Hey," Vicky said.

Anni could hear the chugging of the ferry's engines in the background, and the sound of the wind. She could also hear the fear in her cousin's voice. The same sort of primal fear that had overtaken Anni the moment she had found Arden floating in the creek. The fear and horror of realizing your mother's vulnerability, that she wasn't invincible after all, and that you might not be able to help. It was the moment child turned into parent, caretaker, and protector. It was the moment that changed a child, and a family's dynamic, forever. Vicky was in that moment now, and she had felt it before, learning the news of her father's illness and watching while that illness marched over him, eroded him, and finally took him. But it wasn't the same. Gloria had been there, blocking Vicky from the harsh winds. Now it was Vicky's turn to stand in the winds of change, to step into a role she desperately didn't want, to accept the inevitabilities of what happened when parents aged, became ill or vulnerable. Nobody wanted to accept that role. Anni certainly didn't. But it was not their choice. It was what it was.

Anni told her cousin, as gently as she could, about finding Gloria in the house on Front Street.

"She's confused, Vic," Anni said. "She knew me, but . . . didn't. It's hard to explain. She was probably in some sort of shock from the trauma."

"Was she hurt?"

"Yes," Anni said. "She has a laceration on her forehead, and I think her shoulder is dislocated. That's what I could see, anyway. But remember, she got to the house in Wharton from the crash site under her own power. She had to have walked there herself."

"Okay," Vicky said, sounding calmer now that the realization of what she was facing had settled in around her. "The ferry is just about to dock. I'll call you from the hospital when we know more."

Anni wondered whether or not to tell Vicky about what she had learned about Charles earlier from Nick Stone. In the end, she kept it to herself. That was news best reported in person. She would tell Vicky what she knew the next day at the hospital.

"Remember how twisty the road is just outside of Wharton," Anni said. "Be careful on that stretch."

After talking to her cousin, Anni was convinced that letting go a little and allowing Vicky and Yale to take some responsibility was the right thing to do. Or, at least, an acceptable thing to do. Yale was closer to Charles than any of them—the two had apparently bonded right away—and Yale would shepherd the process of transporting him back to Metsan Valo the next day. Which, given what she now knew, raised more questions than it answered. In the end, Theo was right. Gloria was Vicky's mother, not theirs. It wasn't up to Anni to do everything.

Just then, Anni thought that maybe her family wasn't fracturing after all. Just transforming. The old ways were cracking and falling to earth like shards of clay. Something new was emerging. The elders were moving to the side. First Mummo, and now the Halla sisters. The children were becoming the parents. Whether they wanted to or not.

CHAPTER THIRTY-THREE

Later, Anni was soaking in the hot tub in one of the bathrooms of the two-level suite she and Theo were sharing for the night. She had been in the restaurant at LuAnn's many times growing up but had never been upstairs to the rooms LuAnn rented on a daily, weekly, or monthly basis. The building had begun its life as a boardinghouse for the hardworking fishermen and loggers back in the day when Metsan Valo was new, and Anni liked to think that some of the workers who built it, or maybe even her great-grandparents themselves, had stayed in this welcoming—if slightly eerie—place.

The "taken out of time" vibe the restaurant downstairs gave off was alive and well up in this part of the house, too. Although the inn was more than a century old, the suite she and Theo were sharing looked more like it could've been plucked out of a Northwoods lodge. Even Metsan Valo itself. Hardwood paneling on the walls, a floor-to-ceiling fireplace, overstuffed furniture.

Anni soaked in the bubbling water and tried to read a book she had found on the bookshelf in the living room, but couldn't concentrate enough to follow the story. She had a story of her own swirling around her that was seeming to be more fantastic and stranger than anything somebody else could dream up.

Vicky had called earlier to report that Gloria had been given pain medication and was resting in a room just down the hall from Arden's. Her dislocated shoulder had been set, the gash on her forehead cleaned and bandaged. Charles was sleeping, and Arden was in her same serene state. All was quiet at the hospital. Vicky was planning to stay with her mother for a few more hours, in case she woke up.

So everything was set. Anni was off the clock.

Soaking in the warm tub, with nothing to handle, Anni found herself thinking back to the oddness of the night before. Martin and Meri, the book of their family. The images of her ancestors—if that was what they were—in the great room at Metsan. All that otherworldliness in stark contrast to what was happening in the real world. Arden in the hospital. Gloria off the deep end. It was too much to sort out at one time. Anni decided she'd deal with the mystical Metsan Valo when she was back there. Right now, she had to be focused on the here and now. For Arden. For Gloria. For her family.

Anni's eyes were just drifting closed when they were jolted open by a loud bang. What in the world? Maybe Theo had dropped something downstairs. In any case, Anni figured it was time to climb out of the tub. The last thing she wanted to do was fall asleep and slip under the surface. Another Halla woman going under, so to speak.

She toweled off and pulled on the pajamas she had thought to bring from Metsan Valo that morning. It seemed like such a long time ago that she was there. A lifetime. She saw a white fluffy robe hanging on the back of the bathroom door, and pulled that around her, too, before padding out into the chilly hallway to see what Theo was up to. Maybe they could watch a movie together.

The suite was dark. How long had she been in the tub? He must've already turned in for the night. Anni wondered what time it was. She poked her head into his room—sure enough. He was sawing logs. So much for that movie.

She made her way down the hall to her room and climbed into the antique four-poster, its dark, intricately carved wood set off by a deep blue-and-red floral comforter. Settling into the nest of pillows, Anni thought there was little wonder why people would want to rent this place for the summer. Ultimate comfort. She grabbed the remote off her nightstand and flipped on the news. After a few minutes of local headlines, it was time for the weather segment.

"Severe thunderstorms will be moving into Wharton County tomorrow night," the meteorologist said. Anni sat up to listen. The weather could turn dark and dangerous this time of year, with the winds whipping the lake into an angry, lethal frenzy. It wasn't uncommon for storms to kick up out of nowhere, catching boaters unaware, threatening to take their crafts to the bottom. Anytime storms were actually in the forecast, Anni knew the ferries would stop running. They wouldn't be going back to Metsan Valo the next night, if the forecast was accurate. Anni made a mental note to ask LuAnn if they could stay one more night. She had to admit, she liked the pampering. But they could also move to the house on Front Street, despite the mess in Arden's study. Another mental note: get a locksmith there tomorrow to change all the locks.

Too much to remember, she thought with a groan. She slid out of bed and grabbed her purse and opened it, finding an envelope and a pen inside. She wrote:

✓ *Thunderstorm, P.M.*
✓ *Stay another night at LuAnn's*
✓ *Locksmith*

She stared at the list for a moment, and then added:

✓ *Changes of clothes, pajamas, for G, A & C*

Anni found that, if too many thoughts were rolling around in her mind, she could never fall asleep. Writing them down usually did the trick. She could put her thoughts to the side while she slept, knowing she could pick them up again in the morning.

Anni turned off her bedside lamp and snuggled back down under the covers. Lying there in the dark, she heard the wind picking up outside. It rattled the old windows in her room, slithering through cracks and crevices, whistling in the night. It sounded alive. And angry. Anni pulled the comforter up to her neck. She was glad she wasn't out there in the wind, on that dark stretch of road, like the deer with so much fear in its eyes.

That night, Anni's dreams were hazy and jumbled, nonsensical and strange. She dreamed of the animals along the roadway, her deer, and other, smaller creatures, lurking in the shadows. She saw small folk prodding them on, frightening them into leaping out in front of a car. The image of Gloria swam into view, floating away from the scene of the crash, the car wheels slowly turning, Charles slumped behind the wheel. Hundreds of stars lit up the sky, but soon Anni saw they weren't stars at all, but eyes. Watching. Threatening. Fireflies swarmed, each with a tiny vaki on its back, as though they were assembling for war. And through it all, the wind howled on, calling them, taunting them. Taunting her.

Anni's eyes shot open. She was tangled in the bedclothes, her body clammy with sweat. She blinked a few times. It was okay. She was at LuAnn's. It was just a dream, brought on by the events of the past few days. Anni sat up and reached for the water glass on her nightstand. She took a long drink.

Anni untangled her covers and slid back down into bed. She lay there for a while, listening to the wind. Her eyes began to feel heavy, and she could sense she was entering that vague time just before falling asleep, the time that is neither wake nor sleep, but something of both. She exhaled and let herself fall into it as her pulse slowed.

She was jolted out of it by a heaviness at the foot of her bed. A depression. It felt as though someone had sat down next to her. And now, a hand on top of the covers touched her foot. Grabbed on.

Anni opened her eyes to see Arden sitting there. It was her, but not her, at the same time. Her image wasn't solid. It was light and ethereal, not quite transparent, but very thin. She was wearing the same outfit she had been wearing in the creek. The linen dress, the long strand of pearls. Her hair was illuminated from behind by a light that wasn't there, not in the room with them, anyway.

"Hi, sweetie," Arden said, her voice seeming to come from afar.

Anni scrambled to a sitting position, pulling the covers closer. "Mom?" she whispered.

"Of course it's me, honey. Who else would it be?"

"Mom, you're in the hospital in Salmon Bay," Anni said as a dark and sinking feeling overtook her. Tears pricked the backs of her eyes. "Mom, did you cross over?"

"Cross over where, dear?" Arden said, pushing a tendril of hair from Anni's face.

"Cross *over*," she said, her voice falling to a whisper. "Did you pass away?"

Arden laughed then, a light, musical sound. "No, honey."

"What happened to you? How are you here?"

"I don't know what happened," Arden said. "But I'm here to tell you something."

Anni leaned forward. It seemed like her mother's image was flickering and fading.

"Take me back to Metsan Valo. Tomorrow. Gloria, too. It's important, honey—"

Arden's words were stopped in midair by a noise. After a second, Anni recognized what it was. The beeping of her mother's monitors, back in the hospital. Anni could see a faint, bluish glow in the distance. Arden turned to look at something Anni couldn't see, in a realm

Anni wasn't in. The beeping grew louder. When Arden turned her face back to Anni, her expression was of urgency, even fear. She opened her mouth to say something but didn't get the words out. She vanished, along with the light around her.

In the darkness of her room, Anni put a hand on the foot of the bed where Arden had been sitting. It was cool to the touch. As though Arden hadn't been there at all.

Anni opened her eyes. It was morning. She pushed herself to sit up and took a long drink from the water glass on her bedside table, running a hand through her hair like Theo so often did. There, in the most normal of mornings, with the cheer of sunshine illuminating her room, it was hard for Anni to know if Arden had really visited her or not. It was a familiar feeling since coming home to Metsan Valo. Uncertainty. She was beginning to realize that she had no idea what was real and what was . . . not . . . anymore.

She padded into the bathroom, turned on the shower, and stood under the stream for a long time, thinking about that uncertainty. Was it Anni, losing her grip on reality, or was reality something strange and different now?

After she toweled off and dressed, she was about to head downstairs for breakfast when she spied the envelope on the bedside table. She picked it up to put it into her purse, glancing down at the list she had made. She took a quick breath in when she noticed the last item.

✓ *Changes of clothes, pajamas, for G, A & C*

It was circled with a spidery scrawl, her mother's signature smiley face in a heart off to the side.

CHAPTER THIRTY-FOUR

Theo wasn't anywhere in the suite, so Anni locked the door and trotted down the stairs to the dining room. She found him sitting at the bar. LuAnn was buzzing around tending to a few other tables that were filled with people eating their breakfasts or drinking coffee with the morning newspaper. An altogether ordinary morning after a strange and extraordinary night that Anni still couldn't quite explain.

Anni slid onto the stool next to Theo and noticed an enormous plate of food in front of him—crispy hash browns, sausage, tomatoes, onions and scrambled eggs, all piled high and covered with cheese. Salsa and sour cream sat on the side, along with two pieces of Texas toast.

"Strict keto breakfast?" she said to him, eyebrows raised, amusement buoying her voice.

"Carbs don't count if you're in Wharton." He sniffed. "Don't you know that? It's on all the travel sites."

She laughed at this. "You're seriously not going to eat all of that," she said to him.

He responded by sliding an empty plate in front of her. "I ordered for two, smarty. You were in the shower when I came down. Nobody bathes more than you, by the way. I had forgotten. It's like you're anti-French, taking a bath or shower every hour on the hour."

Gary came over with a cup of coffee and a spatula. He set the coffee in front of Anni and used the spatula to dish some of the decadence up for her. As Gary stumped back into the kitchen, Anni dug into that big plate of heaven gratefully. Comfort food at its best.

She leaned over to Theo. "We really should talk about—"

LuAnn stopped her by sidling up to the bar, a server's notebook in her hand. "Sleep well, honey?"

Anni gave her a long look. "That depends."

"Don't tell me Vivian is at it again." It was Gary, calling out from the kitchen.

Anni furrowed her eyebrows at LuAnn. "Vivian?"

"Resident ghost," LuAnn said, waving her hand. "Harmless. Did she pay you a visit?"

Anni took a bite of cheesy hash browns and considered what, if anything, to say. Under normal circumstances, she probably wouldn't have said anything at all about what had happened in her room the previous night. But something told her she'd have a sympathetic ear from people who had resident ghosts and "passers-through."

"I don't know if it was a dream—" she began.

"It wasn't!" Gary called out.

LuAnn shushed him. "Go on, honey," she said.

"Well, it's just that I'm not sure how it happened, but somehow Mom visited me last night." She winced, looking around.

Gary poked his head out of the kitchen. "What did she want?" This, as though it was the most reasonable thing in the world, someone in a coma having an out-of-body experience and visiting her daughter. Maybe that kind of thing happened all the time at LuAnn's.

Anni noticed Theo wasn't saying anything. She caught his eye. "Well?" he said, frowning. "What did she say?"

Anni took a deep breath. "She said we should take her out of the hospital and back to Metsan Valo today. Gloria, too."

Theo eyed her over the rim of his coffee cup as he took a sip. "That makes sense. Take them away from competent medical care, where they're on monitors checking their vitals constantly, to a place where a squirrel can chew through an electrical cord and plunge the house into darkness at a moment's notice."

His reaction caused Anni's stomach to do a flip. In a way, he was right. It sounded crazy.

"She said it was important," Anni said.

Theo ran a hand through his hair. "You really believe she visited you? Somehow came here from her hospital bed?"

Anni held her brother's gaze for a long minute as LuAnn and Gary discreetly took their leave.

"Are you saying that you didn't just magically decide to walk off the dock in the middle of the night? Or that fireflies didn't swarm us and abruptly disappear? Or that Mom didn't go all Ophelia on us for no earthly reason?" Her voice raised a bit higher than she intended. "And you don't know the half of it, Theo. Weird things have been happening to me this whole time. I haven't told you about meeting everyone in our family tree the other night or how our great-grandfather, who I've seen twice now, still tends the fire at Metsan."

Theo put a hand on her shoulder. "Calm down. I know strange things have been happening. They've always happened at Metsan Valo. Even growing up in the house in Wharton. But Mom's not a ghost. At least not yet. So this is kind of new. Plus, I sort of wanted to put them out of my mind, if you want to know the truth. I never want to see a firefly again. Even a flashlight is too much."

Vintage Theo, diffusing the situation like a pro. Anni smiled at him and squeezed his hand.

"The thing is, I was thinking yesterday how, if she's just resting in the coma-like state she's in and they're not really doing anything for her medically, how long would they let her stay in the hospital anyway?"

"I don't follow," Theo said.

"They don't know what's wrong with Mom," Anni said. "They don't know how to treat her. So they're not. Not really. They're giving her fluids and nutrition and keeping her comfortable, but that's about it. The way I understand it, hospital beds are for people who are being treated for something. Not for people who are in comas for an undetermined amount of time."

Theo nodded. "I guess I can see your point, there."

Anni decided to press that point. "Why can't we take her home and set up, I don't know, a hospital room in the house? We could hire nurses to be there around the clock."

"Would they have to airlift her back? That would cost a fortune."

"I was thinking EMTs, on the ferry. She could go in an ambulance."

Theo took a couple of bites of his breakfast, considering it.

"I'm not conceding that Mom came to you last night," he said. "But . . . there's really no harm in asking what the doctors think about the idea. I mean, I'm sure she'd rather be at Metsan Valo than in the hospital."

He raised his eyebrows at her and continued his thought. "What about the house here in town? It would be more convenient, if she had to go back to the hospital for some reason. Like if she took a turn for the worse. It might be better to have her on Front Street."

Anni knew that made more sense. Of course it did. But something about it didn't feel right to her. Arden had said she wanted to go back to Metsan Valo, whether Theo believed it or not. But she wasn't quite sure how to fight that battle, not even with her twin.

"We'll see about it all when we get to the hospital," Anni said. "But if we do anything about moving her today, it's got to be this afternoon. Thunderstorms are set to move in later."

They finished their breakfasts and took some last sips of coffee. LuAnn came back out into the dining room as they were getting up from their stools.

"Are you two headed off to the hospital?"

"We are," Anni said. "We don't know how to thank you and Gary for your kindness, letting us stay the night. Are you sure we can't pay you anything?"

LuAnn shook her head. "Don't be silly. I wouldn't think of it. But listen now. I was thinking of rounding up my usual suspects and cleaning up the mess at Arden's house this morning. Any objections to that?"

"That would be wonderful," Anni said. She had learned not to try to talk this great lady in leopard print out of anything.

"You let us know your plans," LuAnn said. "The suite is open for the rest of the week if you need it. The house on Front Street will be clean as a whistle if you want to stay there. And, if you're serious about taking Arden back to the island today, let us know that, too. Remember, I'm going to set up a crew to come and sit with her, but we can do that just the same on the island. Everybody is on your side, kids. We're all rooting for you."

Gary poked his head out of the kitchen. "You bet we are!"

Their kindness tugged at Anni's heart. These dear souls. As Anni was gathering her things in their suite, she was overcome with a wave of emotion. She sat down on the edge of her bed, and let the tears flow. Theo was at her side in an instant, pulling her into a hug.

"I know," he said, patting her back. "It's a lot."

"It's everything, all of it," she said, her voice filled with the tears that hadn't poured forth until now. "Gary and LuAnn's kindness sort of pushed me over the edge."

He pulled back and looked her in the eye. "Listen. One: cry all you want to. But for the good of humanity, blow your nose. Two: I'm not going to fight you on this. That was your evil twin talking downstairs. He's gone away now. Vicky and Yale are the difficult ones. Not us. So whatever you want to do, I'm going to back you up."

"Really?"

"Really," he said, handing her a tissue from the box on the bedside table. "As long as the doctors say it's not going to be harmful in any way to take Mom out of the hospital, let's do it. You're right. We can hire twenty-four-seven nurses. We can put them up in the spare rooms in the hallway by the study, or upstairs. We're really lucky that we have the means to do it."

Anni blew her nose. "I know. And I notice you keep saying *we*. But don't you have to get back to Chicago at some point soon?"

"I do, at some point," Theo said, sighing. "But not this second. Jenny is taking care of the business. She'll be here for the wake and wanted to come now because of what happened with Mom. I will have to get on calls with people, work from home, so to speak. Now that Metsan has dragged itself into the digital age, I can do that. Don't worry about me on that front."

"So you think it's best we take her back to the island?"

"A hassle up front, for sure. But it does make sense. Martin and Meri are there to help out. We can house the nurses on site. It's much bigger than the house on Front Street. And we'd have places to escape to—the forest, the lakeshore, Jimmy's, where we can gawk at hipsters in bare feet and man buns."

Anni took a deep breath. She was ready for this. "Okay," she said. "We're agreed. Let's go."

They grabbed their things and headed out the door, saying goodbye to LuAnn and Gary with hugs as they went.

In the car, Anni remembered something. "We need to stop at Front Street," she said. "Mom wants pajamas for her and a change of clothes for Gloria."

Theo shook his head and laughed. "Why does that not surprise me?"

CHAPTER THIRTY-FIVE

Theo pulled up at Front Street and turned off the car, opened his door, and got out. Anni sat there, not wanting to move. The macabre scene of the previous night was replaying in her mind. Gloria, dancing to that old record in Arden's room, wearing Arden's clothes. The singing. The voices.

Theo opened her door and held out his hand. "Come on. Let's do this and get going."

She winced. "It was really creepy last night, Theo."

He looked at her, turned his eyes up to the house, and then looked back. "Do you want me to go in by myself?" he asked her. "I can do that. You just wait here."

Anni thought about that for a second. She was tempted, but no.

"It'll take you forever to find what she wants," Anni said, sliding out of her seat. "I'll come in with you. But if we hear any creepy music, we're gone."

"Deal," Theo said.

He unlocked the front door, and the two of them walked into the house. Anni didn't feel the strangeness, the haziness, she had felt the night before. Nothing odd was hanging in the air. It was just their house on Front Street, as ordinary as it had been on any other morning.

She and Theo went right upstairs to their mother's room, which, of course, was still somewhat disheveled. The bed was mussed, records were strewn here and there. Arden's jewelry box was standing open, necklaces draped everywhere.

She grabbed a pair of Arden's silk pajamas out of her dresser drawer and handed them to Theo, who had found a big tote on the other side of the room.

"What about slippers and a robe?" he asked, rummaging through her closet.

Anni wondered what she should choose for Gloria. Maybe Vicky had thought to bring her mother a change of clothes. Better safe than sorry. She picked a soft pair of yoga pants and a long-sleeved T-shirt, along with one of Arden's many jean jackets. They packed it all in the tote and topped it off with a pair of ballet flats.

Back in the car, Anni eyed Theo. She hadn't yet told him what Nick Stone had dug up about Charles. She tried to think of a delicate way of saying it.

"Charles is a con man," she blurted out.

Theo whipped his head around to look at her. "What?"

"Nick ran his prints. Apparently, he's made a business of marrying rich widows."

Theo heaved a long sigh. "So now we're dealing with that, too. Let him rot in the hospital for all I care."

"It's not really as simple as that," Anni said, but deep down, she agreed with her brother. "We need to find a time to tell Vicky and Gloria, and ultimately they're the ones who will decide what to do about that."

Theo was silent as they drove along. Soon, they came to the twist in the road where Charles's car had gone over the cliff.

"If Charles is conning her for her money, this is a pretty dramatic way for him to go about it," he said finally. "I mean, he might have killed himself in the act. That seems crazy to me."

"That's the whole thing about all of this," Anni said, watching out for the skid marks. "Nothing has made sense since we got to Metsan Valo."

Theo gave her the side-eye. "So, naturally, we should just hurry right back there instead of fleeing to our own lives, where nothing odd or dangerous or creepy ever happens," he said. "We could keep driving right now and be in Chicago in seven hours."

Anni chuckled. "Tempting."

Instead, they pulled into the hospital parking lot and walked into the building in time to see Vicky getting coffee from the small deli and gift shop in the lobby.

"Hey, Vic," Anni said, giving her cousin a quick hug. "What's the latest?"

It was then she noticed Vicky's eyes were bloodshot, dark circles under them.

"I didn't sleep too well last night," she said, raising the coffee cup to her lips with shaking hands. "Mom looked terrible. She was saying all sorts of weird things." A tear ran down her cheek. She didn't seem to notice. Or care. It occurred to Anni that none of the younger Hallas were sleeping well.

"Is she awake this morning?" Anni asked. "Lucid?"

"I haven't been in to see her yet," Vicky said. "We just got here. Yale went to see Charles."

The very name left a bad taste in Anni's mouth. Charles. She eyed Theo, wondering if now was the right time to tell Vicky what they had learned. He raised his eyebrows and shrugged.

Anni took a deep breath. "Vic, about Charles. I hope you don't think I've overstepped, but . . ." She couldn't quite find the words. All at once, what she had done seemed like an enormous intrusion.

"What?" Vicky asked, looking from Anni to Theo and back again. "Overstepped how?"

Anni was beginning to wish she hadn't brought it up. But now she had to see it through.

"I asked Nick Stone to run a background check on Charles," Anni blurted out, the words coming in one long stream. "I'm sorry, Vicky, I know it's none of my business but—"

Vicky put up a hand to stop Anni's words. She was nodding. Her expression was grave. All at once, Anni understood. She wasn't the first one to run a background check on "Charles Wellington."

"Don't apologize," Vicky said. "We did, too. It was just so sudden. And Mom has some money, and she seemed so vulnerable, and he seemed too good to be true. Yale and I hired a private investigator."

Anni squeezed her cousin's arm. "So you know."

"We know," Vicky said. "You may have noticed Yale sticks to the man like glue. He befriended Charles early on. We're watching him."

"What about Gloria?" Theo asked. "Does she know?"

Vicky nodded. "I told her immediately when I found out about his past. She's sticking with him."

Theo and Anni both looked at her, openmouthed.

"Why?" Anni said, her voice raised an octave.

"I can't quite wrap my head around it, either," Vicky said, shrugging. "She said something about kindred spirits, finding her soul mate."

"But that's crazy," Anni said. "And dangerous."

"I know," Vicky said. "That's why I insisted on an ironclad prenup. He'll get a lump sum if they divorce after five or more years of marriage. Nothing if they divorce before that. Nothing if the divorce is because of adultery on his part. And nothing if she dies, unless that death comes after ten years of marriage."

"And he agreed to that?" Now Theo's voice raised an octave.

"He agreed to that," Vicky said.

Anni had her doubts. But this was Vicky's mother, not hers.

Theo put an arm around Vicky. "Okay. Since you've got the Charles situation handled, let's go see your mom."

They rode the elevator in silence, Vicky sipping her coffee and wiping away her tears.

As they walked, Theo rummaged through the tote he was carrying and pulled out the clothes they had brought for Gloria. He held them out to Vicky.

"If she's being released today . . ." he said, handing over the pile.

She looked down at the clothes as though she had no idea what they were. "I didn't even think to bring her an outfit." She turned her eyes back to Anni and Theo. "Thank you."

Anni smiled at her. "It's what we do."

The three of them stood outside the door for a moment before going in. Vicky leaned against the wall. "About her being released," she started, her voice wavering.

Anni knew where she was going with this, and she wasn't about to have her cousin ask her if Gloria could recuperate in the home where she grew up. It didn't matter if Anni owned it now. The house belonged to the family.

"I was thinking Metsan Valo could be Recovery Central," Anni said. "You don't know this yet, but Theo and I are taking Mom home today, if we can get the doctors' blessing. They're not doing much for her here that we can't do at home. I'm planning to hire around-the-clock nursing care for her. So we'll have our own medical team on hand."

"I'm going to arrange for a doctor to visit a couple of times a week, too," Theo said, surprising Anni. *Perfect idea,* she thought.

"You can arrange for house calls?" Vicky said, raising her eyebrows.

"Have you met my brother?" Anni said with a slight grin. "He could arrange for the entire Mayo Clinic to come to Colette if he wanted to."

Theo sniffed and brushed some imaginary lint off his shoulder. "True."

"Given all of that," Anni continued, "it makes sense for your mom and Charles to recover, rest, and get back on their feet there, too. Unless you need to get back to the cities right away and want to take them with you. In that case—"

"No," Vicky broke in. "Yale may have to get back to work, but I'll take some extended time off and stay as long as Mom does. Lichen will, too. She's got school starting in a couple of weeks, but we'll figure that out. Mummo was right. We haven't spent enough time at Metsan Valo. Especially her."

"Wonderful," Anni said. "I don't know if Charles has a family, kids of his own—"

Vicky shook her head. "He doesn't, as far as I know."

"Okay, it's settled, then. I don't suppose you know when either of them will be released?"

"If not today, tomorrow," Vicky said. "That's what they're telling us, anyway."

Anni nodded. That was done. They had a plan. She liked the feeling of taking control of something, finally. It wasn't tragedies happening out of the blue, befalling her family, cursing them. She had reined in the chaos. At least for the moment.

Pushing open the door, they found Gloria sitting up in bed, a tray table in front of her. Her head was bandaged, and she was eating a breakfast of oatmeal with one hand. The other arm was in a sling. Anni saw that her face was turning black and blue, a dark bruise under one eye. Gloria looked up as the three of them came in. She smiled weakly.

"Hello, loves."

Vicky flew to her mother's side and hugged her, which caused Gloria to flinch. She looked so fragile then. As though she were made of glass. Vicky pulled back. "I'm sorry, Mom—" she started.

"Don't be silly, honey," she said. "I won't break. Here, sit beside me."

The same old Gloria, Anni thought. Nothing, not even a trace, of the night before.

"How are you feeling, Auntie?" Theo said, smiling his big Theo smile. "You took quite a tumble."

Gloria raised her eyebrows. "So I've been told. I don't remember much. If anything."

Anni noticed her words were slurring slightly. Pain meds, she presumed.

"What do you remember?"

"I remember leaving Metsan Valo, and being on the ferry. I remember driving off the ferry and . . ." She looked off into the distance, as if trying to see a memory that was just out of reach. "That's about it, I'm afraid." She leaned her head back onto her pillows and sighed.

"That's okay, Mom," Vicky said, reaching out to clasp her mother's hand. "You don't have to talk. I'll be here with you."

Theo and Anni exchanged a look. He cocked his head toward the door. It was time to leave mother and daughter alone. Anni nodded.

"Aunt Gloria, Theo and I are going to check on Arden," Anni said. "She's just down the hall."

"Arden?" Gloria said. "She's okay. She came to see me last night."

Anni raised her eyebrows at Theo.

"What did she say?" Anni asked.

Gloria smiled weakly. "Only that we were going home." Her eyes fluttered closed.

Vicky lifted her mother's hand to her own cheek. "You rest now, Mom."

Just then, Yale came through the door, pushing Charles in a wheelchair. When the man saw his wife, his face melted into a mixture of love and regret and fear.

"Darling," Charles said, conveying everything in that one word, his voice cracking.

Gloria's eyes popped open. She smiled, and it lit up her face. "Oh, my love." She held out her hand.

Yale wheeled Charles to Gloria's bedside. He laid his head on his wife's chest. "I could have lost you," he murmured, weeping. She rubbed his back with her good hand, tears trickling down her battered cheeks.

Vicky backed away, giving her mother and her new husband some privacy. Yale put an arm around her. "Let's go sit in the lounge for a while," he said to her. "You can nap on my shoulder."

The four of them, Yale and Vicky, Theo and Anni, left the room then to the odd union of two seemingly troubled souls.

Theo and Anni headed down the hallway toward Arden's room. "Apparently, Mom was busy last night," Theo said, eyeing Anni and giving her a mock scowl.

She smiled.

The scene in Arden's room was the same as it had been the day before. She hadn't changed, nor had her condition.

"I brought your silk pajamas, Mom," Anni said, taking her mother's hand.

"I'm here, too, lady," Theo said, his voice gentler than Anni had heard it in a long time. "What do you say we spring you out of this joint today?"

Anni sank down into her chair by Arden's bedside. "Maybe you should go find the doctor," she said to Theo. "Float the idea. See what he says."

"Right," Theo said. "Will do."

He slipped out of the room, and it was just Anni and Arden again. As she sat next to her sleeping, enchanted mother, Anni began to wonder what would happen if she never woke at all. The very notion of it filled Anni with an abject fear, as though she were grasping at something that was slipping through her fingers. Her mother was right there, and yet nowhere. Alive, but not living. Would she ever hear her voice again, other than in her dreams, or whatever the visitation of last night was? Wasn't there a way for Anni to help her wake up somehow?

But there was no handsome prince to kiss her mother back into reality. True love's kiss was the stuff of fantasy and folklore. Real life was messier than that. And Arden in an unexplainable coma with no prognosis of when or how she might come out of it was as real and messy as it got.

CHAPTER THIRTY-SIX

A while later, Theo popped back into the room. Anni had her feet propped up at the end of the bed and had been reading the news of the day—focusing on the gossip columns—to Arden from her smartphone.

"Mom is particularly concerned that Prince Harry moved to the United States," Anni reported. "She thinks Prince Charles is befuddled by that turn of events, but the queen is angry."

"Is it bad to say I think I like Mom better this way?" Theo said, grinning. "It's so much easier to have a conversation."

Anni burst out laughing. "You know she can hear you."

"Just kidding, Mom," Theo said, squeezing her foot.

"So?" Anni asked him. "What did the doctor say about us taking Mom home today?"

Theo perched on the edge of his chair, leaning toward his sister. "He wasn't exactly thrilled about it," he said.

Anni squinted at him. "I sense there's a *but* coming."

He smiled. "Indeed. He said he'll sign off on it if we do what we already said we were going to do. Twenty-four-seven nursing care, which we'll get set up. I also suggested that he come out to the island twice a week himself."

"What did he say to that?"

"He wasn't exactly thrilled about it."

Anni grinned. "I sense there's a *but* coming."

"Indeed!" Theo said, laughing. "I reminded him of the sizable donation Mummo made to build a wing of this hospital after Pappa died. I also let him know that you are in control of that fortune now and would be most grateful for the care our mother received."

"So he'll do it?"

"He'll do it."

Anni turned her eyes to Arden. "Hear that, Mom? We're cleared to take you back to Metsan Valo today. Just like you wanted."

Anni could've sworn she saw a slight smile cross Arden's lips, before fading away.

The next few hours were a flurry of activity. With the hospital's help, Theo got in touch with the medical clinic on Ile de Colette and arranged to have a team of nurses who lived on the island set up a schedule for Arden's care, starting the following day. Jane, the nurse who had been attending to Arden at the hospital, would travel with her to Metsan Valo and spend a night or two to get the new team up to speed.

It was really happening.

Anni called Meri to update her on the situation.

"How is your mother?" Meri said as she answered the phone, dispensing with any pleasantries.

"No change," Anni said. "But we're bringing her back to Metsan today." Anni heard Meri take a quick breath in.

"As it should be," Meri said. "I was hoping to hear this news. Bring her home."

Anni then went on to explain the particulars. Meri needed to prepare one of the guest rooms on the first floor to be transformed into a recovery room, with a hospital bed, monitors, and other medical equipment that would be coming over by ferry on a truck along with the ambulance.

"Gloria and Charles will also be recuperating at Metsan," Anni explained. "But we're not sure at this point if they're going to be discharged today."

"Will they be needing hospital beds as well?" Meri asked.

Anni wasn't sure about that, either. "Probably not, but he's got broken ribs and a broken arm. She has a dislocated shoulder and is pretty banged up in general."

Meri thought about this for a moment. "I'll make up one of the other guest rooms in that wing for them," she said. "That way, we'll have all of the patients in one place, whether they're coming today or in a few days. I'll also open up the third room for the nurses to use as an outpost, where they can sleep or relax."

It was all falling into place. While Anni was on the phone strategizing with Meri, a nurse had given Arden a sponge bath, changed her into her favorite silk pajamas, brushed her hair, and even applied a little bit of makeup. She was ready for her close-up.

Vicky poked her head in through the door. "Am I disturbing you guys?"

"Come on in, Vic," Anni said. "What's the latest?"

Given that Anni and Theo were turning Metsan Valo into a medical outpost, the doctors had given the okay for Charles and Gloria to be released, as well. They weren't being treated for anything but pain, and their medications could be managed at home, with the help of the constant presence of nurses.

It was all set, then. The entire family would be going home together.

The truck with a hospital bed and all the monitors Arden needed had gone on ahead, so Meri could supervise preparing the room for her. Jane was catching the next ferry as well. But for the rest of them at the hospital, the next few hours were mostly about waiting. Waiting for the results of the last of their tests, waiting for paperwork, waiting for the doctor to visit Gloria, Charles, and Arden one final time, waiting for all their medications to be transferred to the clinic on the island.

But finally, they were ready to go.

Vicky and Yale would be taking Gloria and Charles in the car with them. Anni watched through the window as staff pushed them out to the car in wheelchairs and helped them settle into the back seat. Their movements were slow and deliberate, their expressions pained.

As Anni was watching Gloria and Charles climb into their car, the EMTs arrived at Arden's room, surprising Anni by opening the door wide and pushing in a stretcher.

"Her chariot awaits," one of the EMTs said as they transferred Arden from her bed to the stretcher. She seemed so limp, so frail. But life bubbled inside her as well. Her skin was pink, almost rosy, not sallow or ashen. She looked beautiful lying there, her hair cascading around her face.

"You ready to go for a ride, Ms. Halla?" the EMT asked, and began pushing the stretcher out of the room. He turned to look over his shoulder at Anni and Theo. "We'll meet you at the ferry dock."

Anni did a last sweep of the room to make sure they weren't forgetting anything, and she and Theo closed the door behind them, one final time.

"Are you ready to do this?" he asked her as they walked down the hallway.

"Ready as I'll ever be," she said. As the elevator doors closed, she looked toward the security and safety of the nurses' station, just down the hall.

When they walked out of the hospital's front doors, Anni saw Arden's ambulance pulling away. No sirens this time. She noticed that Yale and Vicky, with Gloria and Charles in tow, were already gone. They might be able to make the earlier ferry, Anni thought, along with the truck with the hospital bed and equipment.

She looked skyward and saw gray, angry clouds building on the horizon. But toward the island, she saw blue sky. Maybe this weather would hold out until everyone was safely back at Metsan and tucked in for the night, she thought. Then a flash of light sizzled through those gray clouds, and they rumbled deep and low. So much for her hope the weather would hold. It was almost as if Mother Nature had responded to her thought in real time, with a retort.

"Do you think we're okay crossing to the island now?" Anni asked her brother, her eyes still on the sky.

He squinted at the building thunderheads. They looked like billowy animals. The light shining around their edges seemed otherworldly and beautiful. But Anni knew they were a portent of a storm to come.

"I think we've got time," Theo said, turning the car toward Wharton. "But either way, it'll be twenty minutes until we get to the ferry dock. By then, we'll know if the storm is going to hit, or if it will miss us. They won't take the ferry out in bad weather."

He's right, Anni thought. But she kept her eyes on the skies throughout the drive, just in case.

The hospital had called ahead to the ferry dock, and the workers there had been holding other cars at bay until the ambulance and Anni and Theo's car could board.

The attendants waved to them, and they pulled onto the ferry. Theo set the parking brake, but this time, neither of them wanted to get out of the car. They were parked next to the ambulance, and both Anni and her brother wanted to stay nearby.

As the ferry chugged away from the dock, Anni heard another crack of thunder, louder this time. Her stomach twisted at the thought of crossing this lake in bad weather.

"Maybe we should've stayed until the storm passed," she said to Theo. It was more of a question.

He shook his head. "It's going to hold off. You saw the sky to the east. That's where we're going. It might start raining in Wharton soon, but it's going to take a while for the weather to hit the island. We'll be ahead of it."

Anni nodded, but she was unconvinced.

"Right," Theo said, as the ferry jolted and heaved to the side.

Anni and Theo shared a long look, and then both of them got out of the car. They hurried to the railing to look outside just in time to see rain begin to pour down in sheets. Lightning sizzled through the sky.

The swells on the lake were massive, tossing the ferry from side to side like it was a toy. Anni and Theo hung tightly on to the rail.

The ferry's speakers crackled. "This is the captain. Please return to your vehicles and make sure your parking brakes are set. We're hitting some rough water, folks. Life jackets are in the interior cabin."

Anni looked at Theo. "Does that mean we're supposed to stay in the car or go into the interior cabin?"

"Totally unclear," he said, shaking his head. "Let's get to the car. Mom is in the ambulance, and they're certainly not going to take her out to bring her into the cabin. Let's stay near her. But . . ." he started, holding up a finger. He didn't finish the sentence. Instead, Anni watched him take the metal stairs to the main cabin. A moment later, he returned with an armful of life jackets. He gave three to the EMTs in the ambulance—one for Arden—and kept two for himself and Anni.

"Do you really think we need these?" Anni asked him. "It seems like overkill."

"Well, we don't want to go over and be killed," Theo said, handing her a jacket.

They strapped them on and climbed into the car as the ferry pitched and swayed.

She gave Theo a worried look.

"We're almost to the island," he said. "We'll be fine."

But his face told a different story.

Anni watched as other passengers, some with life jackets, some without, returned to their cars to check their parking brakes. Some of them returned to the main cabin. Some stood at the railing to watch the incredible, angry waves. Lake Superior was magnificent and deadly, and usually Anni loved to watch it, safely inside Metsan Valo, while the storm raged on outside. But not this time.

This time, she was part of the storm.

CHAPTER THIRTY-SEVEN

Fifteen white-knuckle minutes later, the ferry pulled into the dock on Ile de Colette. Anni heard cheers coming from the main cabin. People who were in their cars started honking their horns. Even the ferry's foghorn gave three great blasts. They had made it. They had survived Lake Superior's fury. This time.

They drove off the ferry into the punishing rain. But Anni didn't care about the rain, not here. This drive, from the ferry dock to Metsan Valo, was as flat and gentle as could be. She and Theo knew it so well, they could drive it blindfolded. They crept along, leading the ambulance, as the rain turned the view out of their windshield into a mosaic of island scenes—the buildings in town, the grassy fields, the homes that dotted the route, the shoreline. It was like an impressionist painting. *Colette in the Rain.*

Anni could feel her blood pressure dropping, her heart slowing, just from being back on the island. As they turned into the driveway at Metsan Valo, she exhaled. Audibly.

"Tell me about it," Theo said. "The phrase *it's good to be home* was written for this moment, I think."

Martin and Meri were standing under the overhang, holding what looked like a large tarp. At first Anni wondered what in the world it was for, but then she realized. Of course. They were going to shield Arden from the rain. Theo pulled up and let the ambulance get as close as possible to the overhang, and he and Anni hopped out to help Martin and Meri hold the tarp.

The EMTs unloaded the stretcher and wheeled Arden into the house, none the worse for wear. Anni and Theo followed, closing the great wooden door behind them, shutting out the storm.

Inside the house, a fire was crackling in the fireplace. Anni could smell something delicious simmering in the kitchen—pot roast and gravy? Gloria was settled onto the couch, with Charles by her side. Both had afghans draped over them and their feet up on the same ottoman in front of them. Vicky and Lichen were sitting at the game table on the other side of the room, a jigsaw puzzle's pieces strewn everywhere, as Yale looked on with a beer in hand.

A perfect, albeit battered, family portrait.

"Her room is this way," Meri said to the EMTs. Anni followed along, down the back hallway. Meri had transformed the room into a hospital suite, with the help of Arden's nurse, Jane, who had arrived earlier. Monitors were hooked up and blinking, and the hospital bed sat in the middle of the room with a bedside table and comfy armchairs on either side. Anni noticed that the usual stark white sheets and blankets had been replaced with the soft, jersey-knit sheets Arden loved. Fluffy pillows sat propped up at the head of the bed, and a thick down comforter with a floral duvet covered it. A bouquet of fall blooms sat on the windowsill.

Anni turned to Meri and smiled. "This is beautiful," she said. "Thank you."

"So much more comfortable than a hospital room," Meri said, nodding. "This is where she belongs."

The EMTs transferred Arden to the bed as Jane began to check her IV bag and her vitals.

"I'll get her settled," Jane said.

Anni figured that was her cue to step out of the room. "So, Jane, you're spending the night tonight? Maybe two?"

"That's right," Jane said. "The room next door is lovely, so I thank you for that. We've got a team of nurses coming tomorrow morning. I'll get them up to speed and set their schedules for the next month so everyone knows who's on first, so to speak, before I head back to the mainland."

Anni winced at this. "A whole month?"

Jane smiled, rather sadly, Anni thought. "With cases like these, we just don't have any good estimates. Time doesn't matter to the coma. It's not of this world, not really. So that's why I'm scheduling the team a month out, just to cover all of our bases. In two weeks, we can adjust our plan, if necessary."

"Are you going to be supervising the nurses?" Anni liked that idea. Jane seemed the epitome of competence. Just the person to tend to Arden's care.

"Yes, I will," she said. "I'll be in touch with the team daily, and I plan to come to the island weekly with the doctor, just to see how it's all going."

Anni felt a huge burden lift off her shoulders.

"I want you to be prepared for something, also," Jane continued.

Anni winced, bracing herself for impact.

"She may well be in this state for some time. Or she might come out of it tomorrow. Either way, when she does open her eyes and come back to us, it's not like in the movies."

"How so?"

"She's not going to open her eyes, get out of bed, and start skipping through a field of daisies immediately," Jane said. "Sometimes there's a waking-up process, if you want to think about it like that. It's almost as though they're swimming up to the surface from wherever they are. They'll put their faces above the water for a while but then slip back under again. It can happen several times."

Anni shook her head. "Wow, okay. How do we handle that?"

"You're not going to have to handle it. That's what your nurse care team is for."

Anni exhaled. "Good to know."

"Another thing to prepare for. We may be looking at brain damage. She might have to relearn things. I've seen patients who have had to relearn how to talk, walk, the whole nine yards."

Anni glanced over at her mother, looking so beautiful, so unaware she was in any danger of losing her Arden-ness. "But they eventually get back to themselves, right?"

"Sometimes not," Jane said. "But there's a new normal out there."

"You're talking like you believe she's going to come out of this," Anni said.

Jane smiled at her and put a hand on her arm. "Let's assume the best and prepare for the worst. That's how I roll."

Anni left Jane to her work then, kissing Arden on the forehead before going out the door. Back in the great room, Meri was setting the table for dinner—with Lichen's help. Anni caught Theo's eye, and the two of them shared a private laugh. Now it was for certain. The entire world had turned upside down.

Gloria and Charles stayed in their spots on the couch for the meal, tray tables in their laps. The rest of the family gathered around the table, talking about what would happen next. Laying plans.

"I might head back home for a week or so and take care of business, setting myself up to work remotely from here if need be," Yale said, spearing a piece of potato.

"Sounds like a good plan," Theo said. "By that time, we'll have a better handle on Charles's and Gloria's recovery. You might even be able to take them home then."

It sounded reasonable to Anni. A twinge of envy curled its way around her, though. Vicky's mother and stepfather were on a predictable path back into their own lives. Not so with Arden. There were a lot of what-ifs on the road ahead for her.

Later, after they cleaned up the dishes and Meri took a plate in to Jane, Charles cleared his throat. "I want to address what I know is an elephant in the room," he said.

Gloria put a hand on his arm. "You don't have to, darling. It's nobody's business."

Charles patted her hand and smiled at her. "You deserve it," he said, turning his gaze to the others. "I know you all know about my shameful past."

Anni took a quick breath in and glanced at Theo. He raised his eyebrows.

"What some of you don't know is, Gloria has known about it from the beginning. Almost the beginning, anyway."

"We were two broken people," Gloria said. "We found each other and recognized a kindred spirit immediately. It was easy to be honest after that."

"And after we ran the background check," Vicky added. Yale nodded and crossed his arms over his chest.

"You don't owe us any sort of explanation, Charles," Anni said.

Charles smiled. "It's not an explanation as much as it is a defense of my wife," he said. "I don't want any of you thinking she's a doddering old widow who got duped by a con man."

Gloria let out a whoop. "Who are you calling old?"

Charles smiled at her. "From a con man to a changed man. All because of the love of this lady." He turned to the rest of the family. "You can believe it or not. What you believe is none of my business, and none of my concern. Of course, I'd love it if you'd accept what you've heard. Accept me as Gloria's husband. But whether you do or don't, that's not going to change how we feel about each other."

Gloria squeezed his arm.

"But at least now everything is out in the open," Charles said. "I intend to sit down with Arden when she is back with us and talk with her about this, as well."

Theo turned to Anni and shrugged. She knew just what he meant. *Que será, será.* The love between their aunt and Charles seemed as real as anything Anni had ever seen. And if it wasn't, according to Vicky, those two had an ironclad prenup. There was nothing more to say.

With that, Charles and Gloria said their good nights and hobbled down the hallway, leaning on each other.

"See you in the morning, loves," Gloria called over her shoulder, sighing into Charles as they went.

It was funny to Anni. They had been so suspicious of Charles. Even love-and-light Arden was openly hostile about his marriage to Gloria. Rightly so. The man had left a string of women in his wake. And yet, Gloria had accepted him. Made her peace with his past. And here they were, their love for each other radiating out of every pore. Anni wondered why nobody had seen it before. Maybe it was really true. But if it wasn't, Anni trusted Yale to step in.

She marveled at that, too, how Yale had seemed to change into a different person during this time at Metsan Valo. But, as she thought of it, maybe he hadn't changed at all. Maybe it was she who had changed. Or, at least, maybe she hadn't truly seen him before. She and Theo had never given Yale much of a chance. People were too complicated, had too many layers and sides, to judge with only a cursory glance.

After making sure Charles and Gloria got tucked into bed safely, Vicky, Yale, and Lichen retreated upstairs, too. Anni was sure Lichen had had more than enough adult bonding, and Yale and Vicky probably wanted some time alone, too. That left Anni and Theo, sitting by the fire.

Anni curled her feet up under her and settled in. As comfortable as she had been at LuAnn's the night before, she had felt a deep sense of peace when she had set foot back in Metsan Valo. It was home. When that thought struck Anni, a tear escaped from one eye. She whisked it away so Theo wouldn't notice, but of course he had.

"What?" he said.

She shrugged and smiled a small smile. "It's just that, coming back here after everything that went down on the mainland made me feel so glad to be home," she said. "And then it just hit me. I have a home."

Theo smiled at her. "You really love this place," he said. "You're realizing that now. I don't know why you stayed away so long, but, hey, it was Paris. Who wouldn't want to stay there?"

She chuckled at this. "I'll always have the apartment there, thanks to Jean-Paul. Maybe I'll keep it and just divide my time between the two places. Winters here are not ideal."

A darkness fell over Theo's face then. "That's assuming Mom wakes up. Or doesn't."

He was right. She was imagining her future when they hadn't even dealt with the present. Neither of them really knew what the future would hold.

She slid off the couch and padded to the darkened kitchen, where she poured a glass of wine for herself and a beer for Theo.

Handing it to him, she said, "Let's talk about what we don't know."

"I don't know how the pyramids could possibly have been built without alien help," he said, taking a swig of his Scottish ale. "Should we start there?"

She smirked at him. "Or if time travel is real. But I was thinking more of what we don't know about what has happened since we arrived here at Metsan Valo, a scant week ago."

"We don't know who broke into Mom's house."

"Or why."

"We don't know what happened to Mom to cause her to fall into a coma."

"Or why."

"We don't know how fireflies swarmed us and then disappeared— and if you say *or why* again I'll hit you."

"But we don't know why."

"We don't know *why* both of us ended up outside after sleepwalking."

"And we don't know *how* or *why* Charles and Gloria went over the cliff. Although that could've been a deer jumping out into the road."

"We don't know why Gloria went insane for a hot minute and then sobered up again."

Both Theo and Anni sighed.

"We don't know much," he said, taking another sip of beer and gazing out into the rainy night. "There are only questions."

All at once, Anni thought she might know where to find the answers.

CHAPTER THIRTY-EIGHT

Somehow, Anni felt, deep in her bones, that the book, the story of their ancestors, the old tales, had to be the key to it all. Meri had talked about its secrets just a few nights before—though it seemed like a lifetime to Anni. So much had happened since then. But she couldn't deny that a thread of otherworldliness was running through it all.

She said good night to her brother and made her way upstairs to her room.

The book was sitting on the desk where she had left it. She pulled out the chair and sank down into it, kicking off her shoes.

She unclasped the metal hinges and opened the cover. As Anni turned its illuminated, intricately designed pages, she saw that the stories began with the last tale Mummo had told them. She saw an illustration of the dark-haired woman she had seen in the living room a few nights before. There was a hawk, circling above her head. It was Kaija, Anni was sure of it, although she could not read the words. Illustrations depicted her gathering herbs and flowers, sitting on rocks by an angry sea, walking down a village street. A few pages later, a man. A dark-haired man with blue eyes. He looked so much like Patrick Saari, Anni took a breath in. She looked closer. Had the illustration moved? She couldn't be sure. But she was sure it was Calder.

As she paged through the book, she was mesmerized by the illustrations of who she now knew were her ancestors, so far away, and yet so close to her here at Metsan Valo. The longer she studied the pages, the more rapt she became.

Time did not stop for Anni as she looked through the book, but it ceased to have any meaning for her. It was as though Anni was outside of time, someplace where it had no hold over her. She might have been sitting there, at her desk, book open in front of her for a moment. Or it might have been weeks. Months. Even years. And it all took place at the same time.

The storm raged outside her window. Thunder growled through the sky; lightning electrified the landscape with great cracks and bangs. Rain pummeled her windowpanes. But Anni had no sense of it. All she knew was what was on those pages.

Page after page, she studied the illustrations until, all at once, the written words seemed to swim and move on their own. Anni squinted and looked more carefully. Was it really happening? It was as though the words were morphing into something else, just as Meri had said they would.

And then they came into laser focus. She could read the tales, not just look at the illustrations.

Kaija and Calder lived their lives on those pages, there, on the windswept, rocky coast of a northern sea. Anni could smell the salt air, hear the barking of the seals. She could feel the warmth of a reindeer's fur on a bitterly cold day.

She saw Kaija walk out into a storm and calm it. She saw how she summoned protection from the vaki. She also saw the important events in their lives. The births of Kaija and Calder's children, one by one. She watched as Kaija passed from this world into the next in Calder's arms, and felt the anguish and grief he carried with him for the rest of his days.

Other people followed, more stories of adventures, of small moments, of life and death and beyond. She saw, heard, and felt the women of her family doing as Kaija had done, taking control of the world around them. Befriending the vaki. Living side by side with the little folk. Summoning their help in difficult times. Keeping the evil ones at bay. These were the epic tales of her people, told by those who had lived them.

She might have stayed there all night, even longer, immersed in these tales, but something brought her out of the stories and back into her room, into the present. She blinked a few times, realizing she was here in Metsan Valo and not in an ancient land in Northern Europe, where her family tree originated. She was not with Kaija and Calder. They were long dead, dust in the earth. Or were they? Anni had seen their spirits a few nights prior, hadn't she?

She shook her head and cleared her throat. What was she here to do, again? Anni sat there for a moment and then remembered. She was looking for answers to what was happening to her family now. In the present. Not eons ago.

But where would she find those answers? This book was filled with hundreds of years of family stories. Hundreds of years of tales.

And then it hit her. She turned all the pages at once until she reached the last one hundred pages.

And there they were, her great-grandparents. He started the first fire in the hearth at Metsan Valo, just after the house was completed. Anni read that, according to legend, his spirit would have that job until the end of time. It was his charge to tend the hearth here.

She read the stories of vaki in these woods, and in the air, and in the water. She read how the animals talked to them. She saw the vaki take animal form—wolves, bears, foxes. She read stories of protection, and of mischief.

Wendy Webb

She read about vaki attacking humans, running wild, doing damage inside homes and on boats. It was nature out of control. Just like what was happening to her family, right now.

She turned the page and saw Mummo as a young girl smiling back at her. Anni saw a woman she knew to be her great-grandmother taking Mummo out into the woods, telling her about the vaki, showing her their lairs, whispering their secrets.

The next page made Anni gasp aloud. It was titled "The Mistress of Metsan Valo." There was only one illustration. It was Mummo outside, with her arms outstretched.

"Watch over us, my friends in the forest, in the air, in the waters. Keep us safe. We will keep your secrets."

Mummo was doing what Kaija had done, as all the women in their family had done, down through the ages. Making a bond with nature.

Anni saw Mummo walking through the forest, to the creek, with a basket, and settling down next to a huge stone on the creek bank. The stone had small holes that had been drilled into it, almost like cups. Mummo had called it the cup stone. Anni took a breath in, knowing she had seen the stone countless times, but Mummo had told her to stay away from it. Of course, she and Theo would play near it, just because of that warning.

But on these pages, Anni saw what it was really for. Mummo reached into her basket and took out vodka and apple cider and poured it into some of the holes. Next, she reached into the basket and drew out a bag of what looked like leftovers. Scraps of potatoes, carrots, meats. A loaf of bread. She saw Mummo say a prayer.

"Enjoy this bounty, friends of Metsan Valo," Mummo said.

It looked to Anni that Mummo was giving the vaki offerings. In some kind of pagan ceremony. Anni saw these scenes depicted in the book again and again and again. A hazy memory swam into her mind's eye. She had seen Mummo walk into the woods with a basket many times. She hadn't given it a second thought. Was that what she was supposed to do, as mistress of Metsan Valo? Give small offerings to the vaki in exchange for friendship and protection?

She turned the page. What she saw took her breath away. It was her. Anni's own face.

These were the images of what had happened since Anni had arrived at Metsan Valo. She wanted to call out for Theo but could not. She was too rapt by what she was seeing. It was all right there, proof of what she didn't want to let herself believe, but was true.

There were the forest vaki, calling to her in the middle of the night, luring her into the woods. Fireflies, millions of them, screaming a warning that it was all out of control. And Theo, being called out in the middle of the night by the water vaki—she saw them, bobbing on the surface, heard them, calling his name. She heard their laughter, a malevolent and evil sound that echoed in her ears, and in her memory. Anni knew she had heard that sound before, all throughout her childhood at Metsan Valo.

She turned another page and saw their mischief in Arden's house, papers and books flying off the shelves in the office. Mayhem in the basement. She saw them laying out the clothes on Arden's bed, laughing all the while. Anni saw it now for what it was: a message of what was to come. But Anni had not understood it.

Anni gasped as she turned the page and saw the keening spirits, floating in a funeral procession, wailing their grief over what they knew was to come the following day. It was the very scene she had witnessed out her bedroom window, the scene that sent her shrieking into Theo's room in the middle of the night.

So many warnings. But Anni did not know how to listen.

She turned the page and saw Arden, wandering through the forest the morning she disappeared. She saw the forest vaki, evil vaki, following her. Raining enchantment down on her as Arden waded into the creek and lay back on the surface of the water. The vaki gave her a push, and she floated away.

On the next page, there were more vaki, whispering words of madness into Gloria's ears, making Charles see his own wife on the roadway when she was sitting next to him in the car all along.

It was all right there. Evidence of the otherworldly, of the supernatural, of the truth of the stories of her people. This was what happened when there was no mistress. No one to fill the cup stones. Chaos took over.

Anni took a long breath in. Whether she really believed all this or not, she knew it was now up to her to take steps to stop it. She had to try, no matter how fantastic it all seemed. But how? She had seen Mummo's mother taking her into the woods, passing down the ancient secrets. There was nobody to pass them down to her.

And then it hit Anni. Could that be why Mummo had asked her to visit? To pass on the secrets, the ancient ways? She pushed back her chair.

In the hallway, she saw that the house was dark. Everyone was in bed. She made her way downstairs and padded across the living room to the french doors. Rain was still pounding down. But she knew she had to go out there. She had no idea what she was going to do, but somehow, deep inside, something from deep within her cells told her intention was all she needed. Intention would be enough.

Anni took a deep breath and filled herself with the intention of what she was about to do. To take control of what had fallen off the rails when Mummo died. Without a mistress at Metsan Valo, chaos was overtaking her family. That could not continue. She needed to take her place in the role Mummo had bestowed upon her, the role that, perhaps, had always been waiting for her.

It sounded crazy to Anni, even though she had experienced the chaos over the past few days. Fairy tales, the lore and legend of her ancestors just didn't exist in the world today. Unless it did. What would be the harm in pretending?

She strode into the kitchen and grabbed a bag, filling it with leftovers, and a bottle of Mummo's ever-present Finlandia vodka. And then Anni opened the doors and walked out into the rain.

CHAPTER THIRTY-NINE

Anni woke up the next morning with a start. She was in her own bed. She looked around, blinking. What had happened the night before? She couldn't quite remember. She had been reading the book about her ancestors, swept up in their tales. And then what? Had she fallen asleep? Something was scratching at the edges of her mind, but she couldn't quite grasp it.

After a quick shower, she pulled on jeans and a sweater and headed downstairs. It was earlier than she thought—nobody was up yet except for Martin and Meri, who were busy in the kitchen making breakfast.

As she came down the stairs, they both looked up at her, smiling.

"Is there coffee?" she asked, sliding onto one of the chairs at the dining-room table.

Meri poured a cup and set it in front of her, along with a pitcher of half-and-half. Anni poured a splash into her cup and took a sip. Its nutty flavor warmed her from the inside out.

"Wow, this tastes good today," she said. And it did. It was the most delicious coffee she had ever tasted.

Meri smiled. "You'll find many things are different now. Better. Clearer."

Anni furrowed her brow at her, eyeing her over the rim of her cup. "What do you mean?"

"You stepped inside your own skin and became who you are. You're finally home, Annalise."

Anni stared at Meri for a long minute, and it all came back to her.

She had made her way to the cup stone and filled it with small offerings, meats, vegetables, and drink. She said the same prayer of thanksgiving Mummo had said. "Enjoy this bounty, friends of Metsan Valo."

She had stood out in the elements, rain pouring down almost like it was battering her, filling her eyes. Lightning cracked overhead. Thunder rolled through the sky with a growl.

She raised her arms over her head, and there, beneath the wide sky, amid the life-giving forest, on the shores of the greatest of lakes, drenched to the bone, chilled beyond measure, stood Annalise Halla, one small woman standing against the mountainous, incredible rage of nature.

She hadn't known what to say. There was no spell or incantation to follow. Only the resoluteness of her will, which she felt, deep in her cells.

"Help me," was all she could think of to say. So she shouted it into the heavens. And the whole world at Metsan Valo listened.

As she sat in the kitchen now with Meri and Martin, Annalise didn't know if it was good enough. But it was the best she had.

"Is this for real?" Anni asked, holding Meri's gaze. "I saw it all in the book. The vaki, terrorizing and attacking this family. They could've killed any one of us."

Meri nodded, a grave expression on her face, her lips in a straight line. "It is the pact our ancestors made with the vaki, centuries ago. They agreed to protect and empower us against those who would do our people harm. But if we don't honor it, or worse yet, forget it, neglect to uphold our part of the bargain, this is what happens. It's what I meant that night when I said it had begun."

Anni just looked at her, openmouthed. "You know that sounds crazy, right? These are folktales, Meri." But even as Anni said the words, they seemed to dissipate in the air, along with everything she had ever believed about the real world.

"Where do you think folktales come from?" Meri said. "All cultures have stories about worlds within worlds. Faeries and elves and little folk who bedevil and betray and beguile people who aren't aware. Witches and wizards. Shape-shifters. Do you think that's just a coincidence, that so many cultures have similar stories?"

Anni didn't know what to think. "But our world—"

"Is populated by modern people," Meri said, patting Anni's hand. "We have become distracted and distant from the quiet life our ancestors used to live, some in harmony with nature and all that exists in it, others at odds with it. In the fast-paced life in the city, that might not matter much. Here at Metsan Valo, living in harmony with nature is alive and well. And always has been. It's not supernatural. It's completely natural to people with eyes to see."

Anni wasn't so sure. But all at once, it felt like an awesome responsibility had been set on her shoulders.

"And I'm the one who has to tend to this? It's a lot, Meri."

Meri smiled. "It's not so difficult. It was a matter of opening your eyes." She took a sip of coffee and cast her gaze out the window toward the forest. "When a mistress passes on, it's a frightening time for the little folk. They are in danger of being forgotten, relegated to the status of myth and legend. That's what has happened in much of the modern world. I think they were making certain it didn't happen here."

Anni shook her head. "You might have just told me," she said.

"And what would you have thought if I had?" Meri asked. "It has to be self-discovery, if you're not given the knowledge from the one who has come before."

Anni took Meri at her word, but she wasn't so sure. It seemed awfully dramatic and, frankly, unnecessary. "You might have given me the book sooner, though. Like the first night I arrived. That would've helped."

Meri shook her head. "Your grandmother was planning to pass it down to you herself, when you came for your visit. That was the reason she called you back here. But when she was making her video will, she talked to me about what to do if that didn't happen. She asked me to wait until you had heard the story of Kaija and Calder before giving you the book. It wouldn't mean anything to you without that."

Anni nodded. She'd get Theo's take on it when the time came. She sipped her coffee, doubts nagging at her. She had been swept up in something last night, that was for certain. Whether all this chaos would end now was yet to be seen.

She looked at Meri. What was she? What were Meri and Martin? They had been here forever, at Metsan Valo. Were they the guardians of this place? Were they part of this dark fairy tale? Anni started to ask, but then thought better of it. It was too much. She decided to just let it be, for the moment.

But then, Anni shook her head. All of it seemed rather silly in the light of day. She pushed herself up and topped off her coffee.

"I'm going to say good morning to Mom," she said to them. "I don't need breakfast until everyone else gets up, so don't worry about me."

She walked down the back hallway, sipping her coffee. It really did taste delicious. She poked her head into her mother's room. Jane was sitting in one of the armchairs, legs crossed, reading a book.

"How was her night?" Anni asked.

"Fine," Jane said. "Resting comfortably, as usual. Her vitals are strong. No worse for wear because of the journey she took yesterday."

Anni smiled. "Have you had coffee yet this morning?"

"Not yet," Jane said. "But I'll go grab a cup now if you don't mind."

Anni kissed Arden on the forehead and settled into the chair beside her.

"I hear you had a good night, Mom," she said, taking Arden's hand in hers. "I had a strange one."

The monitors beeped happily.

"I read all about our ancestors," Anni went on. "All of Mummo's old tales, and lots that she didn't tell us, too. It's all in a book that Meri says is the story of our family. I got so caught up in it that I went out in the rain and basically commanded all of the chaos surrounding this family to quiet down, already."

Anni chuckled at the thought of it.

"Meri said I became who I am last night. Who I always was. I think it's a little overdramatic. Don't you?"

She thought she saw a slight flicker of a smile on Arden's lips. And then, she felt it. Faint at first, then stronger. Arden squeezed her hand.

"Mom? Mom!"

Anni held her breath until Arden's eyes flickered open.

She looked around the room. "Where am I?" Arden said, her voice a tattered whisper.

"Metsan Valo," Anni said, tears choking her words. "We set up a hospital room for you."

Arden nodded slowly, and her eyes closed. But she held on to Anni's hand.

When Jane returned to the room, Anni turned to her. "She was awake," Anni said, her words tripping over each other. "She opened her eyes and talked to me."

Jane nodded her head. "That's a good sign. Remember what I told you? It might take a while for her to fully come out of it. She may slip in and out. But she is headed back to us."

Anni smiled, a tear spilling out of one of her eyes. "Will you go find my brother?"

Moments later, Theo slipped into the room, his face full of expectation and hope. He sank into a chair on the opposite side of the bed from Anni and took Arden's other hand. "How is she?"

"Her eyes flutter open now and then," Anni said. "She smiles and says a few words. Then she falls back into wherever she goes. Jane says it's normal. It can happen like this when coma patients are waking up."

Theo smoothed Arden's unruly curls. "Are we ever going to know what caused this?"

Anni winced. "You're not going to believe this," she began, squinting at her brother.

"What?"

And she told him everything—the book, their images in it, the vaki having caused all this, her placating them with offerings, her conversation with Meri, all of it.

Theo smirked at her. "Have you eaten any poison mushrooms today? Because that's crazy."

Anni smiled. She didn't know if he'd ever quite believe her. Or if she even believed it herself.

Throughout the day, Arden stirred and fell back into her abyss over and over again. It seemed to Anni that Arden was like a whale or a dolphin coming up for a breath of air before submerging once again.

The twins sat with their mother, each holding one of her hands, until the sun began to set, turning the golden last hour of sunshine into the coolness of evening. But even as darkness fell, Anni could see light.

CHAPTER FORTY

Over the course of the next week, Arden slowly grew more and more awake, more and more herself. A few days after she first opened her eyes, the nurses took her off her saline drip, and she began to eat soft foods, which Meri kept trying to feed to her every minute of the day. Arden objected to all the fuss, but Anni could see how touched she was that everyone was hovering around her.

She hadn't asked much about what had happened to her out in the forest on that fateful day. Anni wasn't sure whether to bring it up. She knew that, in time, they'd talk about it. But she suspected her mother already knew. After all, Arden had grown up at Metsan Valo, had been a child in those enchanted woods.

One afternoon when Anni and Theo were reading the daily news to Arden, she put a hand on Theo's arm. Her eyes brimmed with tears.

"My children. You have been a constant source of love and support as I recover."

"Of course, Mom," Theo said. "We're here for you."

Arden smiled, rather sadly, Anni thought.

"But I haven't been there for you," Arden said. "Not really. Not as a mother should be. Your grandmother filled that role for you more than I did."

"Oh, Mom, we don't—" Anni began, but Arden cut her off.

"I know you don't," she said. "But I do. None of us can change the past. But I want you to know I will be more present in your lives in the future. If you want me to be."

"Now, there's no reason to make idle threats," Theo said, a wry smile on his face. Anni chuckled, and Arden did, too.

"Come on," Anni said, gently pulling her mother to her feet. "It's time for your laps. Twice around the entire main floor."

"Not again," Arden protested, groaning.

"You need to get your muscle tone back, or you and Gloria are going to turn into Baby Jane and Blanche," Theo warned, laughing at his own joke.

"You two are brutal," Arden said, giving each a kiss on the cheek as they took her arms and set off down the hallway.

Anni looked at her brother and saw his eyes were glistening. She felt it, too. The three of them were more of a family now than they ever had been. Anni and Theo had been amusedly tolerant with an undercurrent of resentment toward Arden in recent years, but now, all that had fallen away. Walls had come down. Their mother was more real to them than she ever had been before.

It was strange to Anni that it had taken something like this, the magic, lore, and mystery of Metsan Valo, to make that happen. But maybe that was what family lore and legends were for. Family. Maybe that was all it was. Connecting the past to the present, running an iron cable through it all with the knowledge you had a place in the universe, an unbroken line, a living, breathing history. A home.

As they walked with Arden through the halls of the great house, Anni knew she was right where she belonged.

~❧~

Two weeks later, Meri was buzzing around the kitchen, setting out a spread of hors d'oeuvres on the grand dining-room table. Little sausages wrapped in dough, meatballs swimming in their own gravy, an enormous butcher's board of cheeses, platters of vegetables and dips, smoked lake trout, fresh homemade bread and butter, decadent desserts, and more. Martin was tending to the bar, which he had set up both indoors and out, with red and white wine, ales, and of course, Finlandia vodka.

It was one of those quintessential crisp Lake Superior autumn days. The leaves were blazing with reds, crimsons, and oranges. The sky was impossibly blue and clear. The lake looked like glass, reflecting mirror images of the trees. A fire crackled in the firepit on the lawn.

Anni walked outside with a glass of wine and thought Mummo couldn't have conjured up a more beautiful day for her wake. Or, maybe she had.

As Anni strolled through the yard down to the lake, she reflected on everything that had happened during the previous two weeks. Arden's recovery had been slow, as Jane had predicted. But the doctors had told her, and the rest of the family, that she had suffered no brain damage. There would be no relearning to talk and walk, but it was a struggle all the same. Her strength would come back, the doctors said, but for now, she was still weak and tired easily.

Charles's arm was still in a cast, but he was coming along fine, and Gloria had taken off her sling after about a week and was busy fretting about the scar on her forehead and patting makeup on the bruises that were receding.

The Halla family had made it through the chaos.

"Hey!" Theo called to Anni, snapping her back into the moment. He was standing on the deck with his wife, Jenny, who had just arrived from Chicago. She had come for the wake, and to take her husband home. Anni wasn't sure the two of them were going to make it. Neither was Theo. But, as he had told her a few days prior, fifteen years of marriage was worth fighting for.

Anni trotted up the lawn to greet her sister-in-law, opening her arms and enveloping her into a hug.

"I'm so glad to see you," Anni said.

"Me too," Jenny said. "I understand you've had a pretty odd time of it."

Anni and Theo exchanged a glance and laughed. "I'll tell you all about it on the way home," Theo said.

Patrick came through the french doors and joined them on the deck.

"Arden cheats at cribbage," he reported. "And Meri just condones it."

Anni chuckled and sidled up to him, threading an arm through his. "You know she'll claim it's because of the coma. There's no winning."

The two of them walked down toward the lake together.

"You've been great these past couple of weeks," Anni said.

"That's only because I *am* great," Patrick said with a laugh. Anni pinched his arm and grinned at him.

They walked to the end of the dock and settled onto the bench that Anni's grandfather had built decades earlier. Patrick draped his arm around her shoulders, and she leaned in.

"We haven't talked much during these last few weeks about what's next for you," Patrick said. "I'm curious if you've decided anything. You know, about what's going to happen after the wake today." He was stumbling over his words.

"You're wondering if I'm going to stay," Anni said.

"It has crossed my mind. A few hundred times."

A warmth bubbled up within Anni, as it always did when this man was near. She had known Patrick for only a few weeks. A few tumultuous weeks. But already, she couldn't imagine life without him. He had become such a fixture in her life in his quiet, funny way. They had developed a routine of talking every night before bed, which Anni found herself looking forward to all day. His voice in her ear before she put her head on her pillow.

"I'm staying," she said, surprising herself with the decisive answer. It had been on her mind these past few weeks as well. "I still have my apartment in Paris, but I thought I could use it as more of a getaway than my permanent home, at least for now. My mom is still recovering, and I think it's important for me to be here. And given all that has happened, I want to be."

She looked into Patrick's impossibly blue eyes. Was he one of the reasons she wanted to stay? For Anni, it was too early to say. But she knew it felt right to be with him.

"I'm happy to hear that," Patrick said. "I haven't met anyone like you in a long time. If ever. And I wasn't too enthused about the idea of you going back to Paris just yet. Plus, Pascal likes you."

"That's only because I'm great," Anni said, parroting his words.

They sat there, looking into each other's eyes for a moment, the air around them swirling with electricity. He pushed a lock of hair behind her ear and pulled her closer. His lips met hers for the first time, and in that touch Anni could feel forever laid out before her.

As Anni and Patrick walked back up the lawn toward the house, Anni caught sight of Lichen, sitting in an Adirondack chair on the deck. That morning, Anni had walked into her bedroom and come upon her niece running her fingers over the cover of the book on Anni's desk.

Startled, Lichen had said, "Oh! I'm sorry. I know I probably shouldn't be in here, but I couldn't help but notice . . ."

Anni had smiled. "Not a problem. You were intrigued by the book?"

"What is it?" Lichen had asked.

"Have a look," Anni had said, unclasping the hinges. "It's filled with the stories of our family. From hundreds of years ago up until today."

Lichen had turned some of the pages, a look of wonder on her face. "This is so cool," she had said. "It's hundreds of years old?"

"Yes, it is," Anni had said, pointing to the first story of Kaija and Calder. "These are your great-great-I-don't-know-how-many-times-great-grandparents. Remember that story Mummo told on the video will? This is them."

Lichen had stared at the pages, her eyes wide. Anni hadn't noticed how much she looked like the Halla side of the family until just then.

"I could've been looking at this the whole time," Lichen had said. Anni had laughed. "Next time. It'll be here."

As Anni thought back on that encounter, it warmed her from the inside out. Maybe Lichen would be the next mistress of Metsan Valo. Maybe Anni would have a daughter of her own. Either way, she knew enough to know the future wasn't written into the book. Until it was.

People began arriving all at once—most had taken the same ferry over from the mainland. Nick Stone and his wife, Kate, along with her cousin Simon and his husband, Jonathan. LuAnn and Gary, and Beth St. John from the bookstore in town. A legion of people Anni didn't know, all of whom looked familiar to her. Innkeepers, store owners, long-time residents of both Wharton and Ile de Colette. Young and old. From all walks of life.

Soon the house and the yard were filled with friends and neighbors, all there to honor the memory of a great lady.

Anni looked around and was filled with gratitude, enormous, over-whelming gratitude. These were her people. This was her home.

CHAPTER FORTY-ONE

The sky was full of stars, and the harvest moon illuminated the landscape as brightly as the sun. A fire was still blazing in the firepit. Gloria and Charles, Vicky and Yale, Lichen, Meri and Martin, Jenny, and Arden stood on the lakeshore as Theo and Anni paddled their canoe into the lake, trailing a small kayak behind them.

They had laid the fire before they pushed off. Dry, brittle sticks from the Metsan Valo forest under twigs, which sat under larger pieces of wood from those same trees. Within that nest hewn from the land she had loved for a lifetime, the land her parents had carved from the wilderness, sat the ashes of Taika Halla, the former mistress of Metsan Valo.

"Do you think we're far enough out?" Anni said, turning around to look at her brother.

"I'm more concerned with setting myself on fire, but yes."

"So this is it, then," Anni said, her voice wavering.

"Should we say a few words?" Theo asked.

Anni gazed at the kayak that would serve as the funeral pyre containing their grandmother's ashes, the lake stretching out forever beyond it. She looked up into the sky filled with stars. She turned her eyes to the deep, dark woods and wondered if the vaki were watching.

And she began to tell a story.

"Once, long, long ago, a baby girl named Taika was born to this land, this water, and this house on the shore of the greatest of lakes."

She spun the tale of the mistress of Metsan Valo, growing up in these woods, marrying, raising her family, and then, her grandchildren. And she knew it would all be written in the ancient book of their family when the time came.

She glanced at Theo and saw his eyes were filled with tears.

When she was finished with her tale, she spoke directly to her grandmother.

"As children, Theo and I found love here, Mummo," Anni said. "Safety. Stability. We found our past and our future. Theo and I are the people we are today because of you. Rest in the heavens now, great lady, secure in the knowledge that I am here to carry on your traditions. I promise you they will not dissipate in the wind. They will forever be here at Metsan Valo, as I know you will be."

She and Theo looked at each other. "Now?" he said.

"Now."

Theo pulled the kayak closer to their canoe and, when he could reach it, lit a tightly packed ball of newspaper on fire and set it under the pile of twigs. They watched as the wood began to smoke. Anni said a silent prayer, and the fire erupted in a whoosh, blazing high into the sky.

Theo pushed the kayak forward, and they watched as it floated away, the flames growing brighter and bigger until they engulfed the whole craft.

"We love you, Mummo," Theo said, his voice cracking.

"Thank you," Anni said, tears streaming down her face.

"Taika Halla!" Arden called out from the shore. "Taika Halla!"

The others joined in. Soon they were all chanting her name into the dark, starry night. Taika's name, and her spirit, rose on the flames and was swept into the heavens, until it became one with the sky, as her body became one with the water.

Her family watched until the flames subsided, and the kayak was gone.

~⚘~

Anni rose from her bed, silently called. Stars still shone in the sky, but the moon had dipped under the horizon. Somehow, she knew they were assembling. Waiting for her.

She pulled on her robe, slid her feet into slippers, and padded out into the hallway. All was quiet. She smiled as she walked through the great room and out the french doors, into the night. The chill of the night air nipped at her cheeks. She could still smell the last of the fire, cooling in the firepit.

She made her way through the forest to the clearing by the creek, to the same ring of trees where she had awakened, alone and afraid, when she was a child, so many years ago. A lifetime ago. This place felt enchanted to Anni. Was enchanted. It was where the little folk, the vaki, gathered for their celebrations, both happy and mournful. It was a place of music and dance, of stories by the firelight.

Anni could see them, dozens of them, like tiny lights flitting in the grass. She listened closely, and could hear the music, far away, distant, coming from another realm. She heard the voices, their whispers, the singing.

And soon she saw they were all around her. She held her arms out to the side and moved in a circle, slowly at first. They cheered and sang, the music growing louder and louder.

And just as her ancestors had done before her, Anni danced with the vaki under the starry sky.

ACKNOWLEDGMENTS

When I begin to write a new story, it usually starts with a place. A house, most often. I imagine where the story will unfold, and then I set about finding the story. This book was different. It started with the nagging desire to immerse myself in the folktales of my ancestors. I've always been intrigued by the notion of folktales being real, and the lore and legend of my own culture started to gnaw at the back of my mind.

My mother, Joan Maki Webb, was 100 percent Finn. Her mother, my beloved Gram, was the child of Finnish immigrants and spoke fluent Finn. Her father, who died before I was old enough to know him, came to this country from Finland when he was a young child. My mom, too, was gone by the time I started to write this book, and maybe the whole idea was to connect with her heritage.

When I read that J. R. R. Tolkien took his inspiration for *Lord of the Rings* from the epic Finnish poem, the *Kalevela*, I thought, *Whaa?* I had heard about the *Kalevela* all my life, but I had never heard that. Tolkien even learned Finn to read the *Kalevela* in its native language.

Huh, I thought.

So along with my dear friend and partner in all things otherworldly, Randy Johnson, I began to research Finnish folktales and legends. It's surprising what you might find. Apparently, as the Vikings were raiding and pillaging all over the place, they left the Finns alone. It was because the Finns were seen as the wizards and witches, the keepers of ancient knowledge, able to control the air and the water and the animals around them. The Vikings left them alone in exchange for safe passage through their waters.

Huh, I thought. It's a cool legend. What if that was real?

If that's not the start of a book by me, I don't know what is.

And so, my thanks:

To Randy Johnson, for being the first champion of this idea and helping me research creepy folktales.

To my agent, Jennifer Weltz, and everyone at the Jean V. Naggar Literary Agency for being my literary family, my home base, and my touchstone. You mean the world to me.

To my delightful and insightful editors, Faith Black Ross and Alicia Clancy—it's always so much fun for me to get to the part of the process when you come into it. I love your ideas, thoughts, and suggestions, and I truly enjoy working as a team to make my manuscripts the best books they can be.

To my publisher, Danielle Marshall, and everyone at Lake Union, especially Ashley Vanicek and Gabriella Dumpit, thank you for your faith in me and your tireless work on my behalf.

To Pamela Klinger Horn, the book maven who has done astonishing work for authors (not the least of which is posting photos of our books with her dogs . . . photos that authors now covet as much as a starred *PW* review), thank you for your friendship, kindness, elegance, and grace. To the booksellers who I have missed so much during this year of social distancing, thank you so much for your facilitation of Zoom readings and other events. I can't wait to come back to see you!

And finally, to my readers, thank you so much for sticking with me, enjoying what I write, and getting in touch with me when you can. I feel truly blessed because of you.

BOOK CLUB QUESTIONS

1. Do you think ancient folktales have a kernel of truth in them, or are they just made-up stories?

2. If the folktales and legends in your heritage were true, what would they look like in modern times?

3. What is your sense of the Halla family? Would you want to be part of it?

4. Arden and Gloria both have more than their fair share of eccentricities and even madness. Why do you think that is?

5. What do you think is behind Gloria's desire to become other people?

6. Why did Taika give Metsan Valo to Anni?

7. Is there a deeper reason Anni stayed away for so long?

8. Who are Martin and Meri?

9. Why does Gloria accept Charles, knowing he has been a con man?

10. What is your opinion of Yale? Why is he so misunderstood by the family . . . or is he?

11. Do you believe your ancestors are watching over you?

ABOUT THE AUTHOR

Photo © 2020 Steve Burmeister

Wendy Webb is the #1 Amazon Charts bestselling and multiple award–winning author of six novels of gothic suspense, including *The Haunting of Brynn Wilder*; *Daughters of the Lake*; *The Vanishing*; *The Fate of Mercy Alban*; *The Tale of Halcyon Crane*; and *The End of Temperance Dare*, which has been optioned for both film and television. Her books are sold worldwide and have been translated into seven languages. Dubbed "Queen of the Northern Gothic" by reviewers, Wendy sets her stories on the windswept, rocky shores of the Great Lakes. Wendy lives in Minneapolis, where she is at work on her next novel when she's not walking a good dog along the parkway and lakes near her home. Visit her at www.wendykwebb.com.